ACKNOWLEDGMENTS

"The times when you have seen only one set of footprints is when I carried you."

First, I'd like to thank my family for always being there to show support no matter what! I love you!
Thank you to the online book clubs that embrace and support authors so readily. The encouragement and exposure you provide is immeasurable and I appreciate it from the bottom of my heart.

Thank you to my beta readers, SARAH J. BELK, ANITA TANN, QUANITA JONES, DELORIS HARPER, NASI AL-MAHI, and VICTORIA NIECEY ROBERTS. Love ya'll!
Thank you to my editor, CHYTA CURRY

Last, but not least, THANK YOU TO #TEAM SK!! I took a break and came back to the love and support as if I'd never left. You are the best bunch of reader friends an author could ever have! Thank you for always having my back!
Hugz & Kisses, Peace, Blessings, and Love!

Visit my website at www.skhardy.com

THE PATTELS: HAWK & RAVEN

S.K. Hardy

CHAPTER 1

Raven Randolph sat in the courtroom listening with an impassive expression as the defense attorney questioned his client. She heard the low hiss of disgust that her co-counsel sitting beside her released but didn't let it break her concentration. It wasn't that Raven didn't understand and relate to the emotion. She felt the exact same way. However, she couldn't let it assault her senses or taint her expression in front of the jury.

Years of being an experienced prosecutor gave her insight into lying cockroaches like the one on the stand; she'd dealt with them more times than she could count and right now her bullshitometer was climbing dangerously close to overload status. Raven prosecuted many cases and came into contact with all kinds of ruthless, unconscionable criminals, but the ones she hated most were scum that exploited helpless children and vulnerable women.

Frank Giuliani was a filthy piece of trash who slithered through the fingers of justice an embarrassingly amount of times and landed squarely on his feet like a cat with nine lives. As

Raven listened to the endless litany of lies pouring from his mouth like vomit sullying the inside of the courtroom, she felt the familiar sliver of combative excitement clench the muscles of her stomach. She had him red handed. Today was where Giuliani's luck ended.

That's right, keep talking, asshole. Keep talking.

Suddenly, Raven felt a tingling sensation along the nerve center of her spine that felt like sharp needles pricking each individual vertebra. She brought her hand up and rubbed her nape. Frowning slightly, she squirmed in the chair and arched her neck, but before she could explore the feeling any further it was her turn to cross-examine the defendant. Aaron Rogers, the expensive defense attorney Giuliani hired turned and cast a smug look at Raven as he took his seat.

Deliberately ignoring him, Raven kept her eyes peeled on Giuliani's shit eating grin. Standing up, she rounded the table with her shoulders squared and her chin tilted at a confident angle.

"Mr. Giuliani, can you state for the court exactly what you do for a living?"

"I'm a businessman," Giuliani smirked.

"And what is the nature of your business?"

"Oh, a little bit o' this; a little bit o' that. Why? You in the market to change careers?" he asked with a mocking grin.

"Your Honor?" Raven ignored him and directed her attention to the judge.

"Mr. Giuliani, please answer the question." Judge Warner, known for being stern and no nonsense pressed her fingertips together and cast a strict look at Giuliani who sighed dramatically.

"I own several jewelry stores, nightclubs and restaurants..." he shrugged. "Like I said, a little bit o' this and a little bit o' that."

"These clubs you own... They're strip clubs, is that correct?"

"We prefer to call them exclusive gentlemen's clubs. You oughta come by on amateur night. Show us what you got. Who knows, you might just surprise yourself," he sneered provocatively.

"Is that the line you use to lure unsuspecting young women to work in your 'gentlemen's club'?"

"I don't 'lure' nobody and they ain't unsuspecting." Giuliani shrugged. "They know exactly what the job calls for."

"And does that job description include prostitution?"

"I don't know what you're talkin' about."

"Really?" Raven said glancing at the jury before bringing her attention back to Giuliani. Folding her arms behind her back, she took slow, measured steps towards the witness stand. "Are you personally familiar with the deceased, Faith Hunter?"

Raven didn't miss the cautious gleam that entered his eyes.

"Not personally, no."

"Oh, wait. I'm sorry. When she worked in your 'gentlemen's club' she went by the name Lola. From what I heard, she was one of your favorites. Maybe you remember her now?"

"Ms. Randolph, I have a lot of employees on my payroll. I can't possibly be expected to know every single one of them."

"This is true," Raven nodded, striding with determined steps back to the table. "Which is why I–"

Suddenly, Raven stopped mid-sentence. With her hand outstretched to take the folder her second chair was reaching to her, her eyes collided with a pair of dark, intense ones in the back of the courtroom. She immediately recognized the man looking directly at her with an unwavering stare. Hawk Pattel.

CHAPTER 2

A member of the very crime family the DA's office was actively investigating, Hawk sat in the last row looking extremely relaxed with his elbow bent and resting on the arm of the chair. His finger slowly rubbed his lip. Even from that distance, she could feel the heat of his riveting gaze trained directly on her. Raven swallowed. The connection was so intimate that her body trembled in reaction.

As if he accurately read her mind, the corner of Hawk's mouth quirked upwards in a small gesture that was knowing, seductive and damn near erotic at the same time.

Raven could barely think straight. What was he doing there? How long had he been in the courtroom? And why was he staring at her like…like…*that?*

She pleaded with her lungs to take just one small breath to clear the light-headed dizziness that was threatening to make her knees buckle right where she stood.

Come on, Rae. Breathe…

But just as her lips parted to obediently follow that small directive, a little voice whispered tauntingly in her ear and threw her off balance: *He looks good, doesn't he? Go on. Admit it. Your pulse is racing like you've just finished running a marathon and your heart is in a terrifying free fall...*

Shut up! She growled silently. *Just. Shut. Up!*

"Raven. *Raven?*"

The hushed whisper of her friend and second chair, Gwynneth Jesús, thankfully threw her a much-appreciated lifeline, effectively pulling her to safety out of the drowning depths of Hawk Pattels unwavering stare. Eyes slightly glazed, she forced herself to break visual contact and took the folder out of Gwynn's hand.

"Are you okay?" Gwynn asked leaning forward and murmuring under her breath.

Never looking up, Raven, deftly avoided her probing look and gave her a quick nod. Clearing her throat, she smoothed her face back into what she hoped was a semblance of a woman who didn't plan on take any shit–from Hawk Pattel *or* the defendant on the stand.

She removed one of the pictures from the folder and turned back to Giuliani. "Maybe this will help jog your memory," she stated, giving the image to Giuliani. "That's a picture of you and Faith Hunter–whom you probably know as Lola–at a restaurant a couple of weeks before her death."

Giuliani stared at the picture and shrugged his shoulder. "Still doesn't ring a bell. I have dinner with a lotta people in my line of work."

"Hmmm. Okay. What about this one?" Raven slid another picture towards him, which captured Giuliani and the young, beautiful Lola making out hot and heavy at a table full of other diners who seemed oblivious to the open display of lust.

"Or this one?" The next one showed the two of them leaving the restaurant with Giuliani grabbing a generous handful of Lola's luscious backside. Raven dealt the pictures out like cards on a poker table. "Or this one... Or–"

"Alright!" Giuliani snapped, eyes flashing angrily. Still hesitating, he glanced at his lawyer as if waiting for his intervention, but when there was none, he nodded reluctantly. "Yeah. I...yeah. Now that I see the pictures, I know who she is."

"Isn't it true that you operate a sex trafficking ring out of your clubs; exploiting young girls for the purpose of forced prostitution?"

"That's a lie!" Giuliani answered through gritted teeth.

"Lola was missing for almost three weeks before her body was found. Didn't you wonder why she never showed up for work? Was it because you knew she was already dead?"

"No! I thought she just took off. Look, in this business women come and women go. It's not the kind of job where you give exit interviews. I admit, I knew Lola, but I don't care what it looks like in those pictures. I was never involved with her like that. As a matter of fact–"

"Mr. Giuliani, let me stop you right there. I don't know if your attorney has explained what it means to commit perjury, but if necessary, I'd be happy to break it down in elementary terms that even *you* would understand."

"Objection, Your Honor!" Giuliani's lawyer threw his pen down and shot up from his chair. "Counselor is being unnecessarily demeaning in her tone."

The judge heaved out a put-upon sigh and leveled a stern look of warning at Raven, but before she could deliver the reprimand, Raven quickly spoke up.

"Withdrawn. I have no further questions for this witness at this time."

Turning on her heels, Raven walked back to resume her seat. Unable to stop herself, her eyes went to the back of the courtroom to where Hawk had been sitting. A slight frown wrinkled her brow when she saw the chair he occupied was empty. For the swiftest of seconds, a hint of disappointment caused her chest to tighten, but she pushed it away just as quickly as it arose. Hawk Pattel's presence at one of her trials had nothing to do with her, but it didn't stop her from wondering why he was there in the first place.

After several more witnesses took the stand, the judge called recess until Monday. Slightly preoccupied, Raven placed her folders in her briefcase, half-listening to Gwynn and her paralegal chattering in low undertones. Even though the weekend loomed ahead of her, she knew she would spend the majority of it in her office working. Apparently, so did her co-workers.

"We're planning on stopping by Roxie's after work to grab a couple drinks," Gwynn told her as they walked out of the courtroom. "And before you even say it, yeah, I know you're planning on burning the midnight oil *again,* but come on, *chica,* you gotta relax a little. Blow off some steam."

"Gwynn–" Raven tried to cut in and stop the lecture she knew was coming, but her best friend wasn't having it.

"No, I mean it, mama. You work too damn hard. This is an important case, but admit it, you know it like the back of your hand. Trust, you ain't doin' yourself no good by working yourself into the ground instead of taking a well-deserved break once in a while, *comprendes?*"

Raven slanted a veiled look Gwynn's way, smiling when she heard a hint of the girl from the old neighborhood slipping past her Harvard Law School degree and making itself present and accounted for. Matter of fact, that's where they met. Two outspoken women from the wrong part of town bonding and adding a bit of black and brown girl magic to a sea of melanin challenged yuppies.

More than once, cash fund babies at the school tried to subtly belittle them and make them feel as if they didn't belong at such a prestigious university. However, by the time Rae and Gwynn took turns cutting them down to size with their debilitating tongues and razor-sharp jabs, the snobs quickly discovered they'd bitten off more than they'd bargained for and skulked away with their tails tucked between their legs.

Raven grinned as she thought about the time they staged a protest in the student lounge demanding that the administration make the faculty more inclusive of women and people of color. As president of the Black Law Students Association, Raven took the lead in organizing the demonstration. Suffice it to say, before she graduated there was a ten percent increase in the number of minorities on staff. Not much, but it was a start.

She pushed through the wooden doors and stepped out into the hallway. Her parents worked too hard and sacrificed too much for Raven to let anyone speak to her with anything other than respect. From an early age, she and her siblings were taught that people only treated you the way you allowed them to; they took their clues from *you*. Boundaries in every relationship needed to be respected, whether professional or personal. Which is why she would never understand how her sister, Nikki, put up with Angel LaCroix.

A delicate scowl slashed across Raven's face as she thought about her brother-in-law. Not only was he overbearingly arrogant, but he was the most dangerous man she'd ever met. With all of the criminals she came in contact with in her career, that said a lot.

Angel's illegal activities put Gotti to shame. Murder, drug trafficking, illegal arms dealing, political bribery, money laundering... the list went on and on. His criminal enterprise was a powerful and feared one. There was no way she could allow her sister and nephew to continue to live in such a dangerous and volatile world. Angel might keep Nikki away from the ugliness of his business, but that was no guarantee that it would never touch her.

Picturing him now, Raven supposed she could see the attraction. Angelo LaCroix was a handsome man with a magnetic personality. He could turn on the charm as easily as a light switch with just a few words accompanied by that disarming smile of his. She saw it up close and personal with her own parents, for Christ's sakes. Not long after Nikki and

Angel had first gotten married, FBI agents paid their parents a visit. Even though they denied any knowledge of Angel's affairs, they were followed around and put under close observation, more to intimidate them to cooperate than anything else.

Raven was furious that her parents, the most law-abiding people she'd ever known, got caught up in Angel's crap and she told Nikki as much. Apparently, her anger and disappointment hadn't fallen on deaf ears because some way, somehow, the surveillance suddenly stopped. Her parents were never bothered again and Raven knew it was due to Angel's influence with someone whose pay grade and clearance went high up and that was scary as hell to think about.

It didn't matter because Raven's parents sided with her. They were more determined than ever to get Nikki away from Angel and the danger he represented, but once again, Angel got his way and won them over. After the birth of Angelo Jr., they fell in love with their grandson, and that's how Angel got to them. It had started off subtly enough, nothing too pushy. That wasn't Angel's way. At first, he offered his in-laws access to his private jet so they could fly back and forth as often as they wanted in order to see A.J.

Raven rolled her eyes. *Of course,* they accepted the offer. Who could blame them? Unlimited first-class access to their first grandchild? *Of course,* they didn't turn it down.

After that, he reeled them in a little at a time like precious fish on a hook. They became members of the exclusive Vegas country club Nikki and Angel belonged to and were treated like royalty. Her father was immediately introduced to a golf pro whom he'd admired for years. The two of them played a few holes whenever her father was in town, which all but sealed the deal. Angel somehow became the best son-a-law they could've asked for and could do no wrong in their eyes.

Raven knew better. She'd made it her number one priority to pry that bastard's poisonous tentacles away from her family if it was the last thing she did. Angel was lethal. He'd inevitably go down from all of the dirt he did and when that happened, Rae refused to let him take anyone she loved with him.

Impatiently hitting the elevator button, she glanced up at the number indicator, sighing quietly when she saw it seemed to be stuck on the bottom floor. Raven turned to her co-workers and broke into their conversation.

"Guys, look, if you don't mind, I'm going to have to bow out of drinks tonight." Grinning, she shook her head when they immediately groaned and started a little good-natured ribbing about all work and no play would make Raven a very dull girl. Slowly backing towards the exit that led to the stairs, she added, "Can I have a rain check?"

Gwynn let out a string of Spanish before reluctantly agreeing and changing back to English, "I guess so, but next time, chica, no excuses accepted."

"Thanks, bestie." Raven blew her a kiss and opened the exit door. Before she left, she called out, "And for the record, your girl is anything but dull. Workaholic, maybe. But dull? Never!"

Laughing softly, she closed the door on their replies and headed down the six flights of stairs that led to the first floor. As she rounded the second flight, she felt someone grab her arm and pull her roughly.

"Hey!" Instinctively wrenching her arm away, a surge of anger ripped through her body when she saw a man she recognized as one of Frank Giuliani's goons standing in front of her.

CHAPTER 3

Raven didn't know his name, but it would've been hard to miss the tall, bulky man who attended the trial every day. He wore his hair in a low, buzz cut, but what caught her attention was the half-inch, jagged scar that stood out prominently on the side of his pot marked cheek. He stuck by Giuliani's side like a faithful watchdog and from the look in his eye now, he felt his master was being threatened and didn't like it one bit.

"Don't touch me! What in the hell–" Raven's teeth clamped down to cut off the furious tirade resting on the tip of her tongue, but the look she blazed at him was full of warning. "What do you think you're doing?"

"Shut up, you little bitch!" The watchdog snarled.

Raven's eyes narrowed. She looked him directly in the eye without flinching. "I hope you realize how big a mistake you've just made."

"No, you're the one that made the mistake! But listen closely, I'm only gonna tell you this once." The large man took a step closer and pointed his finger in her face. "Back. Off."

Dropping her briefcase, Raven slapped his finger away and pushed him in the chest. "Get your damn hand out my face and get the fuck away from me. *Now!*" She screamed when he didn't budge, sending her voice echoing throughout the hollow hallway.

"If you ain't noticed, we not in no courtroom no more so you don't call the shots."

He trudged forward, giving Raven no choice but to step back or risk coming in contact with his body. She jumped when the wall brought her to a sudden stop.

He bent down and leaned forward. "Call this shit off now, or we'll your turn your pretty li'l ass out on the street with the rest of the bitches we got walkin' the block." His thick tongue came out to slather his lips with saliva, leaving them disgustingly wet. "I guarantee a sexy li'l piece like you would bring top dollar."

Raven shuddered in revulsion. Her heart beat violently in her chest. She was almost sure the man in front of her could hear it. As much as she tried to keep it at bay, an inkling of fear started to twist and turn in the pit of her stomach, but she'd be damned if she let him know that. She was just getting ready to release a blistering retort when his next words stopped her cold.

"We know where you live, Counselor." He called out the address of her building as well as her apartment number, looking extremely satisfied when her eyes widened in shock. "We know your routine; know that you walk every morning at five and stop by that little coffee shop on the corner on your way home."

Raven's lips parted in shock. "H-how do you...has Giuliani been watching me?"

"Didn't say nothin' about Mr. Giuliani. Just know that we can get to you anytime we want and won't nobody be there to save you. Not one single soul."

"You sure about that Tommie?" A voice from the stairwell behind them asked in a slow drawl.

Raven almost wilted in relief. She didn't have to see the face of the person who spoke in order to match it to the voice because she knew both in her sleep.

The man in front of her spun around, mouth gaping open, watery eyes stretched just as wide. "Yo, Hawk. What, uh…what you doin' here?"

"The question is what are *you* doin'?" Hawk stopped on the bottom step. He surveyed the scene in front of him, Rae obviously backed into a corner with Tommie blocking any means of escape. His cool eyes landed back on Tommie, keeping him locked and loaded in his focal plane.

"Come here, Rae." He extended his hand out for her to take it.

He didn't have to ask a second time. Keeping her body flat against the wall, Rae took a couple sliding, side steps that allowed her to move around Tommie. Without giving it another thought, she hurried to Hawk and slipped her hand in his. She held on tight like a person flailing in rough water grabbing a life preserver.

Once she was safely by his side, Hawk released the other man from visual entrapment and brought his eyes to Raven. "You alright?" He asked quietly, studying her with a thoroughness that told her no matter her answer, he was checking to see for himself. "You're not hurt, are you?"

For some reason his closeness immediately calmed her, acting as a salve to her admittedly rattled nerves and soothing the clenched knots in her stomach. Raven allowed herself to relax a bit. Still, her voice came out a hoarse mess when she ventured to reply to his question.

"Yes. I–" Clearing her throat, she managed to answer more forcefully. "I'm fine."

Still, Hawk's eagle-eyed gaze lingered on her face. When he was satisfied that she hadn't been harmed, he gently pushed her behind him so that his body acted as a protective shield, before turning frigid eyes back to Tommie.

Raven peeked from around him, surprised when she saw what looked to be fear on the other man's face. Good. Now *he* was the one who appeared rattled. It was clear his apprehension came from the fact that he'd angered Hawk and knew that wasn't a good thing.

Nervously rubbing his hands together, Tommie spoke. "I, uh...I'm surprised to see ya' here. How's your father and your uncle?"

"What's goin' on here, Tommie?" Hawk ignored the asshole's attempt at being friendly and fired the question at him in a way that made it clear he expected an answer.

Tommie's glassy eyes went to Raven who was now safe and out of reach behind Hawk. From the way his lips tightened and his jaw clenched, he wasn't happy about the unexpected dent in the plan he had to intimidate Raven and get her to back off.

"Nothin's goin' on, Hawk. Just having a little conversation with the prosecuting attorney here, that's all."

"Looks like it was a lot more than that. Tell you what, why don't we just agree that the conversation is over now."

The nerve at the corner of Tommie's left eye twitched. Slightly fascinated, Raven watched as the weasel hesitated, then nodded. Giving Raven one last glare he moved around them and started back up the stairs. Before he reached the landing, Hawk called his name. He didn't raise his voice, but Tommie heard him and came to an immediate halt.

"Yeah, Hawk?"

"Just so we're clear, don't let there be a need for you to have any further 'conversations' with Ms. Randolph in the future. Matter of fact, I don't even want you to look at her the next time you see her. Make sure you let Frankie know that too, a'ight?"

Raven now stood beside Hawk and boldly stared at Tommie, whose only reaction was to hold Hawk's gaze for several seconds before nodding obediently and leaving out the heavy door. Once he was gone, Raven's breath came out in a soft rush. She closed her eyes for a brief moment. She didn't want it to show, but for a moment, she was scared out of her wits. Even though they were in the stairwell of a courthouse, there was no telling what he would've done to her if Hawk hadn't shown up.

Opening her eyes, she caught Hawk staring at her with an expression that made her body go rigid. Suddenly, the air around them turned claustrophobic and the tension grew thick. The attraction between the two of them?

Unfreakingdeniable.

CHAPTER 4

Raven took a protective step away from Hawk, the same as she did with Tommie, only this time, Hawk wasn't advancing towards her and she wasn't in fear of what would happen. Well, she took that back. She *was* afraid, but not because she thought he would harm her physically. No, physically her body was reacting to something that had nothing to do with fear. It was definitely primal; pure, unadulterated *lust.*

"Rae?"

The familiarity in his voice when he spoke her name snapped her out of her unwanted thoughts and back to the stairwell. Why the hell did he keep shortening her name like that, like he was a friend...or a lover.

"What?" Raven blinked when she heard the breathless quality in her voice.

"You sure you're okay? Did he hurt you, because if he did–"

"No, no." Frowning slightly, Raven shook her head. "He didn't. I'm fine. He just took me by surprise, that's all."

Trying to find something else to focus on other than him, Raven looked around and saw her briefcase lying haphazardly on its side. She moved to pick it up, but Hawk got to it first. Their fingers touched when he handed it to him. The spark of electricity that sizzled from the contact made both of them react in different ways. Raven took in a quick inhalation of breath and held it for several long seconds.

Hawk's head jerked back as if he'd taken one on the chin. However, he recovered quickly when she practically snatched the briefcase out of his grasp and rubbed her palm against her skirt to ease the tingling. Seeing the smirk that tilted his mouth upwards, she scowled.

Squaring her shoulders and lifting her chin, she spoke in a voice that to her relief was strong and clear. "Although your assistance wasn't needed, I appreciate the intervention just the same."

A piercing gleam entered Hawk's eyes. "If that's a thank you, you're welcome."

Raven's hand tightened on the handle of the briefcase. "I had everything under control. We're in a courthouse, for God's sake." Her chin nodded to a corner behind Hawk. "There are cameras everywhere. Believe me, he'll be behind bars within the hour."

"I'm sure Tommie already knew that, but as you can see, he don't give a fuck about no cameras," Hawk answered in a thick, slow drawl. "But don't worry 'bout it, I'll take care of it."

"I don't need you to 'take care of it.'"

"Rae–"

"My name is *Raven,*" she snapped, unable to take another second of her shortened name drizzling off his tongue. It put her in mind of sweet molasses being poured over hot, buttered pancakes. Hell, he didn't know her like that. Nor would he ever. "And anyway, what are you doing here?"

"What am I doing here?" Hawk intentionally repeated. "I thought I was saving you. *Raven.*"

She shifted from one foot to the other when he deliberately called her by her given name. It wasn't much better, though. Matter of fact, it sounded even more intimate and personal. Exasperated by how easily he irritated her, Raven took a deep breath. She tried her best to keep her frustration level low. Why did he have this effect on her?

"I meant what were you doing *here*? Today? In the courtroom." She clarified the question with exaggerated simplicity.

Hawk's shoulder lifted in a casual shrug. "Heard you were trying this case and decided to stop in. Hope I didn't distract you."

"Of course, you didn't," she scowled.

"How are you? It's been a while. The last time I saw you was at Angel's house, right?"

Raven stared at him in silence, hating the fact that the memory forced her to acknowledge that time he caught her eavesdropping on Nikki and her friend, Keisha. After all this time, she still remembered how flirtatious he was, pinning her up against the wall and blocking any means of escape. The provocative words he'd whispered in her ear had screwed with her mind while making her body hot. Thinking about it now, Raven admitted that escaping had not entered her mind in any way, shape, or form. Quite the opposite, in fact.

"I see you remember that meeting as vividly as I do," Hawk purred in a husky voice.

The unadulterated arrogance of the man made Raven grind her teeth. "I don't know what you're talking about. I don't have the time nor the inclination to stand here and play word games with you. The only thing you need to know is that your turn to sit in the hot seat is coming soon, Pattel. I promise you that," she added in an attempt to take the confident smirk off of his face. She should've known it wouldn't work.

Hawk came a few steps closer. "I'm looking forward to it, because I agree, when it's my turn, it's gon' get real hot, real fast, Ms. Randolph. Trust that."

"Keep underestimating me if you choose to. It'll be fun to see how that works out for you."

"Lady, believe me, underestimating you is one mistake I'll never make. Now if there's nothing else you *need* from me..." Hawk smiled suggestively before glancing down at his watch. "I have somewhere I gotta be. It's been fun taking this little trip down memory lane with you, though. Maybe we'll get a chance to create a few more memories very soon."

Raven shook her head at the sheer audacity of the man. Yes, she was appreciative for what he did, but his cocky disregard for the office she held rubbed her the wrong way. He was no better than

Frank Giuliani and his goons. In fact, he and his family were worse and infinitely more dangerous. Unlike Tommie, his threats were subtler; more personal.

Rolling her eyes, Raven turned to leave when she suddenly remembered what the other man revealed about knowing where she lived and her daily routine. A shiver of apprehension crept down her spine when she realized they were watching her. The scary part was that she hadn't had a clue. She'd have to report the conversation to her superiors once she got back to the office. Although she hated the idea of having a security detail assigned to her for protection, it was something she might have to consider until the trial was over. After that, well…

"Raven, what is it?"

Raven stared up at him and found him watching her with his usual focused, unblinking gaze. It bordered on being unnerving, but Raven refused to let herself be intimidated by it. Her lips parted to dismiss his observation, but Hawk wasn't having it.

"And don't tell me it's nothing. I can see from the look on your face that something's wrong. What were you thinking about just now?"

Something told her he wasn't going to let it go without an argument, so she told him with great reluctance. "I...that asshole...he told me something that complicates things. I'm sure it's nothing."

"What did he say?" When she kept her lips glued shut, Hawk practically growled her name. "Raven, answer me. If you won't tell me, I'll track him down and find out myself."

"No!" Any more interference from Hawk would only make things worse than they already were. "Okay, fine. Somehow, he knows where I live. In fact, he seems to know my entire daily routine. He knows that I take a walk every morning, what coffee shop I stop in on the way back, what time I leave my apartment..."

Raven swallowed hard as the gravity of what it all meant hit home. It was possible that she was in serious danger. Tommie's words were meant as a warning. If she didn't fall into line and ease up, she had no doubt they would take steps to get the message across in other ways. She had to finally admit the thought frightened her, and not just a little bit.

"Hey. Listen to me." When she shook her head and kept her eyes averted, Hawk shocked her by placing a gentle finger underneath her chin and turning her face back to him. "Listen to me, Rae. I'll take care of this. He's not goin' to hurt you. There's nothing for you to worry about."

Doubt at his words clouded her eyes. "But–"

"No buts. Nothing will happen to you. I promise you that."

"And I'm supposed to just believe you and leave it at that?" She stepped away from him, immediately missing the warmth of his hand against her skin. "I don't believe for one moment you were in the courtroom out of curiosity. Your family is just as dirty as Giuliani. For all I know, you have a personal interest in making sure he's set free."

"Frankie's been doing shit like this for years. He's taken it too far, this little vice of his. Now he has to face the consequences."

"Wow, that's a revelation. No honor among thieves, I see."

"Don't compare me to him, Rae. I may be a lot of things, but I draw the line at hurting women." A muscle in Hawk's jaw jumped in irritation. "Like I said, I'll take care of this. You'll be safe."

"Why should I trust you?"

"Whether you know it or not, you do, though."

"That's ridiculous," she scoffed.

"When you saw me come down the stairs, I saw the look on your face. You were relieved to see me. Admit it."

"I would've been relieved no matter *who* appeared at that particular moment. There's nothing special about you!" They both heard the vehemence in her voice.

Hawk cocked his head to the side. "Exactly who are you trying to convince here? Me, or yourself."

Raven opened her mouth to retaliate but refused to stand there and go back and forth with him. Her lip curled in disgust, she turned and hurried down the remaining stairs and out the door that led to the main floor. Hawk Pattel could think what he liked. She took an oath to follow the ethical rules of the jurisdiction of the state of New York and to uphold the rules of the constitution of the United Sates to the best of her ability. The day she trusted a Pattel for *anything*, let alone her safety, would be the day she turned in her letter of resignation and personally committed herself into a psych unit.

CHAPTER 5

Later that evening, Hawk sat in the back of his chauffeured car staring out the window as he travelled the route that took him to the woman who seemed to have taken up permanent residence in his thoughts. His intentions were to go to *Club Bliss*, relax in VIP, chill for a while and then bounce, but as the hours ticked by the idea of going clubbing became less and less attractive. If he were being honest with himself, nights like that lost their appeal a long time ago.

For some reason, a picture of Raven flashed through his mind. She was one of the sexiest women he had ever come in contact with. Her sensuality seemed deliberately understated and hidden beneath the guise of her profession. Barely 5'3, her creamy, succulent skin reminded Hawk of addictive dark chocolate. He'd always had a problem keeping his sweet tooth under control; damned if Raven Randolph didn't tempt him to overindulge and go on a sweet sugar high.

What he told her was the truth. She'd been on his mind quite a bit since he saw her at Angel's. Just remembering the way she responded so perfectly to him that day made his dick swell with need. She was ready for him, ripe like a sweet piece of fruit. He wanted to be the one to pluck her from her prudish surroundings and introduce her to the woman she was meant to be. If he had any question of whether or not the attraction between them was still there, those few minutes they spent in the stairwell dispelled any doubt. This...*thing* between them was just as powerful as it had always been. Probably more.

Hawk glanced out the window as Danny, his driver, pulled the luxury car to a stop in front of the building he was directed to drive to. Hawk definitely hadn't planned on making the place one of his stops, but after seeing Raven earlier, she was all he could think about. And this time, it wasn't about any kind of vendetta. No, this was about him and Raven and quenching his insatiable thirst.

When Danny opened his door, Hawk climbed out and took determined steps to the impressive government building where the District Attorney's office was located. Once inside, he reached in his pocket. Pulling out his money clip he peeled off several large faced bills from the swollen stack. He gave it to the security guard before bypassing the security scanner and getting on the elevator. After pushing the button that would take him to the twenty-second floor, Hawk stood with legs spread and arms folded in front of him. The security cameras from the entrance to Raven's office were disabled for thirty minutes. That was more than enough time for him to get in and at least get a taste of what he had been craving for so long.

Once the elevator doors stopped and opened, Hawk stepped out and glanced around, satisfied that he didn't see anyone present in the hallway. Most of the employees left hours ago. Earlier, Hawk put one of his men on Raven as soon as she left the courthouse and told him to report back after she got to her destination. He kept his phone close until he received the call that told him she went back to her office. Only then did he relax enough to focus on the dinner meeting he had with his brother. After they finished, a quick call to his man watching her confirmed she was still in her office. Perfect. He knew there was no way he could let the opportunity pass.

Slow steps brought Hawk to Raven's closed office door. He stood in front of it for a few moments, staring at her name embossed in bold, black lettering before slowly twisting the doorknob and letting himself in.

*****

Raven sat in her office reading over the file on the Pattel family she'd grabbed earlier from the stack resting on the corner of her desk. Most of the information was in her computer, but her eyes grew tired from the strain of staring at the screen for so long so she switched up.

Deciding to take a break, she pulled her glasses off and dropped her head back on the headrest. She thought about the phone call she received a couple of hours ago. Giuliani's henchman was in custody facing a charge of threatening an officer of the court. Of course, Giuliani's lawyer insisted the man acted on his own with no direction from his client. As much as Raven hated to admit it, they had no proof otherwise so she would have to be satisfied with the strict warning the judge gave Giuliani and his lawyer. As far as protection for her, she decided against it. She had a licensed weapon and knew how to use it. From now on, she'd be carrying it with her everywhere she went until she felt she was out of danger.

Sitting up, she slipped her glasses back on. She'd have to be more alert and aware of her surroundings, but Raven refused to let the incident that happened earlier distract her from the job she had to do. She glanced down at the folder in front of her. It had been a while since she'd gone over the information they had on the Pattel family. Seeing Hawk today stirred up the urge to go through it. There *had* to be something they were missing. Yes, they were still working on putting pressure on the confidential informant working for the Pattels, but he hadn't been able to uncover as much as they hoped.

Any other time, Raven would have come to the conclusion that the CI was playing them for fools, but he was well aware of the type of time he faced in federal prison if he didn't come through and give them something substantial enough they could use. The Pattels weren't stupid, they were very careful about who they let into their inner circle. Obsessively so. Isaac and Joseph, the patriarchs of the Pattel family, didn't stay steps ahead of the federal prosecutors all these years by being careless.

Raven turned to the next page in the folder and stared at the picture of a beautiful young woman whose eyes reminded her of the man who had haunted her thoughts all evening. Leah Pattel. To say she was another enigma that Raven couldn't quite figure out would be an understatement.

What she *did* know was that from the day Leah was born, Joseph Pattel's daughter was the darling of the family; spoiled and adored by the Pattel men. She was also loved by the public as well, almost a celebrity of sorts, the same as the rest of her family.

However, five years ago at the age of twenty-one, she dropped off the radar. The DA's office had no information on her whatsoever. Nothing. It was as if she'd disappeared off the face of the earth. The only thing the Pattels would say when asked about her was that she was traveling the world, but Raven knew there was more to it than that. Leah was too close to her family to just stay away from them for no reason. Something happened to make her purposely distance herself from them. *But what?*

Extremely fatigued, Raven propped her head on her hand. What she should've been doing for the last few hours was looking through her notes to prepare for court on Monday morning. It was her intention to do just that until the run in with Hawk.

Raven sighed. The incident at Nikki's house was well over a year ago, but today when she saw Hawk it could've easily been yesterday. What was it about him that still affected her so? She didn't know, but whatever it was, she needed to get over it. The last thing she needed was for Hawk Pattel to have the power to screw with her head, but damned if he didn't make her body tingle in areas they shouldn't. God knows she hated to admit that.

After all the time that passed, she still remembered the words he whispered in her ear in the hallway that night at Nikki's house. Somehow, he knew what she wanted. What she needed. Giving in to temptation, Raven allowed herself to imagine what it would feel like being with a man like Hawk, having him intimately touch her body, discover its secrets and...

Before she could finish the thought, the opening of her door made her sit up straight in her chair. She assumed it was the cleaning staff until she remembered they came and left hours ago. Frowning, she watched with cautious curiosity to see who it was. When she saw Hawk Pattel standing in the doorway, Raven went completely still.

Had her thoughts conjured him up or was it just her imagination?

Raven removed her reading glasses and blinked, but he was still there. Standing slowly, she braced her hands on the desk in front of her for support. "What are you doing here?"

CHAPTER 6

The question earned her a crooked smile from Hawk that did nothing to dispel the sense of dread tightening in her chest.

"I asked you a question," she said when he came in and closed the door behind him. Raven almost stopped breathing when she heard the latch click softly to indicate he locked it. She held a hand up as he stalked predatorily across the room. "I want you to get out before I call security to come and throw you out. I mean it!"

Now two steps away from her, Hawk's mocking smirk unnerved her even more. Raven snatched the phone up to make good on her threat, but before she could push a button, Hawk plucked it from her hand and placed the receiver back on the base.

Determined not to show fear, Raven stood her ground. "I swear to God, if you don't get the hell out of my office, I will scream this entire got damn building down!"

His eyebrows lifting in apparent unconcern was her undoing. Raven tried to dart around her desk, but she waited too late. Hawk caught her arm and pulled her back flush against his body. Raven acted instinctively and stomped the sharp heel of her stiletto down on his foot.

"Shit!" Hawk roared out in pain. "Fuck!"

When his grip loosened, Raven used the opportunity to wrench herself from his grasp, but he caught her before she could take more than a step. Cursing under his breath, Hawk picked her clear up off the floor so that she couldn't use her feet as weapons again.

"Calm down, got dammit!" He whispered harshly in her ear.

His warm breath on her ear had her doing just the opposite. Like a frightened animal caught in a trap, she started clawing at the hands that held her captive and kicking her feet. Hawk moved back just in time when she tried to head butt him in the face.

"Got *dammit,* Rae!"

"Let me go!" She grunted, struggling with everything in her to get free. "Put...me...down...*right...now*!" She inhaled a deep breath in preparation to do exactly as she threatened and scream bloody murder, but before she could get it out, Hawk's hand clamped over her mouth.

"That's enough. Scream or kick me again, I'll put you over my knee and spank that pretty little ass of yours until you can't sit on it for a week." When she let out a shriek from behind his hand in outraged protest, Hawk added in a dangerously soft tone, "Try me if you don't believe me. In fact, I'm *begging* you to."

Raven's eyes widened. Was that the excited anticipation of actually spanking her that she heard in his voice? She abruptly stopped all movement.

Seeing that she had ceased to struggle, Hawk waited a few seconds then slowly removed his hand from her mouth. "Good girl. Now. I'm gonna let you down, but Raven, remember what I said. Do *not* scream and don't fight me."

Hawk waited a few seconds then let her slide down his body one agonizing inch at a time. When her bottom glided over his crotch, she couldn't stop the gasp that came tearing out of her mouth. Their altercation left him unmistakably aroused.

Feeling the floor underneath her feet, Raven was too afraid to move. Even if she'd been of a mind to try, Hawk kept an arm securely wrapped around her waist.

"What are you doing here?" she asked breathlessly.

"What do *you* think?" he countered. "You're a smart woman. Figure it out."

She could hear the amusement in his voice. He was purposely taunting her. "If I knew, I wouldn't be asking."

Hawk gave her the answer by moving her hair to the side and kissing the back of her neck. Raven jumped, biting back a moan of desire just in time. However, there was nothing she could do about the way her body trembled in reaction to the touch of his lips on her skin. Especially her neck.

"You like that, hm?" Hawk murmured in a low, lazy voice.

Raven leaned forward as much as his hold would allow. "No, I don't."

"You might not, but your body does," Hawk teased.

"What I'd *like* is for you to tell me what you want then get out!" She tried to interject a note of authority in her voice in an attempt to sound in control. In reality, she was anything but...and they both knew it.

"Are you sure that's what you want?"

"Positive!" She snapped.

"For some reason, I don't believe you, Raven."

"Hawk–"

"Tell you what. I'm going to give you an opportunity to prove you mean that. If you do, you have my word that I'll leave you alone. I won't ever bother you again."

"Prove it to you how?" Raven asked warily. Of course, she didn't trust a word he said. He was up to something.

"I guess it's obvious that I'm affected by you." Hawk's pelvis cradled her soft rear, leaving her in no doubt as to just how much he wanted her. "I suspect you–" The rest of Hawk's sentence was left dangling in the air as he abruptly stopped speaking.

Raven frowned when all she heard was silence. "Look, if you're finished playing your little game, I want you to get the hell out of my office. Do you hear what I'm–"

This time Raven was the one who let her words taper off when she realized what had gotten his attention. A name from the file open on her desk leapt out at her like a bright beacon. Leah Pattel. Hawk was facing her desk. It was obvious he was looking at the information she'd been reading on his sister.

"Hawk–"

"What tha'…" Keeping one arm tightly secured around Raven's waist, he leaned down and picked the folder up.

Heart thudding in her chest, she twisted away from his arm, lunging for the file and trying to snatch it out of his hand. "Give that to me! Hawk!"

Raven stood on tiptoes then jumped to get it, but it was no use. He was too tall. He easily kept it out of her reach and started reading. "Hawk, you cannot be reading that! It's confidential information!"

Finally, he twisted his head her way and stared at her. Eyes that had only moments ago been warm and aroused were now cold and hard as steel. "What the hell is this? Why are you investigating my sister?"

CHAPTER 7

Raven felt faint when she suddenly remembered that the information on the confidential informant was only a couple of keystrokes away in her computer from where they stood. Extremely nervous, she struggled to keep her voice from shaking. "Hawk, give that to me."

"I asked you a question. Why does the DA's office have a file on Leah?"

She swallowed, knowing she had to tell him something before he went searching for what he wanted to know. "It's just background material. It shouldn't come as a surprise that we have general information on Leah as well as every member of your family."

Hawk's eyes narrowed. He refused to be placated. "What I want to know is why? My sister has nothing to do with our businesses. She left home over five years ago and hasn't been back since. So, I'm gon' ask you again and I suggest you tell me the truth. Why do you have this and why were you reading it tonight?"

Raven licked her lips as her eyes faltered away from his then came back. She had to stall until she thought of a way to get that folder. "Where is your sister if you don't mind me asking? What caused her to leave the family?"

The shutters instantly slammed down over Hawk's eyes. "It's obvious your department is trying to turn her absence into something it's not. Leah went away to school, did a little traveling and then decided to build a life away from New York. That's it."

"A life away from New York or away from the Pattels?" Raven asked.

Hawk flinched as if she touched a nerve before his face went completely blank. "Can you blame her for wanting to get away from scrutiny like this?" He held the folder up. "Unfounded accusations are thrown at us every day. I'm not saying my family is perfect, but we sure as hell aren't what your office is making us out to be; haven't been for a long time. Leah never would have been able to have a normal life if she would have stayed here."

"What about you?" Raven asked in a rush. She gave her desk a quick glance to make sure there was nothing else left out in the open for him to see. "Have you ever wanted that? A normal life, I mean."

"Who's to say I don't have one? My father and uncle worked damn hard for everything they have. They made a lot of sacrifices that they paid for in blood, sweat, and tears. Both of them raised my brothers, cousin, and myself to be strong men, gave us an education and groomed us to take over the family business. Exactly what's abnormal about that, ADA Randolph? It's the American dream, isn't it?"

Raven almost fainted with relief when he tossed the folder back on the desk. "Looking over your shoulder from one day to the next, waiting for the other shoe to drop is what you consider a 'normal' life? If that's true, I feel sorry for you."

"Your sister seems to have adjusted quite well to Angel's 'normal' life, don't you agree?" Hawk shot back. Tilting his head to the side, he watched her closely. "You think my family's nothing more than a pack of rabid animals the world would be better off without, don't you?"

"I didn't say that."

"You didn't have to but let me point something out to you that you seem to be blind to. Your sister is married to one of the biggest, baddest wolves of all, yet Nikki looks to be very happy from what I can see. They have a great marriage and a beautiful family." Hawk shrugged. "If that ain't normal, I don't know what is."

Raven's lips tightened. Even though she knew he was trying to provoke her, she couldn't stop herself from snatching at the bait. "Leave my sister out of this."

"Yet, you think it's okay to involve mine," He countered smoothly, nodding towards the file on the desk.

"You know what, I'm beginning to think Leah is probably the only sane person in your family. At least she got out. Nikki tried, but she wasn't strong enough because she's in love with Angel. I don't agree, but I understand it. That's why I'll be strong *for* her. I won't rest until she and my nephew are safely away from him and everything he represents." Raven clenched her hands into fists, forcing herself to close her mouth when she saw his attentive gaze. She'd already said too much.

Hawk slowly shook his head from side to side. "You should heed the advice Angel gave you a while back. Keep your nose out of things that don't concern you, Rae. The first being your sister's marriage. Angel loves her fiercely and doesn't take kindly to you trying to come between them."

"I'm not afraid of Angel."

The corner of Hawk's mouth quirked upwards at her mutinous expression. "What about me? Are you afraid of me?"

Raven's chin lifted, even more defiant. "Of course not."

"You should be," Hawk came back softly.

Raven stared at him in silence, swallowing nervously. Angel said those very same words to her, but with Hawk, there was a marked difference in the tone. Whereas Angel's sneering comment made her hackles rise like the fur on an angry cat's back, Hawk's taunts caused a completely different reaction. The arousal he made no effort to hide prompted the butterflies in her stomach to do somersaults as if they were trying out for the Olympics.

When he pulled her closer, Raven's nipples tightened. Even *she* could tell the fit of their bodies was perfect, almost as if God Himself molded the two of them to come together that way. She struggled to keep her breathing steady. They stared at each other as the electricity around them sizzled like a violently charged lighting storm.

Hawk seemed as swept up in the intensity of the moment as much as she. When his mouth lowered to hers, Raven used the last bit of her willpower and turned her head to try and avoid what she knew was coming.

"No," she whispered, dreading what could happen, *would* happen, if he kissed her. "Please, don't."

"Why? Because you're afraid?"

Hawk's voice was raw with need, want, and animalistic desire. The sound of it caused a shiver of lust to trickle through Raven's body. When she didn't answer, his mouth remained hovered over hers for several, heart stopping moments. Raven held her breath. Finally, as if coming to a decision, his lips came crushing down on hers, hungrily ravishing and plundering her mouth with his eager tongue.

The kiss wasn't gentle, but it wasn't entirely Hawk's fault. The second their lips touched something exploded inside of Raven. The match was lit and the flame was alive. Raven was on fire. That was the very reason she didn't want him to touch her. She'd known once he did, she would be powerless to fight this uncontrollable side he always brought out of her.

Raven struggled to pull her hands free. She needed to touch him, get closer. When Hawk finally allowed it, her arms found their way around his neck, holding him tighter, savoring the faint taste of clover, vanilla, and fruit that tasted like fine cognac. Raven grew drunk off the flavor. Intoxicated. Her tongue curled around his, seeking more of his taste. Seeking more of *him*.

Hawk abruptly broke off the kiss. His fingers threaded through her hair, holding her head steady as he studied her. Inching her back towards the desk, he growled in satisfaction when he saw her damp, swollen mouth. "I'm gonna make you feel so good, Rae. Relax. Don't think, baby. Just feel. I'll take care of the rest."

Lost in a web of desire, Raven acknowledged what he described was exactly what she wanted.

She didn't want to have to be rational or responsible in that moment. She didn't want to think about what she getting ready to do; there would be time enough for regrets tomorrow. Maybe it was a coward's way out, but she didn't care. Raven closed her eyes, blocking out everything except him. For once, she wanted to kick caution to the curb and just go with the flow.

"Open your eyes." Hawk paused and waited until she complied. "Tell me you want this."

Raven nibbled softly on her inner lip. She stared up at him through her lashes, suddenly hesitant and unsure.

"I want in, Rae. Inside your head and inside your body. Lower those walls for me. Just a little bit. Will you do that for me?" Hawk asked waiting for her to oblige.

Still she hesitated, but finally Raven gave him a small, tentative nod.

Hawk angled his head slightly to the side. "I want the words, baby. Say the words."

Raven's eyes widened in alarm. When she shivered involuntarily, Hawk bent his head and delivered a soft kiss to the spot where her neck met her collarbone.

"I'm waiting, sweetness," he prompted when she whimpered. Deciding to give her a little motivation, Hawk pulled Raven's hand away from where it was clutching the material of his shirt and brought it down to the thick erection outlined in the front of his pants. Her fingers immediately closed around the print. Hawk's bulging sex strained against her hand. He barely managed to hold back his moan.

"Tell me you want it." He pushed the words out from behind clenched teeth.

"Hawk—"

"Tell me," he demanded gruffly.

"Okay, *yes*! I want it!" Raven screamed.

Hawk was on her before the words barely had time to pass her lips. The kiss was wild and hungry. Raven clung to him, mewling in enjoyment. Hawk groaned in approval. He seemed pleased to see his aggressiveness didn't scare her. Instead, it seemed to heighten her desire for him. Arouse her senses. Thrill her to no end.

Yes.

Raven opened her mouth wider to receive his kiss. Hawk had the act down to a science. He absorbed every single part of her essence with an erotic urgency that left her weak. She moaned as his tongue darted repeatedly in and out of her mouth, swirling around hers and stoking the fire inside of her until her entire body burned red hot.

He grabbed the hem of her skirt and without lifting his mouth from hers, mumbled against her lips, "Next time, I promise to go slow, but…"

"Just hurry," Raven interrupted breathlessly. Her arms crisscrossed with his to get to his belt. "I don't want it slow."

"Fuck," Hawk whispered hoarsely.

He finally got the tight, little skirt over the generous curve of her ass then lifted her up on the desk. When she took too long unzipping his pants, Hawk impatiently moved her hands out the way and took over. While he did that, Raven tried to focus on unbuttoning his shirt. Her hands trembled with eagerness. She only managed to undo the first two before Hawk, once again, took over that task and ripped the shirt open.

When she saw an intricately carved '**P**' on the left side of his chest, Hawk's eyes went to her mouth as she unconsciously nibbled on her lip. She pushed his shirt down past his shoulders then lightly traced the letter with her finger before reading the short, but powerful, scripted quote tattooed underneath it. *Family above all else.*

"Nice," she whispered.

Placing a finger under her chin, Hawk lifted her lips and reclaimed her mouth. At the same time, he slipped a finger in the side of her panties and found her creamy, slick wetness.

Raven gasped. She was so ready for him. There was no denying it. She moaned, surprised but turned on when he mirrored the movement of his tongue to the slow thrust of his searching finger inside her hungry body. Her eyelashes fluttered. She threw her head back with a low cry when he caressed the quivering bud of her clit with his thumb. Ripples of pleasure skipped along her spine as she arched into his touch.

"Hawk!"

"I know, baby, I know. I'm gonna take care of you. I wanna taste you so bad, but I *need* to fuck you, Rae. Now, baby." He gripped the delicate material of her sexy, little panties. The thin barrier was all that stood in the way of giving them what they both wanted. Just as he prepared himself to rip them off her cell phone rang.

Out of habit, Raven automatically glanced at it on her desk to see who was calling. When she did, a sudden chill spread throughout her body, effectively dousing the fire Hawk started. The name displayed on the caller ID was not what turned her stone cold sober. It was the sight of the stack of files on her desk full of damning information about the Pattels that snapped her back to reality with a bone jarring intensity that left her head spinning.

She tried to grab Hawk's hand, but still in the throes of lust, he easily evaded her touch. Yanking her hips to the edge of the desk, he slipped her panties to the side. "Hawk, no...*no!*" Panic gripped Raven in its ironclad grip when she looked down and saw him poised and positioned between her widely spread thighs. "*Stop!*"

CHAPTER 8

Finally, the hysteria in Raven's voice penetrated Hawk's brain. He looked up at her through eyes cloudy with need, desire, and anticipation. Mistakenly assuming her nervousness had returned, Hawk was quick to reassure her. "It's okay, baby. It'll fit, I promise."

Raven shook her head violently. Not knowing what else to do, she snatched her cell phone up and answered the call just before it went to voicemail. "H-Hello?"

Hawk scowled at her with incredulous disbelief when she placed a hand on his chest to push him away. For a moment, he didn't move. "You serious?"

She shot him a look to quiet his outrage while exerting pressure on his chest to get him to step back. With great reluctance, he gave her just enough space to hop down from the desk.

"Hello, Raven? This is Wesley," the voice on the other end said. "I hope I'm not disturbing you."

"I...uh, no. Hi. Hi, Wesley."

He hesitated when he heard a slight catch in her voice. "Is everything okay? You sound…distressed."

That was an understatement if she ever heard one. "No, no, no. I'm fine. Actually, uh, I'm glad to hear from you."

"You are?" Wesley's surprise was obvious in the high-pitched lilt of his tone.

"Mmhm." Raven understood exactly why he sounded that way. Wesley was someone she used to date off and on, nothing serious. They acted as the other's escort whenever they had functions to attend and needed a plus one. The last few months, though, she'd been avoiding his calls.

Refusing to look Hawk's way, she felt the anger radiating off his body in waves. Balancing the phone between her shoulder and ear, she concentrated on adjusting her panties and pulling her skirt down. Buttoning her blouse, she half-stumbled around the desk to put some distance between them.

"I'm sorry to call so late," Wesley continued. "I realize you had court today, but knowing you, you're probably at the office."

"Yes. Yes, um, as a matter of fact I am." She finally gathered the courage to look at Hawk. She almost choked when she found him stuffing his rigid package back in his underwear as best he could before fixing his pants.

"I figured as much. We're two of a kind, you and me. I'm actually still up myself working on a speech I'm giving at a seminar I'm attending next month in Wisconsin. I don't think I got a chance to tell you that out of all the top professors in my field, I was chosen to speak on the economic analysis of law and give my views on determining if a legal rule should be declared an administrative law or–"

"Wesley!" Raven gritted her teeth in irritation. He'd only been on the phone for ten seconds and was boring the hell out of her already. The only reason she answered his call was because she needed him as a barrier between herself and Hawk.

Her eyes went to him again. He walked over to the window and was standing with his back to her but Raven could see his reflection glaring at her through the glass. He didn't even pretend to act as if he wasn't listening to her side of the conversation. From the stiff set of his wide shoulders, she had no doubt he was absolutely furious.

"I-I'm sorry, Wesley, I didn't mean to snap. I...I'm just tired I guess. It's been a long day. Actually, I think I'm getting ready to go home. Was there something you needed?" She reached over and gently closed her laptop.

"Well, I was hoping we could see each other before I go to the seminar. You know, just to catch up."

"Yes, well, um...ma-maybe I can cook dinner for you at my place before you leave?"

Hearing the invitation she issued, Hawk slowly turned around to face her. There was a familiar possessive gleam burning in his eyes that she saw before. The first time she thought it was her imagination, but now it was back. With a small frown marring her forehead, she blinked in confusion, but before she had a chance to delve further into what that could possibly mean, the expression disappeared from his face. In its place was the amusement she was so used to associating with him.

Raven's body tensed when he came towards her. "Wesley, I have to go. I'll call you and set up arrangements."

"But–"

"Talk to you soon." Raven quickly disconnected the call in the middle of Wesley stuttering a reply. She bit her inner lip when Hawk came to a standstill in front of her.

"Hanging up the phone when you did was your best out. Smart girl."

"I don't know what you're talking about."

"Yeah, you do." Hawk glanced down at the cell phone Raven clutched in her hand. "Tell me, was that the same Wesley Logansworth you were having dinner with the time I saw you at my restaurant?"

"You remember?" Raven tried not to let her surprise show on her face. That was last year. She would've guessed he had forgotten about that by now, but obviously he hadn't.

"Raven, one day soon, you gon' realize that I remember every single thing about you. Every last sexy detail."

"Too bad I can't say the same." She raised her shoulder as nonchalantly as she could manage when she told the lie. "Now if you don't mind–"

"So. You're cooking dinner for him, huh?"

"Not that it's any of your business, but yes."

"Okay." The ticking of the muscles in his jaw belied Hawk's calmness. "You know, I'll admit, when I heard you offer the invitation I was a little pissed off at first, but then I remembered how bored you looked when I first spotted you in the restaurant with him that night. Your eyes didn't come alive until you saw me walk in." He leaned in closer, making sure to keep visual contact. "For that matter, your *body* didn't come alive until you saw me."

Raven struggled to keep her breathing steady. "You have the biggest ego of any man I know."

Hawk chuckled quietly. "You don't know the men in my family, then."

"If you're finished here, I have a few things I need to wrap up before I leave."

Using a whisper soft touch, he ran the back of his knuckles down her cheek. "This is the last time I'm letting you get away from me. Next time we start this, it'll be someplace where there are no interruptions. I'll make sure of that." His white teeth flashed a smile that took her breath away. Raven could've sworn she swayed in reaction to it.

"Enjoy your reprieve, Raven. It'll be a short one. See you soon."

Raven watched him walk out without turning to look back. The moment the door closed behind him, she rushed forward and locked it just in case he changed his mind and decided to come back. Her hands curled into fists when she heard the unmistakable sound of his low, amused chuckle from the other side of the door. Arrogant son of a bitch.

Her eyes went to her computer. The files saved on the hard drive contained years of wiretaps and interviews with confidential informants, all part of a widespread investigation of a family deeply entrenched in organized crime. Almost any criminal act the authorities could name, the Pattels committed them. They were masters at keeping their illegal activities intricately hidden, which is the reason it was so hard to make any charges stick. The thought of how close Raven came to compromising everything rendered her nauseous.

Yes, she might desire Hawk Pattel, might crave the sexual high he represented, but she couldn't allow herself to lose control again. Hawk was a fantasy. He wasn't real. The quicker she got him and his family off the streets the better things would be for everyone...including herself.

*****

Hawk's thoughts remained on Raven as he rode the elevator down to the first floor. He barely acknowledged the frantic security guard who hurried towards him as soon as he stepped out into the lobby.

"Mr. Pattel! I was wondering what was keeping you, sir. R-Remember, I told you the cameras would only be turned off for thirty minutes. Anything longer would raise suspicion." He tried not to stare at Hawk's shirt, which now missed half its buttons. Not wanting to offend Hawk, he chose his next words carefully. "Y-You've been up there almost fifteen minutes more than we agreed on."

Blowing impatiently, Hawk never broke stride. Reaching into his pocket, he pulled out a roll of bills secured with a rubber band and tossed it at the guard. "Don't worry, I'll take care of it. I appreciate your assistance."

The man stared at the thick roll of hundred dollar bills with disbelieving eyes. As if remembering where he was, he looked around nervously and wiped his damp brow with the sleeve of his shirt. "Th-Thank you, Mr. Pattel. Have a good evening, sir."

Once outside, Danny opened the back door of the car for Hawk, then rounded the hood to slide behind the wheel. "Where to, Mr. Pattel?"

Hawk settled back against the plush seat. He didn't answer right away because quite honestly, his driver couldn't take him where he wanted to be right now. Raven Randolph had a way of getting under his skin like no other woman he'd ever met, but after learning that his sister was part of the DA's investigation, things had changed. What he told Raven was true, Leah had no involvement in his family's business, she never had. It was imperative that her name be kept away from whatever case they were trying to build against the Pattels.

Hawk finally met the driver's eyes in the rearview mirror. "Take me back to my apartment, Danny."

As the driver smoothly merged the car into traffic, Hawk leaned his head back against the leather headrest. Images of Raven flashed through his mind like the pictures on a projection screen. With a growing sense of frustration, he remembered the softness of her skin, the sweet taste of her mouth, how tight her body felt around his finger. She responded to him so perfectly, just like he knew she would. Damn.

Hawk never lost control like he had in her office. *Ever.* He liked to have fun with the best of them, but there were boundaries that he didn't let himself cross. He was normally disciplined to a fault. Unfortunately, Raven Randolph tested the parameters of that discipline every damn time he saw her, making the lines of his boundaries blurred and uneven. Tonight, she bypassed them more easily than he wanted to admit. There was something about her that sparked his interest. She was different from other women he'd been involved with, strong, independent, and self-sufficient, but still...malleable. When she let her guard down he saw a glimpse of a woman who eagerly wanted to give herself over to the right man...and *he* planned on being that man.

For a brief moment, Hawk allowed himself the luxury of wondering what it would be like to actually own a woman like that. To call her *his,* protect her. Spoil her. Indulge her simply because he knew in return, she would give him everything, body, mind, and soul.

Although he'd never experienced it, his cousin, Darrell Monroe, seemed to have that sort of relationship with his wife, Jerra. As a matter of fact, all of Darrell's friends appeared to as well with their respective wives, who were women who spoke their mind, but yielded to their men whenever necessary. Quite honestly, it was the first time Hawk saw relationships like that. If circumstances were different...

But they weren't. Raven was who she was and he was a Pattel. She'd made no secret of the fact that she was coming after his family with both barrels loaded and now that she added Leah as one of the targets, all bets were off. Hawk needed to get the right head in the game and stop letting the one between his legs dominate his actions. His family's freedom depended on it.

Suddenly restless and needing a distraction, he changed his mind about where he wanted to go. "Danny, forget about driving me home. Take me to *Bliss*."

That was his original destination before making the detour to see Raven. If he didn't, he would've been there right now, enjoying the energy and the atmosphere of his club. He needed something to take his mind off the woman who seemed to be dominating his thoughts more than he cared to admit. Good music, a little fun and a beautiful woman to take home with him at the end of the night would do just that.

At least that's what he was betting on.

CHAPTER 9

Later that night, Raven let herself into her apartment and latched all three locks on the door before setting the alarm. She was extra careful coming home. Luckily, her apartment had a 24-hour doorman who was always alert and on his game. As soon as the cab had rolled up, he was there to open the door and escort her to the entrance of the apartment.

Kicking her shoes off, she pulled her blouse out of her skirt and unbuttoned it on the way to her bedroom. After taking a quick shower and slipping her robe on, she hummed under her breath as she took slow steps to the kitchen.

Half way there, Raven picked up the remote and clicked a button so that soft music flowed through the room. Next, she dimmed the lights and lit the new lemon sugar and vanilla candle she picked up for herself earlier in the week. Singing under her breath, she continued to the kitchen and poured a nice, big glass of Bordeaux before retracing her steps back to the living room and curling up on the sofa. Then, and only then, did she allow the long, deep, cleansing sigh that released the week's tension to escape and purge her body.

She was so tired she could barely keep her eyes open. Twelve hours days, endless cases and the stench of criminals like Giuliani were beginning to take a toll on her. Seeing Hawk tonight was the icing on the cake. She still couldn't believe she allowed him to kiss her, touch her like that. If it wasn't for that phone call from Wesley…

Raven shuddered at the implications of what that would've meant. She took a long swallow of the wine that had chilled in her refrigerator all week, patiently waiting for this exact moment. She licked her lips. Just what she needed.

She was in the process of bringing the glass back to her lips when she paused. A tiny smile teetered on the edge of her mouth as she retracted that thought. No. What she *needed* was some of what Hawk Pattel took great pains to stuff back into his pants once she called a halt to what they were on their way to doing in her office. *That's* what she *really* needed. It had been entirely too long since she indulged in that type of extracurricular activity, which was probably why she'd responded so easily to Hawk. At least, that's what she chose to tell herself. Whatever the case, she planned to make it priority number one to satisfy that itch the minute this case was wrapped up.

Of course, it wouldn't be with Hawk Pattel, she reassured herself.

Raven nibbled at the corner of her lip. No, it wouldn't be with Hawk and wouldn't be anywhere near as hot and wild with someone else, but that was okay. She would take safety, self-preservation and self-respect over a few hours of satisfying, lustful sex with Hawk Pattel any day.

"And you are spending way too much time thinking about that man." Raven spoke the words out loud so as to reinforce the sentiment. However, she ruined the effort when she thought about him reassuring her that 'it would fit'.

The grin Raven fought hard to suppress won out and spread across her face. "With his freaky ass."

Humming quietly again, she settled deeper into the plush cushions of the couch and closed her eyes. Before long, she was relaxed and less tense. If a fantasy of Hawk Pattel crept in a time or two as the music continued to cover the room in its smooth, melodic chords, Raven was okay with that. Just for the night, she would blame it on the wine.

The weekend went by far too quickly. Monday morning Raven walked into the courtroom bright and early, ready to put the final nail in Frank Giuliani's coffin. She'd spent the remainder of the weekend working on the case and found a piece of evidence that escaped them before. She wasn't sure how that happened, but it was a much-needed final piece of an intricate puzzle that would seal the deal on Giuliani's fate.

Removing her files from her briefcase, her thoughts briefly went to the conversation she had with Nikki last night. A.J.'s birthday was coming up in a couple of weeks. Of course, Angel and Nikki were going all out, turning their humongous back yard into a virtual set of A.J.'s favorite movie including the characters as well as a maze full of outer space monsters and on and on and on. Raven shook her head but couldn't help smiling. Her nephew was going to have a blast and she planned on having her camera ready to capture every single moment.

She listened as her team chatted quietly for a few moments until the judge entered the courtroom to take the bench. As the bailiff called for them to stand, Raven casually glanced to her right and found Frank Giuliani watching her with his usual arrogant smile plastered on his face. She saw the anger brewing in his eyes as well. Raven knew he had to be furious that his goon was locked up and facing some serious charges, but Giuliani would be joining him in prison soon enough.

Resisting the temptation to give him her middle fuck off finger, Raven brought her gaze forward, settling it on the judge then resuming her seat. Raven felt the familiar sense of excitement she always did the moment a case turned course to her advantage. But that all changed when Giuliani's attorney stood and made the stunning motion to have the charges dropped and the case thrown out.

Raven surged to her feet. "What? On what grounds?"

Judge Warner slammed her gavel three times to bring order. "Mr. Rogers. Ms. Randolph. Approach the bench."

Raven glared intently at Aaron Rogers as they made their way before the judge. Without waiting for him to speak, she hissed in outrage. "Your Honor, I don't know what the opposing attorney is trying to pull here. However, rest assured, it's nothing more than a ridiculous ploy because he knows his client is guilty as hel–"

"Ms. Randolph!" Judge Warner interrupted. "Watch your mouth in my courtroom!" She scolded.

Raven bit down on her tongue to keep herself in check. The last thing she wanted was to be found in contempt. "My apologies, Your Honor."

Judge Warner gave her a hard stare before turning to the defense attorney. "Mr. Rogers, on what grounds are you making this motion?"

Rogers gave the judge a stack of papers bound together before giving Raven an identical stack. "The warrant for the wiretap, Your Honor. If you look at the highlighted dates, you'll see that the detectives started listening in on my client's phone calls before the court issued warrant was granted."

Raven zeroed in on the dates he was referring to. He had to be mistaken. She knew the detective assigned to this case. There was no way he would make such a careless mistake. But when she saw the dates in question, her heart dropped sharply like a cement block in shallow waters. Dammit. Rogers was right. But the time lapse between when the warrant was approved and when the wiretap started was only...

"Eight minutes?" She looked up at Rogers, her eyes widened in disbelief at the lengths he would go to in order to free his client. "Eight. Minutes. You're trying to get this case thrown out over an eight-minute window? Are you serious?"

Rogers gave her one of his disdainful looks before continuing to address the judge. "As I'm sure Your Honor would agree, whether eight minute, eight hours, or eight days, this is a violation of my client's rights. It's clearly a breach of the Omnibus Crime Control and Safe Streets Act, which was designed to strike a balance between the law and the privacy rights of innocent citizens." He glanced at Raven before adding, "Clearly, this was not done."

Raven shook her head. Did he actually use the word "innocent" and "Giuliani" in the same sentence? Raven let out a sound that was a cross between a laugh and a hard puff of air before giving Judge Warner her full attention. If Rogers thought this act of desperation would work, he was in for a rude awakening. Judge Warner, the first African American women to be appointed to one of the highest courts in New York State, was one of the toughest officials who sat on the bench. Highly respected, she earned her success the hard way. Professionally, Raven admired her more than anyone she knew and strived to one day follow in her footsteps.

"Ms. Randolph..."

Raven looked at her expectantly, waiting on the scathing warning Rogers had coming. She could see if the lapse were hours instead of mere minutes. However, what she saw on the judge's face made her pause. "Yes ma'am?"

"Are you denying that the evidence of misconduct Mr. Rogers has presented is incorrect?"

Raven's eyebrows lifted high "Misconduct? I hardly think a perfectly innocent mistake that occurred within an *eight-minute* time-frame, could be labeled as 'misconduct'."

The judge lowered her head and glowered at Raven over the top of her glasses. "The only thing that matters here is the law, not what you *think*, Ms. Randolph."

Rendered speechless by the reprimand, a sudden sense of dread filled Raven's chest. She glanced down at the paperwork in her hands. Yes, technically the detective should've waited until the warrant cleared, and would definitely hear about it but this error constituted the outer most meaning of the word 'technicality'. The judge had the power to overrule something so trivial. Was she actually entertaining the prospect of dismissing the charges? Raven couldn't let that happen.

"Judge Warner, the defense is making a mockery out of the judicial system as well as this courtroom by trying to have this case thrown out."

Judge Warner removed her glasses and folded her hands in front of her. "Ms. Randolph, don't try and use my courtroom to excuse the sloppy work done in your department."

Raven's mouth fell open. "Your Honor–"

"Based on the evidence brought forth, I have no other choice but to have this case dismissed. *With* prejudice."

Raven stood frozen in shock after the judge tacked on those two last words, which meant Giuliani could never be brought up on these charges again. She had to be dreaming. This was *not* happening. "But Your Honor–"

Ignoring Raven, Judge Warner's tone was stiff and no-nonsense as she addressed the defense attorney. "Mr. Rogers, your client is free to go."

Raven gasped. *"Your Honor!"*

Judge Warner's gavel came down in swift anger. "That is enough, Ms. Randolph. My decision has been made."

"But—"

"One more word and you'll be held in contempt." She glared at Raven for several tense moments until she was satisfied that Raven heeded her warning. "Court is dismissed."

Amid the collective murmuring in the courtroom, Rogers sent her a mocking smirk as they turned to go back their stations. Raven silently handed her team the paperwork the attorney presented, momentarily tuning out their hushed questions. Putting folders in her briefcase, she glanced over at the defense table. It took everything in her to keep down the bile bubbling up in her throat when she saw the huge grin on Giuliani's face as he shook his attorney's hand. Their eyes momentarily met. He didn't even try to hide the smug look of victory his face held. When his lips pursed in a mocking kiss, Raven's hand shook with the effort it took to remain calm. There would be time to let her anger out later in private.

She turned to her co-workers. "You guys can go back to the office without me. I have some things I need to take care of."

Gwynn searched her face intently. "Raven, what the fuck?"

"I don't know, but I'm getting ready to find out. We'll discuss it when I get to the office."

Without waiting on a reply, she grabbed her briefcase, determined to find out what the hell just happened.

CHAPTER 10

Raven turned the corner and walked straight to the door that led her to the judge's chambers. Once there, she nodded to Janice Morris, Judge Warner's assistant. "I'd like to speak to her, please."

Normally, she and Janice would have exchanged pleasantries and engaged in small talk, but this day was anything but normal. It was obvious Janice was prepared for Raven's appearance. Her ocean blue eyes blinking wide with concern, she slipped a blonde curl behind her ear and nodded. "You can go in. Judge Warner said to expect you. You have ten minutes before she has to prepare for her next case."

Heart beating wildly in her chest, Raven's legs trembled as she opened the door to the judge's chambers and quietly closed it behind her. Raven watched as Judge Warner hung up her robe and waited for her to acknowledge her presence. It was hard to believe the woman was 58 years old. Her caramel complexioned skin was beautiful, barely touched with lines of age and only a few strands of gray could be seen in her short, curly afro. By choice, she didn't have any children, once remarking to Raven that her career was her child and her work was her life. Now on her second marriage, Raven had to admit that the judge seemed content and fulfilled with her choices.

Judge Warner sat down at her desk and stared at Raven. "Are you just going to stand there or would you like to have a seat, Ms. Randolph."

"Thank you, but I'll stand."

Crossing her legs, Judge Warner's shoulder lifted in a slight shrug. "Suit yourself. I knew it wouldn't take you long to get here. However, before you say a word, please know that I am not here to defend my decision so don't even steer this conversation in that direction."

Raven gripped the handle of her briefcase, forcing her breathing to remain steady. "Of course not, but I can't help but wonder what just happened out there."

"What happened was you failed to make sure your 'i's were dotted and your 't's crossed before you brought this case to my courtroom. This loss is on you, ADA Randolph. Plain and simple. Not only did you drop this case in the defendant's lap, but you gift wrapped it with a shiny red bow for him as well."

"I respectfully beg to differ."

"Of course, you do."

"Was the error a careless one, yes. I admit that. Was it stupid? Yes, I admit that too! But it wasn't one that called for you to dismiss all charges. You could've overruled the motion and proceeded to hear the case. Not only is an entire year's investigation gone down the drain, but you've let Giuliani get away with murder. He can never be tried on these charges again."

"Let's stop right there," Judge Warner snapped. She held up a long, slender finger. "One, you will *not* come in here and attempt to shift the blame for that mockery that just happened in there on me." She held up another finger. "Two, let this be the last time you speak to me in such a disrespectful tone. You do not tell me what I should've or could've done, ADA Randolph. The issue here was not the defendant's guilt or innocence. It's the fact that a simple, idiotic error was made by an overzealous investigator who only had to wait *eight minutes* until his warrant came in to proceed with the wiretap, but he chose not to follow procedure. The evidence establishing guilt must be properly prepared; it's a requirement of the law and those requirements exist for a reason."

"Yes, to protect the rights of innocent people. Not people like Giuliani."

Judge Warner stared at Raven before letting out a deep sigh. "Ms. Randolph, I think we need to bring this conversation to a close. Please proceed more carefully next time, but as far as this case, it's time to let it go."

"But–"

"Goodbye, ADA Randolph!" The words were uttered with firm emphasis.

Raven stood where she was, contemplating whether or not to ignore the dismissal and continue to argue her point. However, she quickly decided against the latter. This was one battle she couldn't win. Plus, she figured she pushed her luck about as far as she could. She wouldn't put it past Judge Warner to throw her in jail for a few hours just to teach her a lesson. Silently admitting defeat, Raven reached for the doorknob to leave when she heard the judge say something that changed everything.

"And just a bit of advice for future reference. I know it's a tactic lawyers use all the time, but you may want to think twice about pulling innocent people into personal vendettas you may have for the sole purpose of using them as leverage against someone."

Raven froze for a split second before whirling around and facing the judge with an expression of confusion. *What was she talking about?* "Excuse me?"

"Good day, Ms. Randolph. That will be all." The judge pulled a stack of papers on her desk towards her and gave them her full attention.

And just like that, a thought Raven never in this lifetime would've associated with the judge hit her dead on. "Someone got to you."

In the act of signing her signature on one of the papers, the judge's pen paused for a split second before scrawling out her name. "Raven, I said, that will be all!"

Her eyes locked on the judge, Raven walked back to the center of the office. It was all making sense now. "Someone got to you," she repeated.

"Who? Judge Warner, if Giuliani has threatened you or threatened your family–"

Judge Warner slammed her pen down on her desk. The tension around her mouth made it stiff and unyielding. "Enough, Raven. Leave. Now!"

But Raven could've no sooner stopped herself from repeating the revelations as they came to her than walking on the moon. "That's why you capitulated so easily to that flimsy technicality that Rogers brought forth. You're aware of what happened to me Friday afternoon when one of Giuliani's thugs accosted me in the stairwell. If they're willing to do something so blatant, then of course they wouldn't hesitate to come after you."

"And who helped you Friday afternoon when you were attacked in the stairwell?" The question was inserted so calmly that it threw Raven off for a second.

"H-Hawk Pattel," she stuttered. Then her body trembled as she made the connection. "Hawk is the one responsible for this?"

Judge Warner held Raven's eye before blinking behind her glasses. "I don't know what you mean. Now, I really must insist you leave." Before

Raven could protest, the other woman pressed the intercom for her assistant to come into the office. She had barely finished the request before Janice was there and holding the door open for Raven's departure.

Somewhat in a state of shock, Raven left without protest. Her mind was too muddled to do anything else. As she rode down on the elevator, she tried to make sense of everything she just learned By the time Raven got to the first floor and started out the courthouse, she had pretty much put the pieces of the puzzle together, save for a few stubborn angles that didn't want to fit. Exactly what did they have on Judge Warner?

When Hawk came to her office Friday night, he talked about the DA's ongoing investigation into his family with almost cavalier disregard, as if they were accustomed to such things and only saw them as a minor inconvenience. It wasn't until he saw his sister's name in the file on her desk that his entire demeanor changed.

What was it Judge Warner said? *"You may want to think twice about pulling innocent people into personal vendettas you may have for the sole purpose of using them as leverage..."*

The Pattels were an extremely close family, protective and loyal to a fault. This seemed to be true tenfold when it came to Leah; Raven was positive it was that way with each of the Pattels. If they felt Leah was threatened in any way they wouldn't hesitate to send a message. Now that they'd done so, it was one that Raven received loud and clear.

CHAPTER 11

"So, you're saying the Pattels are responsible in some way for Judge Warner dismissing the case?"

Raven stood in DA Jeffery Mills', office with her arms folded looking out the large paned window. But instead of seeing the bustling activity below of the unapologetically urban city of New York, her thoughts were on the conversation she had with the judge.

"I'm almost positive," she told her boss. "I got the feeling she was trying to send me a warning."

"Why do you say that?"

"There's no other explanation for what happened this morning. Judge Warner is one of the most principled judges on the bench. It would've taken something catastrophic to make her take the action she did. Giuliani and the Pattels threatening her makes sense."

"What I don't understand is why. Why would the Pattels get involved? What connection do they have to Giuliani that would cause them to bring attention to themselves like this?"

"I think I know." Raven took a deep breath before turning to face Jeff. She dreaded what she was about to reveal, but she had no other choice. "It's because of Leah Pattel."

"What does Leah Pattel have to do with anything?" Jeff's face showed his confusion.

"Judge Warner made the statement that I should be careful about pulling innocent people into personal vendettas. At first, I wasn't sure what she meant by that. Then she made a point of mentioning who came to my rescue Friday afternoon against Giuliani's guard dog. Hawk Pattel."

"Okay, but I'm still not getting it. How does that tie into the Pattels getting involved in the Giuliani case?"

"I don't have all of the facts, but, um..." Raven paused before her admission came tumbling out in a rush. "Hawk Pattel is aware that we've been trying to find his sister. We know how protective that clan is of each other, but it seems intensified when it comes to Leah. I suspect that was the motive. Judge Warner's warning was referencing our investigation of Leah. They wanted to send us a message to back off."

"Wait a minute, back up! How do you know Hawk Pattel is aware of us trying to track down his sister?"

"He came to my office Friday night."

Jeff's frown was instant. "He did *what*?"

"I have no idea how he got up undetected. I was looking over the Pattel files at the time. That's when he saw his sister's name in one of them."

"He had access to the files?" Jeff's eyes burned intense at the mere possibility of that having occurred.

"No! It all happened so fast. He glanced at my desk, the file was lying open with her picture attached to one of the pages."

"And you didn't think to report this, Raven? What the hell!"

"I handled it! I managed to gloss over the information and redirect his attention elsewhere. I knew he was upset about it, but I didn't think he would go to these lengths."

"You didn't think he would go to these lengths?" Jeff repeated giving Raven a steely glare. As was his habit when he became irritated, he ran an impatient hand through his mop of light brown hair. "It seems to me you didn't *think* at all! You should've reported this to me immediately! Do you realize the damage this has potentially done to our case?"

"I know. You're right. I'm sorry."

"What the hell was he doing here in the first place? First, he magically appears in the stairwell just as Giuliani's hired thug is threatening you and then that same night he seeks you out here at your office." His eyes narrowed suspiciously as he began to add things up in his head. "I feel like I'm missing something here. What aren't you telling me? Is there something going on between the two of you?"

"What? No! Of course not!" Raven read his disbelief in his expression at her answer. She couldn't really blame him because even *she* heard the thread of desperation in her high-pitched denial. She made an effort to even out her tone. "Of course, there's nothing going on between us."

"Then why was he here? Especially after hours." Jeff leaned forward in his chair. "Now is not the time for secrets, Raven. We've taken a major hit today. The last thing we need is to screw up the Pattel investigation too. Is there something I need to be worried about with you and Hawk?"

"I swear to you there's nothing. You're right, I should've told you. But I thought I contained the situation. I underestimated him. It won't happen again."

"It had better not. You're an important part of my agenda to rid this city of the culture of corruption and crime it's fallen into year after year. New York is one of the dirtiest states in the country. Extortion, bid-rigging by construction companies, the palm greasing to look the other way are all things of the past. I need to know that you're as committed to this as I am. If you're not, let me know now. I'll replace you with someone who is."

"I'm just as committed as I've always been. After this morning, even more."

"Good." Some of the tension left Jeff's shoulders as he sat back, but he still kept a watchful eye on her. "Let's get to work and take these bastards down."

Raven nodded and turned to exit the office. The main reason she dedicated a good part of her life to the job was because she believed in everything Jeff pledged to do. She was just as fed up with the corruption as most private citizens were.

It was time to put an end to it, or at least a dent that would get them started.

Plus, once they took the Pattels down it was surely only a matter of time before she could find enough incriminating evidence to go after her brother-in-law. That, more than anything, pushed and motivated her to fight with everything she had. They would get Giuliani another time, another way, but until then, they needed to cut the head off the snake, get to the top of the food chain and cut off the supply.

And that meant starting with the Pattels.

CHAPTER 12

"Aunt Rae, Aunt Rae, Aunt *Rae*! Wake up, Auntie Rae!"

Raven moaned softly at the sound of her nephew excitedly squealing her name. She slowly cracked a heavy eyelid open and spied A.J. kneeling in the bed beside her shaking her shoulder to wake her up. She had flown into Las Vegas late last night for his birthday party today but he had been asleep by the time she made it to her sister's house.

"Hi squirt," she croaked. Hearing the hoarse scratchiness of her voice, she cleared her throat. "Wait. Is somebody celebrating a birthday today?"

"Me, me, me!" A.J. shouted enthusiastically. "Today's my birthday, Aunt Rae!"

"You know what, I think you're right." Raven pushed herself up and leaned back against the headboard before opening her arms to her nephew. "Happy birthday, sweetheart. Here, come give Auntie Rae a hug."

She laughed as A.J. launched himself into her arms and hugged her tightly around the neck. Raven inhaled deeply, loving the sweet smell of his little body. She kissed the top of his head. "My gosh, you've grown so much. So handsome."

"I'm the tallest boy in my class. I would be the tallest period, buy Margaret Tolbert is a little taller than me." A.J. wiggled out of her grasp but remained close. "Did you know I was having a party today, Aunt Rae?"

"Well, of course. That's why I'm here. I wouldn't miss it for the world."

"Did you bring me a present?" Hazel eyes with a hint of mint green twinkled as A.J. gave her an outrageously adorable grin which immediately reminded her of his father. Angel could turn on the charm at the drop of a hat when it suited him. Of course, that charm was never directed her way, but she saw him use it to his advantage countless times.

"Now what kind of aunt would I be if I didn't bring you a present? Or two. Or three. Or four." She leaned forward and tickled him until he fell back screaming with laughter. Raven joined in, laughing just as hard.

"Angelo LaCroix Jr., what are you doing in here? I told you to let your Aunt Rae sleep."

Still laughing, Raven looked up as her sister entered the room with a stern look on her face directed at her son. Sharing the same skin tone, high cheekbones and square, but delicately feminine jaw, there was no mistaking the fact that the two of them were sisters. Smiling, Raven gave A.J. several kisses on his cheek before letting him get up.

Stifling a yawn, she sat up in the bed. "Morning, sis. He's fine. I was getting ready to get up anyway. You shouldn't have let me sleep so late."

"You looked like you needed the rest. You need to take better care of yourself, Raven."

"I *do* take care of myself. Things have been a little hectic at work, that's all."

"Hmmm. Well, why don't I take the birthday boy with me and let you get ready. We've eaten already, but I'll ask Mrs. Freeman to fix you some breakfast."

"No, I'm not hungry. Coffee will be fine."

"See, that's what I mean about you taking care of yourself. You've lost so much weight. You need to eat. Don't make me let Mom loose on you."

Raven groaned in response. "Alright, alright. Maybe a boiled egg and a slice of toast."

"Good," Nikki said in satisfaction. "See ya downstairs in about thirty minutes."

Raven smiled as she watched her sister and nephew leave the room. It was good to see them. She'd missed them dreadfully. She lay down in bed a little while longer before getting up and going to the adjoining bathroom. Nikki was right, she *was* tired. She was working a lot of late nights and early mornings for the past couple of weeks, motivated more than ever after the debacle of the Giuliani trial. Raven felt like she let Jeff down and was determined to prove he hadn't made a mistake by putting his trust in her.

Nikki and their parents, who had been in town for a week were disappointed she wasn't able to make it earlier than last night, but with everything going on, it was the best she could manage. It had been her intention to finish up some work when she made it to the mansion and before turning in, but she was so tired that she fell asleep with her laptop open on the bed beside her.

Thirty minutes later, Raven entered the dining room smiling at her mother. She leaned down to kiss her upturned cheek. "Hi, Mom."

"Hello, sweetheart. Did you sleep well?"

"Actually, I did. Where's Dad?" She asked as she sat down beside her mother.

"He's in the back with Angel keeping that grandson of ours busy," she smiled indulgently while shaking her head. "That little boy is so excited about this party he doesn't know what to do with himself."

"I know," Raven grinned. "I wish I could bottle that energy of his up and sell it. I would make a fortune." Seeing the maid bringing her breakfast, the smile on her face slipped a bit when she saw the amount of food piled on her plate.

Seeing the expression on Raven's face, her mother remarked, "Nikki told me all you wanted was toast and eggs, but I asked the cook to fix you a proper breakfast. You need to eat. You've lost too much weight."

"Mom, there's no way I can eat all of this." But after taking a sip of her coffee she picked up her fork and dug in. She closed her eyes in satisfaction when the fluffy pancakes topped with fruit and strawberry syrup practically melted in her mouth. "Oh my gosh. This is so good," she said with a mouth full of food.

"See?" her mother replied in a smug tone, indicating she knew what was best for Raven. "I'd bet anything that you're working endlessly and barely stopping to eat. When you do, it's probably nothing more than that fast food junk or take-out. You need to take better care of yourself, dear."

Raven rolled her eyes as she bit into a slice of turkey bacon. "That's what Nikki said. Have you guys been talking about me?"

"We don't have to talk about you to see what's in front of our eyes. Raven, you're pushing yourself too hard, baby."

"Ma, please," Raven groaned.

"I mean, what else do you do other than work? Do you have friends?"

"Of course, I have friends!"

"What about a boyfriend? Are you dating?"

"Ma!" Raven sat back and frowned at her mother.

"I'll take that as a no. You're not getting any younger, Raven. It's time for you to think about settling down, starting a family. Don't tell me there aren't any nice young men like Angel in New York."

Raven carefully placed her fork on her plate. The appetite she found once she started eating immediately disappeared. "Mom, only *you* would use 'nice' in the same sentence with Angel. Believe me, the last person I'll ever settle down with is someone like him."

"I thought by now you would have gotten over this animosity you have for your brother-in-law," her mother chided. "He's family."

"I'll never get over my dislike for that man," Raven muttered before taking a sip of orange juice.

"Your sister loves him, Raven and Angel absolutely adores her. He's an excellent father to my grandson, takes care of them both, so that they never have to worry about a thing."

"Other than seeing him get carted off to prison," Raven mumbled under her breath.

"Raven!"

"Mom, I don't want to argue about Angel. Not today. Let's just agree to disagree. I don't like him, I'll never like him and I don't think he's good for Nikki or A.J. Bottom line, you can put lipstick on a pig and dress him up in the fanciest of clothes all day long, but in the end, he's still a pig."

"Okay, Raven, that's enough. You're not in a courtroom right now so you don't get to judge. Yes, Angel and Nikki may have been raised differently–"

"That's an understatement if I ever heard one," Raven snorted.

"But they are exactly what the other needs," her mother continued. "You should know by now that life isn't a fairy tale. Your prince may not come in the package that you dream he will. You could be missing out on the love of your life because you refuse to look beneath the surface of what someone presents to you and that, my dear would be an absolute shame."

"I couldn't have said it better myself."

Raven stiffened in her chair when she heard the unmistakable sound of Angel's voice behind her seconds before she saw him walk up to the table. He was casually dressed in a pair of off white slacks, brown leather loafers, and a dark blue button-down shirt he left untucked. The only jewelry he wore was an expensive watch that she was sure cost more than her yearly salary and his gold, diamond studded, wedding ring.

She didn't see him when she made it in last night and for that, she was more than grateful. But Raven had to admit he was still as attractive as ever. Although he was older than both her and Nikki, no one would know it by looking at him. Tall and slightly muscular, Angel took excellent care of himself. With those arresting green eyes, beautifully smooth skin, and the charming smile he wore, he was easily one of the handsomest men Raven ever laid eyes on. She couldn't deny that. But she also knew better than most how dangerous he was.

As her mother put it, it was part of her job to 'look beneath the surface' of people and Angel was just as foul and corrupt as they came. Raven knew for a fact that Angelo LaCroix was in the crosshairs of every major law enforcement agency in the country, including the FBI and the DEA. And he *knew* that she knew. No one had ever been able to touch him, which was a nod to his intelligence, self-preservation, savvy and plain old luck. Thus far, he had avoided getting caught, but with the kind of intense heat he faced every day, it wouldn't last long. He was constantly under surveillance and would eventually get caught; it was only a matter of time. When that happened, Raven wanted her sister and nephew as far away from the fallout as possible.

Biting back an irritated sigh, she remembered the talk she had with herself on the plane ride over. Because it was A.J.'s birthday, she would be civil with Angel if it killed her. She refused to ruin this day for her nephew or cause Nikki undue stress. She would be leaving soon anyway. She could do this.

"Hello, Angel."

"Raven."

She clenched her teeth together and forced herself to remain calm. Even though he only said her name, he uttered it with an intentionally mocking tone, no doubt designed to get under her skin. But not today. She wouldn't let him.

Breaking eye contact with him, Raven stabbed a piece of fruit with her fork and brought it to her mouth. The party would be starting soon. She doubted if they'd even be around one another for the rest of her visit, which would make things a lot easier. Seeing him lean down to kiss her mother on the cheek, Raven couldn't stop herself from rolling her eyes at the way her mother preened under his attention. Ughhh!

"How was your trip, Raven?" Angel asked, turning back to her.

"It was fine, thank you."

"And when are you leaving?"

Raven paused in the act of bringing another piece of fruit to her mouth. He was such an ass. She didn't want to be under the same roof as him any more than he wanted her there. "Tomorrow," she answered in a short growl.

"Pity you couldn't have come earlier. Your parents have been here for a week. It would've been nice if you made more time to visit with them."

"I was telling her the same thing. She works entirely too hard," her mother added.

"I wouldn't have to work so hard if there weren't so many criminals on the street. But it'll be worth it. Before I'm done, they'll all be exactly where they belong–locked up behind bars for the rest of their natural life." Her look told Angel that she included him in that group.

"Good luck with that. From what I heard, you suffered quite a blow in the courtroom with Frank Giuliani a couple of weeks ago. Giuliani is small time. If you can't manage to put him away, what makes you think you even have a shot at getting to those at the top?"

Raven carefully placed her fork down on the plate and wiped her mouth with the linen napkin. "You don't have to believe me. Just watch me work."

"Oh, I will. Count on that."

Ignoring her mother, who watched them through anxious eyes, Raven returned Angel's stare without flinching. The tension in the room grew thick. Neither had to be specific about what they actually meant. The gauntlet was thrown down between them years ago; they both knew where they stood with each another. Raven knew that no matter what Angel may have told Nikki, he still hadn't forgiven her for helping her sister leave him several years ago.

For a short while, Nikki had realized how dangerous it was to be around Angelo. All it took was a phone call from her and Raven jumped into action, helping her submit paperwork for a legal separation and a custody arrangement that had made Angel furious.

However, Nikki hadn't been strong enough to stay away from him; she'd chosen Angel over the welfare of herself and more importantly, her son. But that was where Raven came in. If Nikki didn't have the strength to do what had to be done, then she would do it for her. She would get her away from this monster permanently, one way or another.

"Okay, I think everything is just about done." Oblivious to the tension in the room, Nikki hurried into the dining room, scribbling in a brown leather organizer. "Now we just need to keep the birthday boy out of trouble until the party starts in a couple of hours."

She glanced up with a wide smile, but sensing she walked in on something unpleasant, her eyes went from her mother, to Angel, then to Raven. "Okay, what's going on? Please tell me you two haven't been arguing."

Raven was the first to finally look away. "No. Everything's fine." Before Nikki could follow up with more questions, Raven quickly continued. "And I'm sorry, I should've found you when I came downstairs. Is there anything I can do to help, anything you need me to do?"

But Nikki was clearly unconvinced. "Raven–"

"Sis, everything is fine. Angel and I know how to behave ourselves when it counts. We were just talking about my latest case. I know I should've let it go by now, but it's still a sore spot for me."

Nikki still looked skeptical but decided to follow Raven's lead. "Okay. And no, thanks for the offer. I hired a party organizer to pull everything together. I just needed to oversee the arrangements and make sure everything was done."

"Oversee party arrangements, huh? Good to know that Ivy League education you worked so hard to get hasn't gone to waste." Raven regretted the sarcastic words as soon as they slipped past her lips.

Dammit!

CHAPTER 13

"Raven!" Her mother's face was etched with lines of disapproval as she stared at her youngest daughter.

"What did you say?" The excitement Nikki wore moments ago disappeared.

Angel was the only one in the room who remained silent, but Raven could feel the chill of his glare drilling into her louder than anything he could have said.

"Nikki, I'm sorry, I didn't mean it like that."

"Yeah, you meant it like that. You just didn't mean to say it out loud. That's more accurate, isn't it?"

"Nikki–"

"I guess in your eyes, me planning a birthday party for my child doesn't compare to you trying cases in New York, is that it?"

"No, of course that's not what I meant. I–"

"Let me tell you something, Raven. You may not agree with the things I consider important when it comes to my family, but the operative words here are *my family*. To point out the obvious, you don't have a husband or children so let me clue you in on something; there isn't one single thing I do for *my family* that I ever consider a waste of time."

Raven saw white-hot anger in Nikki's eyes, but she also saw hurt, which left her rightly feeling about ten inches tall. She had no idea why she would say something so bitchy to her sister.

She hurried forward and grabbed Nikki's hand and held it tight. "You're right. And I'm sorry. Of course, I don't think it's a waste of time. Your job as A.J.'s mother is more important than anything I could ever do and I mean that from the bottom of my heart. Please forgive me, Nikki. Please."

Nikki blinked a few times then squeezed her sister's hand and nodded. "It's okay. I forgive you."

"Thank you." A wave of relief almost made Raven wilt. She reached out and gave her sister a hug. After a brief hesitation, Nikki returned the hug before pulling back and mumbling something about going outside to check on A.J.

Raven watched her hurry out of the dining room, mortified by what she'd said. The last thing she would ever want to do was hurt Nikki, but that's exactly what her reckless words had accomplished. Why couldn't she think before she opened her big mouth?

Turning back towards the table, Raven pulled up short when she found Angel standing mere inches behind her. The deep emerald color of his eyes glistened brightly with fury. Already knowing what was coming, she crossed her arms and braced herself for his blistering attack. She didn't have to wait long.

"Proud of yourself?" He asked in a quiet voice, which Raven knew signified how angry he truly was.

"Of course I'm not," she snapped. "I told her I'm sorry and I meant that. I'll make it right, but this is between me and my sister."

"That's where you're wrong. You added me to the situation the minute you hurt my wife." Angel cocked his head back into the familiar, arrogant angle she was familiar with seeing. "You know what, if I didn't know any better, I'd swear you were jealous of Nikki."

"And why would you think that?"

"Because she has something you don't, which is a family of her own. No matter how much you might love your job, it doesn't keep you warm at night when you go home to that cold, lonely apartment, does it?"

"You can't be serious. I'm not jealous of my sister. If anything, I'm angry at the situation she's in, trapped in such a rigid marriage with a control freak like you!"

"Does she look unhappy to you? No, be honest. Does she?"

Raven opened her mouth to deliver a scathing reply but couldn't in all honesty dispute his point because Nikki *didn't* look unhappy. Matter of fact, she was glowing. But sometimes, everything that glittered wasn't always good for you. Case in point, Angel.

"I'm not going to stand here and argue with you. As I said, this is between me and my *sister*."

"Listen to me and listen well, Raven. Make this the last time you insult my wife in her own home. The next time it happens, sister or no sister, you'll find your ass kicked out of this house faster than you can blink an eye. Do we understand one another?"

"Angel." Raven's mother said his name in a soft voice.

His eyes never wavered from Raven. They both knew the only reason he was holding back this much was because her mother was in the room. "If we have to have this conversation again, not only will you not be welcome in my home any longer, but I'll arrange it so that you never see my son again. Are we clear?"

"Nikki would never let you do that," Raven sneered.

"When it comes to my son, I thought you knew not to underestimate my reach. Why would I permit my seed to be around someone whose sole intention is to poison his thoughts and turn him against me?" Angel's brows bunched low over his furious eyes. "You've only received mercy this long because you're Nikki's sister, but I'm begging you, do *not* attempt to test my kindness, because in the end you will be the only one who gets hurt."

"Are you threatening me?"

"I never, ever use threats. I think you know that about me. Now, again. Are. We. Clear."

Raven stared at him with mutinous rebellion, but part of her knew he had the capability to do exactly what he claimed any time he chose. If he wanted to kick her out that very moment, nothing and no one could stop him. And if he went through with his threat to keep her away from her nephew…

"Yes," she answered with reluctance. "We're…clear."

"Good." Angel stared intently at her for several more moments until she looked away. When he seemed satisfied that his words hit home, he walked out of the room without another word.

Raven watched him go, more shaken than she cared to admit. She didn't think her hatred could run any deeper than it did already, but she was wrong. If she could find a way to get rid of him this very minute…

"Why did you have to do that, Raven? Why did you have to be so ugly to Nicole like that?"

"Me?" Raven screeched, thinking about what happened with Angel. "Mom, how about saving at least a corner of that outrage for your other daughter. Did you see how 'ugly' your precious son-in-law was to me just now?"

"Can you blame him? He was defending his wife, Raven. You deliberately said what you did to try and belittle her and I want to know why."

"I didn't mean it." Seeing her mother's dubious expression, Raven sighed. "Okay, I meant it but I didn't mean to say it out loud."

"You know what, Raven, I'm beginning to think Angel may have been right about something."

"Which part? Kicking me out of my sister's house or keeping me away from my nephew."

"I want to ask you a question and I'd like you to give me an honest answer. *Are* you jealous of Nicole?"

"Oh my God, not you too!" Raven groaned. "Why would you even ask me that?"

"Jealous might not be the right word. It's probably more like envy. No, hear me out, Raven. I know you love your sister more than anything in this world. You've looked up to her since you were born and followed in her footsteps the moment you could walk. But then, Nikki deviated from the plan, didn't she? Instead of maintaining the career she worked so hard to advance in, she gives it all up for a man who you don't consider good enough for her."

"And that's what I'm envious of? Her throwing her life away for a man who will eventually spend the rest of his life behind bars?"

"Angel might not be the type of man you would've chosen for her, but it's not up to you. Nicole is happy and content. She has a husband who, for all his faults, worships the ground she walks on, a son who is the center of her world and the family she's always wanted."

"And as Angel said, all I have is a 'job that doesn't keep me warm at night', is that it?" When her mother just stared at her in silence, Raven threw her hands up. "Okay, yes, what do you want me to say, that sometimes I would love to have what my sister has? Come home at night to a special someone I can discuss my day with and unwind. One day have a kid or two? Yes, of course I want that. And I'm happy that Nikki's happy. I just...I just don't understand how she's this happy with *him*."

"It's simple. She loves him. Believe me, when you fall in love with someone, you fall in love with the person they are, flaws and all. One day you'll discover that. Until you do, try not to be so hard on your sister. You can't look down your nose at something you don't understand."

Feeling thoroughly chastised, Raven listened without interrupting. Even though there was nothing anyone could say to ever make her like Angel, she knew Nikki loved him deeply. Anyone with half a brain could see that. Were Angel and her mother right? *Was* she envious of what the two of them shared?

"Go and talk to your sister before A.J.'s party starts," her mother urged. "There's no need to let this remain between you two all day."

Raven nodded slowly and left to do just that. Her mother gave her a lot to think about, whether she wanted to admit it or not. If there was one thing Raven knew about herself, it was that she never avoided a dilemma, no matter how uncomfortable it might be, but she would have to sort all of that out later when she was alone and could dissect the points her mother had made.

Once she stepped out of the double doors that led to the humongous back yard, Raven stopped in her tracks. When Angel first moved there, he purchased several lots to build on, giving him the largest home in the gated community they lived in. A good portion of the back yard was decorated for A.J.'s party and she didn't mean with balloons and streamers like she imagined.

"Wow," she whispered slowly walking out further to get a better look.

The theme was Jurassic Park. The entire backyard was turned into a prehistoric land, complete with mechanicalized dinosaurs that blinked and roared just like the living, breathing thing. Countless cages of 'prehistoric animals' were scattered about, along with caves and mounds of dirt that allowed kids to 'excavate' the land for buried treasures.

Raven saw with her own eyes why Nikki needed a party organizer. This was more than a child's birthday party; it was an event A.J. and his friends would remember the rest of their lives. Of *course* Nikki would've had to be on top of every single detail to insure it all went off without a hitch. Seeing the full display, Raven felt like a selfish little bitch *and* the worst sister ever.

Seeing Nikki speaking to a group of people, Raven walked over checking out the props along the way. A party planner may have organized everything, but Raven had no doubt the entire thing was Nikki's concept.

Once the group Nikki was talking to took off, she glanced towards Raven with cool eyes. "Hey."

"Hey," Raven greeted. "Nikki, everything looks amazing. I had no idea."

"Thanks. Not bad for an Ivy League grad."

"Nikki..." Raven bit down on her lip thoroughly ashamed of herself for even saying something so mean.

"No, Rae, really. I don't understand why you would even put a comment like that out there unless it's how you actually feel."

"My only excuse is that I've been under so much pressure. Getting home late, waking up early. Just going nonstop. Sometimes, I feel like I'm going to snap, you know?" Raven felt a sudden tightness in her chest. Her throat grew thick with emotion. To her horror her eyes watered and threatened to overflow. "And...and I guess I c-cope with it b-by–
"

"You cope with it the way you always have since we were kids, by being a little pain in the ass."

Nikki said finishing her sentence. With a slow shake of her head, she reached out and pulled Raven close. "Come here."

Raven wrapped her arms around her sister, so grateful to have her in her life. "Do you really forgive me?"

"Yeah, I forgive you, but later tonight after everyone has settled in you and I are going to talk." She leaned back and stared Raven deeply in the eye. "And I mean really talk. You're going to be honest and tell me what's going on with you, okay?"

Raven sniffed and wiped her face with the back of her hand. "Okay."

"Promise?"

"I said okay," Raven laughed. "I promise."

"Okay. Well, let's go inside and get ready to–" Her words tapered off as she looked toward the house. A smile lit up her face. "Oh look, Jerra's here. Aleesha and Keisha, too."

"Already? The party doesn't start for another couple hours," Raven commented following behind her sister.

"Yeah, but they said they would come by early to see if there was anything I needed help with. Come on."

"It must be nice to have such great girlfriends like that."

Nikki looked over her shoulder at Raven before reaching back and looping their arms together. "What's even nicer is having such an awesome sister."

They grinned and fell into step with each other as they continued walking towards the house. Nikki's friends, their husbands and kids– along with Angel, A. J. and their parents, were gathering underneath the outside entertaining area that reminded Raven of a miniature country club. Wait staff magically appeared with h'oeuvres and drinks for the adults. Raven and Nikki were several yards away when Raven suddenly spotted a face amongst the crowd that made her come to an abrupt stop.

Nikki slowed her steps and turned to look curiously at her. "What's wrong?"

Raven didn't answer right away. She was busy trying to convince herself that her eyes were playing tricks on her. It couldn't be, but it was.

"What is *he* doing here?" Raven whispered. The question was posed as more rhetorical than anything else. "Did Angel invite him?"

"Who?" Nikki glanced at their guests with a frown.

"Hawk." Raven felt faint just saying his name. "Hawk Pattel."

CHAPTER 14

"Hawk? He's here?" Nikki glanced around with a frown. "Where?"

"There. Talking to Angel." Without being obvious, Raven lifted her chin in the direction of the two men in question.

Nikki stiffened when she saw him. "I have no idea what he's doing here. I swear to God if Angel invited that family here for our son's birthday..." She glanced at Raven. "Are you okay?"

But Raven was busy struggling with the simple task of breathing. Her eyes drank Hawk Pattel in like the thirsty, sex-starved woman she was. Several weeks had passed since the last time she saw him at her office. As always, it momentarily stunned her how good looking the man was, even dressed as casually as he was for the party in black jeans, black and white J's and a gray and black short sleeved t-shirt that emphasized his wide chest and muscular arms. Too fucking delicious.

"Rae?" Nikki called her name then gently shook her arm when she didn't respond. "Raven?"

"Huh?" Raven blinked and turned slightly glassy eyes towards her sister "Did you say something?"

Nikki's eyes narrowed suspiciously. "Yes. Wipe the drool from your mouth."

Raven frowned and actually started to bring her hand up to her face before she scowled at her sister. "I hope you know you're not funny."

"I wasn't trying to be." Nikki glanced behind her then brought her eyes back to Raven. "Is there still something going on between you two?"

"What do you mean, still?" But Raven knew Nikki was referring to the little scene in her house she walked in on over a year ago when Hawk caught Raven eavesdropping. He taunted and provoked her with seductive words that almost ended with a kiss. It *would* have ended with a kiss if Nikki hadn't interrupted them when she did.

Still, the attorney in Raven showed up and showed out in full force to come to her rescue. When all else was lost deny, deny, deny. "Nikki, not that again. There's never been anything between us."

"Don't even try that crap with me, seester." Nikki reverted back to the affectionate term they used ever since they were little. "Something is going on with you and that tall drink of hot chocolate, so spill it."

Although still discombobulated with the unexpected appearance of Hawk at Nikki's house, Raven couldn't help but give her sister a teasing side-eye. "Tall drink of hot chocolate?"

"I'm married, not blind. I might not like Hawk Pattel but no red-blooded woman could help but notice that he's one sexy, good looking man."

"Hmmm. I have to agree with you on that. Personally, I can't stand the man, but he *is* fine as hell. That's not what I meant, though. I just thought you were into vanilla lattes," Raven grinned, referencing Angel's pale complexion.

"You forget my husband is part West Indian, honey. Don't get it twisted. You might not see it but his chocolate lies extremely close the surface, hot and ready to bubble over with just one look or touch from me. And let me tell you, when he gets going–"

"Ewww, stop." Eyes squinting in distaste, Raven held her hands up. "Too much info."

"And I don't have *enough* info about you and Hawk, but don't worry about it. You're safe–for now. But we *will* talk about this, tonight. Full disclosure, remember? No exceptions," Nikki warned.

"Okay, okay. I'll tell you everything, but can you please find out what he's doing here?"

Satisfied that she would be getting the low down later, Nikki slipped her arm through her sister's and led them over to their guests. The next few moments were enveloped in a flurry of hugs and greetings. Nikki waved to Darrell Monroe and Angel's brother, Dominick as they gathered around Angel indulging in a rather intense looking conversation.

Raven noticed that although Hawk seemed to be listening to whatever was being said, even from that distance, she could feel the heat of his gaze attaching itself to her and refusing to let go. Focused on getting the names of all of the kids who had shown up with the group, Raven refused to give him the satisfaction of acknowledging his presence. It wasn't too hard to ignore him given the cuteness overload of the munchkins in front of her.

"Now, Keisha, Christian and Samantha are your only two, right?" Raven asked running her hand over the little boy's curls and marveling how utterly adorable he was.

"Well, we have Dominick's son, Manny, but I claim him as my own, so altogether we have three kids."

"For now-w-w," Aleesha teased.

Keisha rolled her eyes in response, but the happiness on her face negated the gesture. "Sam's at a sleepover with her best friend. And as Aleesha inappropriately mentioned, Dom and I are trying for another one."

"I think they're having more fun *trying* at this point," Jerra chimed in.

"Look who's talking," Keisha fired back. "Raven, FYI, when we were younger, Jerra's the one who always swore she'd never have any kids and now look at her. She has the most out of all of us."

Raven stared in awe at Jerra and Darrell's twin girls, who were absolutely gorgeous. When they blinked up at her from their double stroller with their big, beautiful gray eyes, she could've sworn she felt her ovaries jump in response. "Jerra, they are *so* precious. How old are they now?"

"Thank you. They're ten months," Jerra beamed. "They are definitely daddy's little girls." Everyone laughed when they looked around after hearing the word daddy. "Li'l D. is playing video games with A. J. and Aleesha's other two, Olivia and Dillon, so at least he's occupied right now." Jerra paused, watching as Aleesha placed Addy and Marcus Jr. in the portable playpen she brought. "Got it, sis?"

"Yeah. Thanks."

"You're an expert at that, Aleesha," Raven smiled, watching in admiration as she lowered the first, then the second child into the playpen without incident, in spite of their ever-moving limbs. "They're so active."

"Girl, yes, terrible twos in full effect. They are into *e-ver-y-thing*," Aleesha sighed. "Marcus helps me a lot, though. Thank God for that."

"Speaking of Marcus, where is he?" Nikki asked with a slight frown. "I don't see him over there with the guys."

"He got called into the hospital as soon as we were getting ready to walk out the door. I doubt if he'll be able to make it before we leave."

"Oh, okay. And what about Hawk?" Nikki asked casually. "I was surprised to see him."

Jerra glanced back at the men. "He arrived in town a couple of days ago. He flies in periodically to check on things at *Club Ecstasy* and other investments he has here." Then a thought seemed to hit her. "I hope it's okay that we invited him to come. I just assumed you wouldn't mind since he and Angel..."

"Oh, of course. It's fine." Nikki waved off her concern. "I was just curious."

"He actually purchased our condo a few months back," Jerra added. "Darrell and I hardly ever use it anymore. It was a nice date night getaway when we just had Lil D., but now with the addition of the twins, it's sat empty most of the time so we decided to sell it."

"That makes sense," Nikki nodded.

"That's right, Hawk and Darrell are cousins. I forgot about that," Raven commented.

Jerra hesitated a bit before answering. "Yes, they are."

"So how are things going with that? Darrell being related to the Pattels, I mean." Raven asked the question as casually as she could manage.

However, it was clear Jerra saw right through the ploy. She stared at Raven for several long seconds before answering in a cool tone. "It's fine."

Taken aback by the instant change in her demeanor, it took a moment before Raven noticed the loud silence that suddenly surrounded the group. Then it hit her. They all knew she worked for the DA's office and were unilaterally closing ranks. Even Nikki sat staring at her with a closed, unreadable expression.

An attorney herself, it wasn't too farfetched to think Jerra knew of the investigation into the Pattels. Raven realized that they must have thought she was trying to get information she could use when she asked about Darrell's relationship with the Pattels. No one there would discuss such personal matters with an outsider and definitely not with Raven.

The funny thing was that the investigation into the Pattels was the last thing on Raven's mind. She was just curious about Hawk. Raven could admit to herself that he fascinated her. She couldn't figure him out. Any insight into the man would help her do that, but she realized she crossed an invisible line in the sand and there was no going back.

Knowing she made everyone uncomfortable, Raven was getting ready to excuse herself and go into the house to visit with her parents when out of the corner of her eye, she saw the men coming towards them.

Raven stifled a groan. Although she shouldn't care, she knew if she got up now, Hawk would take it to mean she was running because of him, so she settled back in her chair. Maybe she was being stubborn, even childish, but she refused to give him the satisfaction of thinking he chased her away.

Raven greeted Darrell with a smile then leaned forward to return the hug Dom bent down to give her. When they were kids, her family and Dom and Angel's lived in the same neighborhood. Angel was best friends with her older brother, Jacoby, before he was killed. Raven was younger than all of them but vividly remembered the night Jacoby got shot.

She frowned as she sat down and stole a look towards Angel. She hadn't thought about that in a long time. Funny how far back their history reached. Even now, Raven thought it was a shame that he chose to take the path he did. The man was brilliant. There was no telling how far his intelligence would've taken him *legally*. Instead, he chose to become a common criminal and and showed no signs of deviating from that choice.

"Hello, Raven. We meet again." Hawk Pattel's smooth voice claimed her attention and redirected her interest to him.

"So, we do. Hello." Raven was proud of how normal her voice sounded. Inside, her nerves were in shambles, especially since he decided to stand right beside her chair.

"When did you get into town?" he asked.

"Last night," she answered abruptly.

"Did you have a good flight?" He asked politely.

Raven turned her entire body his way and stared at him. What exactly was he up to with the questions? Changing her mind, she decided that now would be as good a time as any to make her exit. "Uh, fine. But since I got in so late, I think I'll go inside and visit with my parents for a while before the party starts."

"I'll walk with you. I left something in my car that I need to get." Hawk's eagle-eyed gaze lingered on Raven's face to get her reaction to his next words. "On the way, you can tell me a little bit about the Giuliani trial. Tough break, havin' it thrown out like that."

"Are you seriously bringing that up to me, you son of a–" Remembering there were small children present, Raven caught herself just in time. Not trusting herself to speak, she brushed past him without another word, ignoring Darrell's mumble to his cousin that he must be a glutton for punishment.

She waited until they were out of earshot before turning around with claws bared. "What the hell was that back there? Are you trying to be funny or something?" Her face a furious mask, Raven jabbed him hard in the chest with her finger to emphasize her words. "You know damned well my case fell apart because of you!"

"You think it was my fault..." He said smirking and pointing to himself.

"I *know* it was! Yours and that den of criminals you call a got damn family."

Hawk laughed, seemingly truly amused. "Den of criminals? That's something we've never been called before."

"Well, that's exactly what you are. I want to know what you did. What did you threaten Judge Warner with, because I know it was something." Her anger felt good. It reminded her that she needed to ignore whatever attraction she had for this man at all costs.

Hawk took a step closer to Raven. "The Pattels weren't on trial. Frank Giuliani was. We didn't have a dog in that fight. That is, until you pulled us into it."

"What are you talking about? You know what, never mind. I'm not going to stand here and trade puzzle pieces with you to see which one fits so let me get straight to the point. You did this because of Leah, didn't you? It's about that file you saw in my office."

Hawk tilted his head and said in a deceptively quiet voice. "Go on."

"Before Judge Warner threw me out of her chambers, she gave me a cryptic message about proceeding with caution when involving innocent people in my personal vendettas. The Pattels had something to do with that, didn't you? Admit it."

Squinting, Hawk's gaze never faltered. "Maybe we were looking for a way to get your attention. Do we have it now?"

CHAPTER 15

Although Raven knew with every fiber of her being the Pattels had something to do with Giuliani's case being thrown out of court, she didn't actually expect him to admit it. "So, this *is* about Leah. What did you do? Judge Warner is one of the most respected judges I know. What did you use to blackmail her with?"

"Blackmail is such an ugly word, Rae."

"Answer me!" She demanded.

A touch of ice entered Hawk's eyes when he heard her tone. His entire mood changed in an instant. "You're not in the courtroom right now, Raven and I'm not on your witness stand. Don't get outta pocket, alright?"

Something told Raven that she was teetering on the edge of an invisible line she wasn't supposed to cross. She was quickly reminded that although most of the time Hawk came across as fun-loving and playful, he could be extremely dangerous. She could never lose sight of that.

"You look tired," he said suddenly.

And once again, he knocked her off balance. "What?"

Hawk brought his hand up, gently tracing the faint dark circles under her eyes with his finger. "You haven't been getting enough rest. Getting home late and leaving out early in the morning."

"How do you know that?" She asked suspiciously.

"It's true isn't it? You need to take better care of yourself, baby."

The endearment he tacked on at the end confused her. One minute he was practically threatening her and the next, he acted like he cared. Her mind flashed back to the incident that happened between them in her office. Without realizing it, she sighed at the softness of his touch gently caressing her skin.

"That's right, little kitten," he uttered in the same raspy voice Raven found persuasive that night in her office. "Sheathe those claws for Hawk."

Raven blinked and abruptly stepped away from him and back to reality. It was frightening how easily he convinced her to drop her defenses around him with just a simple touch and a soft word or two.

"If I look tired it's because I am. Most people who have to work for a living usually are, but of course you wouldn't know anything about that."

A slight smile tugged at the corner of Hawk's mouth. Cocking his head to the side, some of the amusement returned to his eyes. "You think I don't work hard?"

"Not everyone is lucky enough to be born into a family like yours where everything is handed to them on a nepotistic platter, illegal or not."

A gleam entered his eye that she couldn't quite decipher. It was almost like an inner reflection he was momentarily caught up in. "That's so far from the truth that it's actually funny. Nothing was *given* to us. My father and uncle made sure everything we got was earned the old-fashioned way, through hard work."

Raven leaned forward and cocked her ear close. "I'm sorry, what was that? I couldn't hear you for that silver spoon in your mouth."

Hawk chuckled, lightening the air between them. "You know what, you're funny. One thing I can say about you is that you keep me on my toes. I like that, Raven Randolph."

Deciding it was past time to put things back on track, she steered the conversation around to their original subject. "I'd like to know about Judge Warner."

Hawk glanced around, looking behind him and noticing that although everyone was laughing and talking, covert looks were thrown their way that told him they were being watched. "I don't think this is the time or the place for that discussion. I'll tell you what you want, but not here."

Although Raven didn't believe for one minute that he would do any such thing, he had already admitted the Pattels were responsible for blackmailing Judge Warner. It was possible that if she kept him talking he would let something else slip that could turn out to be important, no matter how small or insignificant it may seem.

"Okay, fine. Do you want to go into the study, or…"

"Nah, I don't talk business in another man's house. I have to leave in about an hour to go *Ecstasy*. Come to my condo later."

"Your condo." Raven raised her eyebrow. "Nice try."

"That's my offer. Take it or leave it."

Raven actually laughed out loud. "You're saying you'll tell me what I want to know if I come to your condo. Would it by any chance be the same conversation you wanted to have in my office a few weeks ago?"

"Only if you want it be. I don't believe in forcing myself on women. Unless you think you would have a problem keeping things strictly professional…"

"Of course, I wouldn't. I'm just not naïve enough to think business is the only thing you have in mind."

"Just so you know, it's not the judge we have something on." From out of nowhere, Hawk casually let that tidbit of information slip out.

"What? Then who?" Raven asked anxiously.

"Like I said, we'll finish this at my place. I'll send a car for you tonight. It'll be late, but I'll make sure you get back to Angel's house safe and sound," he grinned.

"Hawk, just tell me." Raven's tone was impatient.

"That's the deal. Again, take it or leave it."

"Fine! If I come tonight, you'll keep your word?"

"At the end of the day, our word is all we have, right? If I say I'm gonna to do something that's exactly what I mean. After we finish talking, if you tell me you're ready to leave–"

"*When* I tell you I'm ready to leave."

Hawk smirked and slowly nodded his head. "*When* you tell me you're ready to leave, you have my word that my driver will immediately bring you back. No questions asked." Hawk impatiently shifted his weight onto one leg. "So, tell me, what's it gonna be?"

Raven heard the challenge in his voice and for the life of her, she couldn't make herself back down. What was it about Hawk's arrogance that made her take chances she wouldn't normally entertain? "Fine. I'll see you later."

She didn't miss the look of anticipation that spread over his face. It was a reminder to her that Hawk was like most great predators. They employed maneuvering tactics that put unsuspecting prey squarely in their field of view before moving in for the kill. He obviously thought he had her in his crosshairs.

"Good. See you tonight, Rae," He uttered softly before walking away.

Raven stared after him with her arms folded. She knew what he *thought* was going to happen, but she came into contact with people like Hawk Pattel every day; Raven knew exactly how to handle him. As her mother used to say, he who dines with the devil had better make sure they ate with a long-handled spoon. When it came to Hawk, Raven planned to stay as far out of pitchfork range as she possibly could.

*****

A. J.'s party turned out to be a mega hit with everyone. He and his friends ended up having the best time of their young, carefree lives, and after everyone left, it didn't take long for exhaustion to hit him. He offered no protest when Nikki told him that his grandmother was going to take him upstairs to help him get ready for bed.

An hour or so later, Nikki sat snuggled up to Angel on the sofa in the huge family room along with Raven, Dom and Keisha, along with her parents enjoying adult time after an afternoon in the presence of lively, excitable eight-year olds. Christian went home with Darrell and Jerra at their insistence, leaving Dom and Keisha kid-free for the night.

Raven sat curled up on one of the loveseats in the room listening to Angel deliver a particularly funny story that had everyone laughing hysterically. As much as she tried to do otherwise, Raven found herself smiling along with the others by the time he finished. Although she'd only seen this rare side of him once or twice, there was no doubt Angel had a magnetic personality that made people gravitate to him when he chose to bring them into his orbit.

She took a sip of her wine as she continued to watch him. His natural charisma and self-confidence were traits that not many people possessed. Her brother-in-law had what her father called the gift of gab. He spoke eloquently and was well versed and knowledgeable on a multitude of subjects and current events that allowed him to contribute to whatever subject might be the topic of conversation at the time. Witnessing that side of him made Raven easily see why Nikki fell in love with him.

Suddenly, a thought occurred to her. Frowning slightly, Raven realized Hawk had a lot of the same characteristics Angel possessed. He wasn't as polished or sophisticated, but he had what she liked to call the power of presence. Hawk didn't have to say or do anything to draw attention to himself. He easily claimed territory with his body alone, comfortably taking up space to make everyone aware that he was there. With just one look he could make a person feel like they were the only one in the world he was interested in being with at that time. He did it to her on more than one occasion.

Feeling somewhat disturbed by the knowledge, Raven again wondered why she was allowing herself to be drawn into a game as dangerous as the one he clearly wanted to play. The obvious reason was Judge Warner. Raven learned more in two minutes by talking to Hawk than she discovered in the three weeks since the disastrous trial outcome. She knew Jeff told her to move on, but Raven couldn't. If Hawk could give her more insight, it would go a long way to at least helping her gain peace of mind.

So Judge Warner is your excuse? Her subconscious silently taunted. *Really, Rae? Is that what you're telling yourself?*

Raven shifted uncomfortably on the sofa. Okay, fine. Was she attracted to Hawk, yes! Did he fascinate her more than any man she'd ever met, yes, yes, *and hell yes*! But that didn't mean she couldn't manage that attraction and separate it from the job she had to do.

Feeling better since she'd gotten that point straight, Raven was busy mentally patting herself on the back when she heard Nikki ask her a question. It was clear to everyone there that she didn't hear a word of the conversation going on around her. "I'm sorry, what was that?"

"Mom and Dad were telling everyone about the time you set up a protest in school demanding better lunches with desserts for the entire student body," Nikki chuckled. "Daddy was proud of you for taking a stand, but once you got home he tore your butt up for getting suspended."

Raven laughed at the memory and looked at her father. "Hey, but it worked. Even though I got one of Ray Randolph's rare whippings *plus* detention for the rest of the year, it was worth it."

"Look at you, a little rebel even when you were a kid," Dom teased.

"Yeah, and ain't a thing changed," her father added with a deep chuckle.

Raven took their good-natured ribbing in stride, laughing along with them until her phone she held in her hand buzzed with a text. Still smiling, she glanced down and read the message displayed on her screen.

My driver will be there in thirty minutes. That is if I didn't scare you away and make you change your mind…

Mouth tightening in response, she quickly typed, *I'll be ready. Just be prepared to have him bring me back within the hour.*

There was a slight pause before the next words popped up on her screen.

Whatever you say, Rae.

Raven scowled. She could almost hear Hawk's taunting laughter. How it was possible for one man to be such a complete and utter arrogant asshole was beyond her.

"Something wrong, Rae?" her mother asked.

"Hm? Oh, uh no, everything's fine." She got up from the sofa and spoke her next words as casually as possible. "I'm going out for a while. I won't be too late."

"Where are you going, dear? And at this hour?" Her mother glanced at the clock on the wall before looking at Raven with deep concern.

Raven did her best not to roll her eyes. *What was she, sixteen?*

"No, I just found out that a friend from school is in town and leaving early in the morning. We're just going to, um, go out for drinks." Great. Her mother treated her like a teenager and she automatically reverted back to lying like one to take the heat off.

"Who's in town?" Nikki asked. "Which friend?"

"I...you don't know her."

"But—"

"Sweetheart, stop interrogating your sister," Angel cut in, staring at Raven in a way that put her on her guard. "She's a grown woman and shouldn't have to explain her plans to everyone."

Raven shifted from one foot to the other. The irony of the situation was not lost on her. Angel, of all people was coming to her rescue. Eyeing Nikki as she headed out the room, Raven saw that her sister wasn't buying a single word of what she was selling. Raven knew she would have a shitload of questions to answer when she came back, but she would deal with that later. She was almost free and clear when Nikki called her name.

"Yes?" She asked, pausing to glance over her shoulder.

"Do you need to borrow one of the cars?"

"Uhhh, no. She's picking me up."

Raven could've kicked herself when Nikki perked up in interest. "She's coming here? Well, invite her in and so that we can–"

"Goodnight, Raven." Once again it was Angel who ran interference. "Enjoy your night."

Nikki sat up and darted her husband a suspicious look. Seeing that she was distracted, Raven took the opportunity to scurry out of the room like the cowardly lion in the Wizard of Oz. She would just have to wear that label for now.

As she skipped up the stairs, she once again wondered why Angel was helping her, but just as quickly dismissed the question. She had no interest in analyzing his motives. Who knew why Angel did *anything*? Besides, her focus right now needed to be Hawk Pattel, because if he caught her slipping even the slightest bit, she would have hell on her hands keeping her head above water.

CHAPTER 16

Forty-five minutes later, the car Hawk sent for
Raven was speeding off in the direction of his
condo. Raven tried to engage the driver, who
introduced himself as Danny, in subtle chatter to see
what she might be able to get out of him but gave
up after only receiving one word answers and
noncommittal grunts. Settling back in the supple
leather seat, Raven smoothed down the hem of the
belted black and white "shirt" dress she decided to
wear. She paired it with a pair of black, strappy
sandals that gave her a little bit of a height
advantage since she was more vertically challenged
than she liked.

Contenting herself with looking out the
window, Raven occupied the time by trying to get a
script together in her head of how she wanted the
meeting with Hawk to go. It was best for her to take
control and lead the conversation in a direction that
was advantageous to her instead of the other way
around.

It wasn't long before they pulled up in front of an expensive looking high-rise, luxury condominium. After continuing to the garage and parking the car, Danny got out and opened Raven's door before escorting her to the elevator. They rode up in silence. By the time the steel doors slid open on the 42nd floor, she found herself curious to see the place Hawk called his home when he was in Las Vegas.

Raven waited nervously until Danny unlocked the door. When he stood aside for her to enter, she did so cautiously, expecting to see Hawk waiting for her. However, there was no immediate sign of him so she took a couple steps further into the foyer before stopping and glancing around with an expression of awe. Hawk's condo was absolutely gorgeous. Although she expected the modern sleekness of marble floors, stainless steel and other beautiful décor, Raven had to admit it was also very elegant. Each wall boasted floor to ceiling windows that offered a panoramic view of the glitz and glam that was quintessentially Las Vegas. It was even more breathtaking at night.

Raven turned to look expectantly at Danny, wondering why he hadn't announced her arrival to Hawk.

"Mr. Pattel requested that you make yourself at home, Ms. Randolph. He's been unexpectedly delayed but should be here shortly. Would you like something to drink while you wait?"

Raven was still trying to digest the part where Hawk was held up. If tonight wasn't a good night to meet, why didn't he just postpone their talk for another time?

"Ms. Randolph?" Danny prodded.

"Uh, no, thank you. Did he say exactly how long he would be?"

"I'm sorry, ma'am, he did not."

Raven glanced down at her watch. She would give him thirty minutes to get there and after that she was leaving. She looked around the place again. "It's such a beautiful night. I think I'll just go out and wait on the terrace, if that's okay with you."

"Of course. Let me know if there's anything you need." Danny chose one of two dove gray, suede chairs situated in a corner of the spacious room to sit.

Opening the sliding, glass door, Raven stepped onto the large balcony and took in the glittering lights of the city. The stars shone brightly in God's clear heavens giving her a view of a beautiful skyline that was almost startling. It never ceased to amaze her how opulent the other half lived. Surroundings like this probably didn't even faze Hawk. She wasn't joking when she taunted him about growing up with a silver spoon in his mouth. The Pattel's wealth was vast. Purchasing a condo like this one wasn't cheap, but she was sure Hawk hadn't even blinked when he wrote Darrell a check for it.

Leaning against the railing Raven continued to enjoy the beauty of the Las Vegas night and let her thoughts run free. After a while, she lost track of time until a movement from inside caught her peripheral. Turning her head, she saw Hawk striding into the living room, with long, strong steps. Twisting around to get a better look, Raven absently noted that even *that* was sexy. Hawk walked with swagger, like he was in control of himself and everyone around him. It was definitely one of the first things she noticed about him.

Danny gestured towards the balcony. When Hawk shifted dark, almost brooding eyes her way, Raven found herself fighting to remember how to breathe. It was the oddest thing. She'd never been this flustered around a man before. But then, no man had ever affected her the way...

No! Stop it, Rae! You need to get a whole grip on yourself NOW!

It was one thing to be attracted to the man. That didn't mean she had to act on it. Besides, that wasn't why she was there. Again, she reminded herself that she would be leaving once she got the information she wanted. With that course of action in mind, she cleared her throat and squared her shoulders before opening the sliding door to join the two men in the living room.

"Well, I see you finally made it," Raven said to Hawk in way of greeting. "I was beginning to wonder if you forgot I was here."

Hawk blew out a quiet breath. "Danny told you I was gon' be a little late, didn't he?"

"Yes, but if that was the case, you might as well have postponed this meeting. I could've been spending time with my family instead of waiting for you to–"

"Do you wanna leave, Rae?" Hawk interrupted before she could finish her sentence.

Raven was taken aback by the abrupt, almost rude question. "Excuse me?"

"I asked if you wanted to leave. I can have Danny take you back now if you like."

Raven's mouth fell open. She stood speechless and more than a little embarrassed by the way he was talking to her, but she recovered quickly. "You know what, yes. That's exactly what I'd like and for the record? Fuck. You."

Raven rushed forward to get to the door, but before she could pass him, Hawk snagged an arm around her waist and pulled her against his side. "Wait."

"Let me go. I mean it, Hawk, let *go* of me!"

"Look, I'm sorry. I'm tired and I'm in a shitty mood. I shouldn't have taken it out on you."

"No, you shouldn't have." Raven pulled at his arm trying to loosen it from her waist. "This meeting was your idea, not mine."

"You're right. Again, I'm sorry. Maybe we should start over?" Hawk said smoothly. She refused to look at him until he called her name. "Raven. I asked if we could start over?"

Reluctantly, she turned guarded eyes upward to glare at him, but remained silent. She'd be damned if she gave him the opportunity to shoot her down twice in a row.

"We good? You not gonna scream the building down if I send Danny away, are you?"

Although the words were spoken in the form of a joke, Raven didn't see the familiar teasing she was becoming accustomed to in his eyes. He really *was* in a shitty mood. "Fine. I'll stay."

They stared at one another for a few intense filled seconds before Hawk broke eye contact and sent a look to Danny that obviously communicated that he could leave.

Once it was just the two of them, he slowly released his hold on her. "I'm gonna grab a beer. Do you want a glass of wine?"

"No, thank you." Raven folded her arms and eyed him with caution.

Hawk hesitated as if he wanted to say something, but instead turned to go to the kitchen. The open concept floor plan allowed her to watch as he opened the refrigerator door. She frowned when he pulled out a bottle of wine and poured her a glass even though she told him she didn't want any. Deciding it wasn't worth making a big deal over, she took it without comment when he came back and handed it to her. Raven found herself taking a big gulp to steady her nerves.

Without looking at him, she said, "I suppose we should get on with the conversation I came here to have. That way you can get back to what you were doing and I can do the same."

Remaining silent, Hawk kept his eyes on her and brought the bottle of beer to his lips. That action called her attention to him and for a moment Raven stood mesmerized by the way his strong throat worked as he swallowed the beer. It took her a second to realize that his knuckles were bruised and had several cuts.

"Oh my God. What happened?" She placed her wine glass on the glass table in front of her and instinctively grabbed his hand. She winced when she saw how deep a few of the cuts were. "You need to put something on these before they get infected."

Hawk pulled his hand away. "It's fine."

"But—"

"I said it's fine, Raven," he snapped as he moved away from her to go look out the window.

Stung by the harshness of his tone, Raven snapped back. "So, is that what you were doing while I was waiting on you, getting into some juvenile fight at a nightclub?"

Hawk's shoulders stiffened. "Somethin' like that."

Raven let out a soft snort and picked up her glass. "I should've known. Very mature of you."

Hawk slowly turned around and stared at her. Raven did her best to ignore him, but again she thought about the weird mood he was in. Very... unHawk-like. The times she saw him serious—like in the stairwell at the courthouse and even in her office when he found out his sister was being included in the investigation of the Pattels—those times didn't last. Tonight, however, he was almost brooding. There was no question that something was on his mind. What, she didn't know. And it really wasn't any of her business, she reminded herself.

Coming to a decision, Raven once again placed her glass on the table. "I think this may have been a mistake. If you'll call your driver–"

"I wanna ask you something I'm curious about."

The statement took her by surprise. "What?" She asked hesitantly.

"Your relationship with Angel and Dominick. How do you all know each other again?" Hawk slowly paced back and forth, keeping his predator like gaze attached to her.

Taken aback by the off the wall question, Raven struggled to keep up with the swift change of subject. "We, um, grew up in the same neighborhood."

"Really? I didn't know that."

"Is there any reason you should have known?"

Hawk lifted his shoulder in a slight shrug. "Just sayin'. Why is it you seem so friendly with Dom but you can't stand Angel?"

"Because Dominick is a decent man and Angel…well, we both know exactly what Angel is."

Hawk was quiet for a moment as he continued his slow pacing. Raven wondered why he was so unsettled and restless. He reminded her of a big cat roaming around in a steel cage. Seeing that he wasn't ready to discuss what she came over to talk about, she asked a question of her own. "So, aren't you a bit old to be getting into fights in nightclubs?"

"I never said I got into a fight."

Raven frowned. "I thought–"

"Let's just say I was dealing with an issue that's no longer a problem, but I'd rather talk about you." His eyes shifted over her before settling on her face. "So, you got a lil street in you underneath that cool exterior you show everybody. Interesting. You know, you fascinate me, Ms. Randolph. A tried and true 'round the way girl. Gotta say that surprises me."

"And why is that?"

Hawk shrugged. "Just thought you were raised in some middle class, suburban neighborhood that's all."

Raven had to smile at that. "No, my stomping grounds growing up were nowhere near middle class, but I wouldn't change a thing. It prepared me for the real world and helped to shape the woman I am today."

"I heard that. Never would've guessed you grew up knowin' Dom and Angel."

"They were both older than I was, of course. Actually, Angel and my brother were best friends." Raven revealed the information somewhat reluctantly.

"You have a brother?" Hawk asked with interest lighting up his eyes.

"Had. Had a brother. He was killed when I was seventeen." Raven stared down at her glass. This was the second time tonight she thought about Jacoby like that. Sometimes it was just easier to block it out. Less painful.

"I'm sorry to hear that. How did he die? If you don't mind me asking," Hawk added.

"A victim of the streets, which is sad in and of itself. Jacoby was too smart for that, too intelligent a person to take that path. My parents tried to guide him, but he was set on doing things his way.

Ultimately, it got him killed." Raven swallowed as she recalled that horrible night. "He had just turned twenty-one the week before. From what we were told, he got into a confrontation with some drug dealers earlier that evening. Hours later, he and a friend were sitting in a car when they were ambushed. They were shot over thirty times." Raven swallowed hard and closed her eyes to try and block out the violent images of what her brother must have looked like.

"Damn. I'm sorry, baby."

"My parents were devastated, of course. We all were. Nikki and I idolized Jacoby. He was the best big brother anyone could ever have."

Hawk cursed again, but this time under his breath. "Did they catch who did it?"

"The police didn't. As far as they were concerned it was just another case of black on black crime in a poor neighborhood, but…"

"But what?"

She hesitated then said, "Someone took care of the person who pulled the trigger."

"Do you think it was Angel?" Hawk asked. "If that was his boy, I'd put money on it that it was."

"Maybe. The two of them had stopped hanging out as much, but they were still friends. I think Jacoby was a little envious of Angel. He saw the easy money Angel made in the streets and tried to do the same, but in the end it cost him his life. My parents blamed Angel for Jacoby's death for a long time. At first, so did I, but the older I got, the more I began to understand Jacoby had a choice. He knew the risks of that lifestyle, but chose to live it anyway. That's not anyone's fault but his own. Even after all this time, I still miss him."

"Raven..." Hawk put his empty bottle down and came towards her.

Her name spoken with that degree of softness on his lips was her undoing. She turned her back to him to try and get herself under control. "No, don't. Please."

She would *not* break down in front of him. How did they even get on the subject of her brother? She never really talked about Jacoby, not in depth like just now; it hurt too much. However, in the span of a few minutes she laid her soul bare to Hawk Pattel. *Why?*

When Raven inhaled it felt like her throat was on fire from the effort it took to keep the knot of tears at bay. She wiped at the moisture gathering in her eyes and turned to face him. "If you don't mind, I think we should probably talk now. You, um, you said you would tell me more about who Judge Warner was protecting?"

Hawk folded his arms. "No. That's not exactly what I said."

Confusion blocked out everything else for a moment. "Yes, you did. You said that if I met with you tonight you would–"

"I would tell you what you wanted. *That's* what I said."

"Okay, so…"

"I meant what you wanted…when it came to *me.*"

"What? What are you talking about? We were specifically talking about Judge Warner. You told me that she wasn't the one you, or whoever had leverage on. And that you would…" Raven frowned slightly, struggling to remember his exact words. "You would give me something else to go on in the case."

"Nooo." Hawk drew the word out with great patience like he was explaining a story to a child. "I

told you I would give you *something*. And I intend
to."

CHAPTER 17

Raven's mouth dropped as Hawk's meaning sank in. Yes, she suspected tonight wouldn't be *all* business, but after revealing as much as he did earlier, she expected him to tell her a little bit more. Obviously, he had lied to her.

"You are such a got damn liar, you know that?" She exclaimed in outrage.

Hawk's eyes narrowed in warning. "Careful, Raven."

"Oh, go fuck yourself! And since we're taking words literally here, that's exactly what I mean."

His left brow lifted before he chuckled in sudden amusement. "Wow. There she is. I've been waiting for the little wildcat in you to come out."

"You are so full of it! I can't believe I actually fell for your bullshit!"

"It's not bullshit if I deliver what I promised, is it?"

"Just stop! You deliberately misled me into believing–"

"Rae, come on now. Can we be honest with each other for a moment? I know you feel this...*thing* between us just as much as I do." Hawk started walking towards her with those slow, purposeful steps of his. "Are you going to stand there and tell me you weren't expecting this?"

Chest heaving, Raven resisted the urge to run. Things were spiraling out of control and she felt powerless to stop them. "I'd like to go back to my sister's house."

"We're not finished yet." Once Hawk was close, he slowly circled behind her with the unhurried speed of a cat knowing he had his mouse cornered with nowhere to go.

Raven squeezed her eyes closed and forced herself to keep breathing. She could feel him sniffing the air around her, sniffing her scent like a powerful lion preparing to mate with his beta. She had to end this.

Raven blurted out the first thing that came to mind. "I guess you giving me your word that you'd let me leave was a part of your play on the truth as well."

"Not at all," Hawk answered calmly.

Raven shivered. He was standing so close that she felt his warm breath blow softly against the back of her neck when he spoke. She pressed her lips together to stop the whimper escaping that would prove her to be just as big a liar as Hawk.

"As soon as I keep my word and tell you what you want, you can leave after that if you still desire to."

Raven couldn't stand it any longer. She had to get out of there even if it meant calling a cab to take her all the way back to Nikki's house. She took a step to head towards the door, but Hawk anticipated the move and slipped an arm around her waist to keep her in place.

"Not yet, Rae. We're not finished."

She deliberately kept her body stiff and unyielding against him. "Hawk–"

"See, it's not your fault that you don't know what you want. You've never had a real man confident enough to look beyond that bossy attitude of yours and be honest with you."

"And I suppose you, being the real man you are, plan to do just that."

"Damn straight. This attraction you and I share is rare. Raw. Every time we're around each other, the sexual tension is so strong it feels like we're going to explode like an unpinned grenade. You can't tell me you don't feel it."

"You're delusional."

"Am I? I know you, Rae. Better than you think." The hand he held flat against her stomach splayed wide, pulling her closer against him. "It's hard for you to slow down and relax, isn't it? You need somebody to take on that responsibility and help you do that. I know you want to deny it, but no matter how strong a woman is, there's a primal urge in her to just give in, at least once in a while. Do you deny that?" Hawk breathed in her ear.

Raven actually jumped when she felt the soft touch of his lips on the sensitive curve of her neck. "Don't," she pleaded in a hoarse whisper.

"Don't what? Don't stop?"

The fingers of Hawk's other hand slid down and grabbed the mid-thigh hem of her dress. He bunched it up in his hands as he dragged it upward. Raven remained still, as if paralyzed in place. Once he got to the lacy material of her panties, both of their breathing sped up in anticipation. Hawk moved his hand closer to her pulsating treasure and was moments away from cupping it in his palm when Raven caught his forearm.

"No." It didn't even register that her nails were digging into the cuts and bruises on the back of his hand. "We can't. We can't do this."

"Stop fighting me, Rae. Give up control, just this once. I know it's terrifying because you feel safe with it, but trust *me* to keep you safe. Just for tonight. Don't think, Rae, just feel. Will you do that for me? *Can* you do that for me?"

Raven's entire body trembled from desire and fear. Yes, she wanted him. She couldn't deny that, but he was right, she *was* scared. She'd never been more afraid of anything in her life. She *liked* being in control. It allowed her to construct her days just the way she wanted them, with order and structure. Her control was her safety net in a world where the most important things in life could be snatched away before she could blink. If she gave that up to Hawk tonight, that meant she would have to face uncertainty, and she didn't know if she wanted to do that. She didn't know if she *could* do it.

"I promise to make it worth it, Rae. You say I've been playing word games with you, maybe I have. But this is where the games end. The minute you want me to stop, all you have to do is tell me. Things won't go any further. I promise you that," Hawk said breathing methodically on her neck.

Raven shook her head. That was the same thing he told her earlier. She didn't have the strength to comb through his words to find hidden meanings. "I don't believe you."

Hawk's body grew tense behind her. Releasing the hold he had on her dress, he rested his forehead on her shoulder for a moment then slowly stepped back. Raven felt the loss of his body heat immediately.

She turned and saw him take his phone out and dial a number. "What are you doing?"

Hawk watched her in silence before speaking to the person on the other end. "Danny, Ms. Randolph is ready to go now."

Raven frowned. This had to be another of his ploys. "Is this the part of your game where I tell you I've changed my mind and I want to stay?"

The corner of his mouth twisted up. "I told you no more games and I meant it. I'm sorry I wasted your time."

Trying to regain her composure, Raven cleared her throat and tossed her hair. "So am I. Since I don't believe you called Danny, I assume I'll need a cab to—"

The ringing of the doorbell cut off the rest of her sentence. Hawk stared at her for several moments before going to the door. Raven watched as he let Danny in then stood at the door with his hands in his pockets watching her and waiting. That's when the only logical explanation Raven could come up with hit her. This was all an act. He didn't actually think she was going to leave. Unbelievable.

Letting out a delicate snort, she snatched her purse off the couch and marched to the door, aware of how intently Hawk watched her approach them. She would show him that she could play this little game of his just as well as he could. If he wanted her to stay, he would have to be the one to ask.

Once she pulled up even with him, she paused half-expecting him to pull her to him and tell Danny to leave, but he didn't. The longer she stood there, the more awkward she felt because Hawk still made no move to keep her with him.

Which is what you wanted...right? The devil's advocate side of her was in full effect.

"Enjoy the rest of your night," she told him in a stiff voice.

Hawk nodded. "You, too, Ms. Randolph. And if I don't see you again once we get back to New York, take care of yourself."

Raven blinked several times. He was serious. Fine. So was she. Giving him a nod in return, she preceded Danny out the door and started down the hall towards the elevator. Her steps faltered a bit when she heard the soft click of Hawk's door closing behind them.

She waited while Danny pressed the button to summon the elevator, which opened only seconds later. Danny politely stood waiting for her to get on first, but as hard as she tried she couldn't take the couple of steps needed to leave the debacle of a night with Hawk behind. She wasn't ready to leave what he could *give* her behind.

"Uh, Danny, I forgot something. You can go down. I'll be there in a second." But when she turned to go back, Danny did the same. Raven paused and looked at him. "Really, it's fine. You don't have to come with me."

When he refused to budge, Raven rolled her eyes and turned to retrace her steps back to the condo. Once she got to Hawk's door, she glanced up at Danny then rang the doorbell. Raven waited, nervous and at a loss for what she was going to say.

Unsure of what to expect, she cautiously gazed up at Hawk when the door opened. Anything she had time to put together between the short walk from the elevator to now went completely out the window. Her mind went blank when she saw him standing in the doorway with his shirt unbuttoned looking like an entire snack set before her for her consumption. From what Raven had glimpsed in her office that night, she already knew the man's body was insane. Unable to look away, her eyes immediately got distracted by the strip of hard muscle she was allowed a much too brief peek of.

"Raven." Hawk bent his head and lowered his eyes to get her attention. "Hey."

"Huh?" Raven gulped and tried to unscramble her brain. "Oh. Uh."

Geezus, Raven! Really, bitch? How many more times do you want to embarrass yourself tonight?

Managing a ghost of a smile, she tried again. "Hi."

Hawk's expression didn't change. "Was there something else you needed?"

Raven swallowed. "I... I think we need to talk."

Hawk slowly shook his head. "Nah. I think we already said everything we needed to say."

Raven blinked at him a few times before glancing at Danny then back to Hawk. "Okay fine, there's something *I* need to say. In private."

She waited, but Hawk didn't move. For a moment she wondered if he would even allow her to come in. Raven bit down hard on her lip. She already thrown her pride to hell by coming back, so she might as well go the extra step needed to get what she wanted.

"Please," she added.

Hawk folded his arms. "Are you sure? Because once I send Danny away he's not coming back until I decide to call him."

Raven held her small purse in a death grip, but did not look away from him. "I'm sure."

Hawk studied her closely until he found whatever it was he was searching for in her eyes. Then and only then did he step back and open the door. "Come in."

Said the spider to the fly, Raven said to herself as she walked into the condo. While Hawk and Danny spoke in low tones, Raven headed towards the living room, but she only made it a couple steps when Hawk called her name.

Raven turned with an expectant expression. "Yes?"

"Wait for me in the bedroom." He nodded his head in the direction she needed to go. "Last room at the end of the hall."

CHAPTER 18

Raven's feet felt as if they'd been planted in cement. Had she heard him right? Did he actually just order her to his bedroom like some random chick he brought home from his nightclub?

"I, um, thought we could talk. First."

"No. We've done enough talking. Last room at the end of the hallway," Hawk repeated before turning back to Danny.

Seeing that she was categorically dismissed, Raven felt her face burn hot with humiliation. Who did he think he was to treat her like this? Instinctively, she prepared to curse him to hell and back but then she realized…he gave her the choice to leave. It was her decision to come back. He was letting her know this was only happening if they played by *his* rules and *his* rules only. The only question remaining was could she go along with that.

Hawk closed the door after Danny left and turned to stare at her. He waited in silence. Swallowing hard, Raven forced herself to move, putting one foot in front of the other. Now that Danny had been dismissed, it was too late to turn back. Besides, if she were being honest with herself, this was what she wanted, at least for the night. As she continued walking, Raven felt Hawk's gaze on her until she disappeared from his sight.

Once she got to his bedroom, she glanced around the dimly lit area. Distinctively masculine, it was subtly spiced with a gray and cream color scheme. Although minimalistic, the pieces of furniture in the room were bold and dark. Like Hawk, himself. Raven touched the intricately carved dresser. The room was beautiful, but almost *too* perfect. It looked unlived in with no personal touches. While it was obvious Hawk didn't spend much time there, Raven would bet her life she wasn't the first woman he brought to his home. She looked at the bed. For some reason, the thought of being one of the numerous women he had sex with in it brought a sour taste to her mouth.

She shook her head and backed away. This was a mistake. She couldn't do this.

But just as she turned around to leave, she saw Hawk leaning in the doorway with his arms folded watching her. Raven jumped in surprise. "You scared me. How long have you been standing there?"

"Long enough to know that you've succeeded in talking yourself out of staying."

"That's not true." Raven had no idea why she was lying.

"Good. Take off your dress."

"Wait. Before we...start, I think we should get a few things out...out in the...the, uh, open..." Her voice trailed off when Hawk brought his finger up to his lips to silence her.

"How 'bout we not."

"Hawk–"

He swiped an impatient hand over his face. "Jesus, you are one stubborn woman."

"No, I just think–"

"Raven, before you finish that thought let me tell you a quick story, alright?"

"Okay," Raven answered with caution.

"I went out with this artist a few times. Very talented woman."

"I'm sure she was," Raven muttered under her breath. She could only imagine where the woman's talent might lie.

Hawk bit back a smile before continuing. "Sometimes I'd watch her paint. I noticed she always squinted when she worked. When I asked her why she did that, she said it helped her focus on what she was painting and block out any outside distractions. Does that make sense?"

"I guess," Raven said slowly. "What does this ex-girlfriend have to do with me?"

"The point I'm tryin' to get across is that's what I want you to do. Block out everything, including any misgivings you might be having right now and focus on the here and now. Think you can do that?"

"I'll...try, but–"

"No buts, Rae. Don't think. Just feel." He repeated what he told her several times already. "It's that simple. If it gets to be too much and you want me to stop, that's all you have to say. ."

"That's it. If tell you to stop, you will."

"Yes. Will you do as I ask without questioning every little thing?"

Several moments passed before Raven nodded. "I'll try."

"Good." He nodded towards her dress. "Now, take it off."

Raven's heart accelerated to an absurdly fast pace. Before she realized it, she started slipping the buttons free.

"Slowly," Hawk instructed in a deep voice. "Take your time."

Nervously licking her lips, Raven did as he asked.

"Look at me while you undress for me, Rae," Hawk ordered in a seductive whisper.

Raven swallowed hard. Why was she so nervous? She was a grown woman, experienced in the act of sex. The quicker she let him fuck her the sooner she could get him out of your system.

Taking a deep breath, she kept her eyes on him as she untied the belt at her waist and worked her way down to the last button. Raven had to admit, she never thought of herself as a tempting vixen or anything, but the way Hawk licked his lips and kept his attention trained on her gave her a burst of power she never felt before. Raven had never

189

been wanted by a man like Hawk Pattel. The high it gave her was like nothing she'd ever experienced. In that moment, she decided that she would enjoy every single minute of whatever it was he planned to do.

When the dress parted, Raven took her time and shrugged it off her shoulders before letting it drop to the floor.

"Fuck," Hawk whispered once she stood in front of him in her panties and bra.

Raven bit her lip, watching *him* watch *her.* She didn't want to exaggerate things, but he almost seemed...mesmerized. Her eyes drifted down to his crotch. He was *definitely* turned on. *That* was no exaggeration. Whatever part of his brain that acted like a conduit to his desire worked just fine. Any doubt she may have still had about him wanting her disappeared.

Her breathing deepened when he pushed away from the door jamb and walked towards her. His eyes scanned her body from head to toe, lingering on the almost sheer scraps of floral laced underwear. The deep brown lingerie was feminine and romantic, yet sexy at the same time.

Hawk's hand swiped down his mouth. "Turn around."

Raven hesitated for a second before doing as he asked. He was quiet for so long that she started to get a little self-conscious. She knew the lacy boy shorts showed a good portion of her butt cheeks. Was he comparing her to other women he'd been with. Maybe she came up short or wasn't what he'd been expecting. Why wasn't he saying anything?

"Hawk…" Unable to stand it any longer, she tried to turn to face him, but he grunted deeply and placed his hands at her waist to stop her.

"I've imagined you without your clothes at least a thousand times, counselor. Believe me, what I came up with in my mind in no way compares to what I'm seeing now. *Damn*."

Raven melted inside. "You were quiet for so long, I thought maybe you were disappointed."

"You can't be serious. Woman, you are fucking gorgeous. And this lingerie." His hands travelled down to grip and squeeze her ass. "Chocolate over chocolate and then more chocolate. I can't wait to taste you, Rae."

Raven groaned. She couldn't help it. The image of his face buried between her thighs licking her until she erupted with pleasure was almost too much. "I want you, Hawk."

"Do you?" He asked softly.

When she nodded, he gathered her hair in his hand and moved it to the side. Bunching it up in his fist and holding it out of the way, he allowed his lips to follow an invisible line from her shoulder to her neck. Gasping and panting for air, Raven's lashes fluttered until they finally closed. When his lips skimmed over a concentration of sensitive nerve endings behind her ear, her knees almost buckled from underneath her. Was the room spinning or was it just her imagination?

"Tell me how much you want me, Rae," he whispered.

Unable to put the need into words, Raven swallowed nervously. She never spoke explicitly when it came to sex. She didn't know what to say. Why couldn't he just get on with it?

Hawk brought his other hand up and lightly placed it around her throat. Using his thumb, he guided her face towards him and claimed her lips in a kiss that was hot, passionate and so very, very arousing. His tongue boldly plunged inside her mouth, tasting every corner until she swayed against him drunk with desire.

Raven's defenses lowered as he played her body like his own personal orchestra. She gasped for air as the kiss turned her brain to mush. Raven tried to remain lucid, but it was no use. Her surrender was imminent and they both knew it. However, his next words caused her to slowly awake from the lethargic lust coma she found herself falling into.

"Put your hands behind your back for me, Rae."

She blinked in confusion when she turned and saw him holding the belt from her dress. Raven took a step back. Being tied up was *not* something she agreed to. "Uh-uh. I don't think so."

CHAPTER 19

Keeping his eyes glued to her face, Hawk slowly twisted the belt around his hand. "Are you telling me to stop?"

"No, but…"

"That was the agreement, right? If you wanted me to stop, I would. No questions asked. But since that's not what you're saying…" A smile hovered over his lips, but his eyes remained watchful and uncompromising. "Turn around and put your hands behind your back."

Raven hesitated, urging herself to listen to the warning screaming in her ear to put an end to this. However, before she realized what she was doing, she turned her back to him and crossed her arms behind her. She pressed her lips together when he tied a knot with an expertise that told her he was not new to the act of bondage.

Raven closed her eyes. *What have I gotten myself into?*

When Hawk pushed her panties down her thighs, she dutifully stepped out of them and allowed him to help her on the bed. He positioned her on her knees with her head down on the mattress, ass to the sky, and her hands restrained behind her back. Her paranoia went into overdrive. Her heart started pounding in what seemed like a double cadence as panic set in. She glanced around the room. What if she was being recorded?

"Put your head back down, Rae."

Feeling as if she'd been caught breaking some kind of rule, she did as she was told. Alert and hypersensitive to his every move, she heard him rustling around behind her. A drawer slid open. Raven heard him push a few things aside then close it. She twisted her neck to try and look at him, but the precarious position she was in only let her move so far. Her body grew tense when she heard the unmistakable sound of Hawk unbuckling his belt. To her surprise, she felt a sense of anticipation as she wondered what he would do next.

Her heart thumped nervously in her chest when Hawk separated her thighs and exposed her body's most intimate secret. She heard an aroused growl seconds before his tongue came in contact with her quivering flesh. She let out a loud moan when he licked her like a decadent bowl of melting vanilla ice cream. Hawk savored her taste in his mouth before going back for more with hungry intensity.

Her body squirmed from his probing tongue, wordlessly begging for more. Wanting more. Hawk held her steady, wrapping his lips around her clit and sucking it into his mouth. A jolt of electricity vibrated through her body. *What is he doing to me?*

"Oh. God..." Raven's hands curled into fists behind her back.

She struggled to keep her sanity, but Hawk seemed just as determined to steal it from her, working her pussy with the skill and expertise of a thief picking a lock. Patient and in no rush, he used his tongue and mouth to push her to the edge of ecstasy, time and time again, before bringing her back from the brink. For Raven it was pure torture. The sweetest form of it she had ever known, but torture still.

"Hawk...please. *Please!*" Raven cried out for mercy when he curled his tongue in a way that made her thrash back on his face. "Hawk!"

The sound that tore from his throat was pure, masculine pleasure. Giving her what she needed, his tongue moved with lightning speed, beckoning the orgasm that waited in the shadows and finally giving her permission to explode.

The force of her climax shook Raven to the core. It unfolded from the inside out until it consumed every inch of her body. Raven gave herself over to the powerful sensation; she literally had no other choice. It took her hostage and refused to let go until it was ready.

Once the storm passed, Hawk's tongue adjusted accordingly, gentling his touch to soothe and calm. Sinking to her stomach, Raven's heartbeat slowed to its natural rhythm. She was vaguely aware of Hawk untying her hands, but didn't open her eyes. She didn't even have the strength for that simple task and did not move until she heard the unmistakable sound of him tearing open a condom.

With a slight wince, Raven drew her arms forward and turned over on her back. Her eyes stretched wide as she watched Hawk roll the thin, rubber sheath over his impressive length. He was indeed blessed in that area. Raven's mind flashed back to that night in her office when he thought she was worried that it wouldn't fit. Now she understood why. His dick was fucking spectacular.

At full mast its veined shaft hung heavy and curved nicely to the left. All in all, it filled the magnum condom to maximum capacity. Raven swallowed. Maybe there *was* reason for concern. Her eyes flew to Hawk's face when he joined her in bed.

"Open your legs for me, Rae."

After a brief hesitation, her thighs obediently parted. She heard another growl rumble from his throat. Hawk placed a hand on each knee and opened her wider. As he stared down at her, Raven's eyes roamed over his body. She could see why he looked so good in clothes. Hawk was magnificent. There was no other way to put it. Sinewy, sculpted muscles looked like they were chiseled from stone. Raven felt her energy level return. The fantasies she'd allowed herself to indulge in didn't even come close to the reality of the flesh and blood man in front of her. All of a sudden, he flashed her a smile. Raven felt the room spin.

"What's so funny?" She asked with a breathless catch in her voice.

"Just thinking about the things I plan on doing to you tonight." Hawk's eyes went back to the sweet spot between her legs that he seemed so fascinated by. He pulled his lip between his perfectly white teeth. "Did I make you feel good, Rae?"

Raven blinked several times. He wanted to know if he made her feel *good*? He almost put her into a damn coma with that orgasm, but she wasn't going to tell *him* that. His ego was already inflated; she refused to blow it up even more. Her lashes dropped to hide the sudden gleam in her eyes.

"It was okay, Pattel. I mean, you've had one orgasm, you've had 'em all, right?"

Hawk went completely still. "You *do* know you're gonna pay for that, right?"

Hearing the warning in his voice, her eyes flew back to his face. "W-wait, I didn't mean–"

"Don't backtrack now, baby." Hawk stretched out over her and placed a hand on either side of her head. "If that's how you feel, stand by that."

"I'm not backtracking, it's just…that…that..." Raven inhaled sharply when he shifted to place the bulbous head of his dick between her lower lips. Her body tensed. Visions of him ramming *all of that* inside her caused a seed of panic to grow. "Hawk, I–"

But the rest of her words came out as long moan of pleasure when he slipped the tip of his dick in nice and slow. "Ohhhh, shit..."

"That's it," he hissed, kissing the side of her neck. "Relax. Don't think…"

Just feel. Raven automatically finished his words in her head. She was beginning to get it. Eliminate the mental blocks. Let go of her inhibitions.

"Good?" Hawk asked, his voice seductively quiet and low. When she nodded, he rolled his hips forward feeding her a little bit more of his beast.

He watched her closely, noticing her quick intake of breath, the whimpers and moans that escaped, the way she bit down on her lip. Everything he did was intentional. Every look, every feel, every taste was so sensual and deliberate that he effortlessly drew Raven into his orbit. She wanted to stay forever and never leave.

Her nails pierced the taut skin of his wide back. Raven lifted her hips and invited him inside her body. She needed him so desperately, needed him to fill the void inside her. When he obligingly accepted the invitation, her lungs struggled to inhale air. He was so...deep. Deeper than she ever would've thought was possible.

Bursts of color danced behind her closed eyes. The sound escaped her that was a cross between a groan and a mewling purr. "Mmmm. Shit..."

"That's it. Don't hold back," he whispered encouragingly. "Ready for more?"

When his words penetrated her lust befuddled brain, Raven forced her eyes open and stared up at him. "More?"

"So. Much. More." He answered gruffly, thrusting and claiming more depth.

Raven's inner muscles squeezed reflexively. Hawk rolled his hips forward, his movements forceful enough to let her know she wasn't fucking with the average. She did her best to keep up with his pace and rhythm, but she was woefully outmatched. They both knew who was in charge and as the beginnings of an orgasm uncurled from inside her core, Raven was content to just let him be.

"Your body was made to be fucked by me, Raven. Don't ever forget that," he grunted. "You hear me, baby?"

"Yes...Yes!" she cried, arching her hips to meet his. "Oh...Oh, God..."

"I'm layin' claim to this, Rae. All of it. You *do* know who it belongs to, right?"

Raven was out of her mind with ecstasy. She couldn't have resisted him even if she wanted to. This was an entirely different level of sex than the regular. The energy between them was like nothing she ever experienced and she was there for every got damn minute of it.

"Answer me, Rae," he demanded. "I wanna hear you say it."

"Yes! *Yes*, Hawk!" The frisson of anticipation weaved through the emotion in her voice as the onset of her climax teetered on the edge. She tensed for a few heart stopping seconds, suspended in air before she took flight and soared.

Hawk's pace remained consistent. With an expertise that could only be described as an innate gift, he steered her orgasm to a higher plane. The spikes of pleasure reached a fevered pitch, rippling through her nerve endings and consuming her in its flames. Raven fell apart and shattered into a million pieces. She abandoned herself to the spiraling climax as electrifying shudders racked her body.

"You're so fuckin' sexy. You know that?" Hawk said gruffly, his eyes peeled to her face.

Raven groaned in response, blindly seeking his mouth, kissing him deeply as she slowly descended from the powerful release. Tiny tremors of aftershock continued to claim her body in small, pulsating waves. She read about women experiencing orgasm like the ones Hawk gave her, but she didn't believe it for one moment until it happened to her.

"I take it from that smile, I handled my business?" Hawk told her teasingly, carefully withdrawing from her warm, snug grip and standing above her on his knees.

Raven's first reaction was to moan in protest. Without him inside of her she felt so...empty. She stared up at him, once again admiring what a beautiful specimen he was. She saw men who lifted weights and only focused on their chest and arms to get that massive upper body look while their legs and calves resembled sticks in comparison. But not Hawk. His broad shoulders, narrow waist and lean hips gave way to muscular thighs and defined calves. His body was perfectly proportioned.

Raven bit down on a nail. Her eyes slowly ran over the picture he made with the canvas of his bedroom behind him. He was very aesthetically pleasing eye candy that a woman would never get tired of looking at–or fucking. He reminded her of one of those characters hailed as a demi-god whose powers manifested beyond the ordinary. After the heights Hawk brought her to, it wouldn't be too far a stretch to believe.

She brought her eyes back to the magnificent beast resting impatiently at his loins. Raven's heart skipped several beats when she saw how heavy and full it still hung. Then she realized...

"You haven't...you didn't..." She slowly pushed herself back and half sat up on her elbows, "You're still..."

"Still what?" He asked when she abruptly broke off her sentence. "Ready to fuck?"

"Uh, yeah." Suddenly, Raven was mortified. Did she do something wrong? Maybe...Maybe he didn't found her desirable enough. The thought caused her heart to drop. "Do…do you want me to help you, um…finish?"

Thoroughly amused, Hawk threw his head back and bellowed out a laugh. "Ah, no. I don't need any help with that."

Raven's eyes were glued to his painfully erect dick. "Then…"

"Did you really think we were finished?" He stared down at her, head slightly tilted to the side.

CHAPTER 20

Raven blinked up at him with wide eyes. "I...well...yeah."

Hawk bit down on his lip and grinned. "You're cute. Now bring that ass here."

Raven was too caught up in the expression on his face to try and figure out what he meant. "Huh?"

Still grinning, Hawk shook his head. Before she realized what he was doing, he had already picked her up and flipped her over on her hands and knees. When he entered her from behind, the momentum of his thrust almost threw her off balance.

"Oh!" Raven grabbed the headboard with one hand to steady herself.

"That's right. You better hold on," Hawk said in a smug tone.

"I'm good," Raven gasped. "I...I can handle it,"

"You can, huh?"

"Mm…Mmhm." To show him she meant exactly what she said, Raven arched her spine and threw it back at him hard.

"Aw, shit," Hawk groaned. "Fuck."

Raven's confidence grew with each thrust. Being desired so passionately by a man like Hawk Pattel did that to a woman.

Hawk fisted his hand in her thick hair and used it to steer her back on his dick. Flesh slapped against flesh, vigorously and with a steady shared rhythm. "Pussy good as fuck," he muttered in a thick voice.

"You feel good, too," Raven whispered. She never wanted it to end.

A thin layer of sweat covered her skin as Hawk worked her body. He impaled her deeper. Faster. Taming her inner feline until she purred like wild cat that had been domesticated. Their sensual rhythm flowed into a frantic fluidity. His passion ran raw and uncontrolled. Hawk carried them to the edge with steady thrusts. Raven's stomach knotted with anticipation. The violent shudder that assaulted her body was a prelude to the powerful orgasm that hit her only seconds later.

Raven trembled and her limbs grew weak. Her chest slowly lowered until the sensitive tips of her nipples grazed the bed. Sparks of electricity shot down her spine and reverberated through her body leaving Raven light headed and dizzy. Her love flowed down Hawk's dick like warm, thick honey. Raven panted. Her breasts heaved. She savored the sensations that held her hostage for as long as she could before they gradually faded like a thin mist.

Hawk placed each hand on either side of her head to support his weight. His pelvis curled into her once, twice more as he reached fulfillment. *"Ravennn!"* Her name rumbled from his chest in a low, guttural growl. "Awww, shit, baby."

Her fingers clenched the bedding. Delicious currents throbbed through her every time he rocked against her. She struggled speak, to tell him how good he felt, but her brain shut down leaving her mute.

Hawk's body lowered, molding itself to hers. Raven felt the violent beat of his heart hammering in his chest. The warmth of his uneven breathing fanned on her cheek as he held her close. He didn't seem to be in a hurry to move and that was fine with her. As they lay in satisfied silence Hawk pressed his lips to her temple, kissing her and nuzzling his face against hers before finally dragging himself to his feet.

Raven rolled to her back and watched him stumble to the bathroom. Once the door closed behind him, she threw an arm over her eyes and inhaled the sweet lingering musk of their bodies. She tried to wait for Hawk to come back but was too relaxed and his bed felt entirely too comfortable. Giving in to the temptation of blessed sleep, she drifted into semi-consciousness until she felt Hawk turning the comforter back and sliding her under the covers.

"Just a few minutes," Raven mumbled as she turned on her side and snuggled her face deeper into the soft pillow. "Have to leave soon."

She felt the faintest of kisses placed on her forehead. "It's okay. Get some rest, Rae."

Those were the last words she remembered before drifting off into an exhausted but satisfying sleep.

An hour later, Raven hovered somewhere on the threshold of wakefulness. Her lashes fluttered several times, but she fought the urge to open her eyes. Yawning widely, she inhaled a deep breath before releasing it in a long, soft sigh. After several unsuccessful attempts, she finally managed to pry her eyelids open and drag herself out of the fog of sleep.

"Uhmmmm..." she groaned. Remaining curled up in bed, she peered into the darkened room, disoriented and confused. Raven knew she wasn't in her bedroom at home; she realized that right away.

Okay. Flight out to Vegas. A. J.'s birthday party. So, she was in the guest bedroom at Nikki's house...

Raven lifted her head. *No. This wasn't Nikki's guest bedroom.* She frowned and looked around through eyes still bleary with sleep. *This wasn't even Nikki's house.*

Sitting up, her eyes gazed out of a wall made entirely out of glass. She stared at the bright, neon lights flickering against the black canvas of night. There seemed to be a million stars in the sky. That's when she realized she was in the heart of Las Vegas, not the suburban, gated community where Nikki and Angel lived. Raven swallowed hard and became instantly awake. The night's events hit her like an open fist to the chin. Hawk.

Raven slowly closed her eyes and dropped her head back on the pillow. No, no, no, no, no. She had to be dreaming. She did *not* just sleep with Hawk Pattel...*did she*? X-rated images played vividly behind her closed lids as she remembered the things the two of them did and the dirty things he said. Mortified, she covered her warm face with her hands, but the pictures in her head wouldn't go away.

What had she done?

Forcing herself to open her eyes, Raven looked around the room again. There was no sign of Hawk. Thank God. She held her breath and listened carefully, but she didn't hear any movement indicating where he might be in the condo.

Throwing the covers back, she hopped out of bed muttering a string of curses when she stubbed her toe against the bedside table. She turned the lamp on, praying that it wouldn't alert Hawk to the fact that she was woke and bring him to the room.

Spying her panties under the bed, Raven quickly grabbed them and pulled them on. She frantically searched for her bra. When she didn't see it anywhere, she waved it off and snatched her dress off the floor. Slipping it on, she was almost finished buttoning it when she realized she missed a buttonhole.

"Dammit!" She hissed. Raven quickly redid the buttons. She found one shoe then the other after a brief search. Holding them by the straps in one hand, she grabbed her purse off of the dresser.

Glancing around once more for her bra and not finding it, Raven went to the door and opened it with great care. She winced when it made a slight creak. Peering out the narrow crack, she opened the door a little wider and cautiously stuck her head out. She was still in the clear.

Tiptoeing out the room, she kept an ear and eye out for Hawk. Raven knew he told her that Danny would take her back, but if she could get out of the condo without detection, she would just call a cab when she got downstairs. It was a coward's way out, but she preferred not to see him if she didn't have to.

The floor plan was laid out so that the master bedroom was on one side of the condo by itself. She had to pass the kitchen and living room to get to the front door. She prayed Hawk wasn't in either place.

Walking on silent feet, Raven peeked around the entrance to the living area and saw that it was empty. So was the kitchen. She closed her eyes in relief and quickly continued on. Almost home free.

Raven picked up the pace and headed to the door. She was halfway there when she heard a familiar noise coming from the other side of the condo. She knew that sound. Someone was running on a treadmill at an even, steady gait. Raven looked up at the ceiling and mouthed, *"thank you!"* If Hawk was on the treadmill, he wouldn't hear her leave and it would more than likely take a while for him to notice her absence.

Fast walking to the front entryway, she glanced to her right then did a double take. A door across the hall was partially open. Raven paused and tilted her head when she saw a desk with a bookcase behind it. It looked like a home office. She glanced at the front door. Only a few feet away from freedom, but...

Like a magnet, the office beckoned her gaze. Oh, the information she might be able to find in there.

Raven, no! Just go! The sensible part of her brain ordered.

Instead, she remained in the same spot. Raven knew to listen to her inner voice because it never, ever steered her wrong. Resigned to getting the hell out of there, she started walking again, but her feet decided not to cooperate with her common sense. Instead of taking her to the front door, they carried her to Hawk's office.

Just a quick look around, she promised herself. *Thirty seconds. That's it.*

CHAPTER 21

Emboldened by the steady thumping of Hawk running on the treadmill, Raven slipped into his office. She quickly pulled her cell phone out and tapped the flashlight app to use it to illuminate the room.

Dumping her purse and shoes on a nearby chair, she ran to Hawk's desk but was immediately disappointed. No papers or anything lay on the surface, just a laptop. Raven saw that it was locked with a password she knew she would never be able to access. She tugged at the long middle drawer, but found it locked. So were all the other drawers. Glancing at the filing cabinet, she hurried over to try the drawers there, but just as she suspected, they were locked as well.

"Crap," she whispered.

Knowing she was pushing her luck and needed to get out of there, Raven turned to leave. That's when she saw something she'd missed in the dim light. A flash drive plugged into the side of the laptop. Her mouth dropped when she came across the little jewel that probably held a wealth of incriminating information.

Raven pulled the flash drive out of the laptop; she didn't even have to think about it. Heart pounding in her chest, she quickly ran towards the chair and got her shoes and purse. Slightly out of breath, she stood at the door and listened. The continued sound of running on the treadmill almost left her light headed with relief. Hurrying out the office, Raven looked behind her for good measure then made a mad dash to the front door. She was scared to death of Hawk catching her, but she didn't stop.

With trembling hands, she unlocked the door and let herself out. After quietly pulling it closed behind her, she double-timed it to the elevator, slipping her shoes on while she waited for the doors to open. Raven glanced behind her, expecting to see Hawk come barreling out the condo towards her at any moment. She was on the verge of taking the stairs when the elevator quietly chimed and opened to sanctuary. Once inside, she stabbed the button to close the doors so hard, she was almost afraid she broke it, but once they glided shut, she literally collapsed against the back wall of the elevator.

Thank God, she panted. *Made it.*

Staring straight at the mirrored panel opposite her, Raven caught an image of her reflection and grimaced. She looked a hot mess.

No, you look like you've just had the fuck of your life, which is exactly what happened, that damned inner voice whispered gleefully.

Raven used her fingers to comb her hair as best she could then wiped at the faint mascara smudges staining her face. She straightened from the wall and smoothed her hand over the wrinkles in the dress as the doors opened.

Seeing the same concierge behind the luxurious, brown granite desk that she and Danny passed coming into the building, Raven hurried over and gave him a bright smile. "Excuse me. Hi. Could you call me a cab, please?"

The man's brows lifted. When he glanced around behind her, Raven realized he was looking for Danny, who he seemed to be familiar with.

No telling how many women he shuttles back and forth to this place for Hawk whenever he's in town, Raven thought snidely.

Moving a bit to her left, Raven deliberately put herself back into his line of vision. "I'm in a hurry. Could you please call me a cab? Now?" She reached in her purse and pulled out a bill that she slid across the glossy surface. "I need it ASAP."

He quickly recovered and nodded. "Of course, madam. Right away."

"Thank you."

Inhaling a deep breath, Raven released it and walked towards a row of embroidered silk chairs. Taking a seat in one, she looked around, noting how classy the lobby of the high-rise was. The cream-colored marble floors were polished to a glassy shine. Beautiful paintings hung on walls covered in rich golden hued wallpaper, and a gorgeous, crystal chandelier hung from the domed ceiling. Fresh flowers were strategically placed in elegant vases that sat on mahogany pedestal tables, giving off a clean and crisp floral fragrance.

Raven looked down at the flash drive she still held in her hand. Her mind raced with what she might potentially find on it. Of course, she wouldn't be able to use it against the Pattels, but maybe it would give her a much-needed glimpse into what she was up against. The fact that she slept with

Hawk changed nothing; good dick wouldn't stop her from giving her all and helping to build a case against that family.

Hawk was an itch she needed scratched. That was all. However, now that he was out of her system, it was back to business as usual. Reluctantly, she realized that her sexual obsession, or whatever it was with Hawk made it mandatory for her to recuse herself from prosecuting any cases against the Pattels. There could be no hint of misconduct and her personal involvement with Hawk would definitely constitute as such.

Sighing heavily, Raven turned and glanced out the double glass windows, hoping to see a cab. What was taking so long? She was anxious to get back to Nikki's so she could get to her laptop. She was chomping at the bit to see what was on the flash drive.

Raven stood up impatiently with the intention of going back to the concierge to find out why the cab hadn't made it yet, but when she took a step forward and turned to do just that, all the breath was knocked out of her body. Coming towards her with long, angry strides was none other than one pissed off Hawk Pattel.

"Oh...fuck," Raven muttered.

For a second, she was frozen in place too scared to move and too scared to breathe. Then she remembered the flash drive in her hand. Casually opening her purse as if searching for something, she dropped it inside. When she looked up again, it was just in time to see Hawk give the concierge a subtle nod of what appeared to be...thanks.

Her eyes narrowed. She looked at the man staring boldly at her from behind the desk. *That snooty bastard ratted her out!*

She didn't have time to do more than give him a nasty glare before Hawk stepped up close into her personal space.

"Hey," she greeted him in a breathless tone. "What...what are you doing down here?" Raven winced when she heard how trite the question sounded, but it was all she could think of to say.

Hawk tilted his head to the side and answered her with words that dripped with sarcasm. "Oh, I don't know, Rae. Just happened to be in the fuckin' neighborhood."

Raven sucked her teeth and rolled her eyes upward. He was such a smartass. Giving him a cool side-eye, she saw he was wearing a pair of black sweatpants with black and gray running shoes. It looked as if he jumped right off the treadmill when the snitch called to tell him Raven was down in the lobby. The hastily pulled on t-shirt was damp with perspiration and clung lovingly to the ripped muscles of his chest and arms. Lord have mercy, even now, he was sexy per-*fucking*-sonified. It just wasn't fair.

"What are you doin', Rae?" His quietly dangerous voice immediately put her on alert.

She forced herself to look up and meet his eyes without flinching. "Look, I didn't want you to have to bother your driver at this hour to take me back to my sister's place. I'm okay with catching a cab."

"Are you now?"

Raven's eyes flickered away from his before she forced them back. She refused to let him intimidate her. "Yes. I am."

"I appreciate your consideration for Danny, but it's not needed. He's paid extremely well to do what I tell him to do at whatever hour I tell him to do it." He curled his fingers around her upper arm and started pulling her alongside him. "Let's go."

Momentarily stunned, Raven let him lead her a few steps forward until she saw they were headed to the elevator. Warning bells started going off in her head. She snatched her arm out of his grasp and growled from between clenched teeth, "First of all, I don't appreciate you manhandling me, so get your hands *off* me. Secondly, as I said, I'm fine taking a cab so thanks, but no thanks."

Hawk let out a deep breath that told her he was seconds away from losing it. "*First of all*, you didn't seem to mind me manhandling you a few hours ago, so what's the problem now? Matter of fact, I seem to remember the rougher the better."

Raven gasped. "You son of–"

"*Secondly,* you didn't come here in a cab, you won't leave in a cab. And Rae, before you say one more word, if you don't walk your li'l ass to this elevator like you got some sense, I swear to God, I'll throw you over my shoulder and carry you there."

"And I will scream this entire building down if you do," Raven huffed.

"Go on," Hawk shrugged. "I can see the headlines now; Manhattan ADA in altercation with a Pattel in Las Vegas. I'm good with it either way." Hawk folded his arms and stared at down at her. "So, what's it gonna be?"

Raven balled her hands up into tight fists and eyed his square jaw. She'd never wanted to deck someone so bad in her entire life.

Hawk glanced at her hands and easily read her thoughts. Shaking his head, he held Raven's gaze until she broke the stare-down and looked away. "Now are you ready?"

Raven contemplated calling his bluff and refusing to go with him. She would yell bloody murder at the top of her lungs if he tried to make her, but knew she couldn't afford to do that. If even the tiniest whisper of a story got out that she was in a high-rise with Hawk Pattel at four o'clock in the morning, her credibility as a lawyer would be smashed to smithereens. Better to go quietly and with dignity...then light into his ass once she got upstairs.

CHAPTER 22

Holding her head high, Raven marched past Hawk to the elevators. She gave another menacing glare to the concierge, which he resolutely ignored. The weasel. She ought to go over and take her twenty back.

Once they were inside the cab of the elevator and headed upstairs, Raven made the mistake of looking away from the digital panel of numbers she decided to fixate on and glance at Hawk. When she saw him look at her purse then at her, her fingers tightened on the strap. Surely, he didn't discover she took the flash drive. The only reason he came downstairs was because the concierge alerted him that she was leaving. Wasn't it?

The elevator doors opened, leaving her no time to ponder that question. What she needed to do was come up with a plan to convince Hawk to let her leave. She watched as he unlocked the front door to his condo then stood aside for her to enter. Lifting her chin, Raven straightened her shoulders and walked inside. As soon as he closed the door behind them, she immediately went on the offense.

"Since you say Danny is literally at your beck and call, I'd appreciate you calling him now to come and take me home. I prefer not to wait until daybreak to walk into my sister's house and do a walk of shame in front of my parents."

Folding his arms and crossing his legs, Hawk leaned back against the door. "No problem. But first, I wanna see what you're hiding from me in your purse."

Even though she was highly skilled at keeping her emotions from showing on her face in the courtroom, Raven hoped to hell the guilt, fear, and dread she felt now was well hidden. "I don't know what you're talking about."

The corner of Hawk's mouth lifted, but the gesture didn't meet his eyes. "I think you do. Either show me yourself or give me your purse."

Raven took a step back, calling on indignation to get her out of this mess. "You must be crazy, I'm not giving you my purse! I already told you that I don't—"

"Fine." Hawk pushed away from the door and came towards her.

"Alright!" she snapped just as he reached out to grab her purse. Raven's teeth locked together. It was obvious he meant to make good on his declaration.

Her palms grew clammy from dread. In that moment, she regretted the impulsive act that put her in this situation. The only thing it accomplished was making things even more complicated.

Rummaging through the contents, her fingers came in contact with the small item she was looking for. Taking it out of her purse, she hesitated then stretched out her arm out to give it to him. "Here."

She saw Hawk's frown when he looked at the flash drive. So, he *didn't* know she took it. Then it hit her. He figured out she was hiding something when she thought she was sneaking it in her purse downstairs. Great.

Hawk took the flash drive, staring at it as he walked past her into the living room. "You went through my office."

Raven glanced down at her nails as if admiring the new color. Hawk's sentence was constructed as a statement, not a question, so there was really no need for her to reply.

Hawk turned around and threw a veiled look at Raven as she pretended to ignore him. "I thought I locked everything down in case you got any ideas about snooping through my shit. Guess I missed this."

All thoughts of feigning nonchalance left Raven as she frowned at him suspiciously. "What is that supposed to mean?"

"It means I'm not stupid. I knew you'd search my things as soon as you saw an opening, so I made sure my desk was locked and there were no personal papers left out. Don't know how I missed removing this from the USB port." He held up the small electronic device up before slipping it in his pocket and giving her a taunting smirk. "Plus, I was sure I put it on you too good to wake up before I finished exercising. I'll work harder next time."

Raven knew he was intentionally trying to provoke her, but she couldn't help swallowing the bait. "Oh, screw you, Pattel. Just a little FYI, there won't *be* a next time."

"Of course, there will be." Hawk smiled deliberately furthering her indignation. He sat down on the arm of the chair he was standing next to and let his eyes roam over her in an explicitly sexual manner. "Let me ask you a question. You like flowers, don't you, Rae?"

The question threw her off balance but she quickly recovered. Impatiently jutting a hip out, Raven folded her arms and blew out a huff of air. "What does that have to do with anything?"

"Humor me. Do you?"

"Fine! Yes, I like flowers," she snapped.

"Cool. Let me give you a quick biology lesson to show you how I know this ain't over between us. You're familiar with how a flower blooms, right? Specifically, a lily. Days before it's ready, a lily's bud sucks up moisture and grows until its ready to explode. Then, the outer part of the flower gradually peels open like a banana to form a blossom. The whole process of the flower emerging is a slow but steady buildup." He paused for affect then added softly, "Sort of like you last night when I made you cum."

"Oh, that's cute," Raven snapped. "Let me guess, just like the artist, you dated a botanist too?"

Hawk shook his head and said with a straight face, "Nah. She was a horticulturist."

Raven winced as a streak of jealousy hit her. She tried to hide it, but Hawk's quiet laugh told her he saw it.

"I'm kidding. I'm just a man who admires and recognizes beautiful things when he sees them." The amusement slowly faded. The look he gave her was smothered with hot lust. "And you opening up to me like you did last night? That was beautiful as fuck."

Raven gulped and stared at Hawk, caught up in a trance she couldn't seem to break. He kept confusing her by saying the unexpected and that made her nervous...and excited.

A deep throbbing in her core began like a steady drumbeat. It quickly intensified in strength. Nectar pooled from her sweet spot and saturated her panties. Raven struggled to control her desire. For Christ's sake, she was a highly intelligent, professional woman, but she was also street smart and savvy. She could spot a con game a mile away, so why was she entertaining Hawk Pattel's bullshit and letting him get to her? What was it about this man that rendered her a walking, dripping mess of hormones?

Recognizing the weakness she had for him made her panic. She blurted out the first thing that came in her head to wipe the smug look off his face. "Do you really think you're the first man to make my lily bloom? Don't kid yourself, Pattel. I can get what happened last night from anyone."

She felt a thrill in her chest when a flash of anger crossed his face. Finally, she'd gotten him where it hurt and it felt good! Satisfaction showed in the slight curve of Raven's lips, but it didn't last. When he stood up and started walking towards her, dread locked up tight in her stomach and sat there hard and heavy.

Hawk stopped inches from her. "You're many things, Raven, but I never thought you were a coward."

CHAPTER 23

"Excuse me?" Raven squeaked with indignation. She had not gotten to where she was by being a coward and she dared him to say it again. "What was that?"

"You heard me. I've seen you in action in the courtroom. You've gone toe to toe with some of the roughest men out there. You gully as shit and now that I know a little bit about your background, I can understand why. You don't back down and I admire that about you, but when it comes to your personal life, you have a tendency to run away and hide if it's something you don't want to deal with."

"I tell you you're not as special in bed as you seem to think and *I'm* the one who doesn't like to deal with facts?" Raven snorted. "Get over yourself."

"I wouldn't have a problem with accepting it if it were the truth, but we both know it's not." His eyes dropped to her heaving breasts. "I can still hear the noises you made when I touched you. Tasted you. Fucked you." He lifted his eyes to ensnare hers. "Now *that*? That's the truth."

Raven tried to swallow, but her throat was too dry to let her. "Hawk—"

"Those sounds drove me crazy, you know that?" Hawk's hooded gaze came up to lock on her softly parted lips before settling on her face. "Even now, just thinking about the way you begged for it got my beast so hard it hurts."

Of their own accord, Raven's eyes wasted no time travelling down to the front of his pants. Sure enough, the outline of his dick print was painfully long and thick against the material of his sweats.

Raven inhaled, holding on to the breath until her lungs began to burn. It was only when the room started spinning that she blinked rapidly and broke the spell. Her breath came in rapid spurts. Needing to put some distance between them, she pushed past him and went to stand by the window to try and get herself under control. Keeping her back to him, she wrapped her arms around her waist and stared out into the darkness, trying to ground herself. But if she thought Hawk was going to give her a moment to regain her composure, she was mistaken. Like the true predator he was, she saw his reflection stalking her on silent feet until he stood right behind her.

"Please don't." She stated the words with a forced calmness she was far from feeling.

"The men you've been with. Have they taken the time to study the secrets you keep securely locked between those soft thighs of yours, Rae? Did they take notes on what gets you off and turns you on like I did?" He leaned down to whisper seductively in her ear. "Do they know that you like that naughty clit of yours spanked with the tip of the tongue until it makes you–"

"Stop!" Raven found herself pleading with him.

But the seductive words kept coming. "When they fuck you, do they take cues from your breathing and the sounds you make that tell them what you enjoy?"

Raven closed her eyes and shook her head. "Hawk, please."

"And once they find what gets you there, do they settle in for the long haul and stroke that pussy until you cum so much it's like a river overflowing and flooding sheets?"

"I said STOP!" The tingling sensation at the very heart of her femininity vibrated so strongly that

the only thing that would appease it was the beast Hawk Pattel wielded between his legs. Raven shook her head. She needed to get out of there *now*.

Blindly whirling around, she tried to move past him, but he refused to budge. "Move!"

"I've seen the type of men you date, remember? They're meek. Predictable. That's not what you want, baby. You're a strong woman. An extraordinary woman. You need a man who's equally yoked inside and outside the bedroom. A man who's going to bring out that wild side of you like I did. Somebody who'll take control of your pleasure and fuck you the way you need and want to be fucked... fucked like only *I* can fuck."

Raven was all the way shook. The fact that he knew her so well after only a couple hours of sex frightened her. She kept that side of her buried for a reason. Knowledge like that could give a man power over her she didn't want him to have—especially if he knew what to do with it as Hawk obviously did.

"I'm tired of playing word games with you. I-I want to *leave*." The way her voice cracked on the last word revealed just how affected she was by him.

"This isn't a game, Raven. No, listen to me," he insisted when she pushed against his chest. Backing her up against the glass wall, he grabbed her wrists when she continued to struggle and held them above her head in one of his hands. Using his other hand, he lifted her chin up, forcing her to look at him.

"We been circling around each other for a while now because I think we knew what would happen if we ever hooked up. It's true whether you want to admit it or not." Hawk hesitated as if he said too much. That more than anything piqued Raven's curiosity.

"I... I can agree with that," she said tentatively.

Hawk looked away before finding her eyes again. "Maybe this started off as something else, but now that I've had you, I'm not ready to walk away. Be honest with me, are you?" He stared at her so intently it was difficult for Raven to break eye contact.

She opened her mouth to answer him, but the lie poised on the tip of her tongue wouldn't let itself be spoken, so she avoided the question altogether.

"Okay yes, the sex was good, but...we...we can't *do* this, Hawk. If anyone ever found out..."

"Let me worry about that. I'll make sure nobody finds out."

"Let you worry about it? I'm supposed to just trust you like that? I don't think so. I'm not *that* whipped by that monster you have down there," she scoffed. "If...*this* ever got out it wouldn't touch you. *Me* on the other hand? I would lose everything and that's too high a price to pay for toe curling, mind numbing sex." Raven shook her head. "I can't do it. I'll just continue using my B.O.B and be happy with that."

"Battery Operated Boyfriend, huh?" Hawk's quick chuckle brought a reluctant smile to Raven's face.

"Sorry, too much info?"

"Nah, I guess I feel better knowing you use a vibrator instead of the real thing, but damn if I'm not standing here jealous as fuck of it."

"He gets the job done," Raven shrugged. She held his eyes for a long moment before looking away and lowering her lashes. He was so intense. It made her nervous, but she wasn't a coward like he called her earlier, so she brought her eyes back to him and boldly added, "Maybe it's not as good as you, but it takes the edge off."

The savagery that rumbled from Hawk's chest made Raven's stomach clench. Keenly aware that he still held her in a vulnerable position, Raven shifted from one foot to the other. The movement brought Hawk's attention to the front of her dress where her cleavage spilled over the neckline. She held her breath when he brought his hand down to cover her breast. Shivering involuntarily, Raven arched her back and pushed herself more firmly into his hand.

"No bra," Hawk mumbled.

"I... I couldn't find...*ooo*!" She almost choked when he tweaked her nipple between his thumb and forefinger. "Hawk, please."

"Please what. Say it, Rae."

Torn between wanting him so bad that she ached and knowing she shouldn't, sudden tears sprang to her eyes. Why was this happening to her? She couldn't trust him. Her office was investigating his family for God's sake. Nothing good could come out of this and it certainly wouldn't lead anywhere.

"Just like it was your decision to come back to me when you left earlier, it has to be your decision now. Tell me you want this, baby."

Raven shook her head from side to side, trying valiantly to deny the attraction between them. "No."

Hawk blew out a shaky breath, letting her know how much he wanted her. He rested his forehead on hers. When he removed his hand from her breast and stepped back, Raven almost cried out in protest.

"You don't think I get it, but I do. There's no trust because of who we are. Like you said, you have a helluva lot more to lose than I do. I get that too. So how about I even the playing field a little?"

Raven looked at him curiously, watching as he reached in his pocket and pulled out the flash drive. "What are you doing?"

"Here. Take it." He gave her the small device and leaned back in order to see her face. "I'd say that buys me a little bit of trust. Don't you?"

CHAPTER 24

Raven stared at the flash drive lying innocently in her hand before looking up at him with wide eyes. What the hell was he up to now? "I don't understand. Why are you giving this to me?"

Hawk shrugged. "Consider it insurance."

Suspicion clouded Raven's eyes. "Let me guess. It's blank, right?"

Hawk shook his head. "Nope."

"Then whatever is on here has little to no consequential value, is that it?"

"Quite the opposite. Let's just say it would be a game changer if what's on it ever got out."

"Then what's the catch?"

"Two stipulations."

"I knew it. Okay, what's the first stipulation?"

"One, I'm giving it to you for insurance only."

"Now you're being ridiculous. You give this to me, tell me there's information on it but expect me not to look at it."

"Yeah."

"What if I look at it and don't tell you?"

"I'll know. The information on it will cause a chain of events that can't be reversed." Hawk paused before adding. "Not to mention that if you look at it every news agency in New York will know that an officer of the court, sworn to faithfully carry out her duties without fear, favor, or...affection..." He paused at that and grinned at the last part before continuing, "...is sleeping with a member of one of the very crime families her office is investigating. I don't think that would go over too well. Do you?"

Anger simmered steadily in Raven's eyes. "Wait, so you *are* threatening me?"

"Just making sure we're both clear on what's at stake."

Just to humor him, she asked, "What's the second stipulation?"

"For as long as we agree to this arrangement of ours, Rae, you belong to me and only me. You don't see anybody else."

Raven hesitated. Was she really contemplating going through with this just for the sake of sex?

Was she that desperate for a man? But as soon as she asked herself that question, the answer became painfully obvious. No. She definitely wasn't desperate to have sex with a man. She was desperate to have sex with *this* man. Point. Blank. Period. The impression of the flash drive burned a hole in her hand. Holding it tight, she impulsively came to a decision.

"Fine. I accept your offer, but the first time I'm uncomfortable and want to back out, we're done." Raven hesitated then added the next part before she changed her mind. "I have a stipulation of my own. While we're engaging in this little agreement of ours, *neither* of us will see anybody else. There will be no other women. Do you have a problem with that?"

"If I wanted to be with somebody else, I wouldn't be standing here with a hard on from hell trying to bargain my way into your panties."

Raven bit back a smile. "So, that means you agree? I won't have to worry about dealing with artists, or horticulturists, or doctors, or whatever small village of women I'm sure you have waiting in the background?" She fought to concentrate when Hawk gave her that smile that that always made her melt.

"Yeah, I agree with your stipulation, counselor."

"Good." Raven slipped the flash drive in the pocket of her dress. "Well, I, um, guess we have a deal."

"Mmhm." He nodded slowly.

"Good," Raven said again.

"Excellent," Hawk agreed.

Raven laughed nervously then grimaced when it came out sounding more of a girlish giggle. *Get it together, Rae. You're a grown woman. Act like it instead of a young schoolgirl. You can handle this. All you have to do is –*

"Raven?"

Her head jerked up when she heard Hawk call her name. "Huh?"

"Get out of your head and come here." He crooked a finger to beckon her to him.

Biting down on her lip and holding his smoldering gaze, Raven took the couple of steps needed to get to him. Once there, she kept her mouth upturned waiting rather impatiently for him to lower his lips to hers. When Hawk's mouth stopped within inches of consummating the kiss, Raven reached up and pulled his head down and hungrily attacked his mouth.

Groaning harshly from within his chest, his hands came down to grab her hips. He walked her backwards until Raven felt her back touch the glass wall behind her. Somehow she managed to work her hands between them and claw at his t-shirt. She wanted to see his body, needed to touch his skin.

Hawk got the message and yanked the t-shirt over his head. Nibbling at her neck, he finished unbuttoning her dress and dragged it down her shoulders. Raven finished undressing by frantically pushing the dress along with her panties down to her ankles.

She gasped when Hawk placed his hands at the back of her thighs and lifted her up. Wrapping her legs around his waist, her breathing turned ragged and her heartbeat accelerated. It didn't register in her mind that her bare ass was pressed against the glass for anyone with a decent telescope and perverted curiosity to see. Raven needed him.

Wanted him. Anything else that didn't fit into those two categories wasn't important.

Hawk somehow managed to push his sweats down enough to free his erection. Raven turned her head and blindly searched for and found his mouth again. Her tongue curled around his. The kiss was hot, passionate and intense. There wasn't a thing Raven could think about that she wanted more in that moment than–

"Wait," she panted, tearing her mouth away from his before greedily finding it again. "Condom," she mumbled against his mouth.

Hawk groaned in frustration. "Shit. Thank God one of us still has some sense."

"Barely," Raven laughed bestowing soft kisses over his handsome face and caressing the bunched muscles of his shoulders.

Hawk squeezed her ass in his large hands as he turned and headed in the direction of the bedroom. "Just so you know, you ain't makin' it back before daylight so guess you better get ready for that walk of shame you wanted to avoid."

Raven moaned and threw her head back as he sucked the sensitive skin of her neck. Shit, she was grown. They would be alright. "Just hurry up and get to your room. I need you to fuck me before I lose my mind."

Hawk chuckled quietly, sending the chill of goose bumps spreading over her body. "I gotchu, counselor. That I can definitely do."

CHAPTER 25

Early Monday morning, Raven walked into the office with an extra bounce in her strut and a wide smile on her lips. She nodded to several people who greeted her and stopped to briefly chat with one or two of them before continuing on her way.

DeLaney Skye, her assistant who was with her from the beginning, looked up as Raven approached her desk. "Hey, good morning! You look well rested. As a matter of fact, you're glowing. Did you have a relaxing visit with your sister this weekend?"

Raven pressed her lips together to stop the smile on her face from spreading ear to ear. "I had a *very* relaxing weekend, Laney." An image of Hawk Pattel giving her the best sex she ever had in her life broke the smile free from its restraints. "It was just what the doctor ordered."

"Well, good. You work entirely too hard. I'm glad you took some time out for yourself."

"So am I. How was your weekend?"

"It was okay. Took advantage of the weather and hit a few festivals with some friends." She handed Raven a couple of sticky note messages.

"Good for you," Raven called out, heading into her office. "I have that meeting with Jeff at ten. I'm going to take some time catching up on paperwork until then, but buzz me ten minutes before the meeting to make sure I don't get caught up like last time?"

"Will do."

Humming under her breath, Raven closed the door behind her and walked to her desk. She placed her briefcase on the floor and started shuffling through the messages. Seeing that there wasn't anything pressing that needed her immediate attention, she sat down and logged into her computer. Raven grabbed her glasses from beside the keyboard where she left them and started clicking through her emails. It didn't take long for her to become immersed in the usual crazy Monday morning rat race.

Almost an hour passed when her cell phone buzzed with a text message. Raven finished the email she was typing and hit SEND before grabbing her phone. When she saw Hawk's name, her pulse immediately sped up. She sat back in her chair and read the message:

Morning beautiful. How's your day going so far?

Good morning. Typical Monday. How are you?

Other than wanting you? Fine. When am I gonna see you, Rae?

Settling deeper in the chair, Raven crossed her legs. *You just saw me yesterday.*

Exactly. Yesterday. I need to see you again.

A tiny thrill shot up her spine. *When?*

Tonight. What time you get off work?

Raven's mouth twisted wryly at the question. *I get off whenever I finish these days, but tonight's not good. I have a function to go to.*

Alone?

She shook her head at the possessiveness that one word hinted at. *Yes, it's business related.*

I can meet you at your place afterwards.

Raven's fingers hesitated over the keyboard before she answered. *I can't. I won't be home until*

*late and have an early meeting in the morning. I
have to be alert. I already know if you come over I
won't get any sleep.*

You're not blowin' me off are you, woman?

Definitely not. I want to see you too. Then
biting her lip she added: *I'm still sore from
yesterday. In a good way.*

I wasn't too rough, was I?

No. Again she was hesitant, but quickly typed:
You already know I loved it.

Yes. I know.

Raven rolled her eyes. He was so arrogant.
She loved that about him though and couldn't stop
grinning at the phone. *What about tomorrow
night?*

Do I have a choice?

I'll make it up to you. Nibbling on the corner
of her lip Raven added before she could change her
mind. *Anything you want. However you want it.*

Mmmm. That sounds...promising.

You'll enjoy every moment, I promise. Raven
remembered the way he couldn't seem to get

enough of her of her last time and decided she had cause to be a little cocky herself. *I guarantee it.*

You have no idea how hard I am right now. Take care of my pussy for me until I see you.

Raven closed her eyes and squeezed her thighs. Just like that she was instantly wet. *I will.*

You know it's mine, right?

Yes, Hawk. Knowing what he wanted, she added: *It's yours.*

Damn right. See you tomorrow, Rae.

~~Bye baby.~~ Raven grimaced and deleted that. Instead she typed: *Can't wait.*

Raven read over their conversation again and let out a quiet sigh. Closing her eyes, she reminisced on the hours of sex she had with Hawk. She finally had to beg him to stop and give her a break. The man had the stamina of a freaking machine and an iron hard self-control. By the time she awakened yesterday, the morning sun was shining brightly through the window. Raven didn't even trip about it. The night she spent with Hawk was worth every second of the interrogation she knew she would receive from her sister.

Raven opened her eyes as she thought about Nikki because an interrogation was exactly what she got after Danny drove her back. Nikki had sent Raven a couple texts she missed. When she walked in the front door, the first person she encountered was Angel. Even now, Raven's stomach tightened when she remembered the look in his eyes. He bid her good morning and asked how she enjoyed her evening with her *friends*. He emphasized the word just like that, and in that moment, Raven knew *he* knew. Angel was aware that Raven had been with Hawk, but she refused to shrink away from embarrassment.

Nikki joined them a moment later, her all-knowing eyes dragging over Raven from head to toe. Curbing the urge to roll her eyes, Raven had asked where their parents were and could've fainted from relief when Nikki told her they went to worship at one of the churches they found while in Vegas. At least she was spared a cross-examination form her mother for the time being.

Excusing herself, she had gone up to her room to take a shower. Although, she'd taken one at Hawk's condo when she'd gotten up that morning, his horny ass had bent her over a couch and screwed her again before she left. Raven had still been smiling at that memory when she emerged from the bathroom with a towel wrapped around her body. The smile, however, disappeared when she saw Nikki in the room waiting on her...

"Hey," Raven said, deliberately keeping her tone light.

"Hey, my ass. I want to know where you really went. And don't tell me you were with some college friends because we both know that's not true.

"Nikki–"

"You were with Hawk, weren't you?"

Raven thought about denying the obvious but shrugged and answered truthfully. "Yes. I was."

Nikki looked up at the ceiling in exasperation. "Ravennnnn..."

"Before you even start, it's not a big deal."

"Not a big deal?" Nikki squealed. "His dick may have corroded your brain, but let me remind you, you work for the District Attorney's office! You're investigating Hawk and his family! And you're SLEEPING with him? That's as big a deal as I can think of right now!"

"I know what I'm doing, okay? Will you just please leave it alone?"

"Raven–"

"No, Nikki, I mean it. You're worried about me. I know that, but we...Hawk and I...we talked and came to an understanding so..." Her voice trailed off because the stuttering explanation sounded weak and pathetic when she said it out loud.

Nikki looked as if she was doing her best to keep herself from exploding. When she finally spoke it was in a slow and deliberate tone. "You...talked. You came to an understanding. Are you saying you actually trust this man not to use this against you in some way that's beneficial to him and his family? Really, Raven??"

Feeling more like the defiant bratty sister instead of the grown woman she was, Raven just stared at Nikki without answering. The problem was that a part of her knew her sister was right. This thing with Hawk was crazy. There was really no justification for indulging in it but...

Frustrated and needing to think, she walked past Nikki went to the dresser. Pulling the scrunchie loose that had held the thick strands atop her head during her shower, she ignored her sister's unwavering glare and started brushing her hair.

"Can I ask you a question?"

"Nikki..."

"No, answer this question honestly and then I'll leave it alone."

Raven stopped brushing her hair and met Nikki's eyes in the mirror. "Okay, fine. What is it?"

"Do you have feelings for Hawk? Other than the obvious, of course. Are you falling for him?"

They stared at one another for a full five seconds before Raven glanced away, but it was too late. The look in her eyes told Nikki all she needed to know.

"That's what I thought. That's the only explanation that would make this entire mess make any kind of sense." Sighing, Nikki came forward and wrapped her arms around her. She rested her chin on Raven's shoulder and looked at her in the mirror. "It's not as easy as you thought to simply walk away from somebody because of who they are when your heart's involved, is it?"

Raven knew Nikki was referencing Raven's unyielding criticism of her marriage to Angel. Unable to put the obvious answer into words, Raven allowed her silence to suffice.

Nikki didn't push the issue. The last thing she said was, "Just be careful. If you need me, you know where to find me." Then she couldn't seem to stop herself from adding, "And if he hurts you, I swear I'll kick his ass up and down the streets of Manhattan then stomp him into the ground."

A small smile crossed Raven's lips. Her sister barely weighed a buck twenty-five, but she knew Nikki meant every word of it. Even if they didn't agree with each other one hundred percent of the time, they had each other's back no matter what. That was something Raven was extremely grateful for.

Turning back to her desk, Raven's eyes went to her laptop. After a brief hesitation, she leaned forward and googled Hawk's name. Instantly, a slew of information lined the page. Feeling like a schoolgirl stalking her secret crush, Raven scooted forward, clicking on the images and going through them one by one...

Hawk dressed in a tuxedo looking elegant and sophisticated at a fundraiser...Hawk photographed at the opening of the new Pattel restaurant in downtown Brooklyn. Hawk laughing into the camera in reaction to something that someone said to him. Raven propped her chin up on her fist. The man was simply delicious.

Continuing to go through the images, she hovered over one in particular before maximizing it to get a better look. It was one of Hawk, his older brother, Lucas, their adopted brother, King, and cousin, Lorenzo. Spanning every flavor of the chocolate eye-candy spectrum, they were some beautiful ass men. There was no denying that truth. There was also no denying the fact that, in spite of being on the wrong side of the law–in some cases probably *because* of it–they were highly sought after eligible bachelors who had their choice of any woman they desired. Raven shook her head. Handsome, intelligent and educated, there were no shortage of women vying for a spot on these fine brotha's roster.

Allowing herself to get her fix, Raven clicked through several more photos, lingering on the ones that showed him with a slew of stunning women on his arm. She scowled at how possessively they clung to him, as if afraid of letting go for one moment. Sucking her teeth, she continued her cyber stalking and got so caught up that she jumped in her chair when a knock sounded her door.

CHAPTER 26

Raven slammed her laptop closed. Sitting straight up in the chair and hoping she didn't look as guilty as she felt, she cleared her throat. "Come in."

DeLaney came through the door with a face splitting grin. "Look what was just delivered for youuu," she announced in a high-pitched singing voice. Her face alight with animated curiosity, Laney slowly walked up to Raven's desk carrying a large vase with a huge arrangement of flowers. "These are absolutely gorgeous!"

"Oh, my," Raven exclaimed, standing and walking around the desk to look admiringly at the arrangement. "I never receive flowers. Are you sure those are for me?"

"Yes. Your name is on the envelope." Laney plucked the small, rectangular shaped envelope from the cardholder and gave it to Raven.

Sure enough, her name was written across the front and underlined twice. Seeing the dark, bold handwriting, Raven's heart started racing. She looked at the bouquet again. That's when she noticed, tucked within the spray of pink ruffled peonies, fringed tulips, and cluster of soft lavender sweet peas, lay at least a dozen closed lily buds.

Hawk.

She distinctly remembered the analogy he gave her comparing her orgasm to the blooming of a lily...

Days before it's ready, a lily's bud sucks up moisture and grows until its ready to explode. Then the outer part of the flower gradually peels open like a banana to form a blossom. The whole process of the flower emerging is a slow, but steady buildup. Sort of like you when I made you cum...

Raven opened the envelope with fingers that trembled and pulled out the handwritten card: ***Now you can enjoy what I think is the best part of the blooming process. It's all in the buildup. Enjoy seeing it as much as I enjoy you.***

HJP

Raven bit down on her lip to try and stop the grin gaining momentum across her face, but it was no use. She reached out and traced the shape of the tight, delicate lily bud. Now aware that this was how he visualized the most intimate part of her, she

259

knew she would forever be reminded of Hawk whenever she saw a lily in full bloom.

"Well?" Laney asked with barely contained excitement. Raven half expected her to start jumping up and down at any moment. "Who're they from?"

"Just a friend," she answered in a breezy voice.

"An arrangement like this cost a pretty penny. I'm sure he must be more than *just* a friend. Come on, Rae, spill!"

"A girl's gotta have some secrets, Laney." Raven slipped the card back into the envelope. While DeLaney stood there as if she was waiting for at least a clue, Raven propped a hand up on her hip and gave her a direct stare. "Um, I know you have something to do other than stand there trying to get all up in my business."

Giving Raven a puppy dog look of disappointment, Laney turned on her heels and headed to the door. "Fine, fine. Keep your secrets. Just don't forget to invite me to the wedding," she called out half-jokingly before closing the door behind her.

"Nosey little ass," Raven grumbled underneath her breath. DeLaney had tried it, but she knew more than anyone that Raven didn't play that tell all your business shit. Not at all.

Leaning down to smell the flowers one last time, Raven rounded the desk and got her purse out the bottom drawer. After tucking the card securely in her wallet, she put it back and glanced at her watch. She had about fifteen minutes before the meeting with Jeff. Feeling giddy and excited, she picked up her phone and sent Hawk a quick text.

I got the flowers. They're beautiful. Thank you.

You're beautiful and you deserve beautiful things. I'm going to enjoy spoiling you.

Smiling, Raven shook her head. *I have to go. I just wanted to tell you thank you. And that I'm thinking about you.* She held her breath as she waited on his reply to that.

You mean that?

Yes. I do.

His reply took a little longer coming than before.

You sure I can't see you tonight, baby? I miss the fuck outta you.

Do you really or are you just saying that to get some ass?

I don't have to lie to get that, do I?

I guess not.

No guess about it. Let's be clear on that, okay?

Raven could almost see that left eyebrow of his cock up. *Okay.*

What time you want me to swing by?

Raven was tempted, but there was no way she would get through an all-day meeting after a night with Hawk. *I can't. Believe me, I want to, but some people have to work for a living.*

That's the second time you've told me that and it's not true. I'm working now.

Yeah, yeah Raven muttered before looking at her watch. *I have to go. See you tomorrow. Seven okay?*

Alright baby. Tomorrow at seven.

Raven smiled at the endearment. *Talk to you soon.*

Looking at the flowers one last time, Raven left her office and headed to her meeting. The entire way there, her thoughts were consumed with Hawk and the night they shared. The secret smile she wasn't aware was on her face stayed in place even as she walked into Jeff's office.

However, when she saw Gwynn sitting in one of the chairs in front of their boss' desk her smile faltered. She glanced at Jeff, who was talking on the phone. Raven was under the impression she was meeting with Jeff one on one.

Taking a seat next to Gwynn, she leaned over and whispered, "What's going on?"

"I'm not sure," Gwynn shrugged. "I just got an update on my calendar this morning."

Raven lifted her eyebrows and sat back in her chair. The mood in the room was tense and heavy. Something was definitely up. She just wished she had an idea what. Raven didn't like surprises. When Jeff hung up the phone, she gave him her complete attention.

"Morning." His greeting was gruff and brief. "Raven and I were already scheduled to meet, but a couple hours ago, I was just made aware of a situation that we were asked to help out on. It has to do with the Pattels. Specifically, Hawk Pattel. And this time?" Jeff clenched a fist and shook it twice "I think we finally may be on to something."

Raven felt the room take a sharp dip. She gripped the arm of the chair tightly in order to keep herself upright. This. Wasn't. Happening. Not now. Along with a host of other cases, their office had been actively investigating the Pattels since Jeff was elected District Attorney almost two years ago. However, they were never able to find anything. The very moment she let her guard down and became involved with Hawk...

"I just got off the phone with the Las Vegas DA's office," Jeff said. "We're going to be working closely and assisting them on an incident that happened this past weekend at one of Hawk Pattel's clubs. Michael Bernstein, a trusted accountant whose family has a long history with the Pattels, was reported missing by his wife this morning. According to a confidential informant who works at Pattel's nightclub, Saturday night he said he witnessed Bernstein being led downstairs to a room that's off limits to employees. He hasn't been seen since."

Raven kept her attention fixed on Jeff and listened attentively, but her mind immediately went to the cuts and abrasions on Hawk's hands. By his own admission, he'd been in some type of altercation that night. Was this the reason for his foul mood?

Nausea ate at her stomach like a vial of acid. She forced herself to breathe slowly. In. And out. In. And out. Raven swallowed. It wasn't helping.

"Why do we think Hawk Pattel had something to do with Bernstein's disappearance?" She managed to ask in a calm voice.

"Bernstein's wife called the police in a panic to report him missing. It didn't take long for her to come clean about the details of her husband's dealings with the Pattels. He and his father before him, helped the Pattels launder money. Lately, however, it seems he started getting a little greedy. From what Mrs. Bernstein admitted, her husband was stealing from the Pattels, diverting funds and skimming money off the top to finance extravagant trips, jewelry, cars and a nasty gambling habit." Jeff leaned back in his chair and stared intently at Raven and Gwynn before he continued. "According to her, he stole over a million dollars."

"Wow," Gwynn replied.

"Exactly," Jeff said. "To add insult to injury, he was someone the Pattels trusted implicitly. Bernstein's father worked in the organization with the older Pattels so the entire relationship between the two families spanned well over thirty years."

"And she's saying the Pattels discovered him stealing?" Raven asked. "Is she sure? How does she know he didn't just take off?"

"Mrs. Bernstein said her husband was called to a meeting with Hawk, which was unusual for a Saturday night. Especially at a nightclub. He told her before he left home that if she didn't hear from him, something was wrong. He was so wary of meeting Pattel that he even took a member of his company's security team with him. When he didn't come home or answer any of her calls, she knew he was right in his suspicions. The employee who accompanied him can't be reached either. And since she profited from her husband stealing, she's terrified they'll come after her next."

"As well she should be," Gwynn muttered. "This isn't something the Pattels would take lightly."

"Right," Jeff nodded. "At this point, for them it's less about the money and more so about Bernstein's betrayal. Organizations like the Pattel's value loyalty above everything else. I have no doubt they found out and made an example of the man," Jeff concluded.

"Did the CI actually see Hawk with Bernstein?" Raven asked.

"No. For that matter, he didn't see Hawk at all. Just heard rumors that the boss was in the club. I'm sure Pattel's presence can be verified with cameras. We *do* know he was in town though. Someone had to see him."

"I saw him." The words that reluctantly left Raven's mouth sounded as if they were forced out. "I saw Hawk Pattel this weekend."

CHAPTER 27

"You what?" Jeff's eyes bore into Raven as he leaned forward in his chair. "Where? In Las Vegas?"

"Yes, he came to my nephew's birthday party with his cousin," Raven said somewhat grudgingly. The last thing she wanted to do was tell Jeff, but if it came out some other way, she would never be able to explain why she didn't reveal the information from the very beginning. At least this way she had some kind of control over how to spin it.

"What happened? Start at the beginning and don't leave anything out," Jeff demanded. "What did he say?"

"I... nothing," Raven shrugged. "He, um, he didn't say much. We didn't talk long."

"So, there's nothing you remember that could give us a glimpse into his mood that day?" Scowling, Jeff thoughtfully rubbed his chin. "Was he quiet? Angry? Preoccupied?"

Shaking her head, Raven's wide-eyed gaze never left Jeff's face. "Not that I could tell. But as I said, the few words we exchanged were brief. I went back to visiting with my parents and by the time the party started, he was gone."

"Well, at least that's confirmation he was in town."

Raven chose her next words carefully. "Is it possible that Vegas is jumping the gun a bit? There's not very much evidence indicating foul play was involved."

Jeff stared at her and frowned. "The Vegas police are just starting their investigation, but from all accounts the circumstances are more than a little suspicious; especially with everything Mrs. Bernstein revealed. I mean, let's be honest here. We're talking about the Pattels. It's not much of a stretch to believe foul play was involved, is it?" His eyes drilled unblinkingly into Raven's.

Seeing no other out, Raven said the only thing she *could* say. "I agree."

Slightly appeased, Jeff slowly sat back in his chair. "I'm glad we're all on the same page. The Vegas DA is an old friend of mine. He knows we've got files up the ass on the Pattels and their activities here in New York. Raven, what I'd like you and Gwynn to do is pass whatever you're both working on right now to someone else. This takes priority." Jeff stabbed his finger down on the surface of his desk for emphasis. "Raven, you've been gathering information about the Pattels for a while, so I want you to be available for anything the Vegas DA's office needs."

Raven's heart bottomed out. "Of course."

"Quite honestly, I was hoping we would get the honor of being the first to bust a member of that family, but in the end it doesn't matter. There are five more to choose from after this one goes down. I got a good feeling about this. A damn good feeling." Jeff stared over their shoulders, obviously lost deep in thought. Blinking rapidly, he brought Raven and Gwynn back into focus. "I want you both to keep me apprised of everything that happens with this case, no matter how insignificant it might be. Any resources you need are yours. Do either of you have any questions?"

Gwynn shook her head. "No, sir. This has been a long time coming."

"That it has." Jeff's eyes narrowed as they switched to Raven. "ADA Randolph, you seem a little reserved. I thought you would be more excited. This is what we've been waiting for."

"No, uh, I mean yes. I'm...excited. I guess it hasn't sunk in yet. But I'm...I'm ready." Anxiety sat heavy beneath the confidence and professionalism she tried her hardest to convey.

She must not have done as well as she thought. From the corner of her eye, Raven saw Gwynn look at her and frown. She'd have to be more careful. Gwynn knew her better than anyone and she didn't want Jeff to begin thinking too hard about her lack of enthusiasm.

Standing, she gave him a firm nod. "Let's do this."

"We'll meet soon to discuss where we need to go from here." Jeff said in a dismissive tone.

Relieved to finally be making her escape, Raven hurried to the door. Jeff, however, wasn't quite finished.

"Raven."

Her hand poised to grab the doorknob, Raven turned and lifted a brow. "Yes?"

"I need you to stay for a moment. There are some things I'd like to review with you."

Raven didn't like the undertone she heard or the way Jeff was staring at her. She felt like she was being dissected from the inside out. Her hand dropped to her side like a block of cement. Her and Gwynn locked eyes as Gwynn walked out the door. Pushing back her nervousness, Raven reluctantly retraced her steps and sat down.

Seemingly in no hurry to begin, Jeff rocked back and forth in his chair, his laser beam gaze directed solely at her. Raven forced herself to sit and wait patiently. She saw him use that tactic more times than she could count. It was meant to intimidate and make the person in his crosshairs uneasy in order to get whatever information he wanted out of them. It usually worked. But not with her. Jeff was an excellent prosecutor, but there was a reason she was the lawyer he always turned to before anyone else. Raven could be as formidable as him when she needed to be.

"So…" Jeff began. "What's going on with you and Pattel?"

Raven didn't blink, but after hearing the question, she felt every single beat of her heart pound wildly in her chest. "Going on? I don't know what you mean."

"This is the third time that I know of where you've had close contact with Pattel. The first was in the stairwell where he *conveniently* came to your rescue. The second time was when he popped up in your office and saw the file on his sister. We both know how that turned out. He used it as a weapon to manipulate Judge Warner with the Giuliani case. Now, you run into him again at Angelo LaCroix's home the night one of his employees is reported missing. What gives?"

Raven shrugged helplessly. "Coincidence and lousy timing, I guess. Last weekend, he just happened to show up with his cousin, who is a close friend of Angel's. I don't see anything suspicious about that."

"Still, didn't you think that was something you should've mentioned?"

"I haven't had a chance to. Plus, it honestly didn't even register that Hawk being there was anything out of the ordinary. Not only was he there with his cousin, but he's friends with my brother-in-law. Like I told you, we only crossed paths for a few minutes, then he left. End of story."

"Is it?" Jeff shot back.

Raven crossed her legs and directed a sharp glare at him. "What are you getting at, Jeff? If you're accusing me of something, I'd appreciate it if you just came out and told me."

The two of them locked eyes like the clashing of two bull's horns. Neither gave away their thoughts, but if Raven's heart beat any faster, she feared it would burst.

Finally, Jeff broke eye contact. "Of course I'm not accusing you of anything, Raven. You're one of my most trusted ADAs. Just...be careful. I don't trust Pattel. He's up to something. Keep your eyes open."

Feeling lower than dirt for abusing his trust, Raven nodded once and stood up. "Is there anything else?"

"No, we'll talk soon."

She gave him a tight smile and headed to the door. Before walking out, Raven glanced over her shoulder and found Jeff staring after her with a thoughtful expression on his face. It took everything in her to resist the urge to bolt out of sight of the suspicion she saw steadily building in his eyes.

Great.

CHAPTER 28

"Everything okay, Rae?"

To Raven's dismay, Gwynn was waiting for her to come to come out of Jeff's office. They fell into step as they walked to the elevator. "Everything's fine."

"Is it? You forget, I know you, chica. Something's goin' on with you."

Raven blew impatiently. She wasn't in the mood for Gwynn's probing questions. "I guess I'm just a little tired. It was a long weekend. I missed my flight and had to reschedule, so I got home later than I anticipated."

"How *was* your visit? And how's that cutie pie nephew of yours?"

"I enjoyed it. It was nice seeing Nikki and my parents. And A.J.'s great, had a blast at his party. It was just...tiring. Nikki knows how to throw a party, so she and Angel went all out as usual. "

"I can only imagine. How *did* things go with the legendary Angelo LaCroix?" Gwynn shook her head. "As deliciously gorgeous as he is, it's still hard to believe your sister is married to a man like that."

"Surprisingly, it actually wasn't too bad," Raven answered as they stepped on the elevator. "Of course, we bumped heads a time or two, but nothing like we normally do. All in all, it was a good visit," Raven said, clipping her conversation before she caught herself saying too much.

"So, what do you think about the case Vegas is trying to put together on Hawk Pattel? From what Jeff told us, it's almost sounds open and shut."

"Yeah. Maybe." Raven kept her answers as brief as possible.

"Those Pattels have been getting away with a lot of shit for a long time. Maybe this is the beginning of the end for them." When Raven didn't answer, Gwynn angled her head and peered closer. "Rae, you sure there's nothing else going on. You know you can talk to me if you need to."

"No, I promise, I'm fine. Nothing that a good night's sleep won't fix. Hopefully this retirement dinner doesn't last very long." Raven deliberately changed the subject by bringing up the function they were both attending that evening.

"Don't remind me. What time are you leaving the office? Wanna catch a cab over there together?"

"Sure. Sounds great." As the elevator came to a stop on Raven's floor, she squeezed through several people and told Gwynn, "Call you later."

Raven couldn't get to her office fast enough. Just as she passed Laney's desk, her assistant tried to wave her down and stop her. "Raven, wait! While you were in the meeting–"

"Not now, Laney." Raven never broke stride. "And can you hold my calls until I say otherwise?"

Ignoring DeLaney's curious look, she jetted into her office and closed the door behind her. Finally able to grab some much needed privacy, Raven leaned back against the dark, mahogany frame and tried to slow her breathing. She mentally reviewed the meeting she just left. Jeff wasn't stupid. He suspected she was keeping something from him but couldn't figure out what.

Her mind raced with ways to get out of working on this case, but no matter what she came up with, it would still look suspicious. Ever since Jeff became DA, Raven was just as dedicated as he at ridding the city of as much organized crime as they could. Starting with the Pattels. She was upfront with him about seeing the opportunity as a gateway to getting to Angel and permanently removing him from her sister and nephew's life.

But somehow, the script flipped. The joke was now on her. She became involved with a member of the family they swore to bring down. Someone who was the exact type of man she heavily criticized Nikki for marrying.

Her eyes were involuntarily drawn to the vase of flowers. They sat on her desk like a blazing reminder of her betrayal to her position, her grave lack of judgment, her...weakness. The flowers taunted her with memories of how she'd begged him for it. Even now, with everything at stake, the mere thought of sex with Hawk left Raven wet and throbbing. *What was wrong with her?*

Pressing her lips together, she lowered her eyes to the floor. She hadn't worked this hard to get where she was only to have it all stripped away from her in disgrace. The more she thought about the situation she found herself in, the fuller her eyes welled with tears. She desperately tried to keep them at bay, but it was no use. They fell down to the light brown carpet like a slowly, dripping faucet that she couldn't turn off. For a few moments, Raven let them flow unchecked. She needed the quick release they brought, needed to feel the pain, the disappointment she felt in herself.

Finally, she lifted her head and wiped her face. She had never been one to wallow in self-pity for too long. Sniffing, she pushed away from the door and walked determinedly to her desk. Raven whipped a couple of tissues out the box and blew her nose before getting her purse to grab her make-up bag. After repairing the damage she did with her blubbering, she looked in the compact mirror to make sure she restored her protective outer armor as best she could. Satisfied with the cool, calm and professional woman staring back at her, she put her purse away and buzzed her assistant.

DeLaney answered immediately. "Yes ma'am?"

"Could you come in here please? I'd like you to get these flowers and dispose of them," Raven said in a curt voice.

"M-Ma'am?"

Raven gritted her teeth and counted to five before answering. She didn't want to snap at

DeLaney. It wasn't her fault she was in this mess. "I think you heard me. I'd like it done now, please."

Putting her glasses on, Raven turned to her computer and busied herself with typing an email she needed to send out. She kept her eyes on the screen when DeLaney came in. "I don't care what you do with them just get them out of here. Thanks."

"Okay," Laney drawled in confusion. "I, uh, guess I could put them on my desk."

Raven's fingers paused. Removing her glasses, she fixed Laney with a stern look. "Maybe I wasn't clear, so let me clarify myself. I don't want to see them in this building. Throw them away, take them home, I don't care. Just get rid of them."

DeLaney hesitated for a moment. Raven knew she wanted to question her about the odd request, but she also knew when to joke around and when to remain in her place as Raven's employee. Picking the vase up, she was almost to the door when Raven called her name.

"And if any more flower deliveries come for me, please don't accept them."

"Yes, ma'am."

"Thanks."

When the door closed, Raven sank back into her chair and tried to massage away the impending headache that was trying to manifest, but it was no use. Her eyes went to her cell phone. She needed to end things with Hawk. The quicker the better, just...not now. She couldn't muster the energy.

Sitting up straight and squaring her shoulders, Raven made an effort to compartmentalize her issues, something she did since law school to help get her through the hectic classes she took. Hawk, and everything pertaining to him, was assigned to a different space in her head that she would unlock when she had time to deal with it. As for now....

Raven turned her attention to the stack of work she needed to complete before leaving for the party in a few hours. She had more than enough to keep her occupied.

*****

As she'd known would happen, Raven got home from the retirement party later than she intended. It had taken everything in her to keep a polite smile on her face and indulge in the small talk that was expected at those sort of events. Thank goodness Gwynn was there to help her get through the evening. There was no way she could've made it otherwise.

Once she got home, she went directly to her bedroom and started removing her clothes. Although she really wanted to take a hot, relaxing bath, she knew if she did, she'd stay there longer than she needed to, so instead she decided on a quick shower. Afterwards, she dried off and slipped on a pair of panties and comfortable t-shirt. Raven decided to forego her usual glass of wine, being that she had more than enough at the retirement dinner. Exhausted, she pulled the covers back and crawled into bed.

She lay there staring at the ceiling for several minutes thinking about the inevitable. Knowing she couldn't put off texting Hawk any longer, she reluctantly grabbed her phone from her nightstand. However, before she could get her words together, her phone buzzed with a message from the very man at the center of the mini crisis she was experiencing in her life right now.

Hey beautiful. You home?

Raven took a deep breath. *Yes. Just got home a little while ago.*

How was your evening?

As well as those sorts of things can be I guess. Raven hesitated. *And yours?*

Other than thinking about you, it was ok. Miss me?

Raven swallowed. She had to do this now. *Hawk, there's something I need to tell you. I don't think we should see each other anymore. It's just not a good idea. I thought I could deal with it, but...I think we should call this off before things go any further.*

Okay, slow down. What happened, Rae?

Nothing happened.

Don't lie to me, baby.

I just had some time to think and it's for the best if we go our separate ways.

Everything was fine this morning. Hours later you're doing a complete 360. Y?

Raven bit down on her lip and told herself to get it over with. *Because it's what I've decided is best for me. I'm hoping you'll honor what you said. I haven't looked at the flash drive. I don't want to. I'll give it back to you and hope that you'll keep what happened between us quiet.*

There was no response for several moments. Then her phone rang. Jumping in surprise, Raven dropped the phone on the bed like it had suddenly caught fire. She stared at Hawk's number. She didn't know why but she had not expected him to call. Placing her hands over her mouth, she watched the phone until it stopped ringing. Then a text came through.

Answer the phone Raven.

Swallowing hard, Raven picked the phone up. *There's nothing else to say Hawk. Please don't make this hard on me.*

Answer the got damn phone, Rae!

Raven's teeth clenched together when he called back. Once again, she waited for it to stop ringing then typed: *Let me know where you'd like me to messenger the flash drive. Take care, Hawk.*

She immediately turned her phone off after that. Raven took several deep breaths to try and regulate her pulse. Of course, she didn't expect him to give up, but she would just have to stand her ground and remain firm. It was time to woman up and get her priorities in order. As pleasurable as it was screwing Hawk Pattel's brains out...he wasn't one of them.

CHAPTER 29

For the rest of the week, Raven walked on eggshells while waiting for the other shoe to drop with Hawk. When she turned her phone on that next morning after talking to him, she was surprised there were no messages. Still, she wasn't able to relax for the rest of that day, nor the day after that. Every time her cell rang, she looked at it in trepidation, but the caller wasn't Hawk. The stress of trying to keep it together at work while fighting to purge Hawk from her thoughts made her sleep fretfully at night, and it showed. By the time Friday came, she was totally drained.

The case with the Las Vegas PD had no doubt contributed to her angst. She touched bases with the Vegas District Attorney, but with the investigation ongoing, there was little to report. Raven truthfully answered questions he had about the Pattel family and faxed him any pertinent information that might help them. As things progressed, more than likely she would have to fly to Vegas to assist on the case, but as of now there wasn't much point in doing so yet.

By the time the second week passed, Raven started to rest a bit easier or so she told herself. In all likelihood Hawk probably blew her off and went on to the next woman waiting in line to be with him. Raven had to admit she was a tad offended at the thought. Especially when she found out he disconnected his phone.

A couple of days ago, Raven broke down and called him to find out when he wanted to get the flash drive she kept locked in the safe in her bedroom. The gadget was the last thing binding them together. She wanted it out of her possession as soon as possible. Closure was how she looked at it. Apparently, Hawk viewed closure as cutting off his phone, which was her only way of contacting him. Raven couldn't help feeling a bit miffed at the fact that he was able to get over her so quickly. Right then and there, she vowed to do the same.

That night, Raven was determined to relax and indulge in some much-needed self-care which included lighting her favorite candle, drinking a couple glasses of her favorite wine and cozying up on the couch underneath her favorite blanket.

Picking up the television remote, she got ready to Netflix and chill with her damn self. Dimming the lights, she had just settled on the couch and folded the blanket over her legs when she heard a knock on the door.

"Ughhh!" she growled out loud. *Really?*

Who in the hell was knocking at her door this time of night? *Especially* unannounced. That was something she couldn't stand. More than likely it was Gwynn. She was good for doing that shit. The last thing she felt like doing was entertaining guests. Even her best friend. Raven was tempted to ignore whomever it was, but she was sure they heard the television.

So much for quiet, uninterrupted alone time, dammit! She thought to herself.

Impatiently tossing the blanket aside, she started for the door then remembered she was only wearing a t-shirt, panties and socks. When the knock sounded again, this time much more impatiently, Raven glared at the door.

"Just a minute!" she snapped. Another knock sounded as she picked the blanket up and wrapped it around her body. "I said *hold on*! Damn!"

Ready to spit nails, she stomped to the door and tiptoed up to peer out the peephole. When she saw Hawk glaring back at her with a determined look that said he was ready to raise holy hell, her legs almost buckled from under her.

"Shit," she hissed lowering herself down and staring at the door. What was he doing at her apartment? Better yet, how the hell did he know where she lived?

Frowning, she stood on her tippy toes again and peeked back out at him. *Now what?*

"Raven, open the door." It was as if Hawk heard the question and didn't sound too happy about it. "Now."

"What are you doing here?"

"We need to talk. Open the door."

"Hawk–"

"God dammit, woman." She saw him swipe his hand over his mouth and take a breath. "Look, your nosy ass neighbors are already peeping out their doors. I give it five minutes before they're calling the cops to report a strange black man in the building harassing one of the city's ADAs, so if you

want to wait until they show up and explain why
I'm here–"

Raven couldn't unlock the door fast enough.
She knew a lot of guys on the force. The last thing
she needed was anyone linking Hawk Pattel to her
and her apartment.

Throwing the door open, she glared at him and
stood aside. "Five minutes."

Giving her a look that was just as heated,
Hawk walked inside the apartment and stood by as
she locked the door. He didn't comment, but his
eyes took note of the t-shirt she wore, obviously
with no bra and the blanket wrapped around her
waist. After getting his fill of her, he casually
looked around her apartment.

As he surveyed his surroundings, Raven found
herself doing the same to him. She was grateful his
back was turned and he wasn't looking at her
because she needed those few precious moments to
get herself under control.

Even as disturbed as she was about him being
there, she couldn't help but notice how good he
looked. Instead of his usual casual attire, he wore a
custom fitted dark grey suit, white shirt and dark

purple tie with a matching handkerchief in the outside pocket of the jacket. His brown belt matched his leather shoes and the watch on his wrist screamed money. The entire outfit as a whole gave the appearance of a wealthy, sophisticated businessman. Hawk wore the look well.

However, when he removed his jacket and threw it over a nearby chair and loosened his tie, she was immediately shaken out of her little fantasy world. "What are you doing? You're not staying."

"Like I said, we need to talk."

"You ignore me for two weeks, disconnect your phone and *now* you want to talk?" Raven heard the accusing tone in her voice, but she didn't care. She was still a little pissed about it.

"I wasn't ignoring you. I was using an untraceable phone that I switch out periodically. I'll make sure you have my main number before I leave."

"No, thank you," Raven huffed tossing her head. "How did you even know where I lived?"

"The same way Giuliani knew," he scoffed. "You legal eagles types live in a bubble thinking your information is protected when nothing really is. If a person wants to find something out bad enough, there's always a way to make that happen."

"Well it's a good thing I keep protection with me and know how to use it isn't it?"

Hawk's smile came slow and easy. "Was that warning for my benefit, counselor?"

"Take it however you like," Raven replied.

His lazy eyes drifted over her in a way that left no room for doubt about his intentions. "Believe me. I fully intend to."

The suggestive remark winded her. He uttered it with such confidence it was almost impossible for even *her* to doubt he meant it. Raven inhaled, desperate to inflate her burning lungs, but the air wouldn't go past the knot in her throat. She took a step back to put some distance between them. Then another one. Finally, she was able to draw in a gasp through her parted lips that to her relief, opened up her airway for the next breath.

Hawk watched her closely. Seeing her struggle, the corner of his full lips tugged upwards in a subtle smirk. "Calm down. That'll come later. First, we talk."

CHAPTER 30

Raven tried her best to appear unaffected by his remark. In actuality, she was anything but. She hated that he could read her thoughts so accurately. It was infuriating. Especially since his face remained unreadable like it was now.

"You know what? You assume a helluva lot, Pattel."

"Woman, I never assume anything. It's called confidence. I always get what I want." His eyes went over her again. "Always."

Raven started to spit back a sharp reply but was determined not to indulge in tit for tat with him. In an attempt to take control of the conversation, she brought a hand up and waved his statement off. "I already told you there's nothing to talk about. Just so your trip won't be a complete waste, wait right here."

Ignoring the curiosity on his face, she hurried to her bedroom. Closing--and locking--the door behind her, she went to the safe in her closet and got the flash drive.

Once she got back to the living room, she held it out to him. "Here."

Hawk didn't even look at it. "I didn't come here for that."

Sighing impatiently, Raven grabbed the jacket he threw over the chair and slipped the flash drive in one of the pockets. "Maybe not, but now you have it. If there's nothing else..."

Hawk stared at her in amusement. "As a matter of fact, I would like something to drink, if you don't mind."

"No! You *cannot* have something to drink. I want you to leave right now, Hawk!" Raven pointed a finger to the door. She couldn't deal with much more of this, but when he blatantly ignored her and headed to her kitchen, it took several sputtering starts before she could get her words out.

"*Hawk!* I'm not playing with you, get out of my apartment!" She ran behind him watching helplessly as he took out the bottle of wine she opened earlier. "What are you doing!"

While he opened cabinets looking for wine glasses, Hawk glanced at her as if the answer was obvious. Picking up the bottle, he looked at the label and lifted his eyebrows. After popping the cork, he poured until his glass was less than half full, then brought it up to his nose and took a small sniff. Holding the glass up, he tilted it to take note of the color then swirled it around.

Raven rolled her eyes and sucked her teeth. Was he really taste testing her wine?

Noticing her expression, Hawk gave her a tired, sheepish grin. "Sorry. Habit."

Raven's face cleared a bit after the explanation. For a moment she forgot. In addition to owning several nightclubs, he also owned a few legitimately merited five-star restaurants. She watched as he brought the glass up to his lips and took a sip.

"Well? Does it pass muster?" She asked sarcastically.

Hawk slowly nodded. "Not bad. Pretty good actually."

Her lips tightened when he poured more into the glass and pushed the cork back in the bottle. "One glass, Hawk. Finish it, then leave."

"Yes, ma'am," he replied with a wink.

Raven cut her eyes away from him and turned to leave the kitchen. She walked past the sofa she was sitting on before he invaded her home and headed to her bedroom to change.

"Hey." Hawk grabbed her hand and pulled her back. "Where you goin'?"

Raven gestured to the blanket she had wrapped around her waist. "I think it's obvious. To put some clothes on."

"That's not necessary." Hawk shook his head and pulled her behind him. "I've seen you in way less than that, woman. Just sit down and talk to me for a minute."

Raven tugged her hand out of his, choosing the couch while Hawk took the large, oversized chair to her left. She watched covertly as he got a bit more comfortable by unbuttoning the first couple of buttons of his shirt. Like his suit she saw that it, too, was custom made for him. His body was subtly discernible underneath the fabric, a sign of an expensively tailor-made shirt. It fit his chest and upper back comfortably and was elegantly monogrammed with his initials on the side: *HJP.* Hawk James Pattel.

Hearing him sigh loudly as he leaned his head back against the chair, Raven brought her attention back to his face. And what an attractive face it was. Sweet baby Jesus, the man was all kinds of fine. But she could see he was tired too.

Raven didn't want to notice how fatigued he looked. Exhausted, actually. His eyelids were at half-mast, almost closed as he gazed back at her. It was obvious he hadn't been getting enough sleep. Images of him partying and sexing a different faceless woman every night flashed briefly in her head. Jealousy so strong like she never felt made Raven want to scratch the unknown women's eyes out from their sockets. The strength of the unwanted emotion bothered her more than she wanted to admit. She was supposed to be getting him out of her system, but after only a few minutes of being in his presence, she saw that it wouldn't be easy.

"What are you thinkin' about?" Hawk asked quietly.

Raven blinked and brought him back into focus. "I'm thinking that you have ten minutes, then I want you out."

"That depends on you."

"If that's the case then you're as good as gone."

"I want you to tell me what happened. Things were fine after the night we spent together. We both had a good time. Or at least I thought we did."

Raven shrugged as nonchalantly as she could manage. "It was okay."

Hawk smiled. "Okay? First of all, let's agree to start out with some honesty here. Seems to me, I remember you describing it as mind blowing, toe curling sex. That sounds more than just *okay* to me."

Raven casually studied her nails while correcting him. "Mind *numbing* sex, but so what? Sex is sex."

"Do you think that's all it was, Raven?"

Raven froze. She looked at him quickly trying to get a feel for where he was going with his questions, but as always, she wasn't able to figure out his intentions. "Wasn't it?"

"Maybe. Maybe not."

Raven smirked. "So much for honesty in this conversation. Or is that request only for me."

"Touché." Hawk took a sip of his wine, holding it briefly in his mouth before swallowing. "Okay. In the spirit of mutual honesty, I'll confess that it was the best sex I've ever had. And I can't emphasis the word *ever* enough. Is that honest enough for you?"

Raven's mouth went dry with his admission. Leaning forward, she picked up the glass of wine she placed on the coffee table and took several deep gulps. Her specialty was reading people's thoughts. Their actions. Their mannerisms. With Hawk, she was utterly clueless and it frustrated her more than she could put into words. She felt his gaze heavily attached to her but continued to stare at her wine as she answered.

"Then we agree. The sex was good," she responded.

"It was phenomenal. Some people never experience that in a lifetime."

"True. However, it's not something I'm willing to risk losing my career over." Raven bit down on her lip. She didn't mean to say that. She hazarded a glance at Hawk and saw him watching her with an intense interest that told her he picked up on the clue she unwittingly gave him. She quickly tried to change the subject.

"So where have you been all dressed up? A date?" The question came out with a snarky bite she hadn't intended to use.

Great, Raven. Juuuust great.

Hawk took his time answering the question. Finally deciding to let her other comment slide, he said, "I had some business I needed to take care of out of town. Some shit's tryin' to pop off, so I've been flying back and forth with my lawyers to get a handle on it. I came straight here after my jet landed."

Raven knew right away he was talking about the case in Las Vegas. "Oh? Anything serious?"

"They're trying to make it out to be, but my legal team is led by a beast. My cousin, Lorenzo," Hawk smiled. "By the time he finished putting holes in their allegations, the whole thing looked like a slice of Swiss cheese."

"And that's funny to you?" Raven scooted to the edge of the couch and all but slammed the wine glass on the coffee table. Forgetting about the blanket, she stood up in nothing but her t-shirt and glared at him. "You could lose your freedom and you got jokes? What's wrong with you? What's wrong with your family? You all act like something like this is nothing but sport to you!"

"Baby, calm down. I'm not losin' my freedom. I'm not losin' anything–and that includes you."

CHAPTER 31

Raven's eyes filled with unshed tears. Why did he have to say that? Why? She brought a trembling hand up to cover her mouth. She couldn't do this. "I've done what you asked. We talked. I'd like you to leave now."

Hawk placed his glass on the end table beside his chair. "Raven, come here."

She shook her head wildly but didn't answer.

"Baby, it's okay. Come here." Hawk held his hand out to her patiently waiting until she started walking towards him. When she stopped a foot or so away, he reached out and pulled her closer to stand between his legs. "Are you really ready to leave this thing between us alone?"

"Hawk, we can't," she whispered. "Us being together...it's impossible."

"If you really want there to be an us, I'll make it anything but impossible. I just need to know that you're ridin' with me. If you are, then I got this. I'll take care of it."

"How, Hawk? You can't," she said barely above a whisper

Hawk tugged her closer. He held her eyes hypnotized by his as he repeated himself with slow conviction. "If you're with me, I promise I'll take care of it. No matter what *it* is."

They stared at each other in silence. In that moment, Raven realized for certain that he knew about the investigation in Las Vegas. He also had to be aware that she didn't tell anyone what *she* knew. That she kept quiet about it, not only for herself, but for him as well.

Hawk slipped both hands around the back of her toned upper thighs and gave them a little squeeze. "If you want this–want *us*–just let me know. That's all I'm askin'."

Raven had never been more afraid. This moment, however she answered, would change life as she knew it and she wasn't sure she wanted that. But as she gazed into his eyes, it hit her that what she wanted had very little to do with it. She had no choice. As crazy as it sounded she needed this. Craved it, hungered for it in a way she never thought possible.

"I'm scared, Hawk. You have no idea how scared," she uttered in a barely perceptible voice.

But Hawk heard her and understood. "I know, baby. I know what I'm asking isn't an easy thing because of what's at stake for you. Trust me to make it work."

Raven stared down at his upturned face and felt her heart skip a beat. She knew if she told him to leave, he would, but...she couldn't. Raven exhaled as she finally admitted to herself that she was really into Hawk Pattel.

"Okay," she nodded slowly. "Okay."

"Then consider it done." Hawk's chin lifted in a confident gesture, but she saw what looked like relief flickering briefly in his eyes. It came and went so fast she couldn't be sure.

"But Hawk, I don't want to know..." She moistened her lips with her tongue and tried to put into words what she was trying to say. "I *can't* know about anything you're doing..."

"Of course not. This is the last time we'll mention it."

Raven nodded hesitantly. Now that she made the decision, some of the tension left her body. Not all of it though. She would never be good with the decision she made, but...it was done. She was walking into this with her eyes wide open, so whatever happened...

The hold Hawk had on her legs gentled. He ran his hands up and down her thighs, caressing her skin with a light touch that was as soft as silk. Raven reached down and framed his face with her hands. Bending down, she rested her forehead against his and closed her eyes.

"I missed you. Crazy isn't it?"

Hawk's hands moved up to grip her apple shaped, rounded bottom. "Not at all. The connection's been there since day one. We're just catchin' up to it, that's all."

The sentiment made her insides melt. Moaning softly, Raven brought her mouth to his waiting lips and kissed him with all the pent-up emotion she'd carried around the last couple of weeks. She knew she was taking a risk, but she was tired of fighting it.

Raven straightened up and pulled the t-shirt over her head. Hawk growled and bit his lip as he watched her. With a tiny smile, she took her time and inched the tiny, black panties she wore down her thighs and stepped out of them when they hit the floor.

"Damn, Raven. I swear I could look at you all day and never get tired."

"Should I just stand here then?" Raven asked head tilted to the side. "And let you look...but not touch?"

"Nahhh. What you should do is bring that thang here," he said eyes glued to the sweet spot between her thighs. "It's time she and I got reacquainted with each other. It's been too long."

With his hands around her waist, Hawk guided her on top of him so that her legs cradled the outside of his thighs. Watching her closely, he slid his middle finger between the slick crevice of her swollen flesh. Raven's heart fluttered. When he slipped two fingers inside of her, her pussy automatically snapped closed like a trap that captured its prey.

"So, fucking tight," Hawk groaned. He watched the myriad of expressions that crossed her face as he fingered her slow and deep.

Raven grabbed the back of the chair, using it for balance. Her pelvic area circled on top of his fingers, riding them to the promise of ecstasy she knew they would take her to. Hawk's fingertips touched her in places only he discovered, grazing those spots like matches igniting a flame. Raven was helpless to fight it, even if she wanted to.

Using his thumb, he drew light circles around the hooded foreskin protecting her clit. Hawk took his time arousing her, making sure she was feeling it and letting her know there was no rush to get there. When her cream ran thick and plentiful, he tapped his thumb over her clit as he fingered her, paying close attention to how she reacted to his touch.

"Right there, baby?" He asked when a violent shudder ran through her body. "You like that?"

"Y-Yes," she whispered.

"Good," Hawk whispered back. "I want to make sure I give you what you need, Rae."

The entire time he talked to her, his fingers never stopped moving. Instead he increased the intensity of the motions, carefully screwing her deep and fast, then lazy and slow. At the same time, his thumb kept a consistent rhythm that Raven's hips eagerly caught and followed. She tried to slow her movements. She wanted to make it last as long as she could.

"This pussy feels so good, baby, you know that?" Hawk asked. His voice came out raspy and aroused. "You makin' me so fuckin' hungry for it."

Eyes half-closed and lips slightly parted, Raven leaned forward and offered Hawk her breast. She threw her head back and gasped when he sucked her nipple into his warm mouth. The sensation it created acted as a conduit that went straight to her core. The sound that escaped her was so guttural, so desperate that she barely recognized it as coming from her.

This man was like a drug. An addiction. Unfortunately, he was one that no twelve-step program could help her kick because God knows she tried. She read a quote once that said, "the more you engage in any type of behavior, the greater your desire for it will become," and at that particular moment, she couldn't think of one single thing she desired more than what Hawk was giving her. She lowered her hand and covered his as the storm started between her thighs.

"That's it, Rae. You're right there, baby," Hawk whispered, his voice low and intense. "All you need to do is take it."

The fire burning inside of her became a raging inferno. Raven's body arched in anticipation as she waited for it to consume her. *La petite mort*: the little death, the French called it. Funny they would liken an orgasm to death, but that's exactly what it felt like every time Hawk made her cum. Only she didn't pray for a quick ending. No, she wanted it to last, but it was fast on its way to devouring her. With the onslaught of the climax seconds away, her breathing grew ragged. Almost more like an eager pant. Again, she tried to slow the inevitable but suddenly...she exploded.

"Hawk!"

Raven screamed his name as a sensation more powerful than she ever experienced detonated at her center like a bomb set off. A burst of pure ecstasy rushed unbidden through every inch of her body, over every intangible shadow of her *soul*.

Transported to an elevated level of consciousness, she had no control over anything. A steady pounding sounded in her ears. Raven quickly realized it came from within; a rhythmic thumping beating in time with her heart. The muscles of her pussy walls squeezed tight before releasing in a continuously pleasurable spasm. Ecstasy became her mainstay. A gush of warm, thick cream flowed over his fingers and wet his pants. Raven grinded her clit over the heel of his hand as she reached her peak. She soared, suspended in air for several gratifying moments before freefalling from heaven back down to earth. On the journey, her body twitched similarly to an addict already missing her high. Tortuous moans broke free and escaped like long, suffering prisoners finally set free. Raven was right there with them every step of the way.

The entire experience was over way too soon. Dizzy and slightly disoriented, she inhaled deep gulps of precious air. Hawk's hand wrapped around the back of her neck, steadying her. Anchoring her. Raven clung to him like a lifeline. He pulled her head forward seeking her mouth in a kiss that was raw and intense. Tongues entwined like vines on a tree; their mouths opened wide as if they were starving people trying to devour the other for nourishment.

Drained of strength, Raven's body melted against his. Her soft curves conformed to the lean contours of his hard muscles. She sighed contentedly when Hawk wrapped his arms around her and held her close while caressing her back until her trembling subsided. Without a word, he stood up and carried her towards the bedroom.

Eyes closed and her head resting on his shoulder, Raven said in a slow, groggy voice, "I'm not through with you, Pattel. Hope you know that."

Hawk chuckled under his breath and said teasingly, "Just take it easy on me. I don't know how much more of this I can take."

A soft giggle escaped Raven as he approached the bed and plopped her down on the soft mattress. Their eyes met and held, enjoying the moment and each other. It felt good to be open with one another and not having to pretend. As Raven watched him slowly unbuckle his belt, all signs of amusement disappeared, leaving in its wake the anticipation of a long, hot, passionate night ahead.

CHAPTER 32

Raven lay quiet and utterly relaxed as she watched Hawk get dressed. The silence in the room was a comfortable one. No words were needed. Intimate glances and secret smiles more than sufficed.

She glanced at the clock. *4 a.m.* So early. Raven wanted to ask him to stay, but without even broaching the subject they both knew that wasn't a good idea. They couldn't take any unnecessary risks of someone discovering him being at her apartment.

Her attention was drawn back to him as he pulled his socks and shoes on. She sighed in contentment. To use his words, last night was phenomenal. More than phenomenal. Earth shattering. If possible better than before and that was probably because they brought a lot of issues out in the open and dealt with them. Even if some were left unsaid, they were understood. That alone brought a sense of freedom to whatever it was they were indulging in. At least to Raven.

"What are you smiling at?" Hawk asked.

The smile that she wasn't even been aware of broadened. "You," she replied honestly. "And last night."

Hawk stood to buckle his belt. "You damn near drained the life outta me, woman. I'm surprised I can even stand up."

Raven bit down on her lip in an effort to prevent the smile from turning into a goofy one. She was just about to respond with a clever reply when her eyes fell on a large white spot that had long since dried on the front of his pants. It must have happened last night when they were fooling around in the chair. Raven didn't realize she'd been that wet.

She sat up on one elbow. "Baby, your pants. They're stained."

Hawk glanced down. "Yeah, I know. I started to call Danny to bring me another pair, but I'm going straight home. My jacket will hide it."

Raven lowered herself back down to the pillow and folded her arm under her head. "Sorry. It was your own fault for getting me so excited."

Thoroughly amused and delighted, Hawk laughed as he pulled his shirt on and starting buttoning it up. "That's a bit of an oxymoron, don't you think? Sorry but it's your own fault? Come on now, counselor."

"Well, it's true," Raven pouted.

"Yeah, it is. You did cum hard," Hawk came back with his usual arrogance, then nodded towards the bed. "Guess I did that shit all night if we go by the towel we had to get to cover that wet spot in the middle of the bed."

"Hawk!" Now she was embarrassed, but he was right. She came so much she drenched the sheets.

"Hey, you started it," he laughed. Coming over to the bed, he leaned down and gave her a kiss before grabbing his watch off the nightstand and slipping it over his wrist. "What you got planned for today?"

"Nothing much." Raven stretched and groaned. She felt decadently lazy. "Probably meeting up with a couple of friends later for a drink, but I'll be home early. I have some work I need to catch up on."

"Female friends, right?" Hawk gave her a side-glance as he rolled the cuffs of his shirt back on his forearms.

Raven laughed, loving the possessive streak he had. "Maybe."

Hawk went absolutely still. He didn't crack a smile and his eyes thinned to slits. "I'm serious, Rae. All kidding aside. I meant what I said in Vegas. I don't share."

Raven's smile slipped a notch at the seriousness of his tone. "I know. I was just joking."

"Oh, yeah? Well, just so there's no misunderstandings, I wasn't." Hawk stared at her for a few more moments then winked. However, it didn't take away from the layer of steel beneath his brief response.

"There's no one else I want to be with. Just you." Great. Now she probably sounded like the clingy women he usually went out with. It was just...she didn't want to play games. The best way to ensure that didn't happen was to be honest and forthright about her feelings.

Apparently, he felt the same. Their eyes held as another one of those unspoken messages passed between them. Hawk's face finally softened, transforming him back to the lover she awakened with a few minutes ago, but he looked away as if he was uncomfortable about letting her glimpse that side. Raven watched him walk to the living room. She wracked her brain for something to say that would bring back the easy feeling they were experiencing since they woke up, but before she could think of anything there was a brief knock on her door.

Raven sat up straight, alarmed that someone would be coming to her apartment at this time of the morning. She jumped out of bed, scrambling to find something to throw on, but just as she slipped her arms through her robe, she heard Hawk's deep voice speaking to someone before he closed the door.

"Who was that?" She asked when he came back in the bedroom. She peered over his shoulder as if expecting to see the person. "Why did you answer the door? Who was there?"

"Calm down, it was Danny. I sent him a text to come get me and to bring a package up I left in the car."

His words finally penetrated Raven's fear. Her body relaxed as she watched him open the bag he came back with. Hawk sat down on the edge of the bed and took out a small, rectangular box that still had the plastic wrapping covering it.

Raven frowned when she saw what it was, but still asked, "What's that?"

"Well, from the looks of it, I think it's a phone." Hawk glanced up and gave her a teasing grin.

Raven rolled her eyes and folded her arms. "I *know* it's a phone. I meant, why do you have it?"

"It's not mine. It's yours."

Raven shook her head, helpless and frustrated about what the hell he was talking about. Getting information out of him was like pulling teeth, but she knew he wouldn't expound on the answer until he was good and ready. Tying the belt on her short, silk robe, she sat down next to him and watched as he went through the steps of activating the expensive looking device. Her curiosity grew when he added a contact number she didn't recognize.

"Who is that?" When he remained silent, she sucked her teeth but didn't ask anything else.

Hawk took out a phone similar to the one he said belonged to her and hit speed dial. When the phone he just activated rang, he hung up, apparently satisfied that it was working. Finally looking up, he handed the phone to her.

"Here. The number I just called you from and the one I put in your contacts is to this one." He held up the one he took out of his pocket. "Only you have access to it. These are just for us."

Raven frowned as she stared at it. "Okay."

"Raven, look at me." He waited until she complied. "It's important. Only communicate with me using *that* phone. Not your personal phone, okay?"

"I understand." Raven turned it over and gazed at the sleek, rose gold colored device she held in her hands. The thin, titanium-clad gadget was one of the sexiest phones she ever laid eyes on. "Wow. This is one expensive burner phone."

"Got that right, but it does what it's supposed to. It's one of the most secure phones on the market. Now look. See this button right here?" Hawk pointed to a tiny toggle switch on the back. "Make sure that it's always in this mode. Any calls or texts are encrypted and locked down."

Raven leaned her head close to his, watching as he explained the workings of the phone. "Nothing's really secure, though, is it? If someone really wants access to your info..." Deliberately throwing his words back at him, she let the rest of the sentence dangle out in the wind.

"Smartass," he muttered. "Believe me, the federal government ain't tryin' to spend the type of money needed to hack this kind of software. The data's protected and backed up by a security firm in Europe. They monitor the state of the phone and will alert me if anyone attempts to hack into it or tamper with it."

"Wait. Is this like the phone I was texting to before?"

"Yeah."

"And you just...disposed of it. Just like that. A phone as obviously expensive as this."

Hawk's eyes lit up with amusement. "We have stock in the company. I have access to a thousand of 'em if I wanted them."

"Of course," Raven muttered in a dry tone.

Smiling, Hawk stood then pulled her up. "You good? You got any questions?"

"No, I... I guess not." Raven was still trying to wrap her head around the fact that she had to use an encrypted phone to communicate with the man she was seeing. That alone should've been enough to make her run in the opposite direction as fast as she could. Apparently, Hawk read her thoughts, a habit he was becoming unerringly adept at.

"Hey." He paused and waited until she glanced up. "I promised to work it out so that nothing associated with me touches you. This is a small thing. Don't give it more attention than it deserves."

Pressing her lips together, Raven nodded. He was right. If she was going to do this, she had to change her mindset. She had never been involved with a man like Hawk. Raven knew this was only a glimpse of how things were in the world he lived in every day.

"One more thing." He picked up his suit coat that he brought in and laid across the bed. After taking an envelope out of the inside pocket, he handed it to her before slipping the coat on.

"What's this?" Raven asked looking from the envelope to him.

"You'll see. Just make sure you handle your part before next weekend."

Raven's heart took a dip and roller-coastered straight to the floor. Such cryptic words. What exactly did they mean? After everything he promised, was he asking her to do something... *illegal?*

CHAPTER 33

Too afraid to open the envelope, Raven continued to stare at it as she gripped it tightly in her hands. Did Hawk want her to get information for him, something that would benefit the Pattels, or maybe help him with the investigation in Vegas? Something that would put her freedom on the line?

Raven gave her head a mental shake. Oh hell no. *That* wasn't happening. She was already crossing the line and would possibly be disbarred if anyone ever found out about her involvement with him. She would be damned if she set herself up for prison by being a... a mule or informant for a drug cartel. The thought was a sobering one. Raven immediately began to rethink her decision to have an affair with Hawk.

"There you go overanalyzing things again," he admonished, but his tone wasn't accusatory. Only faintly amused. "You don't even know what's in the envelope and you're already coming up with scenarios of what it *could* be. And from your expression, it's not very flattering to me. I'm hurt."

Before she had a chance to voice any of her doubts, her face had apparently divulged them all to him. Raven saw the familiar smirk on his lips seconds before he leaned down and gave her a hard kiss. Moments later, he was gone. She stared after him then jumped into motion ripping the envelope open. Snatching the folded sheet of paper free, she read it with a sense of trepidation. When she realized what the contents of the letter included, it took several seconds for the meaning of it to sink in. Once it did, she took off running after him.

"Hawk Pattel, don't you dare leave yet!" Raven caught him just as he'd opened the front door. She held the letter up to his face and shook it. "What's this? And I swear to God if you give me one of your flip answers I'll kick your fucking ass."

She actually seemed to momentarily surprise him. Letting out a loud burst of laughter, he closed the door then pulled her close. "Well, damn. What happened to the sweet, agreeable woman I woke up with a few minutes ago?" he growled. "Guess I need to tap that feisty ass before I leave to get her back, huh?"

He actually looked at his watch to see if he had time, but Raven slapped his hands away. She refused to let him charm his way out of this. "You went to the doctor and got tested then brought the results to me? You were *that* sure of yourself?"

Hawk's chest rose with the indulgent breath he took. "I'm not an indecisive man, Rae. Nothing was going to stop me from getting what I wanted." He reached out and slipped an arm around her waist again and slammed her back to his body. "Not even you."

Raven swallowed hard when she realized he was fully aroused. "But–"

"Woman, ain't no buts," he cut in. "I don't want no barriers between us when we make love. None. For whatever it's worth, I've never wanted to be like that with another woman." He paused, peering at her closely before continuing. "If I'm correct, we made headway last night breaking down a few roadblocks. It's time to break some more. Starting with me being inside of you and feeling you wrapped raw around my dick with no protection."

Raven fought to remain unaffected, but her juices started flowing the moment he pulled her to his body. His explicit proclamation only intensified her desire. She realized he was telling the truth about why he cut off his phone. It wasn't because he didn't want to be with her anymore. This was proof he was thinking about her the entire time the same way he was in her thoughts. Moisture coated the juncture where her thighs met her sex. She literally throbbed. God, she wanted him so bad.

"You on the pill, right?" he asked.

"IUD."

"Good. Then I expect you to have the results of your tests by next weekend." He leaned down and captured her lips in an explosive kiss that left her weak.

Hawk finally let her go and opened the door to leave, but not before he popped her on the ass and reiterated his request. "No excuses. Alright?"

Raven had to grab the doorknob to keep herself upright. "Y-Yes. Alright. But wait. Wh-What's happening next weekend? I'm seeing you tonight, right?"

Hawk shook his head with reluctance. "I have to fly out to Miami this evening for the rest of the weekend. Matter of fact, I should be there right now but I had something more important I needed to handle." The heated look he gave Raven left no doubt he was talking about her.

"Oh." Raven tried to contain the burst of pleasure she felt at his unexpected admission, but she couldn't. The warm and fuzzies started and refused to stop. This man did it for her effortlessly.

But then right on cue images of hot blooded women on the beach in G-string bikinis and up in his nightclub scantily clothed sprang to mind. Jealousy hit her like a pain in her stomach when she thought about Hawk sampling what she was almost sure they would be offering him. Her hand curled up into a fist, crushing the letter she forgot was in her hand.

"You could always come with me," he added head tilted to the side waiting on her response to the suggestion.

Raven realized he was studying her face the whole time and was once again aware of what she was thinking. For the briefest of moments, she was tempted to take him up on his offer. She wanted to, but...

"I can't," she finally sighed. "It's probably not a good idea."

Hawk nodded slowly. "I figured. That's why I didn't ask you to begin with."

"When will you be back?"

"Probably not until next Friday. After I leave Miami, I have to fly to LA." Hawk wearily rubbed a hand over his face. "We're in the process of opening a new restaurant. I need to check on the progress and meet with some people while I'm there."

"Oh. Okay." Raven tried to keep the disappointment out of her voice. "So... next weekend?"

"Yeah. I'll talk to you before then though."

"Alright." Wanting to stretch out the moment before it was time for him to go as long as she could, Raven reached up and caressed his beautiful face. She couldn't believe she actually thought at one time he didn't do any real work. If anything, it seemed he did so obsessively. "You look tired. Hopefully you can find some time to relax and get a little rest."

Hawk turned her hand over and kissed her palm. "That'll come next weekend when I'm with you," he grinned.

Raven smiled. "I'll make sure."

"Good. Talk to you soon." Hawk gave her one last, lingering stare before walking out. After three steps, he stopped and glanced over his shoulder. "Lock the door, woman."

Raven nodded. "Call me when you get there. Just to, um, let me know you made it safely."

Hawk gave her a soft smile. "I will."

Before she could change her mind, she blew him a kiss. Raven's heart two stepped in her chest when he blew one back. Giving him a small wave, she closed the door then locked it. Walking back into her apartment, which now seemed unusually quiet, she thought about how far next weekend seemed. Sitting down on the couch, she looked at the letter again.

She thought about what Hawk said regarding them being together without using protection. Raven wanted that too. She decided to call her doctor first thing Monday morning to make an appointment. The thought of being able to feel him moving inside of her without the thin barrier of a condom between them...

Raven closed her eyes and fell back on the couch. Next weekend couldn't come fast enough.

CHAPTER 34

Later that night, Raven sat on the main floor of one of New York's hottest nightclubs with Gwynn and a couple more of their friends. When she agreed to go out, she had in mind a relaxing night at a lounge or jazz club. Once Raven found out where they intended to go, she'd tried to back out, but Gwynn wouldn't let her.

Now, she wished she would've stuck to her guns. With the roar of loud music blaring in her ear and the bass thumping like a giant heartbeat, the area was rapidly swelling up with a people. Raven needed to go to the bathroom, but she didn't feel like navigating through the massive crowd. Even with her reluctance at being there, she admired the venue though. It was quite gorgeous, especially in VIP where they were sitting. Plush leather banquettes, marbled floors, large display monitors on the wall...Extremely luxurious.

Raven picked up her drink and took a small sip. It wasn't that she was a stick in the mud or anything, but club scenes just didn't do it for her anymore or at least not every time they went out. At thirty-three, she considered herself far from old, but she mellowed quite a bit from her younger years. Gwynn, however, had not.

Raven looked at her and smiled. Her girl was having the time of her life dancing with one guy after the other. As well she should. She worked hard and deserved to play even harder. They both did. The only problem was the person Raven was in the mood to play with wasn't there.

She looked at the cell phone she kept a tight grip on since they got to the club. Even if what Hawk told her about it being truly hack proof was true, the last thing she needed was to set it down somewhere or lose it the same day he gave it to her. She unlocked the security code to see if he'd sent her a text, but nothing after the brief message he sent her earlier letting her know he made it to Miami and that he would call her later.

Trying to ignore the stab of disappointment she felt, Raven sat back and glanced around thoroughly bored. Raven was so lost in thoughts of Hawk, she jumped when Gwynn snuck up from behind and shouted in her ear.

"Alright, bitch, spill! Why the hell you keep lookin' at your phone? Who you waitin' on a phone call from?"

"Gwynn! You scared the crap out of me." Raven glanced down to make sure the message wasn't still displayed on the screen. "Your ass is tipsy."

"I ain't tipsy! I'm drunk!" Gwynn plopped down on the cushioned seat next to Raven and laid her head on Raven's shoulder. "Stop tryin' to change the subject. Who you texting? And is that a new phone?"

She tried to grab it to get a closer look, but Raven switched it to her other hand and kept it out of reach. She shook her head at her friend and laughed. Gwynn was a hard party girl for as long as Raven knew her. In school, she'd go out clubbing on the nights before they had exams and easily ace the tests the next morning. Now, in adulthood, nothing changed. She was a brilliant attorney, but when the mood hit her, the loud and brash BK girl from the block was never far away.

"I'm not texting nobody, I'm just bored."

"Bullshit!"

Raven winced when Gwynn yelled in her ear.

"You been mopin' around the office the last couple of weeks like you lost your best friend and I know that's a lie because that's me!" She pointed to herself and fell out in a fit of giggles. "Tell the truth. You got some, didn't you?"

"What? From who? You know I'm not seeing anybody."

"Come on, Rae. You been acting mighty secretive lately. Wait!" Gwynn's head bounced off Raven's shoulder to glare at her as if she'd just thought of something. "Please tell me you didn't screw that corny ass Professor What's His Name."

"Who, Wesley? Ugh!" Raven's face scrunched up in distaste. Wesley was very good looking and a certified genius, but the attraction was just not there for her. "Not a chance."

"Thank *God*." Gwynn picked up Raven's drink and took several big gulps. "Then who? And don't tell me nobody. Give a bitch some credit. I've known you for fifteen years. I know when you're lying."

Raven let out a sigh. Before she could think of something to get Gwynn off her case, her cell phone rang. *Hawk*. She mumbled an excuse to Gwynn and hurried to find a quiet spot to talk. When the phone rang twice more, Raven pushed the button to accept the call so he wouldn't hang up.

Frantically glancing around, she brought the phone to her ear. Pressing a finger to her other ear, she tried to try drown out the noise. "Hello? Hawk?" She heard the rumble of his deep voice but couldn't make out what he was saying.

"Wait! Hold on!" She yelled, ducking out the door to the entryway where it was bit quieter. "Can you hear me?"

"Yeah. I can hear you." Another pause, then he slowly asked, "Where are you?"

Raven smiled into the phone. He sounded so good. To say she just saw him earlier that morning, she missed him more than she thought she would. "I'm out with my friends. How are you?"

"I'm good. Where did you say you were going again?"

Raven told him the name of the club. "I'm glad you called. I've been checking my phone all evening," she confessed with a self-conscience laugh. Just as quickly, she rolled her eyes at herself. *Girl, get it together.*

"You remember what I told you, right, Rae?"

"Huh?" She frowned, truly confused until she realized he was referencing what he told her that morning. "I told you I was going out with friends. I'm not doing anything."

"Let's keep it that way, okay?"

Hearing the hint of censure on the other end, Raven felt herself starting to get a bit perturbed. This morning was the second time he made it a point to tell her that he didn't share his women. She got it. She told him she didn't share either. That should've ended the conversation, but the suspicion and mistrust in his voice said otherwise.

Raven took a deep breath, trying to keep her temper in check. "Is there a problem, Hawk?"

"I don't know, baby, you tell me," he said, using the same tone she did. "Is there?"

"Whoa! Wait a minute!" Even though he couldn't see her, Raven held a hand up for him to slow his roll. "Let's rewind a bit here because things went left in this conversation *real* quick. Obviously, you're mistaking me for one of the weak bitc-" Raven caught herself just in time. She refused to let him take her out of her character. "Weak *women* you spend time with. Just to make things clear, I answered your question the last couple of times you brought the subject up because I *wanted* to–not because I felt compelled to answer *to* you. There's a difference."

"Raven–"

But she wasn't finished. "I only have one man I call Daddy and his name is *not* Hawk Pattel," she hissed twisting her neck. Belatedly remembering where she was, she made an effort to lower her voice but her words were still heated. "I'm a grown woman, Hawk. I expect to be treated like one and more importantly, *respected* like one. If you can't do that then..."

Angry tears sprang to her eyes. Things were difficult enough. Why was he intentionally trying to ruin things after they left each other on such a high note? Glancing around, she wiped the tears away as inconspicuously as possible. The silence on the other end stretched on for so long that Raven thought he hung up. She was just getting ready to disconnect on her end when he answered.

"Look, enjoy your night with your friends. Holla at me later."

"Hawk..." Raven paused. She didn't really know *what* she wanted to say, but she knew she wouldn't beg.

"It's cool, Rae. This one is on me. Just tired, I guess."

"What's wrong?" She asked in a hushed voice when the sentence trailed off. "Did something happen?"

"Don't worry about it. Seriously, everything's good."

"Okay, but...are *we*?" As much as she hated to, Raven couldn't stand to not ask for clarification. "Still good, I mean."

"Yeah. We're good, baby, but..."

"But what?" Raven held her breath as she waited for him to answer the question.

His voice lowered an octave to the intimate level that made her melt every time she heard it. "You know it's not in my nature to pass up a challenge. That part about not callin' me daddy..." His sexy laugh sent a thrill of electricity crackling through the line. "Yeah."

"Oh, God, baby..." Raven closed her eyes and bit down hard on her lip. "Stop."

"Be careful getting home. Matter of fact, call Danny when you're ready. I'll text you his number."

"That's not necessary, Hawk. I–"

"Humor me. For my own piece of mind. New York is a crazy city, especially at night for a woman."

"I've been navigating the streets of New York by myself since I graduated law school," Raven grinned relieved that some of the tension between them passed. "I'll be okay."

"I know you will, but the difference is you're not by yourself now. I don't want you catching cabs at all hours of the night. Will you let me do that for you? Come on, indulge me."

Smooth, Pattel, Raven acknowledged with a slow shake of her head. *Real smooth.* Still. The warm and fuzzies started fluttering in her stomach right on cue. "Okay. Thank you."

"Of course. Talk to you soon."

With an expression of what Raven decided to call *'deep like'* on her face, she hung up the phone and bit the inside of her cheek. Sighing quietly, she turned to go back to the VIP when she came face to face with Gwynn who was standing a few feet behind her. The look on her face was enigmatic, which made Raven panic. *How much had she heard?*

CHAPTER 35

"Hey. What's up?" Staring at Gwynn, Raven deliberately kept her voice bright and upbeat. "What are you doing out here? I know you're not ready to leave, are you?"

Gwynn studied Raven as if trying to figure something out. "No. Just making sure you're okay."

Raven waved her hand. "I'm fine. Thanks for checking on your girl though." Just as Raven walked past her, Gwynn stopped her with a question.

"Raven, who was that on the phone?" she asked quietly. "This new mystery man of yours?"

"I told you there's no mystery man. At least not in the sense you mean. Just... a friend."

"You and your *friend* seemed to be having a heated discussion when I walked up." Appearing more than a little suspicious, Gwynn folded her arms. "You sure there's nothing you want to talk about, Rae?"

"I'm positive, now come on. That's my song!"

"Raven–"

"And since you guzzled my last drink, it's your turn to buy the next round."

Raven grabbed Gwynn's hand and pulled her back inside before she could probe any further. Heading straight to the dance floor, Raven waved over a couple of their other friends to join them. Slipping the phone securely in the back pocket of her jeans, Raven did her best to put on a show of enjoyment to distract Gwynn, but all she could think about was if she heard Raven call Hawk by name? Had she been overly loud during the conversation?

Raven knew she had to be extremely careful, especially around Gwynn, who had a tendency to pick out the smallest things that a lot of people skipped and dissect the hell out of it. It was a good talent to have as an ADA, but not right now–not when there was so much at stake if it got out that Raven was sleeping with a member of the top crime family in the city.

A couple hours later, amid a chorus of rowdy protests, Raven was finally able to beg her way out of staying any longer. The group had gotten wound up and planned on getting something to eat afterwards. Raven sent air kisses to everyone at the table and told them to have fun but be careful.

She had already texted Danny to let him know she was ready. Raven had to admit it was nice to be able to walk out of a busy nightclub and have a driver standing by a luxury car ready to whisk her off to wherever it was she wanted to go.

She smiled her thanks at Danny when he opened the back door for her. Once they were on their way, she told him, "I'm sorry if this is an inconvenience. Hawk insisted I call you and well, you know him better than I do. It seems when he's made up his mind about something that's it."

"It's no inconvenience at all, Ms. Randolph. As a matter of fact, Mr. Pattel has asked me to be available to you for the rest of the week. Call me if there's anything I can do or anyplace you want to go."

Raven looked at him with surprise. "Oh, I didn't know that. But it won't be necessary. I appreciate the offer, though."

"Of course, ma'am."

After that, the rest of the ride was made in silence. Once they got to Raven's apartment, Danny escorted her inside the building before nodding and bidding her goodnight at the elevator. Releasing a sigh of relief when she walked into her apartment, Raven locked the door then kicked off the heels she had on all night. They were cute, but definitely not made for dancing. That was for sure.

Suppressing a yawn, she headed directly to her bedroom and pulled her clothes off. The bathroom was the next stop, where she ran a scented bath and relaxed for a while. Once she dried off and slipped a gown on, she grabbed her phone and got into bed.

Looking at the clock, she saw that it was still fairly early. Raven started to text Hawk to let him know she was home safely, but she wanted to hear his voice. Especially after the words they exchanged earlier. Hitting speed dial, she put the phone on speaker and waited for him to answer, which he did after the second ring.

"Hey, baby. You locked in safe and sound?"

Raven smiled. It was nice to have someone checking to make sure she was safe. Adjusting the pillows behind her head, she sat back and got comfortable. "Yes, I made it home about thirty minutes ago. I took a bath first and yes, I double checked the doors and now I'm in bed."

"Good. Only one thing missing from that picture."

Raven's smile grew wide. "Oh yeah? What?"

"Me, of course."

"Is that so, Mr. Pattel?"

"It is, Ms. Randolph."

"I have to say I agree with you. You being here now would be just perfect."

"Glad you agree." Hawk's laugh warmed her through the phone. "Did you enjoy yourself?"

"Aagghhh." Raven grimaced. "It was okay. I was expecting to go somewhere more low key, but I was outvoted. I just wasn't in the mood, I guess."

"Yeah. Gets old after a while, doesn't it?"

"I don't see how you do it so much. The club scene, I mean."

"I used to enjoy the fuck out of it. Women, drinks, music. It's a single guy's dream, but quite honestly, it's becoming more of a chore than...wait. Hold on a minute, baby."

Raven heard him talking to someone in the background and giving them instructions about what he wanted done. "I'm sorry, I didn't even ask if you were busy before I started running my mouth," she told him when he came back to the phone. "You can call me back if you need to."

"Nah. What I *need* is physically impossible with you in New York and me in Miami, so talking to you is the next best thing. I would video chat with you, but I got people running in and out of my office."

"I understand. I'm happy just to be able to talk to you."

"Even after I pissed you off earlier?" He asked in amusement.

"Yeah. Sorry about that. It feels like I may have overacted."

"Got a temper on you, don't you? I like that. Keeps things interesting. Can't wait to find out more about you, Raven Randolph. Matter of fact, I'm looking forward to it."

"Same here," Raven let out softly.

"So, tell me, what...hold on, Rae. Damn. Baby, I'm gonna have to call you back; looks like I

347

got a mini crisis here that I have to deal with before it blows out of control. It may take a while. If it's not too late, I'll call you back, but if I don't talk to you, rest well."

"Okay." She wanted to tell him it didn't matter what time he called, but that sounded a little desperate. "Again, you try to get some rest, too."

"I will. Talk to you soon. And Rae?"

"Yes?"

"Dream about me."

Raven smiled as she hung up the phone. Afterwards, she lay in bed wide awake thinking about Hawk and their situation. She really, *really* liked the guy. A *lot*. It would be so easy to let herself pretend they were just two people in a relationship getting to know one another, because truly that's how it seemed but...

Raven turned over on her side. She was too tired to analyze what was happening. She just didn't have the energy. She wasn't looking for a happily ever after with Hawk and she was sure the same was true for him. Raven made the decision last night to *feel and not think*. Call it stupid, naïve, whatever. She planned to enjoy every moment of it.

And with that being her last thought, she drifted off into a deep sleep with images of Hawk Pattel lingering behind her closed lids.

The weekend went by much too soon and before Raven knew it, Monday morning was upon her bringing all of its typical madness right along with it. Once she fixed a cup of coffee and entered her office, she barely had a chance to sit down when she was summoned to Jeff's office.

Raven's head dropped back, but after exhaling loudly, she stood up to go and see her boss. She and Gwynn arrived about the same time. Raven raised an inquiring eyebrow when she saw Gwynn looked as if she barely had any rest over the weekend.

"Rough night?" Raven asked. "You don't look so good."

"Gee, thanks," Gwynn answered sarcastically. "Just a little bit too much partying I guess."

Raven shook her head and sat down in front of Jeff's desk. "Morning, Jeff."

"Good morning," Gwynn mumbled.

"Unfortunately, there's not a damn thing good about it."

Raven exchanged a cautious look with Gwynn before asking, "What's wrong?"

"I just got off the phone with the Vegas DA and it seems like the case against Pattel has started falling apart, that's what's wrong."

Raven's shock turned to caution mixed with hope. "What happened?"

"Pattel admits to being at his club the night in question but denies seeing Bernstein. Says he's not sure where that story came from, but he hasn't seen him in several months. He allowed the authorities to search the downstairs room where the CI claims Bernstein was taken, but nothing came up. It's mostly just used for storage and nothing looked out of place. To compound the matter, no cameras inside the club show Bernstein was even there that night. However, video surveillance in a reserved parking spot yield a blurry image of a man that resembles him getting into a car later that night and driving away. Investigators thought they were on to something, but that person has surfaced." Jeff threw the pen he was holding on his desk and glared at Gwynn and Raven. "Turns out it was an acquaintance of the manager, not Bernstein."

Raven did her best to hide her surprise. Months ago, she would've been just as outraged as Jeff that the Pattels seemed to be slipping through their fingers yet again, but not now. No, now relief overshadowed any and all other emotions. Her head practically spun from the strength of it.

"On top of all that," Jeff continued, "Pattel has an alibi for the time Bernstein was supposedly seen at the club. A female friend of his stated they were together at his condo later on Saturday night and didn't leave until early Sunday morning. Cameras in the lobby corroborate her story. They show her coming and then leaving just as she said. It doesn't show the two of them together, but the concierge stated she's a frequent visitor ever since Pattel purchased the condominium a year ago."

Raven's hand tightened on the pen she held. The only explanation for her not surfacing on that video was that Hawk somehow doctored the footage to erase her presence.

"What about the informant?" she asked. "I thought he saw Bernstein in person on more than one occasion and swore it was him that night."

"That's another thing. The CI's credibility is being called into question. It seems a large number of opioids were found in his locker. He admitted to selling the pills to club goers on the side, but swears he's telling the truth about what he saw. Doesn't matter now. He could tell us the sky is blue and the grass is green and it would be shot down as a lie and inadmissible by Pattel's lawyers."

"Shit," Gwen whispered.

Raven cleared her throat. "So, is it possible Bernstein may have skipped town after all?"

Jeff's gaze sharpened. "Yes. You don't seem too upset about it though. I wonder why."

Raven frowned at his attack. "What are you talking about? The fact that Vegas had an unreliable CI who gave them bad information is not on me, Jeff. I've always done my job and would never, ever compromise my position here. I resent any implication that says otherwise."

"Raven's right," Gwynn added. "This case was a little flimsy to start with. The LVPD were so eager to try to pin this on Pattel that I think they rushed it and jumped the gun. They never should've shown their hand and gone after the Pattels on such weak evidence. Like Raven said, that's on them. Not us."

Raven never broke eye contact with Jeff. No matter what, she couldn't allow him to think she had anything to hide.

Finally, Jeff's eyes dropped away. "That's all for now. If anything changes I'll update you both accordingly."

Gwynn nodded and immediately stood up, but Raven hesitated. She felt there was still something Jeff wanted to say and if he did, she didn't have a problem with—

"Ready, Rae?" Gwynn asked pointedly.

"Well, I—"

Gwynn placed a hand on her shoulder and gave it a subtle squeeze. Raven instantly got the message: *Bring yo' ass on.*

Reluctantly standing as well, she tried to catch Jeff's eye, but he made a big production of turning to his computer and staring at a document he pulled up on the screen. Raven turned and followed Gwynn out the office. The moment the door closed, Gwynn gave her a slanted look from the corner of her eyes.

"You need to pick and choose your battles, girl. Now was not the time to force whatever issue you and Jeff are having to the forefront. And before you say it's nothing, save it. You don't have to tell me what's going on, but Rae..." Gwynn turned around so that the two of them were eye to eye. "Whatever you're doing–*who*ever you're doing–be careful."

Raven opened her mouth to protest, but Gwynn brought a hand up to Raven's face. "Don't. Just remember what I said."

Giving Raven one last meaningful look, Gwynn left her standing in the busy corridor alone. Raven's shoulders lifted with the deep breath she took. She would have to track Gwynn down later and smooth things over, because something was definitely wrong; but for now, she wanted to wallow around a bit in the relief she felt in Jeff's office.

The fact that Hawk might not be involved in Michael Bernstein's disappearance was not a possibility she'd entertained. Bottom line, he was a Pattel and she knew what the Pattels were capable of. It wasn't too farfetched to believe he actually did what he was being accused of, but if he wasn't involved...

Raven pushed that line of thinking aside. She already made her decision to keep seeing him, at least for the moment. She had no idea where things went from there, but she planned to live in the moment and play things by ear. Raven wasn't stupid by a long shot. She realized it wasn't a smart thing to do. However, it *felt* good, so yeah, for once she was going to throw caution to the wind and enjoy the feeling.

A sharp emotion she didn't want to put a name to hiccupped in her chest as she thought about seeing him the coming weekend. With a tiny smile hovering around her lips, she stepped on the elevator to head back to her office. Raven didn't have time to stand around mooning over Hawk, she had more than enough work to keep her busy, but first...she needed to make that appointment with her doctor.

CHAPTER 36

By the time Friday rolled around, Raven was torn between excitement and nervousness. She'd spoken to Hawk several times that week and although she'd refrained from asking him exactly when she was going to see him, it didn't mean the question wasn't been constantly on her mind.

Usually, Raven's daily schedule was jammed packed with appointments, meetings and court dates, giving her little time to even grab lunch on some days. That's the way she preferred it. She thrived on the rush.

However, this week showed her that if she *really* wanted to make room for something, she could definitely do it. The doctor's appointment she went to Tuesday morning normally would've been scheduled out weeks or even months in advance. She made it happen in a day. The manicure, pedicure, hair appointment and bikini wax she squeezed in were indulgences she saved for the weekend. Not the case *this* week. Having those things completed before she saw Hawk was a must.

She was at her desk admiring the manicure she got yesterday when the phone Hawk gave her rang. Determined not to appear too eager, Raven let her finger hover over the **ACCEPT** button and forced herself to wait until the second ring trailed off. Then, taking a deep breath, she answered the call.

"Hello?" She shook her head when she heard the breathy quality of her voice. So much for trying to project the cool image she was going for. Epic fail.

"Hey, beautiful. How are you?" Hawk's deep voice seeped through the phone and landed straight between her legs. Raven swallowed. Would there ever come a time when she didn't become moist from just the sound of it?

"I'm fine. How are you?"

"Couldn't be better now that I know it's almost time to see you."

Warmth covered Raven's body like a favorite blanket. She had to admit, that was one thing she liked about him. While she always tried to sound unaffected when talking to him, Hawk never shied away from letting her know that he wanted her. It was a refreshing change to deal with a grown man who knew what he was about and didn't play games.

"I'm looking forward to seeing you this weekend, too," she answered honestly. Deciding to take it a step further, she asked, "When ...um, when will that happen?"

"When will what happen?"

Raven heard the teasing lilt in his voice and dropped all pretense of trying to remain cool. "Pattel, you do *not* want to play with me right now. Trust me on that. For once, just answer the damn question."

"Ahhh, there's my little corporate thug in a skirt. I was wondering how long it would take her to make an appearance," he chuckled. His tone clearly told her that's what he was waiting on.

"Hawk." The way she said his name told him she wasn't screwing around. She wasn't for the shits and giggles right now. "When?"

"Tonight okay with you?"

The tension melted from Raven's body. "It's perfect," she whispered. "What time?"

"Well, I was hoping you could leave work a little early. Would that be a problem?"

"Not at all." Raven deliberately left her workload light for that particular reason.

"Great. Sorry for the short notice, but I wasn't sure I would be able to make it back into town tonight, but I worked my ass off to make it happen. Think you can be ready around three?"

Raven glanced at the small clock on her desk. It was just after twelve. If she left as soon as they got off the phone, it would give her enough time to take a nice relaxing bath and get ready without having to rush.

"Three sounds perfect." Visions of tearing his clothes off as soon as he stepped through her door danced unchecked through her head. She couldn't wait.

"Good. Danny will be waiting outside your apartment to pick you up."

The vision starring him and her in living color instantly dissipated. "Wait, pick me up? I thought we were going to...well, you know. Stay in." *And fuck our brains out*, she thought silently.

"We are. But not in the city. I want to be able to enjoy you with no distractions this weekend."

Raven gulped. The weekend? The *entire* weekend? A frown appeared on her face and deepened as Hawk continued.

"Oh, and you don't need to pack anything. I've taken care of all that. The only thing you need to do is give yourself over to me for the next forty-eight hours. Think you can do that for me, baby?"

"Wait, slow down a minute," Raven laughed nervously. "I don't understand. Where are we going? And what do you mean I don't have to pack anything?"

"Okay, look. I know it's hard for you and that Type A personality of yours to hand control over to someone once in a while–"

"If that ain't the pot calling the kettle black," she muttered, twisting her lips.

"But I'm asking you to do it now. For me? I realize it hasn't been that long since we've been seeing each other, but I'm hoping you feel comfortable enough to trust me just a little bit..." Hawk let the sentence dangle in the air inviting her response.

"I, well, yes, it's not that." As far as Raven was concerned she already went above and beyond her norm when it came to trusting him, but...

"Good. Then you'll be ready when Danny gets there, right?"

"I... I guess so," Raven answered reluctantly. Now she'd have to regroup and recalibrate. She hated not being prepared. "Can you at least tell me where we're going?"

"Nope."

"But what if–"

"Woman, enough. I'm gonna teach you how to let loose and have fun if it kills me."

Raven sat up straight in the chair. She felt a bit insulted. "I know how to have fun, dammit."

"Then no more questions, right?"

Raven opened her mouth to ask just one more, but snapped it shut and stewed in irritated silence.

Apparently, Hawk was aware of how much it was costing her to remain quiet. "And just to show you how much I appreciate your effort, I promise to give you a reward later."

Raven's tongue came out to wet her lips in anticipation. "Oh yeah?"

"Mmhm."

"Well. Okay. In that case." She smiled when he let out an amused laugh.

"Alright, I'll let you go. See you this evening, Rae." His voice was soft and soothing, instantly easing any anxiety she might have at the change of plans. "Don't forget, the only thing I wanna see when you get outta that car is you. No suitcase, nothin'. I got this."

"Okay," she responded just as softly then suddenly remembered something. "Oh, wait. Aren't you going to ask me if I took care of that...thing?" She was referring to the tests she took earlier that week. Was actually staring at the results on her computer now.

"Nope."

Raven eyebrows went skyward. "No?"

"I don't have to ask. I know you womaned up and handled it. Wanna know how I know?"

"Please. Enlighten me." The corner of Raven's mouth lifted. This should be good.

Hawk's voice lowered to an intimate level that instantly ensnared her in its tentacles. "I'm positive you did because you want to feel me unsheathed, experience the friction of me sliding inside you, skin to skin with no barrier between us. And when you cum, Rae? I can't tell you how much I'm looking forward to feeling your warm, wet cunt gripping my beast so tight that it feels like a hostage situation of epic proportions."

Raven slowly sat back in her chair, astonished at his ability to work her up into a frenzy verbally as easily as he did physically. Her breathing accelerated dangerously quick, like a car whose gear jumped from one to five and bypassed everything in between. The only thing that mattered in that moment was getting to him *now*.

"What time did you say Danny would pick me up?"

"Three o'clock."

"I'll be ready."

As she promised herself, as soon as she hung up the phone with Hawk, Raven finished tying up a few loose ends well enough so they would hold until she came back Monday morning. Passing

DeLaney she gave her a warm smile and a finger wave.

"Don't stay too much longer," Raven told her.

"I won't. I'll leave as soon as I finish this report," Laney grinned. "You got something special planned for the weekend?"

"I sure do."

"Good. Have fun."

"I intend to. Enjoy your weekend."

When she got outside, Raven swiftly hailed a cab. Once they were on their way, she sat back to think about the next couple of days with Hawk. To say she was excited was an understatement. It was still so hard to believe what was going on with them. Raven had never been one to get so emotionally involved with a man. For as long as she could remember, she was so driven to excel in her career, she never had the time nor the inclination to pursue what she called frivolous relationships. Especially not with a man like Hawk Pattel. She'd always loved confident men, but Hawk was confidence on steroids.

A hint of a smile rested on her lips as she pictured him in her mind. He walked around like he knew he was the shit and damn if that wasn't a turn on. As strong a woman as she was, Raven never dreamed she would be attracted to someone as dominating and arrogant as he was. His direct and straightforward personality was a breath of fresh air, even while his enigmatic mind frustrated her. All those traits worked together to capture her interest like no one or nothing else ever had. Hawk fascinated her. As busy a man as he obviously was, the fact that he took the time to plan this mysterious weekend for them only served to intrigue her further.

Seeing that the cab was pulling up in front of her building, Raven pulled out the fare and leaned forward to give the bill to the driver, who gave her a face splitting grin when she told him to keep the change. Once she got to her apartment, she kicked her heels off and went to her bedroom. Pausing, she shot a glance towards her closet where her overnight bag was stored. Raven chewed at the corner of her lip. She was tempted to pull it out and at least pack a few essentials, but she decided to give Hawk the benefit of the doubt. If he claimed she didn't need to bring anything, she would take him at his word.

After finishing her bath, Raven applied her favorite scented lotion over every inch of her skin, leaving it silky smooth to the touch. Humming underneath her breath, she wrapped her body in a towel and headed to the kitchen to pour herself a glass of wine. She still had a little over an hour before it was time to leave and would probably need every minute of it to calm herself down.

The doorbell rang just as Raven turned to go back to her bedroom. Frowning, she padded to the door. She wasn't expecting anyone and it was too early for Danny to be there. Looking cautiously through the peephole she saw her doorman standing in the hallway holding a couple of wrapped packages.

"Just a minute," she called out before hurrying to the bedroom to grab a robe. Snatching the towel off, she quickly slipped the robe on and went to open the door.

"Hi, Ben," she greeted with a smile while looking curiously at the boxes he was holding. "What's this?"

"They were just delivered for you, Ms. Randolph."

"Oh? Um...Okay. Just a sec." Slightly perplexed, Raven went to grab some money out of her purse to tip him for his trouble, but he shook his head and held a hand up to stop her.

"No need, ma'am. It's been taken care of."

Extremely curious at as to what she got and who it was from, Raven held the door open for him to come in and sit the packages on her sofa. Ben tipped his hat, waving away her thanks and left her to open her surprises. Hurrying back to the couch, she tore the dove gray wrapping off of the larger package to reveal a box in a lighter shade of gray. Raven recognized the fancy monogrammed words of an expensive French boutique on Madison Avenue she and Gwynn visited before.

The store's European molding, marble floors, and gray and blush color schemes was as extravagant as their clothes. But so were the price tags. After casually browsing around, Raven deemed it too rich for her blood, but Gwynn's ghetto fabulous ass purchased a dress just to spite the snooty saleswoman. She left the price tag on it and wore it out to the club that night, then took it back to the store the next day. Raven shook her head at the memory before going back to the mystery in front of her. *Who would be sending me...*

Before she even finished the thought, the answer came to her in an instant. Hawk.

Mouth agape with excitement, she lifted the top off of the box. On top of the wispy sheets of tissue that covered the items inside lay a handwritten folded card with her name written on the front. Raven picked it up and eagerly read it: *Can't wait to see you in this. Looking forward to seeing what's underneath it even more.*

HJP

CHAPTER 37

Raven's hand trembled as she read the message again. She couldn't believe he did this. Placing the card on the sofa beside the box, she eagerly peeled the thin sheets of tissue away and lifted out a sexy, but tasteful little dress the color of rich cognac. After admiring it with wide eyes, Raven carefully placed it on the couch and dove back into the box. The next item she pulled out was a skimpy silk and lace thong in a slightly darker color than the dress.

Seeing them both together, Raven was reminded of the comment Hawk had made when she undressed for him that first night in Vegas...

Chocolate over chocolate. And then more chocolate. I can't wait to taste you, Rae.

Her excitement growing, she opened the next box and found a pair of strappy taupe stilettos and a clutch to match. Raven looked at all of the goodies. Everything was the correct size. She shook her head in disbelief. He was too much. But she loved that he paid such close attention to detail. It was a very attractive quality in a man.

Raven reached for the last box, which was much smaller than the other two. By the size of it, she was sure it was some type of jewelry to go with the dress. She guessed right, when she unwrapped it and found a velvet rectangular box.

Biting her lip in anticipation, she slowly opened it. Once she saw what was inside, Raven's hands trembled so violently that she almost dropped it on the floor. "Oh. My. God!"

Lying on a bed of luxurious, black velvet was an oval shaped, yellow diamond, surrounded by a circle of brilliant, white diamonds that hung from an 18k gold chain. Nestled in the middle of the jewelry box was a pair of matching, canary yellow earrings. They were the most exquisite pieces of jewelry Raven had ever seen. She slowly lowered herself down until the coffee table met her bottom. Extending her trembling hand out, she gently traced the necklace, admiring its unique and brilliant beauty, then did the same with the earrings.

Finally managing to tear her eyes away, she surveyed the gifts Hawk gave her with a sense of awe. No one had ever done anything like this before for her. She still couldn't believe it. It was too much, especially the jewelry. She would wear the earrings and necklace to meet him this afternoon, since he obviously picked it out specifically to complement the champagne undertones in the dress, but when she left at the end of the weekend they would stay with him. There was no way she could accept such an expensive gift.

Feeling a little better now that she made that decision, Raven gathered everything in her arms and hurried to the bedroom. Once again, Hawk Pattel had knocked her off balance and as a result, she was now running late. Danny would be downstairs in forty-five minutes.

She had to admit, however, that Hawk choosing every single item she for her to wear made it a lot easier to breeze through the dressing ritual which she would have fretted about until she walked out of her apartment. Raven was completely dressed in less than twenty minutes. It didn't take long to apply her make-up since she didn't wear very much. Eyeliner, a swipe of cinnamon colored lip gloss and a couple coats of mascara did the trick. Ten minutes–done. Turning to look in the full-sized mirror, she studied herself with a sharp, critical eye.

She couldn't lie. The man knew his stuff when it came to clothes. The figure flattering dress fit her to perfection. Thin, spaghetti straps showed off her glowing, toned arms and shoulders while the plunging neckline showcased her cleavage so that the necklace fell just shy of the valley between her breasts. The middle of the dress cinched in to accent her waistline before lovingly outlining the curve of her backside to stop several inches above her knee. Provocative and sexy while still decidedly elegant.

"Not bad, Pattel," she murmured after studying herself from all angles. "You did good."

Hearing her phone buzz, Raven picked it up and saw that it was a text from Danny letting her know he was downstairs whenever she was ready. Fluffing her hair around her shoulders, Raven checked herself out in the mirror one last time. After making sure she had the letter from her doctor in her purse, she took a deep breath then left the apartment. Right then and there, she made a decision to have the time of her life over the weekend. How did Hawk put it? Let loose and have fun.

Taking the elevator down and stepping into the lobby, Raven smiled at several people who either stopped to stare at her pass by or who actually gave her a double take. Their reactions did much to ease some of the nervousness she still felt. After all, the only person whose opinion really mattered had yet to see her. She hoped he was just as impressed.

Once outside, Raven walked to a black luxury car with tinted windows parked on the curb that was different than the one she rode in before. She smiled at Danny, who nodded and held the door open for her. Her pleasure intensified when she sank down into the plush, leather seats where a bottle of expensive champagne sat nestled in a silver ice bucket along with a crystal champagne flute beside it. A tray of strawberries, cheese, and crackers sat securely on a folding tray table attached to the full-length center console.

Oh. My. Raven sighed in amazement. *Is this how the other half lives?*

Before Danny pulled out into the heavy, afternoon traffic, he turned around in his seat to look at Raven. "The ride to your destination will take roughly two hours. Maybe a little less. Mr. Pattel wanted to make sure you were comfortable. If you'd like to turn the television on, the remote is to your left. If you prefer, you can listen to music. Mr. Pattel has a wide range of choices, so hopefully you'll find something you enjoy."

Raven's head was spinning, but not so much that she didn't hear the first part of his little speech. "Danny, what do you mean it'll take two hours to reach our destination? Where exactly are we going?"

Danny's lips tightened in what she imagined was a smile. "Mr. Pattel instructed me to tell you to sit back and enjoy the ride. If you need anything, just press the intercom." With that being said, he turned to face the front without answering her question. Seconds later the partition slowly raised up.

Mumbling that she would get an answer one way or the other, Raven reached for her purse and pulled out her phone. After unlocking it, her fingers hovered over the keys. Then, blowing sharply, she placed the phone down beside her on the seat. Hawk was probably expecting her to call and question him. However, no matter how tempting it might be, she wouldn't do it. As hard as it was, she would show him that she knew how to relax and give over control once in a while.

Raven grabbed the bottle and poured herself a glass of champagne, instantly closing her eyes in appreciation after tasting it. Absolutely delicious.

Raven took another sip and savored it on her tongue before swallowing. Giggling to herself, she looked around the luxurious interior of the car. She could easily get accustomed to this treatment.

Picking up a fat, juicy strawberry, she dipped it into the bowl of cream on the tray and carefully bit into it. She let out a low groan at the decadent, sweet taste. Deciding to listen to some music instead of turning the television on, Raven picked up the remote and pushed a button. In an instant, the sounds of a favorite artists' smooth voice drifted from the surround sound speakers. Perfect. Sighing in pleasure she sat back and closed her eyes.

Yes, she could definitely get used to this. And she would. But just for the weekend.

CHAPTER 38

The trip to meet Hawk was so relaxing that the ride seemed like mere minutes instead of two hours. After the third glass of champagne, Raven's head had started to spin a bit so she cut herself off half-way through the trip. She needed a clear head to handle Hawk Pattel–as much as any woman could possibly handle a man like that.

Raven glanced out the window, having figured out some time ago that they were on their way to Connecticut. Raven had visited the New England state a time or two before with friends, but that was years ago. With its mix of coastal cities and rural towns, she'd enjoyed herself immensely.

The county she saw they were heading towards was one that was a popular retreat for well off New York business types. The scenery was absolutely gorgeous. The covered bridges, rich forests and relaxing rivers took her breath away. Worlds away from Manhattan, it was the perfect weekend escape from the hustle and bustle of city life, but definitely pricey.

After a while, they turned down a quaint, country lane that ran for quite some time until Danny finally slowed down. Raven sat up with interest when he pulled into the driveway of a picturesque estate in the middle of what seemed to be acres and acres of thickly, forested hills. What caught and held Raven's attention, however, was a classic Georgian mansion that Danny brought the car to a stop in front of. Even with the waning light outside, she could see it was set high on the property to no doubt take advantage of what had to be beautiful views from every direction. And in front of the breathtakingly handsome home stood an even more breathtakingly handsome man with his hands in his pockets waiting on her.

Hawk.

Casually dressed in a pair of dark, denim jeans, a white pullover shirt and dark brown boots, he made a sexy picture poised against the backdrop of the elegant home behind him. He looked so damned good. She couldn't take her eyes off him. Still tipsy from the champagne, her inhibitions were dangerously low. Raven knew such a state could potentially contribute to extremely risky behavior in a person and lead to life changing repercussions. She was all in.

Raven had been a good girl all her life. She kept her grades up in school, received a scholarship to college then went straight to law school after graduation. Once she entered the workforce, she fell into a routine that she memorized and followed, line by line like the pages of a life script. It was her comfort zone, a place where she felt at ease and in total control. Now she wondered if she'd missed out on actually *living*.

Maybe. Maybe not. But what she *did* understand was that Hawk might be her chance to rewrite her script, break down the walls of predictability and comfort. With him she could be as bad as she wanted to be and not get judged for it. Seeing the wicked grin on his face as Danny helped her out the car, Raven couldn't help but smile. No, this one would never judge. He understood the concept because he was so good at being bad himself.

Raven started walking towards him, but Hawk remained where he was to get a good look. His eyes devoured her the entire way. When he slowly nodded to himself, it was clear that he approved of what he saw—as well he should since he purchased every single thing she had on. His grin widening, Hawk took his hands out his pockets and met her the last few steps. Bending slightly, he wrapped his arms around her waist and lifted her feet up off the ground. Raven laughed and held him tightly around the neck as they hugged.

"Missed the fuck outta you, you know that?" He whispered in her ear.

"I missed you, too," Raven whispered back without hesitation. *Full disclosure*, she reminded herself. "I missed you a lot."

"Glad to hear that."

Still holding her off the ground, he pulled his head back until they were face to face and smiling at each other. The kiss that followed happened naturally and ended with a few slow pecks before their mouths reluctantly parted.

Hawk looked at his driver. "I'll see you Sunday, Danny. Enjoy your weekend."

"Thank you, Mr. Pattel. You as well, sir." Danny nodded his head, blue eyes twinkling in amusement.

"I intend to, my friend. I intend to," Hawk answered. His eyes remained glued to Raven's face as he carried her inside and closed the door behind him. "How was your ride here?"

Still holding on tight around his neck, Raven threw her head back and closed her eyes. "It was the most enjoyable ride I've ever taken. It was so smooth that it didn't even feel like I was in a car. And the strawberries. And cream. And *champagne*?" Raven couldn't emphasize that enough. "Mmmmm."

Hawk's white teeth flashed brightly against the smoothness of his unblemished brown skin. Her enthusiasm seemed to be catching. "I thought you'd like that."

"Looooved," Raven grinned.

"I can see that," Hawk chuckled, finally lowering her feet to the floor. "I wanted to make the trip as pleasant as possible for you."

His eyes swept over her in appreciation; he didn't miss one single detail on the visual journey. Similar to a shrewd shark circling helpless prey before an attack, he slowly walked around her. Raven shivered, but fear wasn't one of the many emotions churning through her at the moment. No, that would be desire and anticipation–the nervous energy kind. She could almost feel his eyes physically caressing every inch of her body. When his steps halted behind her, Raven's stomach twisted into a ball of knots as she waited.

"Damn, Rae. You are one gorgeous woman. You *do* know that, don't you?"

Pleasure flowed through her veins like an infusion into her bloodstream. Her words came out breathless and paper-thin. "I'm sure the outfit you bought for me has something to do with that. But thank you."

"Nah. You can't really believe that. You wearin' the hell outta that dress–not the other way around. Not every woman is honestly able to say that about a dress like this. That's why I bought it for you. I knew what you would look like in it." Still standing behind her, his vocal chords dropped to a rich, silky baritone pitch that reverberated down her spine when he leaned forward and brought his lips close to her ear. "But as much as I'm enjoying looking at you in it, I'm even more excited to see you out of it."

The sensuality in his voice wrapped around Raven like a pair of strong arms. She held her breath and waited for him to touch her. Kiss her. Anything. She was moments away from ripping the dress off and begging him to take her right there when he stepped back. She immediately missed his body's warmth.

"Come on. Let me get you a glass of wine then show you around." He took her hand in his and led her further inside the house.

Raven tried to swallow her disappointment or at least not let it show. When he looked over his shoulder at her and teasingly pushed his bottom lip out, she had a feeling she didn't do a good job.

Quiet laughter rumbled from under his breath. Hawk stopped and pulled her to him. He lowered his head and gently nibbled on her pouting lip. "Let me try to explain something you might not have picked up on. You already know I want you, Raven. More than I've ever wanted any woman in my life and that's a big admission for me say out loud."

Hawk paused. An emotion she couldn't quite place flashed beneath the surface of his playful expression, but it was gone before she had a chance to decipher what it might mean. Raven filed the moment away for the time being and listened attentively when he spoke again.

"This weekend is about more than just sex. I brought you out here intentionally, away from the problems, away from all the craziness that's goin' on right now in the real world we live in. I wanted to give us a chance to enjoy each other without having to sneak around or be uncomfortable because somebody might see us. That make sense to you?"

"It does," Raven nodded glancing around. "It's beautiful here."

"Maybe by the time we leave here this weekend things will be a little clearer about what the hell is exactly happening between us, because other than the physical, something *is* happening. Do you agree with that?"

"I... guess so. Maybe." Raven knew her reply was cautious, but understandably so. Where was he going with this?

Hawk immediately caught on to her hesitation. He took a step back and folded his arms. "Maybe?"

"I mean..." Raven peeked up at him from underneath the safety of her lashes trying to gauge his mood, but it was impossible. "This is kind of coming out of nowhere. I thought this was just a hookup. You know?"

Hawk's frown was instant. "Hmph," he grunted quietly. "Just a hookup, huh?"

"Well...yeah." Trying to lighten the mood, she unfolded his arms and slipped in between them. "You did say my job was to relax you this weekend, didn't you? So, let me take care of you."

But Hawk wasn't buying it. "Is something wrong, Raven?"

"No, nothing's wrong. I..." Raven was at a loss for words. Dropping her arms from around his waist, she moved back to put a little space between them. No matter what it sounded like, she didn't believe for one second that Hawk Pattel was catching feelings for her. "I'm just not sure where all of this is coming from. I... I don't trust it."

Hawk's eyes never left her face. "You don't trust *me*, you mean."

CHAPTER 39

Raven's brows lifted and fell in a quick shrug when she heard Hawk speak her thoughts out loud. "I'm sorry. I guess I'm putting a damper on this weekend before we even get started."

The words lay between them in the silence that followed. Raven tried to read Hawk's thoughts but of course it was impossible. Was he angry with her? And if so, how was she going to fix it.

"Hawk—"

"No. It's okay, Rae. I appreciate your honesty. And I didn't mean for this to get all heavy, but I think you know by now that I'm not a man who bites his tongue when he has something to say. Let's agree to save this conversation until later. I just want you to relax and enjoy the next couple days. Deal?"

Some of the tension rolled away from Raven's shoulders. "Deal."

Hawk smiled and took her hand again. He led her through a space that Raven assumed was the family room. Complete with a fireplace and cream-colored furnishings, it was pristine yet welcoming at the same time. She immediately noticed pictures of his family scattered around the room, whom she of course recognized, but two photos in particular caught her eye. One was of his sister, Leah. She was the spitting image of the woman in the other frame, leading Raven to assume she was Hawk's mother. They were extremely beautiful women with thick, shiny hair and large brown eyes that were surrounded by a thicket of long dark lashes. Both had the same exact smile.

More than a little curious, Raven looked closer at the picture of the older woman then glanced at Hawk. "Is this your mom?"

"Yeah. That's her." He reached past her and picked up the picture and stared at it. "She and my sister could pass for twins, couldn't they?"

"They seriously could." Raven paused, aware that his mood suddenly turned somber. There was almost no public information regarding any of the women in the Pattel family, which was odd. Raven was too curious to let a chance like this one slip by. "How old were you when she died?"

"Young. Barely five years old." Hawk replaced the picture back on the shelf. "Leah was even younger. Just a baby."

"So sad. Did you at least get a chance to know anyone on her side of the family? Was she close to them before she married your dad?"

Hawk's narrowed eyes cooled several degrees. "Why? Are you asking as prosecuting attorney?"

"No," Raven answered calmly. "Any time I'm with you, I'm not a prosecuting attorney and you're not...who you are. It's just us. Raven and Hawk. But if you're not comfortable talking about it, I understand."

He studied her face for several seconds before looking away. "Yeah. I'd rather not."

"Okay. That's fine. What about this house? It really is a beautiful place. Whose is it?" She placed her hand in his as they started towards the kitchen.

"It's mine."

"Yours?"

"Why do you sound so surprised?" Hawk asked looking down at her.

"I don't know. As beautiful as the Vegas condo is it's the complete opposite of this place which is homey...cozy. Do both homes represent the different sides of Hawk Pattel?" She asked, half-jokingly. "One a sophisticated, mysterious man of the world and the other more a regular homebody?"

Hawk cocked his head to the side as if thinking about her observation and nodded. "Yeah, I guess you could say that. They serve their intended purposes. I wasn't necessarily going to buy a place in Vegas, but I'm there fairly often to check on the club. Plus, my cousin and his family are there. We've gotten to be pretty close. When Darrell mentioned he was putting the condo up for sale, it made sense to buy it."

"And this house?" Raven asked. They had just reached the gourmet kitchen, which featured black, stainless steel appliances and beautiful stone floors. Cream subway tile backsplash wrapped around the walls to the adjoining breakfast nook. "I absolutely love this kitchen."

"Thanks." Hawk took a bottle of wine out of the refrigerator and grabbed a couple wine glasses. "I bought this house a couple of years ago, had it completely gutted and renovated. I'm not here as often as I'd like, but when I get a chance to steal a couple of days off I enjoy coming here to unwind and decompress, if that makes sense."

"It does and I can definitely see why."

"It's getting dark outside now, but we'll explore the property a little bit tomorrow if you want to. Guess I'll let you come up for air enough to do that." He smiled as he handed her a glass.

Hiding a grin, Raven took a sip of her wine. Her eyes widened and went to the bottle on the counter when she realized it was her favorite. She didn't even notice when he took it out of the refrigerator.

"You picked up a bottle of my wine? Thank you."

"You're welcome. It's good. I'm thinking about adding it to the wine lists in my restaurants. Can't have you coming by for dinner and not having your favorite wine available, can I?"

If Raven's chocolate skin could've produced the blush that spread under the surface it would have. She could easily fall for Hawk Pattel. He checked so many boxes on her list she hadn't even realized she had of her perfect man.

Except for that pesky last name, she thought wryly.

Suddenly remembering the test results from her doctor, she placed her glass on the counter and unsnapped the opening of her purse. Feeling a bit awkward, she took the white envelope out and handed it to him. "I almost forgot."

Hawk took it from her and placed it on the counter in front of him. "Thank you."

Raven glanced from him to the envelope before bringing her eyes back to his face. "Aren't you going to open it?"

"I will. Later."

"Oh. I mean, I thought you'd be curious to, uh...well...you know. Look at it."

Hawk smiled. "You did what I asked. We're good, Rae."

Trying to figure out his angle, she stared at him a bit puzzled. Whatever. Picking up her glass she shrugged. "Fine."

Laughing at her slight display of attitude, Hawk put the bottle of wine back in the refrigerator. "Come on. Let me show you the rest of the house, then we can eat."

Raven lifted her nose and sniffed. "It smells good. What are we having?"

"Glazed salmon, rice pilaf, and vegetables."

"Mmm. That sounds delicious."

"My chef just finished everything and placed it in the oven for us. He left before y'all drove up. We're on our own for the rest of the weekend."

"Who's going to cook?" she asked, eyebrows raised.

"Yours truly, of course."

"Oh, God," Raven groaned teasingly, following him out the room.

"Really, woman? I'll have you know I can throw down in the kitchen just as good as I can in the bedroom." A smile hovered over his mouth when Raven almost choked on her wine. "Yeah. Think about that."

"Can we eat *now*?" He laughed but Raven wanted to tell him she was *so* serious. The sooner they ate, the sooner they could...

"Get your mind outta the gutter, Ms. Randolph." Hawk looked back at her with a knowing smirk.

Raven stuck her tongue out at him before following behind him to see the rest of his house, which looked to be just as impressive as what she saw so far. With hardwood throughout, the formal dining room opened up to another living area. There were a total of four bedrooms and three and a half bathrooms. Hawk told her all of the bedrooms had fireplaces.

They toured two bedrooms on the first level before going upstairs where Hawk showed her a third bedroom that looked much the same as the other two. However, when they entered the master, Raven instantly fell in love. It was intimate and serene, yet fabulously sophisticated. How great would it be to curl up in the huge bed on a cold night in front of the large, brick fireplace? Raven could only imagine. She followed Hawk out a door that led to a large deck that looked tailor made for drinking a cup of coffee in the morning or relaxing in the evening with a glass of wine and watching the sun set.

Once inside, Raven remarked how extremely spacious the room was. There was not one, but two, large, walk-in closets. To her surprise, in one of them she saw newly purchased clothes and shoes all in her size and her style. There was also a lingerie tower full of bras, panties and other delicate intimates. Raven looked at him with wonder in her eyes as she took in the neatly arranged space he carved out for her.

Next, Hawk showed her the high-end bathroom. The color scheme was light and relaxing with textured marble slabs, gleaming granite counter tops and walnut framed mirrors. Although the bathroom reminded her of a luxurious spa, it was timeless in its beauty and style. Thick, fluffy towels were neatly arranged on shelves. Hawk pointed out that the floors were heated for those cold winters that Connecticut was known for.

Raven eyed the focal point of the room, which was the sleek, oversized, bear claw bathtub centered in front of a bay window. Hawk opened a cabinet and showed her where an assorted array of oils, bubble baths, soaps and bath bombs were stored. Giddy at all of the goodies at her disposal, Raven couldn't wait to fill the tub up with hot water and indulge herself in paradise.

When he opened more drawers and cabinets, Raven saw a flat iron, still unopened and in the package, along with hair supplies and facial cleansers. That would've been amazing all on its own, but what made it even more so was the fact that they were all just about same brands she used at home. Apparently, Hawk remembered them from when he was at her apartment last weekend. His attention to detail and the fact that he made such a humongous effort to make sure she was comfortable was not lost on her.

After the tour, they headed back to the kitchen. Hawk poured them another glass of wine and started taking some plates down. He nodded towards a pair of French doors that opened out onto an outdoor patio area.

"Why don't you go on out and have a seat. I'll have everything ready in a minute."

"Okay. Are you sure there's nothing I can do to help?" Raven watched, fascinated as he started fixing their meal. This was a side of him she never imagined she would see.

"No. The table's already set, so the only thing you need to do is take your lil fine ass outside and relax," he answered, sending her a sexy smile that made Raven's body tingle.

"I think I can manage that." Giving him a small wave, she left through the door and stepped onto the stone terrace.

Well lit, it overlooked a luscious landscaped garden that had an abundance of path lights nestled into the ground. An endless row of bulbs illuminated the cobblestone walkway, which led to an infinity edge swimming pool. More customized lighting highlighted water features and architectural elements in the clear, blue depths of water. The mood created an ambience that was soft, soothing and utterly romantic.

Raven sat down and sipped her wine. Deep in thought, she looked out into the distance and let her mind run free. *Hawk said this weekend was about more than just sex. What exactly did he mean?* No matter how much they might pretend otherwise, they were two people who lived in two completely different worlds; it was hard to get much farther. Sure, the chemistry between them couldn't be denied. She would even expound on that observation and admit the initial spark that lit up when they first met at Angel's house was instant. But...

You're thinking it so you might as well say it, Raven. You're not sure if he's just using you for information and you'll never be sure.

"Alright, I can see the steam coming out of your head, so let's put all the heavy thinking away for now."

Raven jumped when she heard Hawk behind her. "You really think you know me, don't you?"

"I'm beginning to. Why? Was I wrong?"

"You know you weren't." Raven playfully rolled her eyes, but when he lowered their plates to the table, her attention was immediately captivated by the delicious looking food while her senses grew intoxicated by the aroma. "Wow, this looks amazing."

She barely got the words out before her stomach growled in agreement. Her mouth literally watered as she eyed the salmon with a honey garlic glaze, vegetables, and rice pilaf. Raven barely noticed that Hawk went back in to get the bottle of wine and a basket of warm, homemade dinner rolls. She didn't realize how hungry she was. Starved, actually. The appetizers in the car on the ride over was all she ate since breakfast and that was only been a bagel she picked up outside her building.

Once he sat down, she picked up her fork ready to dig in, but noticed just in time that Hawk had bowed his head to silently say grace. Embarrassed and more than a little shocked, she bowed her head as well. Again, another side of him she didn't expect.

"Amen."

"Amen." Raven stared at him for a few minutes longer before hunger overrode her curiosity. The first bite of the succulent salmon made her slowly close her eyes. She moaned with pure pleasure as it practically melted in her mouth. So. Good.

"Whoever your chef is, don't ever let him go. This is the best salmon I've ever tasted in my *life*."

"Don't worry, he's not going anywhere. I make sure of that by paying him very well." Hawk brought his glass up to his lips and took a long swallow of wine before setting it down again. "I'll be sure to pass on your compliments, though."

Raven smiled and went back to her food. Everything was cooked to absolute perfection. As they ate, the conversation was casual and light. They talked about everything from the restaurant he was in the process of opening in LA to politics and world issues. Before Raven realized it, she scooped up the last bit of food onto her fork, leaving a clean, empty plate. Sitting back with a satisfied sigh, she was convinced she died and went to heaven.

"That was delicious."

"I'm glad you enjoyed it. Hope you saved room for dessert, we're having strawberry cobbler and ice cream."

Raven started shaking her head back and forth before he even finished. "Uh-uh. There's no way."

"You sure?" Hawk grinned.

"I can't. Can we save it for tomorrow?"

"Of course."

"What is it with you and strawberries? Is that like your favorite fruit or something?" She asked, thinking about the strawberries in the car.

"No. *This* is my favorite fruit." Before she realized his intention, Hawk reached over and slipped his hand between her legs. "You eating strawberries beforehand is a bonus."

CHAPTER 40

"S-So you like the way it tastes after a woman eats strawberries?" Raven bit down on her lip to stifle her moan when his thumb ran over her sex.

"I *love* the way it tastes. Wet. Sweet. Juicy." Hawk slowly licked his lips as if he could taste her flavor. "Nothin' else like it."

When he tugged her thong to the side and gently caressed her silky flesh, Raven's lashes fluttered as if in crisis. His touch was unexpected, but so...*wanted, so welcomed*. She tried to speak, tried to tell him how good it felt, but she couldn't concentrate long enough to remember how to speak.

"Look at me, Raven. Baby, look at me," Hawk whispered when she squeezed her thighs, trapping his finger to the spot that craved it most. Once her eyes were open, he continued in the same low voice. "This weekend, I plan on fucking you. A lot."

Raven was already thoroughly and irrefutably aroused, but his intentional, verbal seduction brought her so close to the edge she trembled. She was helpless to do anything but sit there at his mercy and wait for him to finish.

"I'll be very demanding, but hey..." He bit down on his lip, his gaze practically smoldering hot. "There's no need to dance around the issue, we both like it that way, don't we?"

Raven nodded. He was right, she saw no need to be coy. Surprisingly, she felt no shame about it. It just happened to be her preference. When Hawk dominated her in bed, it elevated her pleasure to a whole other level. He awakened a part of her she didn't know existed. But honestly, how could she have? Raven couldn't imagine she would react the same way with any other man *but* him. Matter of fact, she knew she wouldn't.

Hawk's answering growl was wild and primal. "You love me owning you like that because make no mistake about it, I mean it in the most of possessive of ways. You belong to me. Mine. It turns me on to know how classy you are in front of everyone else, but how nasty you get when you're in my bed. But then again, that's the way it should be between two people who care about each other."

"I agree." Raven did her best to sound as normal as she could, but she was beside herself with frustration. Hawk continued to touch her as he talked, but not enough to give her the relief she sought. She reached down to cover the hand between her thighs. She needed more, but his grunt of warning made her reluctantly move her hand away.

"I don't need no help," he drawled in a voice that dripped sex. "But thanks."

"I know. Its jus that.." Her sentence trailed off as she struggled to put her feelings into words.

Hawk pushed his chair back and stood up. Leaning over her, he gripped the back of her chair with one hand and while his other separated the tender folds of her sex to insert two fingers inside her snug opening.

"Fuck." His warm breath fanned over her parted lips. "I plan on being all up in this every chance I get."

"Hawk, please," Raven gasped.

His thumb lightly caressed her swollen clit. "I love the way you cling to me and make those sounds in the back of your throat when I'm deep inside you. Makes me feel like I'm that dude, you know what I'm sayin'? Every man enjoys that feeling when he's with his woman."

Hawk moved his head the inch or so needed to mesh his lips to hers. Raven's mouth opened eagerly her tongue rushing to find his. She brought her hands up to cup his face attempting to deepen the kiss, but he moved out of her reach. Hawk nibbled his way down to her throat opening his mouth wide and tonguing that one little spot he knew drove her crazy.

"I want you so bad." Raven's voice sounded hoarse and choked. She reached out to squeeze his dick through his pants moaning almost desperately when she felt how thick, hard and aroused he was. "I need you, Hawk."

"Don't worry, baby. You'll be well fucked and satisfied before you leave on Sunday. I promise you that."

Hawk stood up and reached for Raven's hand. Pulling her out of her chair, he leaned down to blow out the candles on the table before leading Raven into the house and up the stairs.

*****

The next morning after the two of them finished eating breakfast, Hawk and Raven spent the rest of the day enjoying their time together, starting with a tour of the outside grounds. Hawk's estate spanned over eight wooded acres. Raven was thoroughly enchanted with the idyllic and postcard-ready picture it made. The land had a natural beauty that wasn't seen in the city. She could understand why Hawk claimed it as his peace.

The time they spent on their mini nature hike allowed Raven to see a different side of Hawk. The man was like a chameleon–he could adapt at the drop of a dime to fit into the environment around him. During this trip, she felt as if she finally got to see the man behind the mask he so easily donned and it made her fall for him even more.

Raven thought about the night they shared after dinner the previous evening. Hawk was an excellent lover. A generous one. Throughout the night, he explored her boundaries and tested her limits. When it came to sexual proclivities, to his satisfaction–and her embarrassment–nothing was off limits with him. Somehow, he knew her innermost secrets, those fantasies she never told another living soul, and exploited them shamelessly.

Raven allowed Hawk liberties she never would've even entertained with anyone else.

She bit down hard on her lip as she remembered how, at one point, he'd pinned her against the wall, driving into her body again and again as if he couldn't get close enough. *Deep* enough. The man easily crawled inside her mind as well as her body and drove her absolutely insane. Before the night was over, Hawk had brought her in tune with her body in a way that allowed her to obtain complete and absolute gratification. It was everything she anticipated, and so much more.

"What are you thinkin' about, woman?" Hawk asked as he chopped up the array of crisp, colorful fresh vegetables for their salad.

The question abruptly brought her back to the present. They were in the kitchen getting ready to eat what was supposed to be a late lunch, but turned into an early dinner. Comfortably clad in a pair of shorts, tank top and footies, Raven sat atop the large island watching Hawk. She wanted to witness firsthand this cooking skill he said he possessed. She had to admit that he knew his way around the kitchen. Interesting.

"Just how much I've enjoyed myself so far." When he held a slice of carrot out to her, Raven leaned over and ate it from his fingers. "You really do know how to cook, don't you?"

"I may have picked up a thing or two from the chefs in my restaurants." He gave her a quick smile before turning to drop the cobs of corn into the boiling water on the stove. "You didn't believe me when I told you I could cook, did you?"

"No, I didn't," Raven laughed. "I stand corrected."

Hawk shook his head and grinned. "Man, you and your half-assed apologies."

Raven's stomach chose that moment to let out a low, whiney growl. "I'll apologize once I have some of that food in front of me," she pouted, grabbing her stomach. "How much longer? I'm starved."

"And whose fault is that? We could've eaten an hour ago, but–"

"But you and your sex fiend tendencies got in the way," Raven interrupted cutting her eyes away from him.

Hawk wiped his hand on the towel and came over to stand between her legs. "Alright. I'll take the charge for that one. Is it my fault you're so got damn irresistible that I can't keep my hands off of you? Like now?"

Looking into his adorably handsome face, Raven melted. When he leaned forward to kiss her neck, she closed her eyes and wrapped her arms around him. "Well. I guess since you put it that way, we can share the charge."

A growl rumbled from Hawk's chest. "Mmmm. You smell so good."

"So do you."

Hawk leaned back to glare at her. "I smell like that girly shit from the bathtub. If the fellas got a whiff of me now, they would never let me live it down. Next time, we take a shower."

"But we had so much fun in the tub, though, didn't we?"

"Yeah. And we had the mess to clean up afterwards to show for it."

Smiling, Hawk stole another kiss before going to the stove to check the water for the lobster. After seeing it was boiling, he retrieved a huge lobster from the sink and slowly lowered it in the pot, then got the other one and did the same.

"There we go. Tell your stomach the food will be ready in fifteen minutes," he told Raven.

"Can't wait." She followed Hawk's movements as he got the bottle of wine out to refill their glasses. He looked relaxed in a pair of faded jeans, plain white t-shirt and black leather slip on shoes. "Ya' know, you're gonna make some woman a great catch one of these days."

Hawk slanted a low-lidded glance at her and picked up his glass. "Thought I already made somebody a great catch."

Lowering her lashes, Raven fought to keep the smile off her face. She knew he didn't mean it, but it made her feel good anyway. Plus, it gave her the opening she needed to ask a question that had been popping up in her subconscious lately.

"Why is it no one has snatched you or the other gorgeous men in your family up yet?" When he lifted a sharp brow at her reference to how good-looking his brothers and cousin were, she rolled her eyes. "You know what I mean. So, what gives? Why aren't any of you in serious relationships?"

Hawk lifted his shoulder in a casual shrug. "As I'm sure you've noticed, the Pattels and the word relationship don't exactly go hand in hand. It would take a very special woman to accept our...lifestyle. It's just been easier not to get too deeply involved. Less complications."

"So, you'll just stay single forever? No family of your own? No kids?"

"If you'd asked me that a year or so ago, I would've said you hit the nail right on the head, but now..." Again, the slow shoulder shrug. "I would say I'm open to the possibility of it happening one day."

"What made you change your mind?" Raven probed even further.

"You want me to be honest?"

"Please."

Hawk was quiet for so long Raven wasn't sure he was going to answer the question, but then he said, "I've never had the opportunity to be around anybody in a healthy relationship. My pop and uncle raised us to believe women were nothing more than a distraction and needed to be treated that way. The only woman we trust is my sister. That's it. But let's just say that lately, I've had the opportunity to witness relationships that made me start to rethink my viewpoint." His eyes grew steady and intense. "Why? You applying for the position?"

CHAPTER 41

Raven had just taken a sip of wine, but almost spit it out when he asked that question. "What? No! Of course not!"

"Just thought I'd ask. What about you? Would you like to get married and have a family one day?"

Raven was slow to answer. She was still trying to mentally crawl out of that last question. "I guess so. Maybe. If I find the right man."

"And what type of man would it take to secure a woman like Raven Randolph?"

This time it was her turn to shrug. "I don't know. I guess I want what every woman wants."

"I'm not interested in what every woman wants. I asked about you."

Raven blinked at the rapid reply. Now things were getting a bit awkward. She wasn't as comfortable as Hawk was when it came to sharing something so personal, but by the way he stared at her it was obvious he wasn't going to let her slide.

She cleared her throat. "I want a man who's honest. Trustworthy. Listens to me."

"Save the standard textbook qualifications. Tell me what you *really* want."

"That's what I'm doing."

"Yeah, I believe you, but you're also staying on the surface with your answers instead of going deep and telling me what I want to know. Don't be a coward, Rae. Tell me."

"Fine. I want all of the things I said, but I also want a man who says what he feels and means what he says. Someone who makes mistakes and owns up to them. A man who takes care of his family above all else." Her eyes dropped to the spot on his chest where he had his tattoo then brought her gaze back to his. "Most importantly, I want someone who tells me his absolute worst truth instead of feeding me his best lie because if I've chosen to be with him, that means I'm all in. I can forgive anything. Just don't lie to me."

Silence fell over the room when she finished. Water from the pots boiling on the stove sounded like loud, steam engines. She could hear the soft music he put on, but it sounded faded and far in the distance as they continued to stare at each other. It was as if their eyes were connected by an invisible string. Normally, she would've looked away, uncomfortable at baring her soul so completely, but not this time. She didn't know what possessed her to tell him something so deeply personal, but she couldn't take it back. Besides, he asked.

Jumping off the counter, she flounced past him with more confidence than she actually felt. Opening the cabinet door, she got two dinner plates and two salad bowls and placed them on the island. Next, she grabbed a couple forks. The entire time, Raven felt his eyes following her every move. When she couldn't stand it any longer, she turned around and glared at him.

"What?"

Hawk's eyebrows bunched together in confusion. "I didn't say anything."

"No, but you keep staring at me."

"I always stare at you. You fascinate me." His eyes slowly ran over her. "Even more so now."

"Why? Because I gave you my list of requirements of what I look for in a man? Are you planning on applying for the job?" She meant to throw his earlier question back at him, but as soon as it left her lips, she wished she could snatch it out of the air.

Before Hawk could respond, the timer on the stove went off, indicating that the lobster was done. She let out a low sigh of relief as they went about the task of fixing dinner. Raven went to the refrigerator and got the bowl of salad while Hawk finished up the garlic butter for the lobster. Everything looked delicious, but Raven's thoughts were on the idiotic statement she made about him applying for her heart. Luckily, Hawk seemed gracious enough to spare her any further embarrassment on the subject–or so she thought.

Just as she got ready to pick up her plate and bring it to the dining room table where they were eating, Hawk hooked a finger through one of the belt loops of her shorts and pulled her up against his body. He lowered his head so that they were face to face and eye to eye.

"I didn't forget about your question. I think we both know I check off the majority of those requirements you listed, so as far as applying for the job, I'm well qualified. You just make sure there aren't any other applicants who think they have a chance of being hired for the spot. *My* spot."

Raven's mouth dropped open. Hawk took full advantage by pressing a hard, possessive kiss on her lips. She was too surprised or maybe the correct word was shocked, to do much more than hold on.

Once he lifted his head, Hawk's narrowed eyes roamed her face, as if studying her features and committing whatever he saw reflected there to his memory bank. Once satisfied, he nodded and smiled. "Let's eat."

*****

"I can't believe you have a copy of a whole motion picture movie that hasn't been released yet. And it's not bootleg," Raven added, staring at the images on the large screen.

After a delicious dinner, they retreated to the basement of the house where Hawk's media room was set up. It was damn near a mini theater that enhanced the experience of watching movies at home. The large room boasted contemporary chairs and theatre seating throughout. Hawk and Raven were at the back on the raised level, reclining on a huge wrap around sectional. Raven lay curled up under Hawk's arm with their legs stretched out on the recliner.

"Bootleg?" Hawk repeated with distaste in response to her observation. "Hell, nah it ain't bootlegged. I don't roll like that."

"Well how did you get it then?"

"Ya' man is just that dude. You haven't realized that yet?" Hawk answered, eyes still fixated on the screen as he absently ran his hand down her side to her butt then back up again.

Raven turned her face up to him, studying his features in the dim, recessed lighting. She was having such a wonderful time with him. She felt...content. She almost wished she could stay here and never go back to the hectic pace of the city.

Hawk tore his eyes away from the screen and when he noticed her staring at him he asked, "What?"

"My man," huh?" Raven asked half-teasingly.

"That's what I am, right?" Hawk answered with a lift of that arrogant brow of his. "I thought we established that fact in the kitchen when I told you to send out notices announcing that particular job was now filled."

"Oh, is *that* what that meant?" Raven grinned.

Hawk's hand grew still. "Don't play with me, woman. Let me know if there's somethin' I need to make clearer for you so we don't have no misunderstandings."

"No, I think I got it, Mr. Pattel."

She slowly closed her eyes when Hawk leaned down to give her a sweet kiss that quickly ignited to turn fiery and passionate. Raven's breathing turned shallow and shaky. She was enjoying the movie because it was one she planned on seeing when it came out in theaters, but the minute Hawk kissed her, she forgot all about it. He had her complete attention. It felt so right being in his arms like that it was almost scary. It made Raven think that maybe it *was* possible for this *thing* between them to work out.

They both groaned when his cell phone suddenly rang. Even though it was nice to get away from the headaches of the real world, they couldn't escape reality altogether. Each needed to be available in case an emergency came up and they needed to be reached.

Hawk reached over and picked up his phone from the table beside the couch. Glancing at it, he frowned. "Excuse me, baby. I gotta take this."

Chuckling at having to extricate himself from her limbs, he stood up and walked out so that he could talk in private.

Raven lay back against the cushions and stared at the screen, but instead of seeing the images from the movie, she replayed the weekend she had so far with Hawk. She tried desperately to hold on to the walls she erected to protect herself against what was happening between them, but she couldn't. It was too powerful a force. Raven had to admit that frightened her. Still, she knew nothing and no one was perfect, but the Hawk Pattel she got to know damn near was. Yes, he was arrogant and at times demanding, but she liked that. Things were never dull with him. He was so charming. And could be so sweet. And so funny.

But...he was a Pattel. And she worked in the DA's office. No matter how much she tried to skirt the issue, those two things were facts that would never change. Hawk would always be a Pattel. *Would she always be an ADA?*

Raven's heartbeat raced as the ramifications of what that question could possibly mean. Was she actually contemplating giving up the career she'd worked her ass off to build for a man? Suddenly afraid that it was exactly what she was doing, Raven swallowed hard. Of course, she couldn't do that. Raven wasn't *that* woman. She wasn't the woman who followed her dreams and remained laser focused on what her end game would be only to give it up for a man. She wasn't the woman who put a man before anything and everything just because of how she felt about him. She wasn't her sister. *Was she?*

"Oh God," Raven whispered sitting up.

A sudden vibrating from her phone on the end table called for her attention. Blinking rapidly to try and dispel the mood she'd fallen into, Raven picked it up and looked at the caller ID. Seeing that it was Gwynn, she put it back on the table without answering. She would call her when she got back to the city tomorrow.

Raven curled her legs up under her and stared at the screen, but it was hard to get back into the movie. Besides, how could she think about anything else other than the bombshell she subconsciously dropped on herself about the option of leaving the DA's office so she and Hawk could be together. That was just...*crazy!*

Before she could delve further into that line of thought a series of sharp beeps from her phone told her that she had a couple of text messages. Blowing impatiently, she picked her phone up again. Both texts were from Gwynn.

Something's happened! Where are you!!!

Pick up the phone! NOW!

Raven slowly sat up. A shimmer of fear crept down her spine. Her first thoughts went to her family. Did something happen to her mom or dad? Couldn't be, Nikki would've called her. And if something had happened to Nikki, her parents or Angel would've called. So...

As soon as the phone rang, Raven pushed **ACCEPT.** "Gwynn? What's wrong?"

"It's Judge Warner. Jeff just called me."

The chill that shot through Raven's body went so deep she literally felt it in her bones. "What about Judge Warner?"

Out the corner of her eye, she saw movement by the door. Turning, she found Hawk standing there still on the phone but staring intently at her.

"Rae? Baby, what's wrong?" He asked.

But Raven ignored him and concentrated all her attention on the phone call. "Gwynn, answer me. What happened?"

"Raven, she's dead. Judge Warner is dead."

CHAPTER 42

"What?" Raven shook her head. No. Gwynn had to be mistaken. Judge Warner...*dead*?

Standing slowly, she pictured the judge wearing the half-smile that always seemed to be present on her face. To Raven it somehow suggested the world was trying to turn her into a cynic, but she was doing best to hold on to the last bits of her ideals.

"I don't know all the details," Gwynn continued. "Jeff didn't say much. It hasn't gotten out to the press yet, so no one else knows."

"H-How did she die? A heart attack? Car accident?"

"No." A pregnant pause stretched the silence between them before Gwynn answered. "Raven, Jeff said she committed suicide. No one's sure why."

"What? Gwynn, no. *No.*" Raven shook her head vigorously. "That's not possible."

Hawk stepped in front of her, his serious expression showing his concern. "Raven, what's wrong?"

Raven turned away, still trying to process what Gwynn just told her. "She would never *do* that. *Never.* She enjoyed her life too much to ever contemplate suicide."

"Raven, who was that?" Gwynn asked with a hint of suspicion. "Who's with you?"

Still distracted, Raven asked impatiently, "What?"

"Who's there with you?" Gwen asked a bit more forcefully.

Realizing Gwynn heard Hawk's voice, Raven's eyes flew to his. Hawk stood several feet away to give her space, but his arms were folded as he watched her and continued to listen to her side of the conversation.

"I, um. Gwynn, I'm on my way back to the city. I'll–"

"*Back* to the city. Where are you? Raven, what the hell is goin' on, chica? You been actin' strange these last few weeks. Honey, talk to me."

Last few weeks. For some reason that made Raven pause. Had it only been weeks since her world was turned upside down by Hawk Pattel? Strange. It seemed like a lifetime.

"Raven. Are you still there?"

"Gwynn, we'll talk when I see you. I'll call you when I get back to my apartment. Bye." She hung up in the middle of Gwynn still shouting questions at her. Gwynn was her best friend and Raven knew she was only concerned about her, but Raven's relationship with Hawk was something she couldn't share with her. Not now. Maybe not ever.

"So, you know about Judge Warner." Hawk's deep voice interrupted the weird silence that fell in the room. "I'm so sorry, Raven."

Still in a fog of disbelief, Raven stared at Hawk. "I can't believe it. I admire..." Realizing she was using the present tense, Raven closed her eyes and corrected herself. "*Admired* her greatly. I used to love to listen to her talk about the struggles she faced and the walls she knocked down in her career to make it easier for young, black women like myself to walk through the door. I could listen to her speak all day. She was a wonderful woman."

"I'm sure she felt the same way about you. I know the two of you shared a special relationship, sweetheart."

The reaction was delayed, but something in his voice finally penetrated Raven's grief. Once it did, it acted as an electrical current to her brain, giving it a much-needed shock and waking it up from the mush ball it had been all weekend. The chill that had seeped into her bones inched into her eyes like water transforming to ice. When she spoke, her voice held more than a tinge of bitterness she didn't even try to hide.

"Yeah. You *did* know, didn't you? That's how you knew you could use her against me during the Giuliani case, right?"

Hawk's entire body went completely still. He immediately saw where she was steering the conversation. Raven knew it was dangerous territory. It was understood between them and never spoken that they stayed away from anything that had to do with their real lives, but she couldn't help herself. Judge Warner's death brought everything to the forefront.

"Raven, I realize you're upset, but I don't think now is the time to do this. You've just suffered a loss that's gonna leave a huge void in your life. Let me help you get through this."

Raven's brows shot up. She took a step back, then another while glaring bullets at him. "*You* don't think this is the time. *You* know what a huge loss this is for me. *You* want to help me get through this? Please don't talk to me in that condescending tone. Especially after what you and your family did to blackmail one of the strongest women I know as a means to your own shady end!"

Squinting, Hawk's eyes grew hard. "**This wasn't all on us.** If she was as strong as you think, she would've told us to go fuck ourselves when we told her what we wanted her to do. Think about that."

While he was delivering his nice/nasty reply, Raven saw that something clicked inside him the same way it did for her. Gone was the sweet, attentive lover who was by her side all weekend making her feel like she was the most special woman in the universe. In his place was someone she didn't recognize. And Raven didn't like him one single bit.

"That was cold and uncalled for, you son of a bitch."

His face suffused with a burst of anger. Hawk took a quick step forward, then stopped just as abruptly. He inhaled deeply as if forcing himself to calm down before speaking. "I'm gonna let you have that one because I know you're upset, but–"

Raven bristled with indignation. "I don't need you to *give* me a pass about a damn–"

"But, I ain't gon' let too many go." Hawk's deep voice easily talked over her to finish his sentence.

"Screw you!"

"Raven..." Hawk's chest expanded from the breath he took in and held for several seconds before releasing. His jaw worked furiously as he met her mutinous glare. His next words were slow and emphatic. "Maybe I phrased that wrong, but what I was *trying* to say was that everybody got a choice. *Everybody.* Judge Warner could've told us to get the hell out of her face and done the right thing and reported it, but she didn't. Instead, she chose to protect–" Hawk stopped abruptly as if knowing he was on the verge of saying too much, but Raven wasn't about to let it go.

"She chose to protect *who*? Hawk, tell me. Who was she protecting?"

"It doesn't matter now," Hawk said gruffly.

"It *does* matter." Anything that would give her insight into what Judge Warner was thinking would help. Especially if she died the way Gwynn said she did.

Raven went towards him and reached for his hand. "Hawk, please. I need to know. They're saying she..." Raven swallowed several times before continuing to implore him. "They're saying she committed suicide, but no one knows why. If you care about me at all, I *need* you to give me this."

Hawk lifted his hand and gently caressed her face with his fingertips. "You know I care, Rae."

Raven burrowed her face in his hand. "Then tell me. *Please.*"

Hawk slowly moved his head from side to side. "I'm sorry. I can't."

It took a moment for his words to sink in. Raven dropped his hand and moved away from his touch. "Can't or won't."

"Both. You don't need to get pulled into this any more than you already are."

"Why do you keep telling me what I need?"

"Because I told you I wouldn't let anything touch you and I meant it. Rae, let me take care of this. Take care of you."

"I don't need you to take care of me!" she snapped. Throwing her head back, she closed her eyes. "You know what, I'm not doing this. You don't want to tell me, fine." Looking at him, she let her eyes drag over him dismissively. "So much for you checking all of those boxes you mentioned earlier, though. Honesty and trust was at the top of that list."

"Dammit, Raven! This has nothing to do with you not being able to trust me. I think you know that."

She could see she hit a nerve, but obviously not enough for him to tell her what she wanted to know. "What I know for sure is that we've been fooling ourselves these last couple of months by pretending that anything could ever come out of this. Bottom line, we're two different people from two vastly different worlds. It never would've worked."

She turned to leave the room, but he grabbed her arm to keep her in place. "Don't do this. What happened to Judge Warner was a tragedy, but it ain't got nothin' to do with us. Baby, me and you? We're good."

"No, Hawk. We're not."

"You tryin' to tell me we didn't have an amazing weekend together, just the two of us? That you haven't enjoyed yourself? Enjoyed being here with me?"

"Of course, I did. This weekend *has* been amazing, but it's not real." She gestured around the room. "This is a beautifully controlled environment where everything is set up to be perfect. No Pattels, no DA's office. Just us, but it's not realistic."

"Raven–"

"How did you even find out about Judge Warner so quickly? It just happened, but you knew before I did."

"That was Lorenzo who called. I was on my way back to tell you when I heard you on the phone."

Raven couldn't find fault with his answer. Being that Lorenzo was a lawyer himself with deep connections, that made sense. Still, she felt like she was missing something. "Why would he call you and tell *you*, though?"

"He knows we're involved, Rae. He thought that I'd want to let you know as soon as possible."

"Or warn you so that you could get your stories straight."

Hawk snorted softly. "As usual, you're overthinking things and projecting your own suspicions on to me."

"Or I'm right and you're trying to deflect the truth and make me *think* I'm overthinking. Maybe I am, maybe I'm not, but that only makes the point I brought up earlier. I can't trust you. I can't trust anything you say, Hawk."

"Have I ever lied to you, Rae?"

"No, but that's because we have an unspoken rule to stay away from subjects that would force either one of us to."

"Jesus," Hawk whispered under his breath. "Okay, look. Emotions are running high. Maybe we should just call it a night and sleep on this. Things might look a little clearer in the morning."

"No. You know what? I think I'm going home."

"Now?" Hawk asked, frowning. "Raven–"

"You don't have to bother Danny, I'll call a car to pick me up."

The more Raven thought about it the surer she became. Tomorrow, she would go by Judge Warner's apartment and pay her respects to her husband, who she knew had to be devastated. Raven had met Robert Warner many times. He was a good man and he loved his wife very much. She could only imagine how lost he must be right now.

"Rae, just wait until the morning. Baby, we need to talk about this."

Raven shook her head. "No, I'm leaving tonight. Do you mind telling me the address so I can give it to the driver?" Hawk simply stared at her without replying so Raven shrugged. "Never mind, I'll just use the location services on my phone to find out where I am."

The silence lengthened between them. When Hawk finally answered her, his words shot out like bullets discharged from a gun. "That's not necessary. If you want to go tonight, I'll take you home."

He was furious. Raven could hear it in his voice and see it in the tense set of his features. His jaw was locked so tight it looked like it would break to pieces if he turned his head wrong.

"Thank you," Raven said. "I'll go get dressed."

Giving him one last look, Raven left the room. She was only a couple of feet out the door when she heard a loud crash, as if Hawk had thrown something or swiped items to the floor. Raven paused mid-step, but she didn't stop. He could be mad all he wanted, but she meant every word she said. If he couldn't be honest with her, when she needed it most, then the two of them had a huge problem.

The roughly two-hour drive back to the city was made in relative silence, which was fine by Raven. She wasn't in the mood for conversation and it seemed neither was Hawk. She texted Gwynn to find out if she found out any more information, but she didn't. The two of them agreed to meet at Judge Warner's home the next day around noon.

Still trying to process the fact that Judge Warner was gone, Raven stared out the window for the majority of the ride. What did Hawk mean when he said she chose to protect someone. Who? And why the hell wouldn't he tell her? The more Raven thought about it the angrier at him she became. She thought they were closer than that, but obviously she was wrong.

By the time Hawk pulled up in front of her building, Raven was ready to jump out of the car just to get away from the suffocating tension between them. The ride had not been comfortable; far different than the trip she made going. Her doorman, Ben, came to the car and stood patiently, ready to assist her inside the building, but when Raven tried to open the door she found out the safety lock was on.

Sighing heavily, she reluctantly turned to look at Hawk and found him holding a square box. Raven immediately recognized it as the jewelry box she brought to leave the necklace and earrings he bought her. From the beginning, she was hesitant about accepting such an expensive gift, but with the latest turn of events, she *knew* she couldn't so she left it on the dresser in the bedroom. Hawk must have picked it up before they left.

"You forgot something," he said.

"I didn't forget. I intentionally left it. I can't accept it, Hawk. It's too much."

"No, what it *is,* is a gift."

"Hawk–"

"I bought it for you, so I want you to have it. We can sit here all night until you decide to take it. It doesn't make a difference to me."

Raven bit down on her tongue and counted to ten. Knowing he wouldn't let her out until she took the damn jewelry, she snatched the box from his hand and gave him a pointed look. "Can I go now?"

"I'll check on you tomorrow. If you need anything, let me know."

"The only thing I need are answers. If you won't give me that, then I'm good." Her hand went to the door handle. "Can I please go now?"

Hawk waited several beats before finally unlocking the door. Once she was free, Raven quickly jumped out the car. Nodding to Ben, she hurried into her building without looking back; she could feel Hawk's eyes on her. She half expected him to get out the car and follow her. Raven didn't breathe a sigh of relief until she got on the elevator and was headed up to her apartment. At least she could thank him for that.

CHAPTER 43

Around one the next afternoon, Raven and Gwynn went to the Warner's apartment as planned. By that time the press was aware of the news. The media was posted outside the building and clamored for any piece of information they could get about the death of the high ranking, esteemed judge who had seemed to have it all. Reporters shouted questions at Raven and Gwynn once they realized the two women were with the DA's office. They both breathed a sigh of relief once the elevator doors closed to the crazy and chaotic scene.

They joined other well-wishers inside the apartment, including Jeff who was good friends with Robert Warner. Robert tried to put on a brave face, but it was evident he was taking his wife's death hard. Jeff told Raven and Gwynn that as of yet, no one knew why Judge Warner decided to end her life; *if* that's what happened.

Not wanting to overstay their welcome, Raven suggested they take their leave after about an hour. They were walking towards the front door when Gwynn spotted someone she wanted to have a brief word with. While she waited for her, Raven studied the photos of Judge Warner and her husband visiting various countries. Raven smiled when she saw how relaxed and happy the judge seemed. She definitely enjoyed life, which made it so hard to believe the circumstances of her death. Raven was glad there would be an investigation before cause of death went on the record. She had a feeling there was more to the circumstances than any of them knew right now.

Raven picked up a particular picture of Judge Warner, Robert and some friends standing in front of a famous landmark in London. A sad smile tugged at the corners of Raven's lips. She was going to miss talking to her mentor, miss soaking in the little gems of wisdom the judge dropped that were so helpful and so very much appreciated. Raven wished she would've had the chance to ease some of the tension that fell between them after the Giuliani case, but it was too late.

She carefully replaced the photo and glanced at a couple paintings on the wall. Her eyes lingered on one in particular, admiring the clean lines of the abstract painting. She wasn't an expert by any means, but one of Raven's favorite pastimes was visiting art galleries and showings in the city whenever she had time. She folded her arms and peered closer. The painting she studied piqued her curiosity and her imagination with its layers of vivid colors and sand-like gritty texture. One of her favorite quotes by *Arshile Gorky* came to mind as she studied it: *Abstraction allows man to see with his mind what he cannot see physically with his eyes.* It definitely fit in this instance.

"I see you're admiring my painting, Rae."

Raven turned and saw Janice, Judge Warner's assistant standing behind her. Her blonde hair was slicked back into a sleek bun. The black dress she wore contrasted vividly to her pale coloring. After the two women hugged each other, Raven gestured to the piece of art. "Did you paint this?"

"Yes," Janice nodded. "I dabbled, for years. When the judge found out, she asked to see a few of my pieces and chose this one for her home and one other to hang up in the office," she said sadly.

"I'm so sorry, Janice." Raven reached out and gave her hand a quick squeeze. "I know you and she were close."

"I'm gonna miss her, Rae. All of this is just so hard to believe. Why would Judge Warner..." Unable to finish the sentence, Janice could only helplessly shake her head "She loved this painting, you know."

"I can see why," Raven commented staring at the fascinating piece of art. "It's breathtaking. You have a real talent for the craft. How long have you been painting?"

"Ever since I was a young girl." The smile that crossed Janice's face took away a little of the sadness. "I remember my mom would always come in my room and catch my squinting at the canvas. She thought maybe I needed glasses or something, but I told her I did it because it helped me focus on what I was painting and block out the distractions of the outside world. I know it sounds crazy, but..."

Janice continued to talk, but something she said stole the heat from Raven's body. Her words brought back a memory of the conversation she had with Hawk at his condo that first night in Vegas...

"Let me tell you a quick story. I went out with this artist a few times. Very talented woman. Sometimes I'd watch her paint. I noticed she always squinted when she worked. When I asked her why,

she said it helped her focus on what she was painting and block out outside distractions. Does that make sense?"

"I guess. And what does an ex-girlfriend have to do with me?"

"She wasn't a girlfriend. Just someone I dated once or twice. But anyway, that's what I want you to do. Block out everything, including any misgivings you might be having and focus on the here and now.

A chill ran through Raven's body, leaving her icy cold. Was it a coincidence that Janice used the same phrase as Hawk to describe her way of achieving focus while painting? Maybe it was a common term among artists or maybe...

Raven suddenly felt sick to her stomach. An artist using almost the exact same words Hawk quoted from a woman he dated might *possibly* be written off as a coincidence. But when the artist in question is the assistant to a judge the Pattels blackmailed in order to sway her cooperation to benefit their interests? No. Raven couldn't explain that one. Besides, too many coincidences had a way of becoming facts.

Did Janice betray Judge Warner by passing on sensitive information to Hawk that could be used against her? And if so, how did Hawk 'persuade' Janice to break trust with a woman she seemed so undeniably loyal to?

But the answer to the last question was painfully apparent. It didn't take a genius to come to the conclusion that more than likely, Hawk slept with the woman and manipulated her with nothing more than that monster of a dick he wielded between his legs. That thing was positively lethal when he let it loose. Raven knew from experience. Every time he touched her, she was like putty in his hands. She hadn't gone as far as Janice to betray her position at the DA's office, but getting involved with him wasn't exactly ethical.

"Rae? Raven? Are you okay?"

It took several seconds for Raven to realize Janice was calling her name and looking at her with an expression of concern. "Uh, no. I'm ...I'm fine. Just a little tired, I guess. Everything is still so hard to process."

"I know exactly how you feel."

"How long did you work for Judge Warner again?"

"Seven years."

"Wow! Well, you were someone she trusted and depended on. I *do* know that. And I'm sure you do too."

And that's when Raven saw it. It happened so quickly. Anyone else may have missed it, but Raven was an expert when it came to studying expressions of witnesses on the stand and if they would have been in a courtroom, Janice would've just given her a kill shot. The guilt on her face said it all.

"Yes, I... I suppose so. I mean, sometimes it felt like I could never get anything right as far as she was concerned, but..." Janice stared at the painting as if remembering incidences from the past. "The judge was just so much of a perfectionist, you know? And she wanted everyone around her to be perfect. She wasn't an easy woman to work for." As if realizing she may have said too much, Janice gave Raven a self-conscious smile and tried to clean up her revelations. "But I loved her, Rae. I have a lot of regrets, but who doesn't, right?"

"What type of regrets?" Raven asked trying to keep the woman talking. "It's okay, Janice. It might make you feel better to open up to someone and–"

"You ready, Rae?" Gwynn chose *that* moment to appear beside them.

Raven could've screamed. "Can you give us just a minute? Janice and I were in the middle of something."

"No," Janice said quickly. "I should go, um, check on the other guests. It was good talking to you, Rae. You two take care." Before Raven could say anything to stop her, she was gone.

"What was that about?" Gwynn asked.

Raven continued to stare at Janice, who made it to halfway across the room. She glanced over her shoulder to see if Raven was still there. When she saw Raven in the same spot staring at her, she quickly turned around and made a big production of nodding at something the man in front of her was saying.

"Nothing," Raven said to Gwynn. "Just having a little chat with Janice to see if I could gain any insight into what was going on with Judge Warner."

"Did you find out anything?" Gwynn turned to stare at Janice as well. "What did she say?"

"Nothing really." Raven decided to keep her suspicions to herself for the time being. She glanced at Gwynn and headed to the door. "Ready?"

Once Raven made it home, she kicked off her shoes and went straight to her bedroom to change clothes. After they left the Warner's home, she and Gwynn stopped at a restaurant they frequented a lot, but neither had much of an appetite. Gwynn probed into where Raven was over the weekend, and for the first time since their friendship, Raven lied to her. She made up a story about going on a last-minute trip with Wesley to a conference in Philadelphia. She didn't think Gwynn believed her, but she really didn't care because that was the least of her worries. Hawk took front and center stage in that department.

He had texted her several times to check on her, but Raven didn't answer. She needed time to process everything that happened in the last twenty-four hours; Judge Warner's death, her suspicions that Janice deceived and betrayed a woman who trusted her implicitly and last but certainly not least, Hawk's role in the whole affair. He seemed to be a lot more involved than she originally thought, but how deeply entangled was he in all of this?

Raven was turning everything over in her head, trying to figure out the answer to that question and so many others when she heard a knock on her door. Exhaling harshly, she closed her eyes. She should've known it was wishful thinking to hope Hawk would respect her wishes and give her some space.

Raven slipped on a pair of gray tights and an oversized pink and gray t-shirt. Exuding much attitude, she walked to the front door and swung it open, ready to let loose with both barrels, but the person on the other side of the door wasn't Hawk. It was a man who unmistakably favored him, just older and not as tall. Even if she hadn't seen his photo at Hawk's estate, Raven still would've recognized him anywhere.

Joseph Pattel. Hawk's father.

CHAPTER 44

Not much shocked her these days, but Raven had to admit she Joseph Pattel was the *last* person she expected to see at her front door. She hated to be caught unawares and that's exactly how she felt right at the moment. *What now?*

"Ms. Randolph? I'm–"

"Joseph Pattel. Yes, I know who you are. What I *don't* know is why you're at my apartment. And how the hell did you know where I lived?" Raven felt a sense of deja vu hit her. She'd asked his son almost the exact same question.

"I think we need to talk, you and I. May I?" He gestured beyond her to indicate he wanted to come in.

Raven hesitated, torn between letting him come in and slamming the door in his face. In the end, her curiosity won out. Stepping back, she opened the door wider, silently inviting him. Closing the door behind him, Raven watched him closely as he glanced around her apartment.

Joseph Pattel was an impressive figure, very handsome and fit for his age. Raven noticed right away that his eyes were the same deep brown as his son's. His skin tone, a shade deeper than Hawk's was smooth with very few wrinkles, but the lines that deepened into his face only made him more distinguished. It was fascinating to see how Hawk would look in thirty years. However, there was a seriousness about Joseph that she only saw in his son on a handful of occasions. Raven hated to admit it, but it left her slightly unnerved.

It was best she find out what he wanted so she could bring the unexpected visit to an end as soon as possible. "Mr. Pattel, what can I do for you?"

"How was your visit at my son's home in Connecticut this weekend, Ms. Randolph?"

Raven did her best not to show her surprise at his question. She never took in consideration that anyone in his family knew she and Hawk were seeing each other. But from what Hawk said, Lorenzo was aware and now Joseph.

"How did you know I was at Hawk's estate this weekend?"

Joseph's quick smile made Raven catch her breath. He looked so much like Hawk when he smiled. Back in the day, Joseph Pattel must have run women as crazy as his son did now. With his looks, money and charm, Raven didn't doubt he probably still had his choice of whatever woman he chose to spend time with. She suddenly remembered the photo of Hawk's mother. She and Joseph must have made a striking couple.

"You'll find there's not much that happens in my family and I don't know about it," Joseph said watching her closely. "For instance, it seems my son is quite smitten with you."

"Your son is *smitten* with a lot of women, Mr. Pattel," Raven answered dryly. "Please don't read too much into it. We're merely acquaintances."

"Oh, I think you're a lot more than that, Raven. You don't mind if I call you Raven, do you?" Without giving her a chance to answer, he continued. "I have a feeling we're going to be seeing a lot of each other, so I thought it best we bring everything out in the open."

Raven's eyes narrowed. "I'm not sure I understand," she said slowly. "I have no intention of hanging out with you and your family, Mr. Pattel. And I think you know why."

"Yet you've been sleeping with my son for weeks even though the Pattels are the subject of a witch hunt by your department and your illustrious district attorney, Jeffrey Mills." Joseph spat Jeff's name out as if it left a bad taste in his mouth. "Yes. I'd say we'll be seeing quite a bit of each other in the future, Ms. Randolph." Catching himself, he held a finger up and gave her a charming smile. "Raven."

What the fuck? Raven screamed in silence. From experience, she was able to keep the appearance of an unruffled exterior, but inside she trembled. *Was he threatening her?*

"I have no idea what you're talking about and I don't want to know. But what I *do* want is for you to leave my apartment before I call the police and have you thrown out."

"Oh, I wouldn't advise that."

"I don't care *what* you advise." Raven marched to the door and snatched it open. "I want you out. Now!"

"Close the door, Raven."

"Did you hear what–"

"Close the got damn door." Joseph didn't raise his voice, but his facial features shifted. No longer was he the charming, older gentleman who was making pleasant conversation with subtle innuendoes sprinkled throughout. He turned cold and dangerous. "If I leave here now, news of your tryst with my son will be front page news by morning. Is that what you want?"

Raven's heart jolted in her chest and started beating with an uneasy rhythm. For a moment, she stood too shocked to do more than stare at him. All the Pattels were ruthless men, but Raven heard if you could avoid crossing one in particular, make it Joseph Pattel. Rumor had it that you would never see the blow coming, but when he decided to hit you with it, it brought you to your knees. Her senses went on full alert. Knowing she had to tread lightly, Raven slowly closed the door. Staring at him with arms crossed, she waited.

Seeing her comply accordingly, Joseph lifted his head at an arrogant angle and returned her stare with a threatening one of his own. Finally, he reached into his pants pocket and pulled out a flash drive and held it out to Raven.

"I believe my son gave you a copy of this, but you didn't look at it. I'd like you to do so now."

"I have no interest in knowing what's on it. That's why I gave it back to Hawk."

"I understand that, but it's crucial that you watch it before we go further. It'll make things a lot easier for you to understand."

"I don't think–"

"It'll also give you some insight into why Judge Warner killed herself. You *do* want to know that, don't you?"

Raven's wide eyes went from Joseph's face to the flash drive he held in the palm of his hand. Such a tiny, innocent looking device. Was it possible that it held the answers she was torturing herself with ever since she found out about Judge Warren?

Knowing there was no way she could *not* look at it now, she slowly walked forward and took it from his hand. Going to the couch, she sat down and reached for her laptop. She typed in her password and inserted the flash drive into the USB port and clicked on the file that appeared.

Aware of Joseph standing directly behind her, Raven kept her attention on her computer. When she saw Jeff and Robert Warner on the screen talking, her stomach dropped to her feet. Robert and Jeff were roommates in college, so they knew each other for years. At first glance, it wouldn't be odd for the two of them to be having a conversation, but something about their expressions told Raven that whatever they were discussing was very intense.

Leaning forward, she looked closer. Were they in Jeff's *home*? Her heart was still resting at her feet but realizing the Pattels had Jeff's home under surveillance made it jump back into her chest and began to beat with a vengeance. How the hell did the Pattels gain access to the District Attorney's house and install cameras to spy on him? Who *were* these people? An even scarier question for Raven was who was the man she had been sleeping with these last couple weeks. She thought she knew, but now she had no idea.

"Watch, Ms. Randolph," Joseph urged softly from behind her. "It's about to get very interesting."

Raven turned her head slightly. From her peripheral, she saw him studying her intently. If Joseph was anxious to have her see what was on this file, it couldn't be good.

Bringing her eyes back to the laptop, she gave her full attention to the conversation happening between the two men. The body language was off. Robert kept pacing back and forth ringing his hands nervously until Jeff got up and made them both a drink.

"Here. Take a sip. Calm down. And tell me what the hell is going on, Rob."

Robert took the glass out of Jeff's hand. Bringing it to his lips, he swallowed the entire drink at once, wincing at the burn of the strong liquid hitting his throat.

"I need your help, Jeff. I've gotten myself into trouble. Big trouble."

"Okay. What happened?"

"I... I've been seeing another woman."

"Dammit, Rob..."

"You know things haven't been good between me and Denise. She barely wants me to touch her and when I do, it's like she's only tolerating me. I have needs. I wasn't getting them met with my wife, so I went elsewhere. Robert glanced at Jeff cautiously. *She...the other woman...she was an escort"*

"Are you out of your fucking mind!" Jeff screamed. *"Rob, I've known you for a helluva long time. You've done some crazy things over the years, but this? What the hell were you thinking?!"*

"I didn't plan it, it just happened. I was sitting at the bar nursing a drink one night and she sat down beside me. I knew what profession she was in, but the attention felt good. One thing led to another and well, we...we ended up at a hotel. After that, we met each other twice a week for months."

"Jesus Christ, Are you fucking insane? Why would you do something like that?"

"I told you why! Please, Jeff, just...just let me finish before I lose my nerve."

"Fine! Go on.

"Like I said, we began seeing each other a couple of times a week. Things were good, I was happy. But..."

"But, what?"

"Jeff, you know I love Denise. She's the only woman I've ever loved. We decided to go to counseling to get our marriage back on track. I was committed to doing that. I told Lola that I couldn't see her anymore".

"Wait a minute! Lola? Are you talking about the same "Lola" who's at the center of the DA's case with Giuliani?"

"Yes."

"Rob! What the fuck!?"

"I know, I know! When I tried to break things off, she decided to blackmail me. She threatened to not only tell my wife about the affair but go to the press and every news show she could book and tell them about the affair she was having with the federal judge's husband. She...She had pictures. Compromising pictures." A broken Rob sat on the couch and dropped his head in his hands. *"If they would have gotten out it would've destroyed me and my wife. Denise's career would be ruined from the scandal."* Shaking his head, he looked up at Jeff with tears in his eyes. *"I couldn't let that happen. I couldn't let her hurt my wife like that."*

Something in his tone must have alerted Jeff that there was more. *"What did you do?"* When Robert only stared at him without answering, Jeff screamed, *"Rob, what the hell did you do!?"*

"I... I had to shut her up. I had to stop her. I... I killed her, Jeff. I killed the whore!"

Raven slammed the laptop closed. She didn't want to hear anymore. She stood abruptly and walked several paces forward, keeping her back to Joseph. She could feel him tracking her with his eyes.

So many things were now crystal clear. The Pattels must have used this information to blackmail Judge Warner into dropping the charges in the Giuliani case. That snake might be guilty of a lot of things, but it seemed Lola's murder wasn't one of them. And Jeff knew it. He intentionally let her go into that courtroom and prosecute a man innocent of those particular charges. All of this had to have played a part in Judge Warner's suicide. She was a very principled woman and must have been in hell the last couple of months. Everyone she trusted betrayed her. Raven brought her hands up and massaged her temples with her fingers. This couldn't be happening. It just couldn't be.

"I see you've mentally untangled all of the intricate details that came out in the video."

Angry and needing to take it out on someone, Raven spun around and sent him an ugly glare. "Why did you show me that? Exactly what were you hoping to accomplish?"

"Are you saying you would've rather not known?"

"Don't act like you did it for me and my peace of mind; we both know that's not true. I'm asking you again. What. Do. You. Want?"

Joseph nodded once in acknowledgement. "Fine. Jeffrey Mills has to go. Once he's out of office, we'll need someone to take his place. You fit the bill quite nicely, Raven."

CHAPTER 45

Rendered speechless, Raven gave Joseph a stare strong enough to bore holes in him. When his words finally sank in and registered, her expression turned comically incredulous. She scrambled desperately to get her brain working.

"What are you talking about? And what do you mean once Jeff's out of office that I'm to take his place?"

"Exactly what I said," Joseph answered somewhat impatiently. "I realize this is coming at you fast, but I need you to keep up. Things are getting ready to move at a rapid pace. Just as I'm here speaking with you, someone is having a similar conversation with Mills. He's expected to submit his resignation within twenty-four hours. Once that happens, an interim DA will be assigned to the position. That interim DA will be you until the election. At that point, the position will become yours permanently."

"What?" Raven shook her head and couldn't seem to stop. "What are you *talking* about? I don't know who came up with such an idiotic plan but

count me out! I am *not* stepping into Jeff's position to be controlled by you."

"You really don't have a choice, my dear."

"The hell I don't!" Raven snapped. The more she thought about what he proposed, the angrier she became. "Who the hell do you think you are? I don't know what universe you reside in, but in the one the *rest* of the world lives in, there's a little thing we follow called *the law*."

"Was Jeffrey Mills following the law when he helped cover up a murder his best friend confessed to then tried to pin it on an innocent man?"

Raven's mouth snapped shut. There was nothing she could say to defend that. If she hadn't seen and heard it for herself, she wouldn't have believed it. How could Jeff do something like that? Friend or no friend, he should have turned Robert in the moment he confessed what he did. What would happen once it got out that the DA's office covered up a murder? Raven didn't even want to think about it, but it seemed as if Joseph Pattel was more than happy to tell her.

"You have two choices," he started off, advancing until he got right in front of Raven. "You can do as I say and go along with the script that I just laid out for you or let the newspapers find out you've been sleeping with a Pattel. They'll also receive a copy of the flash drive as evidence of Jeffrey Mills' gross abuse of power. Every case he's ever prosecuted, every case he's ever assigned to his ADA's, every case he put as much as a pinky finger on will have to be reviewed and possibly retried due to prosecutorial misconduct. By association, you and the other lawyers who work for Mills will be scrutinized and put under a microscope as well." Joseph paused, his eyes squinted as he went in for the kill. "Evidence may even surface showing you knew the entire time you were prosecuting Frank Giuliani that Mills was setting him up to take the fall for his buddy. Who knows? Maybe you were in it on it from the very beginning."

"That's a lie and you know it!"

" I do, but the authorities that investigate your role in this entire mess might not. As a matter of fact, I'll make sure they won't."

Silent screams of denial reverberated in Raven's ears. Her stomach churned in tense knots causing her to feel nauseous and weak. For the first time since Joseph Pattel stepped inside her apartment, Raven felt pure, unadulterated fear. She did her best not to let it show on her face, but this bastard had her shook.

Raven's hands clenched into tight fists, her nails dug into the softness of her palms. When she finally responded her voice was eerily and scarily calm. "I just want to know one thing. Why are you doing this?"

"Why? Raven, my dear, there's a reason my brother and I have been able to survive and retain our freedom and status for so long and it wasn't by sitting back and hoping things didn't cave in and bury us alive. We need someone in the DA's office who is going to look out for our best interests. That person is you. It's as simple as that."

As the enormity of what he was suggesting hit her, panic set in. "I don't want anything to do with this. I just want to be left alone."

Joseph's smooth brow arched high. "So *now* you want us to leave you alone. Don't' forget, your sole intention since you've been with the DA's office has been to bury the Pattels, lock us up and throw away the key. *You* came after *us*. Well, guess what, Raven, now you've got us. There *is* no leaving you alone now."

Raven's mind raced for a way out of this mess, but her thoughts were too scattered. The best she could do right now was try to stall. "Okay, fine. But I need more time."

"That's one luxury you don't have. As I said, things are getting ready to move at lightning speed. We have a lot to discuss. I'll be sending a car to pick you up in a couple hours to bring you to Pattel Manor. We'll talk more then."

Raven stared at him in shock as he turned to leave. "Wait! What do you mean a car's going to bring me to Pattel Manor?" Raven shook her head. "That's not something I'm comfortable with."

With his hand on the doorknob, Joseph paused. "I don't give a damn if you're comfortable with it or not. If you're not there at the appointed time, I'll take that to mean you've declined our offer. If that turns out to be the case, you already know the consequences for that decision. You're an intelligent woman, Raven. I'm sure you'll choose wisely."

And with that proclamation, he was gone. The minute the door closed behind him, Raven rushed forward and turned the locks on the door. Walking to the middle of the room on legs that literally trembled, she sat on the couch and covered her face with her hands. Her brain struggled to make sense of what just happened, but she couldn't. She felt as if she were dangling off a high building, kicking her feet and hoping to find solid ground below, but instead there was nothing but empty air. No matter how hard she tried to think of a way out, she came up with nothing. There was no one she could call. Definitely not the authorities. Raven had no reason to doubt Joseph's influence reached high in the police department. If she reported what happened, there was no way she could be sure he wouldn't be informed the minute she hung up the phone.

Before Raven realized it, an hour passed and she still didn't have a solution. The only thing she could do for now was pretend to go along with Joseph until she could figure out what to do, because she damn sure wasn't going to be a puppet for the Pattels. Knowing the car he was sending would be coming soon, Raven reluctantly stood up to get dressed. Entering her bedroom, her cell rang.

Hawk. She hesitated for a moment, torn between answering his call and never speaking to him again.

However, reasons she wasn't brave enough to examine made her grab the phone and answer it before the call went to voice mail. "Yes?"

"Hey, I was just calling to check on you. How are things?"

Raven let out a harsh, rage filled laugh. *How dare he?* "How are things? Oh, they're just peachy. Thanks for asking."

"Raven, I'm trying to be here for you, but you're not making that easy for me, baby?"

"Easy?" Raven screeched. "You want *easy*, Hawk? Okay, fine. How about I ask you a question that's so *easy* it'll only require a yes or no answer. We can't get much *easier* than that, can we?"

"Rae, what are you..." He cut the rest of the sentence off and released a hard breath. "You know what? Fine. What's the question?"

"Did you sleep with Judge Warner's assistant in order to get information you could hold over the judge's head?"

The silence on the line was suddenly deafening. She waited for Hawk to speak, but as the seconds ticked on, his lack of response told her everything she needed to know. The knowledge that she was right felt like a knife being plunged into her vulnerable flesh. It was true. He was guilty. But she needed to hear him say it. She needed to hear him admit what he did.

"Yes or no, remember." Raven cleared her throat as her voiced cracked. "That's all you need to say."

"I told you I'd never lie to you, Rae."

"Yes. Or no, Hawk."

"Yes. I slept with Janice to get information on Judge Warner."

His admission twisted the knife, sending it deeper and deeper into her chest. Biting her lip to keep a choking cry inside, Raven slowly sat on her bed.

"I can't believe I was so stupid." Raven thought she was thinking the statement in her head, but apparently, she said it out loud.

"You aren't stupid, Raven. What I did...it was before we grew...close. It didn't mean anything."

"It meant everything, Hawk!" Raven screeched. "You're a user. You use women, including *me*. It's like you're paying a board game and the woman you choose next is nothing more than a way to bring you closer to whatever goal you're trying to reach."

"I never claimed to be perfect, Raven. I'm far from that. I admit I've used women for my own advantage, but I think you know as well as I do that it was never that way with you."

"Oh yeah? I think it was. Tell me, was this your endgame all along? To strategically break me down little by little until I was so far gone that you were able to bend me to your will?"

"Raven–"

"I never took you to be a coward, Hawk. I thought you would at least have the balls to deliver the kill shot yourself instead of letting Papa Pattel do it for you."

"Wait, wait, wait!" Hawk broke in to interrupt her tirade. "What the hell does my father have to do with this?"

"Don't act like you didn't know he was going to pay me a little visit."

Another one of those tense silences fell over the line between them before Hawk spoke in a slow, measured tone. "You saying my father came to your apartment? When?"

"He just left. And by the way, he made sure I viewed the contents on that flash drive. Really, Hawk? You should've told me what was on it. Instead, I get blindsided by your father who now informs me that I'm to step into Jeff's spot to be the next Pattel puppet." Raven's throat was tight with unshed tears.

"Fuck! Raven–"

"That's not the best part!" Now that she started talking she couldn't seem to stop herself. She had to tell somebody and whether she liked it or not, Hawk was it. "Joseph is blackmailing me. If I don't do as he says, he'll expose our relationship to the news media and make it seem like I was in on the cover up with Jeff."

"What?" Hawk snapped. "My father told you that..."

"Do you think I'm making this up?!" Raven yelled, on the verge of losing what little control she had left. "He's sending a car to take me to Pattel Manor so we can, as he put it, continue our discussion."

When she heard herself double breathe a crying hiccup, Raven could've kicked herself for getting so emotional. Angrily wiping the tears streaming down her face, she did her best to calm down as she waited for Hawk to say something. Say *anything*.

Gradually, she became aware of him breathing heavily into the phone, slow and deep, similar to a furious bull eyeing a red cape and pawing at the ground. Then she heard him growl to someone in the background, "Turn the plane around, we're going back."

Raven frowned in confusion. *Plane?* Was he...?

"I don't give a fuck *how* close we are to Miami!" Hawk roared in response to something that was told to him. "Turn this bitch around *now!*"

"Where are you?" She asked cautiously.

A string of muffled curses came through the line before Hawk seemingly got his anger somewhat under control. "Rae, listen to me, baby, nothing's goin' to happen to you, alright? I'll deal with my father. Fuck! I *told* him..." He clipped the rest of the sentence, but it was too late. Raven jumped on what he *didn't* say with the quickness of a hound sniffing out a rabbit.

"You told your father what? You knew he was going to do this, didn't you? Is this what the Pattels planned all along?"

"It was...discussed before you and I ever got involved."

"What was discussed? Tell me dammit!" She demanded when silence met her question.

Hawk's next words came slowly, almost reluctantly. "Did I plan on manipulating you like I've done with countless women before you, yeah. I did. But once I started seeing you, getting to know you–"

"Stop," Raven whispered closing her eyes. Why hadn't she been able to see what was going on? "You bastard. Don't you dare say I was different from the others!" All the hurt and bitterness Raven felt at the moment could be heard in her voice.

"It's true, Rae. I told my father to leave you out of it and find another way. I know you don't believe me, but I swear on my life I'm telling you the truth, baby."

"The *truth*, Hawk? You wouldn't know the truth if it came up and bit you on the ass. God, what's *wrong* with me? I *knew* better than to get involved with you." Raven had never been more disgusted with herself than she was at that moment. "You fed me lie, after lie, after lie and I stood there and ate up every bite like I was starving for it. I ignored my gut feeling and fell for every single thing that came out of your deceitful ass mouth!"

"I never lied to you, Raven. Not once."

"Lying by omission is just as bad! I *knew* you couldn't be trusted, yet..." Yet she allowed herself to fall under his spell and give him the benefit of the doubt. Something her mother used to always say suddenly came to mind: *if you tell half-truths you'll get half-baked answers. And that's exactly what she got from Hawk.*

"Raven–"

"You know what, I don't have time for this right now. The car your father is sending will be here in less than an hour. I have to go so I can decide what I'm going to say to buy myself some time."

"No! Raven, listen to me, you're not going! You understand me? I should be landing in less than two hours. I'll handle my father."

"Yes. You've done such a bang-up job handling him so far, haven't you?"

"Got dammit, Raven!"

"I don't trust you! Do *you* understand *me*? I'll just take my chances on my own."

"Raven!"

She hung up in the midst of him cursing a blue streak and yelling her name. Raven did her best to put him out of her mind as she changed clothes. As she told him, she didn't trust Hawk to put her best interests above the interests of his family, no matter what he said. The Pattels were a bunch loyal only to each other. It would do her well to remember that from this point on.

CHAPTER 46

A little more than an hour later, the car Joseph sent for Raven slowly pulled around the wide, circular driveway and up to the front door of one of the grandest homes she ever saw. The sprawling structure was colossal. Almost intimidating.

It probably took a small army of employees to upkeep such a huge space. Half of the rooms were probably never even used, Raven thought.

When the car came to a stop, the driver came around and opened her door. Taking a deep breath, Raven got out and walked up to a set of heavy, wooden double doors that opened once she stood in front of them.

Once inside, she followed a proper looking butler past a grand entrance that was two stories in height and surprisingly elegant. Raven glanced around her surroundings as they continued on until they came to a great room that was bigger than her entire apartment. Ornate chandeliers hung from high, cathedral ceilings in a room decorated in masculine tones of crème, tan and brown. A large, flat screen television over the fireplace was hidden behind a specially built panel that merged seamlessly with the wall when not in use. The furnishings were obviously expensive but chosen to ensure comfort. Raven was so busy looking around that she jumped when a deep voice called her name.

"Raven, I'm glad to see you made the right decision." Joseph Pattel came towards her and guided her further into the room. "As I said, you're an intelligent woman. I think our business arrangement will work out wonderfully. Come, let me introduce you to my brother."

The surreal vibe of the moment wasn't lost on Raven. She couldn't believe she was actually in a room with both Isaac and Joseph Pattel. It had to be a nightmare and Raven prayed she would awaken from it soon.

But as she stood in front of the other patriarch of the family, she realized the moment was all too real. She, of course, knew who Isaac Pattel was but, the same as with Joseph, she never saw him in person. The pictures didn't do him justice. Tall like the other men in his family, Isaac came across as a very serious figure. Whereas Joseph turned the charm on whenever he chose, Isaac's demeanor was more calculating. His piercing, dark eyes seemed almost bottomless. They drilled into her with an intensity that made her want to shrink inside of herself just to get away from the scrutiny. Instead, Raven lifted her chin and made direct eye contact. Even though she was slightly intimidated by the man, she was determined to make sure she didn't show it.

"Mr. Pattel, I'm–"

"Raven Randolph. Yes, I know, it's a pleasure to finally meet you. Would you like something to drink?"

"This isn't a social call, so no. I don't plan on being here very long so let's get straight to the matter of why I'm here, shall we?"

Isaac appeared momentarily taken aback by her candor. He glanced at his brother before bringing his attention back to Raven. If possible, his eyes turned even colder. "Let's get something straight, Ms. Randolph. You might be accustomed to running things in the courtroom, but here you don't run shit. Is that clear?"

"And neither does my son," Joseph added. Taking a seat, he crossed his legs and fixed Raven with a penetrating look. "I know you called him as soon as I left."

"*He* called *me*. I understand you don't know me very well, but I'm not some helpless woman who needs to go running to a man to save me from the big bad wolf," Raven said with a bite in her voice. "Besides, Hawk is the last person I would go to for help. I think less of him than I do the two of you."

"Interesting," Joseph remarked. "Does *he* know that? He was quite upset with me for going to see you."

"I would rather not talk about Hawk. I only came here to tell you once again that–"

"Ah, there she is. I was beginning to wonder what was taking you so long," Joseph cut in. Both he and Isaac were looking past Raven to someone who entered the room. "*Now* we can begin."

Frowning in confusion, Raven turned to see who they were talking to. She wasn't aware that anyone else was supposed to be joining them, but when she saw who was standing in the doorway, confusion turned to shock. Every muscle in her body froze as her brain tried to register what her eyes were seeing.

"Gwynn?"

Shocked and speechless, Raven stared at her best friend. Gwynn was the last person she expected to see. Raven had briefly contemplated calling her to tell her what was going on but decided against it. Gwynn would've insisted on coming with her and Raven didn't want to get her involved, but it looked as if the Pattels had other plans.

Eyes wide with fury, she spun around and glared at the two brothers. "Why did you call her? She has nothing to do with this."

To her surprise, Isaac let out a deep rumble of mocking laughter while Joseph only stared at her with an enigmatic expression on his face.

"How noble of you to be so protective of your *friend*," Isaac chuckled. His gaze slanted mysteriously from Raven back to Gwynn.

Cutting her eyes at them both, Raven rushed forward and grabbed Gwynn's hands. "What are you doing here? I'm so sorry they've dragged you into this." Her voice lowered so that only Gwynn could hear her. "Do you know about Jeff too? About what he did?"

Gwynn's eyes welled full of unshed tears. "Raven–"

"It's okay. We're not letting them get away with this. What Jeff did was wrong, but we won't let them use us to do their dirty work."

His eyebrow lifted high in amusement, Isaac ignored Raven to address Gwynn. "Would you like to tell her, or shall I?"

"Tell me what?" Raven snapped. Still gripping Gwynn's hand, she spun around to glare at Isaac.

"No, please," Gwynn whispered, shaking her head furiously, but Isaac's attention was squarely on Raven.

"Ms. Jesús is a highly valued asset of ours, has been for some time. She'll be a great help to you in making your transition."

"What are you talking about?!" Raven spat. "I told you, I'm not going to step in as interim DA and neither is Gwynn. You can threaten us all you want, but the sooner you understand that the better."

"I don't think you understand, Ms. Randolph, but you will," Isaac mused. His eyes still on Raven, he said, "Come here, Ms. Jesús."

Raven glared at Isaac with a hatred she never knew she could feel for another human being. "I've had enough. I'm not staying here another moment and neither is..." Her voice trailed off, then stopped completely when Gwynn reluctantly pulled her hands away from Raven's.

"I'm sorry, Rae," she whispered before slowly walking over to stand behind Joseph's chair.

Raven stared at her lost and more than a little confused. "Gwynn? What's going on?"

"What's going on is that Ms. Jesús has been working for us for over a year," Isaac informed her with an arrogant tilt of his head. "Is that clear enough for you?"

Raven shook her head in denial. "You're lying. That's not true."

"Haven't you wondered why we've always been two steps ahead of you all this time? Why you've never been able to pin anything on us that would stick? As I said, she's become a valuable asset to the Pattels. Very loyal."

"I don't believe you!" Raven said, but the guilt on Gwynn's face said it all. No. *No!* It couldn't be true. The person she had known all these years would never...

Gwynn stared at a point beyond Raven's shoulder before finally bringing her eyes to Raven's face. "I'm sorry," she said.

"You're...*sorry?*" Raven screeched. She struggled desperately to connect the dots that were all over the page. "Is it true? You've been working for the Pattels...all this time..."

Raven's stomach lurched at the sight of Gwynn standing there, siding with the enemy. For a moment, she was unable to comprehend what she was so obviously seeing. Her brain registered several emotions that hit her at all once. Anger, disbelief, hurt, the pain of betrayal...

"Gwynn, why?" She asked. "How could you do this?"

Gwynn shook her head helplessly. "I never intended for it to go this far, but the money was too good. At first, they didn't ask for much. Just a heads up if it seemed we were getting too close. Before I knew it, I was in too deep to get out."

A revelation suddenly hit Raven and left her faint. "The case in Vegas. It was you. You fed them information about the investigation."

Joseph waved her statement off. "That case was flimsy at best, but I wasn't taking a chance that you would somehow tie it to my son."

Raven glared at him before directing her attention back to Gwynn. "You knew about Jeff. You knew he was covering up for Robert, didn't you?"

Gwynn hesitated before answering. "Yes."

"And you went along with me prosecuting Giuliani anyway?" Raven shook her head. "I guess I don't know you at all, do I?"

"This has all been very amusing, but you two can iron out the details later. We don't have time for all of this female melodrama," Isaac said with slight edge to his voice. "This is why I hate working with women. You're too emotional, too needy."

"Is that why there are no women in this family?" Raven returned with razor sharpness. "Because they're emotional, needy? Cause too many problems?"

"Precisely," Isaac snapped. Joseph, however, watched her with cautious eyes.

"Is that what happened to Tina Monroe, your son's mother? Did she *cause too many problems* so you ultimately silenced her?"

Isaac eyes narrowed threateningly. "Watch yourself, Ms. Randolph."

"It was just a question. Why are you getting so...emotional? So, upset?" Raven taunted with a smirk.

CHAPTER 47

Beneath the confident façade she wore, Raven was a nervous wreck about what she was about to pull. On the ride over, she'd broken down and called Jeff. Although she was furious with him, she needed to talk to someone. The moment he realized it was her, he had immediately launched into an explanation of his actions, which he admitted he regretted.

Her eyes on the driver, Raven kept her voice to a whisper and stopped him in the midst of his uncharacteristic rambling; she wasn't his judge and she wasn't his priest. He would have to find a way to deal with what he did, but right now she needed his help. He owed her that much. She quickly brought him up to speed on what was happening with the Pattels and how they wanted her to step into his shoes.

"I can't do it, Jeff," she told him. "There's no way I can live with myself allowing those people to pull my strings for the rest of my life."

"Maybe you won't have to," Jeff answered slowly. "There's nothing I can do to save myself, but I owe it to you to help you get out of the mess I've inadvertently dragged you into. And I think I know exactly how to do it."

That's when Jeff told her his suspicions regarding something that wasn't even on Raven's radar: Tina Monroe's death. Tina was a woman Isaac Pattel was involved with years ago. Their relationship had been tumultuous and complicated, especially after Tina gave birth to two of Isaac's sons, Lorenzo Pattel and Darrell Monroe. Although Isaac raised Lorenzo from birth, he never met Darrell until recently. Raven was aware of that part.

She remembered the first time she spotted Darrell with his cousins at a restaurant the Pattels owned in Manhattan. She wasn't exactly sure of the ins and outs about what went down, but after a strained relationship between father and son, in the end Darrell and Isaac had called a truce. Raven didn't know how often they were in contact, but she *did* know Darrell was extremely close with Hawk and his brother, Lorenzo.

Raven heard about Tina's death because of her connection to the Pattels. At one point, Darrell was a suspect in her murder, but it was discovered that she was killed during a botched robbery attempt.

The man who confessed to the crime got convicted and died in prison a couple years later. Or at least that's the story they told. It turned out that Jeff suspected there was more to it than what was discovered.

Joseph got up and stood beside his brother. "It sounds like you're doing the same thing Mills tried to do with Giuliani, trying to blame an innocent man for someone else's crime. Just in case you're not familiar with the case, the man who killed my nephew's mother was a career criminal. The day Sims Goodman was arrested, he was attempting to rob another woman. Plus, he confessed to the crime."

"Did he?" Raven countered swiftly. "Or was he coerced to take the fall?"

"Exactly what are you getting at, Ms. Randolph?" Isaac's tone did little to hide his impatience. It did, however, contain a warning Raven knew she probably should heed. "If you have something to say, I suggest you say it."

"Fine. It seems everyone involved with the case profited greatly from Mr. Goodman's conviction. The detectives who arrested him suddenly started spending money like it was water, buying luxury cars, going on lavish trips abroad that they couldn't afford on a cop's salary. The family of the convicted also seemed to get an influx of cash that has never been explained. Mr. Goodman took the fall to cover for someone, and I think that someone was you."

"I agree with my brother," Isaac commented in a bored tone. "It's not very responsible of you to throw around unfounded accusations."

"I wonder how your sons would feel about my unfounded accusations? Maybe I should call them and tell them my theory. Should I start with Lorenzo or Darrell?"

Isaac's body grew rigid, his eyes hard and emotionless, his stare was lethal. Raven got the distinct impression that he was trying to decide what part of her he would tear apart first. She knew she had crossed an invisible line, which was her intention, but it didn't stop the vein in her neck from hammering erratically from fear. She knew what Isaac Pattel was capable of. If he wanted to kill her right now, there was nothing and no one to stop him. The odds went up that Raven wouldn't make it out alive. She thought about her parents and her sister. They would never know what happened to her.

When Isaac lunged towards her, Raven backed away and turned to flee, but it was too late. She felt his hand grab her ponytail and snatch her back so hard it felt like needles piercing her scalp. Sudden tears sprang to her eyes as she reached back and frantically clawed at his hand, but that only made Isaac's grip tighten. Her entire head ached.

"Let...me...*go*...!" she screamed. Her breathing turned ragged and harsh as she tried to extricate herself from his grasp.

"Raven!" Gwynn ran forward to help her but before she took more than two steps, one of Pattel's men was there to pull her back. "You're hurting her! Let her go!"

Raven trembled when she heard Isaac's voice hiss in her ear. "You little bitch. You have the nerve to stand there and threaten *me*? Threaten my family? You obviously have no idea who you're dealing with." His laugh was evil and chilling. "People have died for less."

Terror left Raven unable to formulate a thought. She tried to remain still because struggling only led to more pain.

"It would be so easy to snap your neck like a weak twig on a branch, you know that?" Isaac continued to calmly rage. "But I won't. There are other ways to control you and gain your cooperation. If you choose to do this the hard way, that can be arranged. But hear me and hear me well." His voice low and threatening Isaac jerked Raven's head back to make sure he had her attention. "Don't ever try and back me into a corner by coming at me through my family. I promise you, it won't end well for you."

And with those words of warning, Isaac tossed Raven onto the chair in front of her like she was a toy he grew tired of playing with.

Raven brought a violently trembling hand up to massage the back of her throbbing head. From her sprawled position on the chair, she locked eyes with Isaac, letting all the hatred she felt for him show on her face. She thought about the gun she kept locked in the safe in her apartment. She started to bring it with her but decided against it at the last minute. That decision was probably for the best because if she would've been able to put her hands on it at that exact moment–

"What the fuck is goin' on!"

Raven turned her head in surprise when she heard Hawk's voice. She blinked several times, but it wasn't her imagination. He stood in the doorway, taking in the scene in front of him with an expression of icy anger that would've made her tremble if she hadn't been so damned glad to see him. Raven briefly closed her eyes as she fell back in the chair. Her relief was so powerful it left her weak. He came for her.

CHAPTER 48

Joseph stared at his younger son with a somewhat disbelieving expression. "You seriously had the jet turn around and bring you back? Really, Hawk?"

But Hawk's attention was glued to Raven. His eyes carefully ran over her, his temper clearly rising with each passing second. In a moment of clarity, she saw what he surely saw, her cowering in a chair with a mixture of fear and anger on her face while his uncle stood over her, fists clenched and a look of murder on his face. Hawk turned eyes full of raw rage towards Isaac. His breathing was deliberately slow, as if fighting an internal battle to hold on to a control that was quickly unraveling.

"Get away from her. Now." Although he didn't raise his voice, no one doubted the fact that he meant every word.

Isaac's brows bunched low over his eyes. "What did you say to me?"

Hawk slowly advanced into the room. Several of his uncle's men who were standing in the shadows took cautious steps behind him, but

Hawk's gaze never faltered from Isaac. "You heard what I said. Get the fuck away from her!"

Raven's eyes went from Hawk to Isaac, whose momentarily shocked expression would've been comical if the situation weren't so serious. She blinked and brought her attention back to Hawk. She saw him upset before, even slightly angry, but she never witnessed *this* type of fury from him. There was a danger about him that he didn't even try to mask. It radiated throughout the room; every one of them felt it. Raven's first thought was that she was looking at a person she didn't recognize, but just as quickly she realized it was a side of him that was always there. Of course, it was. He was a Pattel.

Startled when Isaac barreled towards him, Raven pushed herself back in the chair and sat up straight. The tension in the room grew thick. She glanced at Joseph. *Do something*, she wanted to scream, but it looked as if he planned on letting the scene between his brother and nephew play out. Raven got the feeling it wasn't the first time they clashed.

She held her breath when Isaac came to a stop in front of Hawk. Her nails dug into the soft leather on the arms of the chair as she watched Isaac shove his face close to his nephew's. She could practically see the flames burning in his eyes, ready to ignite anyone in its path.

"How dare you speak to me in such a disrespectful way. Who the fuck do you think you're talking to, boy?" His pupils were slits of blazing rage. They reminded Raven of a deadly snake in a viper pit spitting venom.

Hawk, however, didn't flinch. It seemed to Raven as if he was accustomed to the heat of his uncle's anger. "I told you months ago to leave Raven out of this. I meant that! Yet you go around me and come after her anyway?" His next words, spoken slow and precise, left little room for any misunderstanding. "She belongs to me which means she's off limits. Don't ever come near her again." His gaze finally left his uncle and fell on his father. "That goes for both of you."

Isaac positively seethed. "You arrogant little–" Stopping abruptly, Isaac glared ferociously at Hawk. "If I didn't know any better I would swear she had you pussy whipped, boy. Is that what this is? After everything you've been taught, you're letting a *woman* run you? Is she controlling things now because if she is—"

"That's enough!" Joseph interjected sharply. "*Both* of you."

But Isaac wasn't finished. Raven gasped and covered her mouth when he slapped his hand roughly on Hawk's chest where his tattoo was and bunched the material of his shirt up in a meaty fist. "Have you forgotten what this means? *Family above all else.*" He quoted the words through clenched teeth. "That means family above every*thing* and every*body*."

"You don't have to tell me what it means. It's been grilled into me since I spoke my first words," Hawk shot back. "I am and will *always* be loyal to this family. I didn't think I needed to convince *you* of that."

The two men stared at each other until Isaac grunted out a sound of frustration and released the hold he had on Hawk. He sent a hot glare towards Raven. "I hope you know what you're doing. She's not easily controlled and that can be dangerous." Isaac's clipped tone was like the sharp point of a knife. "I'm holding you responsible if she tries to use what she knows to come after this family."

Snorting from the 'not easily controlled' comment, Raven gave them both a look that was full of animosity and disdain. "If you're finished talking about me as if I'm not in the room, I would like to leave now."

Isaac glanced at Hawk in annoyance, silently telling him that Raven just proved his point. Shaking his head in disgust, Isaac cut his eyes away from them and walked over stare out the window, effectively dismissing them both.

Hawk went to Raven and silently held his hand out. He waited until she somewhat reluctantly grasped it with her own and stood up. When she tried to pull free, Hawk held on tight and pulled her towards the door. Raven caught the dark glare he sent his father. It communicated without words that they would be speaking later.

As she turned her head and glanced at the Pattels, her eyes happen to collide with Gwynn's. Raven easily read the plea Gwynn gave her to help. As angry and disappointed as she was, Raven couldn't just leave her there. Her feet slowed as she tugged on Hawk's hand. Looking back and giving her an inquiring look, his mouth tightened in a grimace when he followed her gaze to Gwynn.

"She comes, too," Raven said in a firm voice.

"Don't push it, Ms. Randolph," Isaac responded his back still to the room. "She stays."

"Hawk, please." Raven ignored Isaac and kept her eyes trained on Hawk.

"Rae–"

"Let her go," Joseph cut in. "We have Mills. We can work with that for now."

Isaac slowly turned around and fixed his brother with an unwavering stare. Being accustomed to getting what he wanted, it was obvious he wasn't pleased with the way things were turning out. They had a plan. Isaac was furious that they were now deviating from it. He watched as Gwynn hurried across the room to stand beside Raven before unleashing the fire in his eyes on his nephew.

"We need to talk, Hawkins." Isaac's voice sliced through the thick tension in the air like a hot knife cutting butter. "*Tonight!* You've had your fun. It's time to get back to business."

Hawk swiped his hand over his face and let out a long, tired sigh. The look he sent his uncle was chillier than an arctic wind; it was so sharp that it cut past the white meat and went straight to the bone. Without answering, he kept a firm hold on Raven's hand and left the room with Gwynn following closely behind.

Neither women spoke as Hawk led them through the house to the front door. Once they were outside, Raven saw Danny standing by the now familiar black town car parked in the circular driveway holding the door open. She was so happy to see him that she could've thrown her arms around him and given him a big hug.

When Raven started towards the car, Hawk fell back and tightened his grip on her hand. Coming to a stop, Raven looked up at him inquiringly, but his attention was on Gwynn.

"You can get in the car. I need to talk to Raven," he told her rather brusquely.

Gwynn's steps slowed. Her eyes went from Hawk to Raven before coming back to rest on him. "Hawk, maybe you should..."

Slightly taken aback, Raven glanced at Gwynn when she heard the familiar way she addressed him. After trying to hide the relationship with Hawk from her all this time, it was still odd to her that the two of them knew one another. That would take some getting used to.

"I didn't ask you to weigh in with your opinion," Hawk replied in a chilly tone. "Get in the damn car."

Raven looked from one of them to the other. The air suddenly flowed so dark that it coated Raven's lungs as she breathed it in. She watched as Gwynn hesitated before slipping into the back seat of the car. Danny closed the door behind her before walking around to the driver's side of the car and getting in so Raven and Hawk could have some privacy.

Hawk pulled her to him and banded his arms around her. After a brief moment, Raven gave in and wrapped her arms around his waist. Feeling safe and protected, she closed her eyes and rested her head on his chest. She remembered how relieved she felt when she looked up and saw him standing in the doorway. Maybe she should still be upset and angry with him, but at the moment those were too emotions it was impossible to conjure up.

"Thank you," she said softly. "Thank you for coming for me."

Hawk's wide chest expanded with the breath he took. His arms momentarily tightened as he kissed the top of head. "I'll always be there when you need me, Rae. I want you to remember that."

Hearing something strange in his voice, she lifted her head so she could see his face. As soon as she did, his lashes dropped, effectively acting as a barrier to hide his thoughts. Raven didn't realize how much she was beginning to know him, but bit by bit she was. Something was up. *Now* what? Apprehension caused the muscles in her stomach to cramp.

Hawk framed her face with his hands. He stared down at her for several moments without speaking, his eyes tracing her features as if memorizing the shape of her jaw. Her mouth. Her eyes, cheekbones and eyebrows.

"Hawk, you're scaring me," she told him in a low whisper. "What is it? What's wrong?"

Exhaling, he brought his mouth down to gently cover hers in a brief kiss. "I need to tell you something."

Raven's apprehension turned to out and out fear, but she did her best to remain calm. "Okay. What?"

Looking away briefly before gathering his words, Hawk brought his gaze back to her and stared at her intently before speaking. "First, I want you to know I plan on being with you for a long, long time. Indefinitely."

Raven bit down on her lip. A short while ago when they were at his house in Connecticut, she might have felt a burst of happiness if she heard those words, but now they only sounded like a preface to something disastrous, so she remained silent and decided to let him finish.

"I realize it won't be easy for you to forget what you found out these last couple days. You'll need time and I plan on giving you that, but in order for us to move past this and continue to build on what we have, you need to know everything."

"There's more?" Raven asked the question she thought she was only thinking in her head.

Hawk's eyes moved past her to the darkly tinted windows of the car where Gwynn was sitting before bringing his attention back to her. "For as long as I can remember I've used women to get what I've wanted or just to simply satisfy my needs. Most of the time they were just a means to an end. But like I told you before, it's never been that way with you. Ever."

Her heart beating wildly, Raven pulled her arms away from the warmth and security his body represented. This was not going to be good. She could just feel it. Raven steeled herself for what was coming next. "Just tell me."

Hawk's jaw worked for several moments, as if determined to keep the words he wanted to say kept inside and unspoken. Finally, they slipped free aimed straight at her. "When Gwynn first started working for us, she and I had a... relationship. Not even a relationship. It didn't last long and it didn't mean anything, but–"

"Wait. No, wait." Raven took a step back and held a hand up to stop him when he tried to reach for her. She needed clarification as to what he meant because he couldn't possibly mean...

"When you say relationship..." Her stomach clenched violently when she repeated the word he used. Raven did her best to swallow the bile that rose up in her throat as an image of Hawk and

Gwynn together sprang vividly in head. "You admitted to sleeping with Janice to get information on Judge Warner. Are you saying that you...you slept with Gwynn *too*?"

His eyes fixed intently on her Hawk nodded slowly. "Yes. I did."

CHAPTER 49

Raven heard a whimper in the distance that sounded like a wounded animal caught in a trap. It took several moments for her to realize that the sound came from her. Her eyes were drawn to the back seat of the car. She couldn't see inside, but she knew Gwynn was looking at her.

Turning so that her back was to both of them, Raven wrapped her arms around her waist and bent over. For a moment, she visibly wilted. She felt shattered, her heart in disarray Betrayal ate away at her like a hungry beast destroying the lining of her stomach. Squeezing her eyes shut, Raven fought to keep the nausea at bay, but that only made it worse because behind her closed lids, she kept seeing Hawk fucking Gwynn and the two of them enjoying each other's body.

No!

"Raven. Baby, come here." Hawk placed his hand on her arm and tried to turn her to face him.

His touch made Raven snap. Jumping away from him as if she'd been burned, she spun around, her eyes promising violence if he didn't back the fuck up. "*Don't* touch me! Don't you *dare* touch me!"

Hawk held his hands up and stepped back. When he spoke, his voice was quietly calm in direct contrast to hers. "Raven, let me explain."

"Explain? You fucked Gwynn! *You. Fucked. Gwynn.* What else could there possibly be to explain?!" Raven didn't know if she was repeating herself for his benefit or to make herself believe it was true.

"It happened before you and I ever got involved. Swear to God it didn't mean anything."

"Stop saying that! Do you think that makes me feel better?" She screeched. Raven brought a trembling hand up to cover her mouth. The anger she felt was only a shield to temporarily ward off the pain, but she would take it. "How could you keep this from me all this time? You *knew* she was my best friend! Did the two of you just plan on not telling me? Would you have *ever* told me if you hadn't been forced to?"

"I never expected to have feelings for you, Rae. I'm telling you now because I want everything out in the open. No more secrets."

Raven's chin trembled. His words stung and added fuel to an already fast burning fire. The anger engulfing her felt good though. She clung to it eagerly, letting it take over and using it to replace the sudden emptiness she felt. The pain surrounding her heart turned cold. Raven felt herself go completely numb.

"I don't believe you. I don't believe you and I don't trust you. In fact, I'll never trust you again. *Never.*"

"Raven–"

"You're a user, Hawk. You said it yourself." Raven's laughter came out sounding more like a choking sob. "First you sleep with Janice, then you sleep with a woman who I thought of as my best friend. Did you sleep with her after she started doing your family's dirty work or before? Was dicking her down an incentive to make her betray the people she worked with? To betray me?"

Hawk opened his mouth to answer, but apparently decided against it.

"Oh, you takin' the fucking fifth, now huh? Afraid that anything you say might incriminate you further in this whole mess?" Raven sneered. "Well, don't bother. Your silence tells me everything I need to know. Besides, I wouldn't believe anything you said anyway."

Raven didn't think she could feel any more foolish than she did after she found out Hawk slept with Janice. He even had the nerve to quote something she said as a means to get what he wanted from her, which only added insult to injury. But now finding out he'd slept with Gwynn as well? She'd never felt more stupid in her entire life.

"I just want you to know I hold you personally responsible for Judge Warner's death. You killed her, all of you! You and your family, Gwynn, Jeff..." Raven's breath hitched as a ragged, gasping sob claimed her voice. How could she have been so naïve? So gullible? Her intuition tried to alert her that she was crossing into dangerous territory, but even knowing how accurate it *always* was, she ignored it time and time again because in spite of the fact they lived in two different worlds, she wanted to believe Hawk so badly.

Did he and Gwynn have a good laugh at her expense? Hawk said they hadn't slept together since he started seeing her, but how could she be sure? The blood in Raven's veins ran ice cold. A bitterness she couldn't control built up and clogged every pore in her body. No more. She was through. Lesson learned.

"After tonight, don't contact me. Don't call me. Don't text me. Don't try to see me. Save every one of those lies you tell so beautifully and use them on someone else because you've made a fool of me for the last time. I'm done." Her voice had an air of finality that conveyed to Hawk nothing he said from that point on would change her mind about her decision. Ever. Each word she spoke was like a brick she stacked on top of each other to erect a protective wall around her to keep him out. "If I see you on the street, walk past me like you don't know me, because that's what I intend to do."

She thought she saw his eyes flicker with an emotion that would be called regret on any other person. Whether real or imagined, she didn't care. Self-preservation was the only thing that mattered. Opening the back door of the car, Raven climbed inside. She felt Gwynn's eyes on her, but refused to look her way. Before she could close the door, Hawk grabbed it and held it open.

Bending down he peered into the car, but Raven determinedly looked straight ahead. "Do you remember what you told me last weekend? You want someone who tells you his worst truth instead of feeding you his best lie. You said you could forgive anything as long as he didn't lie to you. I've told you everything, Rae. I've given you my worst truth. Are you saying you won't even try to forgive me?"

Raven rolled her eyes hard as he threw her words back at her. "This is different and you know it."

"Why? What makes this so different, Rae?"

"There are some things that are unforgiveable. You may not have said the words, but the lies were there. So many of them."

"I understand you're upset with me. You got a right to be." When her eyes swung swiftly to his in a hard stare, he met them head on. "But understand this, I plan on doing whatever it takes to make this right. I'll ride out the storm no matter how rough it gets. I ain't goin' nowhere, Rae. When you're ready, I'll be here."

Raven raised her eyebrows in disbelief. *Was he serious?* "Do you really think I'd give you the chance to hurt me again? Only a fool let's a wound heal then turns around and pulls the scab off. If you care for me at all, which I highly doubt, you'll let me wake up from this nightmare so I can get on with my life–a life that doesn't include you or your crazy family. Now can I please go?"

Their eyes remained locked. For the briefest of moments, Raven wondered if Hawk intended to keep her there, but finally he straightened and closed the door. Danny started the car after Hawk moved back. Although she knew he couldn't possibly see her through the dark windows, his eyes remained unerringly trained on her watching as the car pulled off and headed down the long driveway. Raven tensed when she saw another car coming in and passing them headed to Pattel Manor. She didn't even want to know who it was, and didn't breathe a sigh of relief until the heavy wrought iron gates opened and allowed them to drive through to freedom.

CHAPTER 50

The air in the car remained suffocatingly thick as Danny turned onto the highway that would lead them back to the city. Raven kept her head turned towards the window. The stars hid behind the dark, gray heavens, reminded Raven of a low, gloomy ceiling. The feeling was decidedly ominous.

Perfect, she thought wryly. *Tailor made for the evening I've had.*

"Rae, I think we need to talk."

Raven sighed heavily and closed her eyes. She knew it was pointless to think she and Gwynn could make the trip back to the city in silence, but still. She hoped.

"I know you're angry and disappointed in me."

Raven rolled her eyes in the dark interior of the car at Gwynn's woe is me tone. It sounded like she'd lost her best friend. And she had.

"Please give me a chance to explain."

"What the hell were you thinking to get involved with those people, Gwynn?" Raven's promise to remain silent flew out the window.

"Raven, you know I basically support my entire family, including helping with my youngest brother's tuition. That's not easy to do on an ADA's salary."

"So, you decide to go and work for one of the most dangerous crime families in New York? To just break the oath you took at the District Attorney's office? You could've found any number of ways to make extra money other than breaking the law."

"Of course, you wouldn't understand. Everything has always come so easy for you, Rae. Plus, you only have yourself to look out for. I did what I had to do, chica. You can't judge me for that."

"You did what you had to do? That's your excuse? And what about Judge Warner? Like I told Hawk, I blame everyone involved in this travesty, but *especially* you. How can you live with yourself?" A knot of emotion, including anger as well as grief, swelled in Raven's throat. "Does it even bother you how helpless Judge Warner must have felt towards the end? How alone she must have felt? Do you feel guilty at all about the role you played in this?"

"Of course I do! I admired her just as much as you, but there was no way I could get out at that point. I had to go along with whatever the Pattels said. You saw first hand how they evil they can be!"

"That's because they're extremely dangerous people! You know that as well as I do!" Gwynn sitting there and acting clueless was pissing her off even more. "Yeah, they let you walk out of there tonight, but don't think for one second they've loosened their hold on you. Once you're in bed with men like the Pattels there's no getting out."

"You would know, wouldn't you?" Gwynn muttered under her breath.

Raven's expression grew hard as stone. *No she didn't...*

"You bitch. Are you fucking serious? You wanna go there, Gwynn?"

Gwynn's expression grew just as fierce. "You've done your shit too, Rae. Or is fucking Hawk Pattel, a member of one of the 'most dangerous crime families in New York', different.

We took the same oath, mama. It's not like you wouldn't get disbarred right along with me if anyone ever found out."

"Screw you, Gwynn. It's not the same thing and you know it!"

"Fuck you, Rae and yes the hell it is! I was suspicious when I saw the new cell phone you had at the club that night. The only people I've seen with those are the Pattels, but I didn't know for sure until I walked up behind you and heard you call his name. It didn't take much to put two and two together to figure out he was the mystery man you were seeing."

"Then why didn't you say anything?"

"Because I was waiting on you to tell me! Waiting on you to confide in me!" Gwynn twisted her body in the seat so that she was facing Raven and looked at her beseechingly. "Rae, Hawk told you the truth. What happened between him and me...it happened before you two ever hooked up. Like he said, it didn't mean anything."

"And that's supposed to make me feel better? Finding out you slept with the man I..." Raven shook her head. She refused to get into an argument with Gwynn over Hawk, especially now that she knew he was nothing but shared community dick. "It doesn't matter. I'm finished talking about this. It was crazy for me to even get involved with him in the first place."

"I know you care about him, Rae. You might not want to hear this, but I think he really cares about you too. I can't believe I'm saying this, but maybe you should–"

"I said I'm finished talking about it," Raven snapped. "Besides, you're the last person I would take advice from, so just shut the hell up. I don't want to hear shit else you have to say...about *anything*. How 'bout that?"

"Fine," Gwynn said, turning around in her seat.

"Fine," Raven reiterated.

Thankfully, the rest of the ride was made in silence. Danny dropped Gwynn off at her apartment building first. Before she got out of the car, she looked as if she wanted to say something, but when Raven kept her eyes averted, Gwynn sighed and left without a word. By the time Danny pulled up in front of her building, Raven had come to a decision.

After Danny opened the door for her, Raven walked into the lobby with him following close behind her. She wanted to tell him she was fine from there, but it wouldn't do any good. She knew Danny had a standing order to walk her to the elevator and not leave until she got on it safely. He was loyal to one person and only took his orders from one person and that was Hawk.

Once she got to her apartment, she locked the door behind her and went straight to her laptop. The letter she typed up was brief and to the point. It served as her resignation effectively immediately. Raven pointed the mouse to the send button but hesitated before clicking on it.

For a moment, she questioned whether or not she was doing the right thing. Being an attorney was all she ever wanted to do. The end game was to eventually have a seat on the bench, but now that would never happen. As much as she loved her job, there was no way she could stay now, especially knowing the Pattels would be the ones running the District Attorney's office and pulling the strings. Shaking her head at the thought, Raven hit **SEND**. She sent a copy of the letter to Jeff as well as human resource.

Mentally ticking that task off her list, Raven went to her bedroom and pulled her suitcase from under the bed. She quickly threw whatever she thought she would need into it and zipped it up. Now for the hard part.

Sitting down on her bed, she stared at her cell phone for several long moments before taking a large breath and dialing a number. Bringing the phone up to her ear, she waited until the line was connected.

"Rae?"

The minute she heard her sister's voice on the other end, it acted as a catalyst for her pain. Raven broke down. She hadn't intended to, but it was as if a dam broke and let loose the stress from the last few hours. From a seemingly far off distance, she heard Nikki call her name in a panic as raw emotional sobs tore from her throat.

Raven's hand shook horribly as she pressed it against her mouth to try to keep her cries within. She didn't call Nikki to upset her; she just didn't want her to worry when she didn't hear from her for a while. However, the minute she heard her sister's voice, it was as if the wall she built to get her through the last few hours collapsed into a pile of rubble.

"Raven, where are you? Are you alright?" Nikki's voice cracked with emotion. "Sweetie, calm down and stop crying so that you can tell me what's wrong."

"I'm okay. I'm okay," Raven managed to whisper hoarsely. God, why couldn't she stop crying?

"Raven, where are you?"

"Apartment." Raven's voice was paper thin as she tried to answer. She was hanging on by a thread that was quickly unraveling.

"Are you hurt?"

Was she? No. Not physically. Emotionally she was devastated.

Knowing she was scaring Nikki, Raven took deep, hiccupping breaths, as she struggled to get herself under control. She heard Angel's voice in the background asking Nikki what was wrong, but at that point Nikki was almost as hysterical as Raven.

Angel must have taken the phone out of Nikki's hand because the next instant Raven heard his deep, commanding voice on the line. "Raven, it's Angelo. Tell me what's wrong."

His voice had the desired effect of ice-cold water being dumped over her head. Wiping her face with the sleeve of her blouse, Raven sniffed and cleared her throat. "N-Nothing. I'm f-fine."

She heard Angel sigh impatiently. "You're not fine. Tell me what's wrong," he ordered again. "Now."

"I..." Raven squeezed her eyes shut and tried to concentrate. "Nothing. I... I'm just going away for a while. I didn't want Nikki to worry."

"Going away where?" Angel's authoritative voice was razor sharp and demanding.

"I don't know! Just...away!" Raven could feel herself getting flustered. Angel had a way of doing that to a person. She was not in the frame of mind to go head to head with him. "Can you just–"

"Where's Hawk?"

The question immediately threw her off balance. It was the last thing she'd expected him to ask. "Hawk?"

"Yes. Do I need to call him?"

"No!" Raven stood up shaking her head from side to side as if he could see her through the phone. "Don't!"

A brief silence fell over the phone before Angel spoke. "Is he the reason you're upset?"

Raven bit down on her lip as her eyes watered up again. She heard Nikki in the background firing question after question and asking Angel to give the phone back to her, but Angel remained on the line waiting for Raven's answer. She tried to say something. Anything, but she couldn't. Her lack of response seemed to tell Angel what he wanted to know.

"You're at your apartment?"

Raven nodded. "Yes."

"Can you get to JFK tonight?"

"I... yes." Raven frowned. "Why?"

"I'm going to have a jet waiting for you. It'll take you to my island if you need to go somewhere private."

Raven slowly sat on the bed, trying to keep up with the swift turn of events that were being thrown at her. She thought about his private island, *Angel's Cove.* It was where he and Nikki had gotten married. Raven nor her parents attended the wedding. They stayed away in protest of Nikki marrying Angel. Raven regretted it now, wishing she would've gone if for no other reason than to support her sister.

"Raven." Angel's voice whipped through the phone waves. "Did you hear me?"

"I... yes, but...why? Why are you doing this?"

"Because it'll put your sister's mind somewhat at ease knowing you're there instead of you going away and not knowing where. As I said the island is private. There's a full-time staff that can provide anything you need. If you would like to go there, I'll make the arrangements as soon as I get off the phone."

Raven's first instinct was to decline, but the more she thought about it, the more appealing Angel's offer became. But...

"If I go, I don't want anyone to know where I am." They both knew she was talking about Hawk.

"I won't tell him."

"I mean it, Angel. Promise me."

"I said I wouldn't and I meant it. One thing you apparently don't know about me is that I keep

518

my word," Angel said in a cool, clipped voice. "I'm giving the phone back to Nikki then I'll call to make the arrangements for your flight."

"Okay. And Angel..."

"Yes, Raven?"

"Thank you."

He'd made it clear he was only doing this for Nikki, but Raven didn't care. No matter what Hawk said, he wouldn't stay away. It wouldn't surprise her if he came straight to her apartment when he left Pattel Manor.

Even though she was furious with him, Raven didn't trust herself to be around him. She hated to admit it, but Hawk controlled her body far better than she did. If he got it into his mind to use sex to break her down, she knew she would be powerless to stop him and once that happened, she wouldn't be able to resist.

Once Nikki got back on the phone, Raven was surprisingly calm. She reassured her sister that she was fine, especially now that plans were underway for her to get away from New York.

And Hawk Pattel, she added silently.

Promising to call her as soon as she got to *Angel's Cove*, Raven hung up the phone. After making sure she had everything she needed, Raven rolled her suitcase into the living room. She took the phone that Hawk had given her and placed it on the coffee table. There was no need to bring it with her. She wouldn't be needing it.

Looking around one last time, she left her apartment and went down to the lobby. As she waited for Ben to hail a cab for her, Raven thought about how quickly things changed. Just days ago, her life seemed perfect. She had never been happier. Now her life, her career, everything was in shambles. All because of one man. Raven foolishly put her trust in Hawk, had been ready to give up everything to be with him.

But never again.

As she climbed into the cab, Raven was honest enough to admit she was running away to lick her wounds. In doing so, she made a promise to herself that when she came back, she wouldn't be the same woman who left. She was paying the price for believing the lies Hawk told her and she accepted responsibility for it. That was on her. But him coming into her life and deliberately destroying everything she worked so hard to build, her happiness and peace of mind? Oh, that was on him.

Yeah, hell hath no fury and all that. A woman scorned could be a very dangerous adversary. As her mother used to say, Hawk poked the bear and now he would suffer the consequences. She didn't know how or when, but he would pay for making a fool of her. And she would get him right where it hurt most.

The Pattel's electrifying saga continues in the

next book of the series featuring:

LORENZO & CEECEE

Coming soon!

Made in the USA
Middletown, DE
19 December 2022